Love's Golden Destiny

**Center Point
Large Print**

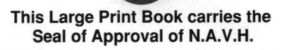

**This Large Print Book carries the
Seal of Approval of N.A.V.H.**

ॐ श्री गणेशाय नमः

Love's Golden Destiny

Patricia Matthews

Center Point Publishing
Thorndike, Maine • USA

Bolinda Publishing
Melbourne • Australia

This Center Point Large Print edition
is published in the year 2001
by arrangement with the author.

This Bolinda Large Print edition is published in the year 2001
by arrangement with the author.

The text of this Large Print edition is unabridged.
In other aspects, this book may vary from the original edition. Printed in
Thailand. Set in 16-point Times New Roman type by Bill Coskrey.

US ISBN 1-58547-128-3
BC ISBN 1-74030-500-0

Library of Congress Cataloging-in-Publication Data

Matthews, Patricia, 1927-
    Love's golden destiny / Patricia Matthews
        p. cm.
    ISBN 1-58547-128-3 (lib. bdg. : alk. paper)
    1. Large type books. I. Title.

PS3563.A853 L59 2001
813'.54--dc21

                                                                    2001028169

Australian Cataloguing-in-Publication

Matthews, Patricia, 1927-
Love's golden destiny / Patricia Matthews.
ISBN 1740305000
1. Large print books.
2. Historical fiction.
3. Love stories.
I. Title
813.54

British Cataloguing-in-Publication is available from the British Library.

≈1≈

The year was 1898, but as Belinda Lee looked landward from the deck of the *Chilkat,* it might have been a hundred years earlier. The shallow, mountain-bound harbor of Dyea was crowded with all manner of vessels, some so old and decrepit that she had to wonder how they had ever made the passage. In front of them stretched an interminable mud flat, across which laboring men, looking like great bears in their heavy clothing, were attempting to push, pull, or carry huge piles of gear and supplies.

Gold had been discovered in the Klondike, and the rush was on, bringing thousands of gold seekers into this small harbor, the beginning point of the arduous trek over the Chilkoot Pass into Canada, and the Klondike gold fields.

Belinda shivered, and tucked her mittened hands into her armpits. It was iron-cold and the distant mountain range was covered with snow and ice, although it was the month of April. For the first time since their embarkation from Seattle, she doubted the wisdom of her decision to make this trip.

On board ship there had been much talk of the difficulties of the landing at Dyea, but somehow she had not imagined that it would be as bad as this. It was said that the tide at Dyea had a spread of twenty to twenty-five feet, and that the tidal bore came in at a frightening speed, often sweeping precious cargoes out to sea.

Belinda had drawn a good lot, Number Ten, but she still had to make arrangements to get their gear from the water's edge up past the high-tide mark.

The ship carried several landing scows, crude objects hastily knocked together for the trip, and Belinda had made sure to reserve a place for Annabelle, herself, and their gear. But, since passage did not include landing costs, each passenger had to arrange those details himself.

She turned to her sister Annabelle, who stood beside her, her cheeks and nose pink beneath the dark fur of her hooded parka. Annabelle's full mouth was turned down and her chin was set. Belinda sighed, and for the hundredth time wondered what had possessed her to agree to let her older sister accompany her upon this most important venture of her life.

This was no place for Annabelle, with her dark, artfully arranged curls, pansy eyes, and pouting lips. She belonged at home, back in New York, where she could go dancing with her beaus, visit the theaters and fine restaurants, and be adored by her circle of admiring friends, mostly male. Why had she insisted on coming? And, more importantly, why had she, Belinda, allowed her to come?

Around them the bustle of the landing activity grew insistent. Men were rushing to and fro, shouting, cursing, and hauling out their gear. Great excitement was in the air, but somehow she did not feel caught up in it.

There were few women present. Belinda had been warned that the life here would be difficult for a woman. But up until now, she had not faltered; not even when the passage was rough, the food indifferent at best, and privacy nonexistent. Even the sight of the few primitive towns along their sea route had not dampened her enthusiasm, yet the view of this dreary mud flat, and the urgency of getting their mountain of belongings ashore, especially the expensive photographic equipment, had temporarily unnerved her.

Then she smiled to herself. Temporarily, my dear, is the operative word, she thought. You aren't beaten yet.

She started to speak to Annabelle, then hesitated as she stared at her sister's lovely petulant face. For an instant she wondered how *she* looked to Annabelle.

Did Annabelle find *her* attractive? Belinda pictured her own face in her mind. Her chin was more pointed than Annabelle's, her nose less retroussé, and her eyes, while shaped much the same, were gray instead of blue; she also lacked the full lower lip, which gave her sister that popular pouting expression. For this Belinda was just as glad, for she did not care for the current look, although it was much admired by many. Her hair, while almost as dark a brown as Annabelle's, did not curl at all, but hung shining and straight almost to her waist, although she had trimmed it considerably shorter in preparation for this trip.

Looking at it as objectively as possible, Annabelle might be more beautiful, yet Belinda knew she was the stronger; and that was why she should have stood firm. It was a mistake to have allowed Annabelle to accompany her. As they stood side by side looking toward the shore, Belinda had the feeling that in the future she would regret her decision even more.

Using her binoculars, she scanned the tidal flat. Among the landing passengers from other ships, she saw the hurrying forms of small, squat men, bearing huge burdens on their backs. They must be the local Indians, the Chilkats, who hired out to transport cargoes over the ever-dangerous

7

Chilkoot Pass. She had heard that they were capable of carrying incredible loads.

The first mate was calling out the lot numbers now, and as each number was announced, the goods of the number holder were put over the side, into the scows.

Belinda touched her sister's arm. "We'd better see to our gear, and pray that we get some help. I understand that no one is supposed to claim their possessions on the beach until it is all unloaded, but I've heard that most of the passengers don't abide by this rule, because they're anxious to get their belongings safe above the water mark before the tide comes in."

Annabelle smiled brightly. "Oh, we'll have help, Bee. I've already asked several of the young men."

She looked so pleased with herself that Belinda, about to scold her sister for her flirtatious ways, held her tongue. With as little sarcasm as possible, she said, "How very kind of them! However will we thank them?"

Annabelle looked at her a trifle sharply, but did not comment, as Belinda led the way aft to the large pile of canvas-covered trunks and crates, neatly stacked and lashed to the rail.

Two young men, in the motley attire that marked many of the passengers who had not had time to purchase proper clothing for this country, were already untying the canvas covers. They both tipped their hats as the two women approached.

"Oh, Ned," Annabelle called out gaily. "And Freddy. How nice of you both to help us! I'm sure we'd never be able to manage alone."

Belinda clenched her teeth. It was true, of course. They

8

could not manage alone, yet it went against her grain to trade on feminine wiles to get the help they needed, and it always upset her to see Annabelle blithely making implied promises with her eyes and manner that she knew would never be kept. Men were such fools, Belinda thought angrily; all it took was a pretty face, and they fell all over one another to fetch and carry.

As the shorter young man, the one called Freddy, started to lift one of the crates, it slipped slightly and Belinda cried out, "Careful, please! That's irreplaceable!" Her whole reason for being here was in those trunks and crates.

Freddy blushed and adjusted the crate. "Sorry, ma'am. It's all right now. I've got it firm."

Belinda sighed in relief, and her breath made a frosty circle in the air. The Graflex, which was in the valise at her side, and the new cut film, had cost a small fortune, but the convenience they offered should be well worth the price. The preparation of wet plates, in this climate, would be an unpleasant and very difficult process, and even dry plates were cumbersome and fragile. This new camera was smaller and easier to handle than the old view camera, and the experimenting she had done in New York before their departure had convinced Belinda that this new system would soon replace the glass plate method.

Ned and Freddy were now joined by two other young men, who in turn touched their hat brims, nodded self-consciously to Belinda and Annabelle, and then proceeded to help load the women's belongings onto the scow, after which they hurried away to get their own goods unloaded.

Belinda had marked each of their trunks and crates with their last name, Lee, in bold letters. Despite Belinda's dis-

9

approval, Annabelle had brought along two large trunks of clothing; in fact, her personal belongings occupied almost as much space as the photographic equipment and food.

As soon as the last item was on the scow, they took their places on board the heavily laden craft. Now that their gear was safely off the ship, Belinda felt her spirits rise. This was part of the landing process accomplished; surely the next part could be managed as well.

She sniffed over at Annabelle, who sat crowded in next to her, but her sister was looking the other way, boldly eyeing the young man on her left, while poor Freddy sitting opposite vainly tried to catch her eye. Belinda sighed in exasperation. She was going to have to give Annabelle a severe scolding—not that it was likely to do much good.

The moment the scow reached shore, Belinda jumped out and was immediately up to her ankles in muddy sand. Undaunted, she pulled her trim boots from the muck and began searching for a teamster as yet unbooked.

The beach was a scene of utter confusion. Many of the men were porting their own supplies, carrying them load by load to a point above the high-water mark. Others were dickering with the teamsters, whose sled-like vehicles dotted the beach between piles of gear.

Belinda's heart sank as she remembered the horror stories she'd heard on board the ship, and she had a vision of her precious supplies being carried by the waves, out into the bay.

As she turned back toward the scow, she saw a large dray pulled by two ill-matched horses. The apparent owner was talking to a broad-shouldered man in a heavy fur parka. Both men were gesticulating; it seemed to Belinda that they might be arguing about the fee.

Making a sudden decision, she hurried over to the men. "Pardon me," she said, looking the owner of the dray full in the face, "but whatever this man is offering you, I'll pay more!"

So far she had avoided meeting the eyes of the man in the parka, but as his breath exploded in a mild oath, she turned to face him. He was older than she, but still a young man. He was only a little over average height, yet his heavy shoulders and long legs made him appear taller. His face was clean-shaven and strong-featured, with a bold nose and strange, ice-blue eyes that were arresting in the intensity of their gaze.

Momentarily nonplussed, Belinda looked away. "I'm sorry," she said stiffly. "But it's important that I get my things safely away."

He gave a harsh bark of laughter. "And you're alone in that condition, are you? What in the holy hell do you think I'm trying to do here? Is my gear less valuable than yours? Is that it?"

He was right, of course. Belinda was prepared to be ruthless, but it was more difficult than she had thought. Nevertheless, it must be done. There was too much at stake for her to quibble over a matter of business ethics. "I am sorry," she said again, more stiffly than before, and turned to the teamster. "Sir?"

The man scratched his head. "Well, the price for hauling is twenty dollars an hour, seeing as how the tide's still out. But if this feller argues with me much longer, the tide will begin coming in, and it'll go up to fifty an hour."

"I'll pay you thirty dollars an hour," Belinda said recklessly, "if you start right now!"

"You've got yourself a deal, little lady! Where's your stuff?"

Belinda turned and pointed to Annabelle, who was standing by their gear. Evidently, her feminine charms had worked again. Freddy was just unloading a last trunk, and placing it beside the others.

As Belinda mounted the seat next to the driver, she turned to look at her victim—she couldn't help but think of him in those terms.

His full mouth was set in anger, but she thought she saw a trace of something else in his face. Could it be amusement?

Well, it didn't really matter. The only thing that mattered was that she get their gear safely out of harm's way, and she had the dray!

Once again, the great pile of goods was loaded with the help of Annabelle's "friends," this time onto the dray.

It took two trips of the large, sled-like vehicle to carry all their material a quarter-mile back from the edge of the beach. But at last all of the precious trunks, boxes, and crates were neatly stacked, high above the water line, and covered with canvas.

The wind whistled coldly over and around the piles of goods that covered the beach in all directions, for the Canadian government required that each person venturing into the gold fields must have enough supplies with him to last one year.

Ned and Freddy lingered long enough to set up the tent beside the stack of gear. Belinda overrode Annabelle's protests about spending the night there.

She said firmly, "I have no intention of leaving everything here at the mercy of thieves. Even if I went to the expense of hiring a guard, whom could I trust?"

"But we could find a hotel in town!" Annabelle said.

"This is a boomtown, Annabelle. Any hotel room would be exorbitant, probably no more than a knocked-together cubicle, and vermin-infested at that. You'll be warm and comfortable, once you're in your sleeping bag. Now, you stay here and watch our things, while I try to engage some bearers."

Ignoring her sister's pout, Belinda struck out determinedly, with no actual destination in mind. The beach was a scene of great confusion, and Belinda was amused at many of the items she saw piled there. Stoves, kegs, brass bedsteads, even pianos, all littered the sand like the flotsam of some strange tide.

Looking seaward, she saw that the tide was coming in. Facing about, she saw, about a quarter-mile distant, a single muddy street forming a division between raw board buildings. She could hear the faint sounds of raucous, drunken voices, punctuated by a gunshot.

Belinda shivered, hugging herself, glad that she had been firm with Annabelle. A night spent in the town of Dyea would be dismal and likely dangerous, especially for two women alone.

She jumped as a gruff voice spoke at her elbow. "Little lady?"

She looked around into the face of the lanky teamster who had carted her goods. "Yes?"

"You said you were bad in need of bearers to get you over the Pass. I may have one for you. Told him you paid real good."

He turned to clap a swarthy, grinning man on the shoulder. The stranger was squat, with powerful shoulders, a round face adorned with a sparse moustache, and dark eyes with an Oriental slant. He was dressed in rough clothing and muddy boots, but sported a pair of bright-red galluses under his open mackinaw. He leaned his weight on a thick stick, with an L-shaped handle.

The tall teamster said, "This here is one of the local Chilkats. His Indian name is a real tongue-twister, so most folks hereabouts just call him Charlie. Charlie, say hello to the little lady."

Charlie ducked his head shyly. " 'Allo, little lady."

Since Belinda was taller than he was, she thought the appellation hardly applied. She said, "My name is Belinda, Charlie, Belinda Lee, and I do need bearers. What do you charge?"

Still grinning, Charlie said, "Charge thirty-five cents a pound, Miz Belinda. Goods must be packed square. Charge more, odd-shaped bundles. Two-hundred-pound loads."

Belinda was calculating swiftly. "And just how far do you pack for this price?"

"This end Lake Linderman. Twenty-seven mile."

"I may need you longer than that, and I will need at least two more bearers. Can you get them?"

"How much pay?"

"You said thirty-five cents . . . oh! I'll pay *you* forty cents a pound, the other bearers the going rate." Privately, she despaired of her extravagance; she had spent money lavishly since leaving New York and her funds were growing low. Long-ago words of advice from her father came to mind: "Money, that's what paves the way in this old world, girl." And if things turned out as she hoped, the money would be well spent. She became aware that the smiling Indian had his hand out.

"Got deal, Miz Belinda. Shake on bargain?"

She took his hand, and had to refrain from wincing; she felt as if her bones were breaking. She did not reveal her discomfort by word or gesture, and from the glint of approval in Charlie's dark eyes, she gathered that she had been put to a test, and had passed.

"You sleep now. Charlie find other bearers. We start morning, early. Make it to Sheep Camp."

With a duck of his head, he started off, walking with a cocky strut.

The teamster said, "Charlie is the best bearer around, Miss Lee. I leave you in good hands."

Belinda started back to their tent. She had read everything she could find about this area and the gold rush in preparation for the trip, and she knew that Sheep Camp was a staging area for the assault on Chilkoot Pass. It was thirteen miles from Dyea and was relatively easy traveling most of the way, but they had to pass through Dyea Canyon, which was only fifty feet wide, and taken up almost entirely by the Dyea River. The canyon would be crowded with pack animals and humans. She was glad she had a competent, dependable bearer.

In the tent, Annabelle was already asleep in her sleeping bag. Belinda removed only her outer clothing and her boots, then crawled into her own sleeping bag, welcoming the warmth.

She didn't go to sleep right away. She had planned this journey for several months, and now that she was in sight of her goal, her excitement was at a high pitch.

The impetus for the arduous, expensive trip had been her father, strangely enough—a man who had deserted his wife and two girls when Belinda was only seven. But such was Morgan Lee's strong personality, sense of fun, and gusto for life, that he remained etched vividly in his daughter's memory, and likely would forever.

Belinda remembered him as a handsome man, with sweeping moustaches, who used to roar with laughter as he tossed her high, and whose moustache tickled her deliciously when he kissed her. Belinda had worshiped him, and cried herself to sleep every night for months after his sudden departure.

"Your father is a ne'er-do-well, a reprobate, a rover. He has no sense of responsibility, and I never should have married him." That was the only explanation Belinda's mother ever gave for her husband's disappearance.

For a long time Belinda thought her father had died, and no one wanted to tell her. Then, a few years later, she found out that once or twice a year her mother received bank drafts, sometimes for large amounts, sometimes for very little. There were never any letters, no return addresses, but the banks on which the drafts were drawn ranged all over the United States, and the last one, four months previous, had come from Dawson City.

That was when Belinda had begun to think of going to the Klondike. Of course she realized that Morgan Lee would probably be long gone before she ever got there, but she was bored with the photography studio in New York

City. She had supported herself and Annabelle with the studio for three years, ever since their mother's sudden death, but Belinda had visions of traveling to far places, supporting herself by selling her pictures to newspapers and magazines.

When she conceived the idea of going to the Yukon with her cameras, she soon discovered that most editors of publications using pictures were reluctant to hand out assignments to women. The majority of them laughed openly, deriding the idea of a female in a profession not only comparatively new, but belonging exclusively to the male.

Brenda got a few half-hearted assurances that her pictures would be considered, but only after the fact. It was up to her to arrange and finance the trip; not a single publication would advance her any money. One of the most prestigious publications, *Leslie's Weekly*, received her more warmly than others, yet even its editors balked at advancing her funds. But this dim promise encouraged her and she went ahead on her own. It took most of the money she could scrape together to purchase materials, pay train passage across the continent, and book the ship passage to Dyea.

Annabelle's decision to accompany her did not help, since it served to double their transportation expenses. At first Belinda was adamant in her refusal, and was amused when Annabelle insisted on going. She thought that it was only one of Annabelle's whims and would soon be forgotten; but, as preparations progressed, Annabelle showed no signs of changing her mind, and finally Belinda had been forced to flatly refuse to allow her to make the trip.

It was then that Belinda discovered a streak of steel beneath her older sister's soft, pretty exterior. She had never been able to cope with Annabelle's tearful, dramatic outbursts; and after a week of tears, pleading, and accusations, she relented, admitting to herself that she had rather dreaded the idea of traveling alone.

Although Belinda knew that their funds would be dangerously low when they reached the Yukon, she hoped to earn some money by taking portraits. She figured that men up there, especially those with paying claims, away from home and family, would be willing to pay well for portraits to send home. Also, she was confident enough of her ability, that she was certain she would be able to shoot pictures of this exciting frontier country that would be accepted by various publications. If the pictures she took were good enough, the fact that she was a woman would be overlooked.

She had absolutely no interest in looking for gold.

Charlie awakened Belinda for the trip to Sheep Camp early the next morning, although it was morning only by the clock, so far as Belinda was concerned. She doubted that she would ever become accustomed to the long nights and equally long days here. There were places here, she had read, where the sun did not rise at all for a month in winter.

Charlie had two other Indiana bearers with him, younger replicas of himself. He did not bother with introduction, saying merely, "Do not speak good English like me." He grinned. "But good bearers. Not strong like me," he added, flexing his muscular shoulders, "but good. We start now."

Without further ado, he started to take down the tent. Annabelle, still asleep inside, awoke with a startled cry.

"Belinda!"

Stifling her laughter, Belinda said, "My sister isn't up yet, Charlie. You start moving the other things first. By the time you get back from the first trip, we'll have the tent down and ready."

The Chilkat shrugged philosophically. He and the other bearers lashed together the trunks and crates, fastened them into harnesses, shouldered the packs, and started off. Belinda was amazed at the loads they carried, seemingly with ease; they had taken more than half of their goods.

Stepping into the tent, she saw that Annabelle had snuggled down and gone back to sleep. Unceremoniously, she nudged her sister with the toe of her boot. "Up, dear sister. It's time to move out."

Complaining bitterly, Annabelle got out of the sleeping bag and put on her clothes. Belinda cooked their breakfast over the alcohol stove. Then she collapsed and folded the tent into a pack, receiving only token assistance from her sister. It was well past noon by Belinda's pocket watch when the three bearers returned. She offered to carry some of the smaller bundles.

Charlie drew himself up, and said huffily, "Charlie hired to transport goods."

Hiding a smile behind her hand, Belinda hastily dug the tripod out of one trunk, then trailed after them, carrying only the tripod and the valise holding her camera. She wanted to take some pictures of Dyea.

Trudging along beside her, Annabelle muttered angrily as she had to pull her boots out of the mud. "What a dreary place! It's fit only for roughnecks and," indicating the bearers, "savages like those."

"Hush, they'll hear you," Belinda scolded. "And stop complaining! Do I need to remind you that it was your idea to come along, not mine?"

"I didn't think it would be this bad," Annabelle said, pouting. "Why, even the men up here are too maddened by gold lust to take time to pay proper respect to a lady!"

"You should probably consider yourself lucky." Belinda said dryly, "if the men we have seen so far are typical."

They were passing by the last of the sleeping tents now, and entering a muddy street, lined on every side by tent saloons, gambling establishments, clapboard hotels, and log cabin restaurants. Belinda saw a crude sign on a leaning post: TRAIL STREET. She knew that Dyea, once an Indian village of some two hundred people, had swollen considerably since the discovery of gold, with the population now estimated between five and ten thousand.

Vultures, she thought, thousands of vultures feeding on the gold seekers.

Trail Street was crowded with traffic—men toting packs, pack animals heavily laden, even a dog sled. There were no sidewalks, but hitching rails before most of the buildings provided a narrow space packed with men watching the parade of gold seekers. Most of them were hawking wares of various kinds, and others were trying to lure passers-by into the saloons and casinos. Belinda even noticed several heavily painted women darting out into the foot traffic, attempting to entice men with flirtatious winks and whispered promises.

Belinda took her sister by the arm and pulled her out of the flow of traffic. She called, "We'll catch up, Charlie. I want to take a picture."

She set up the tripod and placed the camera on it. Directly across the street was a long, wooden building in better condition than the others. What had caught Belinda's eye was a large mural across the front, depicting a barroom scene, with men drinking at a long bar, a roulette wheel surrounded by players holding pokes of gold, and an audience of men, and brassy-looking women in skimpy costumes. In bold letters across the top of the mural were two words: LESTER'S PLACE.

Belinda thought that the mural epitomized how this town catered to the gold seekers—to their lusts, greed, and appetite for drink. It would make a good picture, if she could get it right.

Adjusting her camera, glancing up from time to time, she noticed a tall man wearing a derby hat, a fancy suit, and a topcoat with pearl buttons—far better apparel than most of the other men had. His face was long, divided horizontally by a dark slash of moustache, and pitted with smallpox scars.

He was standing before Lester's Place and, suddenly, Belinda became aware that he was watching her intently with hard black eyes. There was something malevolent about his stare, and she was relieved to see him turn back inside. But he was back almost immediately with another man. The second man was enormously fat, with a huge belly protruding from his unbuttoned topcoat. He was also tall, almost the same height as his companion, and as nattily dressed, although his clothing did not fit him as well as that of his slimmer comrade.

With a thrill of apprehension, Belinda saw that the man with the moustache was pointing at her! Now, in tandem, they started across the street, picking their way through the traffic, clearly heading for her. But what could they do to her? She'd done nothing wrong!

By now they were close enough for Belinda to see the fat man's face—beardless, round and pink—wearing a jolly smile. His small brown eyes twinkled at her. Belinda relaxed. Despite his size and girth, he had none of the menacing manner of his companion.

Breathing heavily, he stepped out of the traffic, swept the derby hat from his head, and bowed. Belinda stifled a cough of laughter. His head was bald and shiny as an egg!

In an unctuous voice, he said, "Ma'am, may I introduce myself? I am Lester Pugh, and I am the proprietor of that establishment, which I gather you are about to photograph. This gentleman is my friend and associate, one Chet Harter by name."

The pockmarked man's expression did not alter in the slightest.

"I am Belinda Lee," she said tightly, "and this is my sister, Annabelle. Is there some reason why I cannot take a picture of your establishment?"

"That, Miss Lee, would depend on your purpose."

Belinda said, "I am a photographer by trade. I intend to sell portraits while I am here. I also hope to sell my pictures, if they are of interesting subjects, to *Leslie's Weekly, Harper's,* and other publications."

Out of the corner of her eye, Belinda noticed that Chet Harter was studying Annabelle boldly, and her first impulse was to reprimand him sharply. Yet, why should, she? Annabelle was of age, it was her idea to come along, and given her flirtatious ways, this would not be the first man to have designs on her.

Annabelle had remained demurely quiet all the while, but she had taken note of the pockmarked man's bold eye. He had a strong presence, but he certainly could not be called handsome—not with his pitted face—and something about him frightened her. Even so, she found him fascinating. All the suitors she had known had been in awe of her beauty, and polite to the point of dullness. Whatever else he might be, she sensed that this man would not be dull. She felt a shiver go down her spine, and she felt sure that this was not the last she would see of Chet Harter. This country held the promise of some excitement, after all!

Belinda, her full attention on Lester Pugh, saw his eyes brighten. "Now that, Miss Lee, would be a purpose I could agree with. Free advertising, so to speak, for my establishment! Feel free to take all the pictures your heart desires!"

"Perhaps you and your associate would like to pose in the picture?"

For just a moment the affable man vanished, and she recoiled at the naked rancor staring out at her from his small eyes. Then he was genial again. "I must beg off. Let us say that I am shy, and unaccustomed to having my picture taken. I wish you good fortune in your venture into our north country, Miss Lee." He dipped his head and replaced the derby. "Oh . . . if, your pictures are used, I would much appreciate a copy of the publication. Just send it C.O.D. to Lester Pugh, Dyea. Everybody knows me . . . come, Mr. Harter, let's leave the lady to the pursuit of her trade." He swiveled his head when there was no response, and seemed to notice for the first time Harter's interest in Annabelle. Although his genial manner did not change, Pugh's voice took on a rasp. "Mister Harter!"

Seemingly unperturbed, Harter took his gaze from Annabelle. "Yeah. Heard you the first time, L.P."

The pair moved off, soon disappearing into Pugh's establishment. What an odd pair, Belinda thought, and strangely disturbing—especially Chet Harter.

Annabelle's giggle sounded. "The tall one's rather attractive."

"Attractive!" Belinda shuddered. "He's the ugliest man I've ever seen!"

"I know," Annabelle said complacently. "That's what makes him attractive."

Long accustomed to her sister's whims, Belinda dismissed Harter from her mind, and went about taking the pictures. She waited patiently for a lull in the traffic along Trail Street, so her view would be unobstructed. Finally, her chance came, and she pulled the shutter lever on the camera.

Then she replaced the camera in the valise, folded up the tripod, and beckoned to Annabelle.

Although Charlie and the other bearers were long out of sight, they had no trouble finding the way to Sheep Camp, since the canyon was narrow and all the traffic had the same destination.

Their tent was already up when they arrived at the camp, a place of incredible clutter and confusion. The only permanent buildings were two log cabins, but there were a number of tents clustered together as if huddling for protection against the elements.

Charlie had set up the camp stove and was cooking supper; the other bearers were not in sight.

"It isn't necessary for you to cook for us, Charlie," Belinda said.

The Chilkat shrugged. "Charlie good cook. *Like* to cook."

Belinda had the feeling that Charlie had adopted them, but it was a comforting feeling. She wondered if it would be possible to hire him to accompany them all the way to Dawson City.

Studying a sign in front of one of the log buildings, she saw that she had further reason to be grateful to Charlie. Tired as she was after the long hike, she had thought of buying their supper tonight. The sign said: THE MASCOT—HOT DRINKS AND MEALS—SUPPER—ONE DOLLAR.

Belinda had been warned that the prices up here were outrageous. After the heavy expenses she had already incurred, she could ill afford two dollars for their supper.

So, she was happy to eat Charlie's cooking—tinned beef, gravy, sourdough biscuits, and peaches. She was more determined than ever to make every effort to keep Charlie with her.

Both women were exhausted. Charlie warned of an early start the next day, so both Belinda and Annabelle crawled into their sleeping bags immediately after supper and slept soundly.

The next morning, April 3rd, shortly before noon, Belinda stood next to their pile of remaining gear and looked about her in awe. She was in a shallow valley called the Scales, situated at the foot of Chilkoot Pass. She was alone. Annabelle had gone on ahead with Charlie and the other bearers. At the summit, Charlie would leave

Annabelle to watch the goods ported on their first trip, then return for Belinda and the rest of their possessions.

The squat Chilkat had insisted that they start out early this morning. It had been snowing off and on for days, and several feet of snow had been deposited atop the already heavy pack. Charlie had explained that he wanted to be well over the pass before the midday temperature softened the snow pack, increasing the danger of an avalanche.

Belinda gazed at the mountainside—dark lines of men labored up the slope, a lock-step procession moving up a flight of twelve hundred steps worn into the frozen snow. The pace of the line was determined by the slowest man. To step out of line for any reason often meant a wait of several hours before being permitted back in. The ascent was 1,950 feet in the first three miles, and 1,250 feet the final mile.

Looking back the other way toward Sheep Camp, where they had spent the night, Belinda saw that the line of men stretched out of sight in that direction as well.

Suddenly, she was seized with a feeling of great excitement. What a marvelous picture this scene would make!

Hastily, she took the Graflex from the valise. The snow here, about twenty yards from the trail, was packed down hard, so she had no trouble setting up the tripod.

Ready to take the picture, she took a few moments to decide which view would make the best composition. She was momentarily distracted by a familiar-looking figure in the line of men. Then the figure turned slightly, and she saw that it was the broad-shouldered man whom she had outbid for the dray. He was carrying a bulky pack that must have weighed close to two hundred pounds, yet he walked easily, without the pronounced stoop of his fellows. Now, as though feeling Belinda's gaze on him, he looked directly at her, his ice-blue eyes as cold as the snow underfoot.

She glanced hastily away, feeling color rise to her cheeks, and concentrated her attention on the job at hand, focusing the camera on the upper half of the Chilkoot Pass.

As she snapped the shutter, she heard a sharp report, like the crack of a whip, followed by a booming sound, above her. Looking quickly up the trail, she saw a wall of snow at least thirty feet high, which had broken loose from a cliff overhanging the trail about halfway up, moving at terrifying speed, covering the trail as it went.

Belinda saw a whole section of the line of men simply disappear, as though a giant eraser had eliminated them, and then she realized that the avalanche was coming directly at her, like a giant tidal wave. . . .

Startled into immobility, Belinda could only stare at the wall of snow and ice coming toward her. She knew that she must move—there was no way of knowing how far down the avalanche would travel—but somehow the message from her brain did not reach the rest of her body. Her only thought was what a magnificent picture it would make!

Suddenly her eye was distracted by the movement of a dark object to her left, but before she could turn her head, she was hit from the side. As she tumbled into the snow, she saw thick legs in heavy boots churn past her; then, as she raised her head, she could see the whole man, a bulky figure in a hooded parka, reaching toward her camera where it rested on the tripod.

Confusion and anger filled her. What was going on? What was he trying to do?

Hastily, she scrambled to her feet. The man's back was to her as he fumbled with the camera, and without hesitation, Belinda flung herself onto his back.

The man staggered briefly, and then, without even turning his head, he flung her aside with frightening ease. Belinda hit the ground hard, and the air left her lungs in a rush. Stunned, she could do nothing but watch, as her assailant grabbed the camera and tripod and began to hurry off. This simply couldn't be happening!

Then a shout sounded behind her, and she turned her head to see a second figure moving swiftly toward the first. This man appeared shorter than her attacker, yet he was easily as broad of shoulder and he moved with the quickness of a cat.

The first man flung a frightened look back over his shoulder. He tried to move faster, but the front end of the avalanche had reached him now. Most of its force had been dissipated, but about two feet of snow was swirling along the ground, hampering the fleeing man's movements.

Belinda watched with breathless hope, as the second man caught up to the fleeing thief, and seized him roughly by the shoulder. Now she winced as the thief let the precious camera fall to the ground, and turned to face his pursuer.

Oh, God! Please let the camera be all right! Please! And then, guilty at the realization that her first thought was for her camera rather than her rescuer, she added a plea for him, too. Let him win, dear God. Please let him win!

The two figures, looking ridiculously small and puny in the vast, white landscape, struggled back and forth in the icy snow, and now Belinda could not tell which figure was which.

It occurred to her that she should approach them and retrieve her camera while they were engaged, but as she started to put this plan into effect, one man struck the other a mighty blow, and just like that the fight was over.

Now, one man lay in the snow, limbs spread, and the other bent over to pick up her equipment. Oh, dear God! Please let it be the right one!

Belinda waited in agonizing suspense, as the man shouldered the tripod and camera, and began to move toward her. Behind him, the man on the ground got awkwardly to his feet, and staggered off until he was lost among the other men milling about in consternation and panic.

It was not until her rescuer was standing before her that Belinda recognized him. When he was near enough for her to see into the dark recess of his parka, she felt the shock of recognition, as she stared into ice-blue eyes. It was the man from the beach at Dyea. The man she had treated so rudely. Despite the biting cold, she felt her face grow hot.

He paused in front of her, his breath a frosty cloud hovering between them, and smiled. Rather wolfishly, she thought.

"I believe these belong to you, ma'am." He held the tripod and camera toward her, and Belinda took them with what she knew was indecent haste.

Quickly, she examined the Graflex for damage. Thank heaven, there was nothing broken, and the exposed film was still inside. It seemed almost like a miracle.

Only after her examination of the camera did she give him a smile. "I owe you a great deal," she said, "and an apology, as well."

His smile widened and—as a photographer, of course—she was struck by the rugged good looks of his craggy features. When he smiled like this, his cold eyes appeared to thaw.

"Well, that's a pleasant surprise," he said dryly. "Somehow, when we met before, you didn't strike me as the grateful sort. Now why do you suppose I thought that?"

Belinda felt her cheeks grow hot again. How ridiculous, she thought, he's got me blushing like a chit of a schoolgirl! However, she was in his debt, and it would be rude of her not to admit it.

"I *have* apologized!" she said with some asperity. "And I have acknowledged my debt. I am grateful."

She experienced a sudden urge to explain her actions to him, but pushed the thought away. He wasn't interested in the story of her life, and she didn't really have to justify herself to a stranger.

He shoved back his parka, and the thin sunlight caught in the thick, coppery gold of his hair. "Now," he said, "about this debt you admit you owe me, how do you propose to repay me?"

His tone was serious, but his eyes were amused, and Belinda, who had heard this type of gambit before, felt a rush of disappointment and annoyance. So he was just like all the others, quick to turn the conversation into a game, a sexual ploy, hinting for kisses, and heaven only knew what else. Well, she was not Annabelle, to flap her eyelashes and simper sweetly while she implied promises that she would never keep. If he wanted repayment, he would get repayment, although not in the currency he evidently expected.

"How much do you want?" she said coldly. "I'm afraid that right now my funds are a bit low, but if you can wait . . ."

He looked at her strangely and moved a step back, as if to see her better. A brief, lopsided smile touched his mouth, then disappeared.

"I'm afraid you mistook my meaning, ma'am," he said, coolly and politely. "I was only making light conversation, a thing I'm not particularly accustomed to, and clearly not good at. No payment is necessary. Just consider what I did the act of a Good Samaritan, shall we say, which someday you may pass on to someone else."

Belinda felt a rush of embarrassment, the now-familiar blush touching her face and throat. Stepping back from him, she stumbled, and, losing her balance, sat down abruptly on the snow.

Dreadfully embarrassed now, she struggled to rise to her feet, as he stood watching her, an unreadable expression on his face.

Full of anger, at both herself and at him, Belinda regained her feet and hurriedly straightened her clothes.

"I would have helped you up," he said seriously, "but then I figured that you might feel *too* indebted to me. And that would be a heavy load of 'grateful' for a girl like you to be carrying around."

She tried to stare him down, without success. She said frigidly, "I appreciate your consideration, and I understand perfectly."

"Do you now?" he said cryptically.

31

Their gazes locked, and for a moment Belinda felt much as she had when she saw the avalanche approaching—frightened and fascinated.

It seemed very quiet on the mountain now, except for an occasional shout in the distance. Belinda tore her gaze away, for the first time in several minutes remembering the avalanche and the men on the trail.

Looking up the mountain, she saw that the top part of the trail had been obliterated by a thick blanket of snow. The black, ant-like row of climbers was gone, scattered into individual specks of darkness that floundered through the soft snow, searching for buried supplies and, perhaps, buried men.

Belinda shivered, suddenly aware of how cold, tired, and sore she was, and how close she had come to death. She needed rest and food . . .

Her gaze again went to the trail. Everything she had, except for the camera, tripod, and what she wore on her back, was up at the top of the pass. A wave of depression rolled over her and her body sagged.

"Are you all right?"

She had forgotten that he was there. "Oh, yes. I'm fine." She gestured. "But those poor men . . . there must be several buried in the snow."

"I'd say so, yes. Probably a large number. It's a harsh country here. But you now . . . where are your supplies, the rest of your things?"

Wordlessly, she pointed to the top of the trail.

"There'll be no getting up there until tomorrow at the earliest. It'll take at least that long to clear the trail. You'll need a place to spend the night and something to eat."

To her chagrin, Belinda felt the prickling of tears behind her eyelids. She blinked angrily, and for the first time the reality of her situation overcame her. The impersonal cruelty and the brutal threat of this beautiful, frozen land overwhelmed her, and for just a moment, she was conscious of her own insignificance and frailty.

Then she thought of the clown. And her spirit revived.

When Belinda had been a little girl, her father had taken her one Sunday to a puppet show in the park, in which the main character, a small harlequin clown, suffered much adversity. But always, in the play, the clown had survived. No matter how beaten down or oppressed, he had always gotten to his feet; slowly sometimes, even reluctantly, but always the small, bright figure had at last stood upright, triumphant.

Something in Belinda had identified with that small, brave figure, and after that, whenever things were bad for her, whenever life knocked her down, she thought of the little harlequin clown who had forever and always got to his feet, and it had helped her to do the same.

She tried to smile. "Well then, I suppose I'll just have to manage, somehow, until tomorrow . . ."

As she spoke the words, a wave of dizziness struck her, and she swayed and nearly fell.

In an instant his arm was firm around her waist, and she found herself leaning against his strength. She heard his voice against the hood of her parka. "I have a small tent and some food in my pack. You can stay with me until morning."

This time there was no joking about gratitude or repayment, and Belinda, tired as she was, appreciated his sensitivity, for she certainly did not have either the strength or the will to banter or argue back. She let him lead her away from the spot where they had been standing; he found a partially sheltered hollow between two large boulders.

"This looks like as good a spot as any." He seated her on a smaller boulder. "My name is Joshua Rogan, by the way, Josh to my friends."

"I'm Belinda Lee."

"Fine, Belinda Lee," he said briskly. "You stay put until I get my tent set up."

When the tent was erected, it looked barely large enough for one. His voice direct and impersonal, Josh said, "Get inside, and wrap up in the blankets. I'll get the stove going shortly and cook something to eat."

Inside the dark cocoon of canvas, Belinda wrapped herself in blankets and stretched out on the ground. She was shivering, but slowly it subsided. As she grew warmer, she dozed.

She awoke to the smell of food cooking and her stomach proclaimed its anger at not being filled. She sat up, keeping one blanket around her. His back to her, Josh squatted in the tent opening. Scooting over to him, she saw that he had something simmering in an iron pot on the camp stove.

"Hello, Josh," she said tentatively.

He twisted around to face her. "Feel better?"

She nodded. "Yes, much. But I'm starving. The smell woke me up." She nodded toward the bubbling pot.

"It won't be a meal to please a gourmet, but well have something hot in our bellies. It's almost ready, Belinda. Would you like to get the plates and utensils from my pack?"

Belinda took two tin plates and a pair of spoons from Josh's pack. She gave the plates to him to fill. The stew, or slumgullion as he called it, was tasty and rapturously hot. She finished her share, along with a thick chunk of bread, and wished there was more.

Then they sat before the stove, sharing its meager heat and drinking tea made from melted snow—just as if they had known one another for years. After the prickly edges were rubbed off, she found Josh a comfortable person to be with, intelligent and aware of other people's feelings.

"How do you and your sister happen to be here?" he asked. "It's unusual, you know, to see a young and beautiful woman in these parts, much less a pair of them."

Belinda, warming to his interest, told him her story without embarrassment.

"I wish you good luck," he said, "and I think you'll do whatever you set out to do. You're a strong woman, Belinda Lee."

Belinda was surprised at the pleasure she felt at this compliment. "And you?" she said. "What brings you up here? Searching for gold? You strike me more as a professional man."

He looked away, and was silent for a few moments before answering. "Well, you might say that all my life I've been a searcher, and I guess I'm still searching. And I'm not the only one, it would seem. There are hundreds of professional men out here, scratching for gold side by side with ex-roustabouts and laborers." He looked up at the Chilkoot Trail, which Belinda could see had been partially cleared now. "There are all kinds here, crooks as well as honest men." In profile his face seemed to harden. "And some who'd rather kill a man for his poke, than work for their own.

"Well!" He slapped his knee. "I suggest that we both get some sleep. They should have the trail cleared by morning, but it will probably be rough going. We'll need our strength." He stretched elaborately, yawning.

He turned off the stove. "You'd better get inside," he said, his voice flat.

For a moment Belinda stared back into the tent; the vision of them lying side by side made her face hot and her throat tight.

He scowled at her in annoyance. "It's a matter of survival, Belinda. We'll just have to put our personal feelings aside, and you will have to accept my word that I'm a gentleman, and won't take advantage of the situation."

She nodded, still unable to speak; but she felt awkward and provincial in her hesitation. Quickly then, she bent down and crawled through the low opening. As she settled herself in the blankets, she felt Josh crawl in after her.

She tried to make herself as small as possible, but the narrow confines of the tent, barely wide enough for the two of them, forced his body alarmingly close to hers. She felt as if she was blushing from head to toe, and pulled the blanket she had worn outside, close to her body, like a shield. Then she felt his fingers gently tugging at it.

She choked back a cry, and held onto the blanket for dear life.

"Belinda," his voice was gentle, "I'm not going to touch you, but we must share the blankets. Our body warmth is vital here. I mean, together our bodies will generate more heat. It's more efficient if the blankets are over both of us, and then tucked in."

Belinda relinquished the blanket quickly, chiding herself for being a prude and an idiot. He was right about two bodies generating more heat. Her own certainly felt warm right now.

For several moments he was in motion, arranging and tucking in the blankets, and then he was finally still, the warmth of his breath fanning her neck hairs.

Belinda lay rigid, unable to shed the years of training in propriety so quickly.

She wondered if he was as tense and uncomfortable as she was, and then was startled to hear his gentle snore. He was asleep! Here she lay stiff as a board in embarrassment, and *he* was asleep! She felt outraged and somehow cheated, but her commonsense came to her rescue. She laughed quietly at herself. This relaxed her, and she grew warm and drowsy, gradually slipping into sleep.

During the night she drifted in and out of sleep, until at one point the eerie, frightening sound of a wolf's howl brought her sharply awake.

The tip of her nose, protruding from the blankets, felt icy, and she pulled the blankets over her head to warm it in the woolly dark.

Behind her, Josh stirred, and she realized that in sleeping they had assumed the position of two fitted spoons. He was curled around her body, with his front snuggled against her back. He moved again, and made a strange, half-strangled sound in his sleep.

It was then that she became conscious of his hand, which had somehow crept up under her parka and was now resting over and around her right breast. For a guilty moment, she admitted that it felt nice there, warm and comforting, and then she realized the full import of their position.

And now his hand moved, gently squeezing her breast. For a blinding instant a warm flood of feeling traveled along the nerves of her body, originating in her nipples and coursing down to the secret parts of her body. She had the most awful feeling of "wanting." But then she grew frightened, for behind her, through the thick trousers and woolen underwear she wore, she could feel an insistent pressure.

Panic filled her. Who was this man, this stranger? Belinda had had little actual experience with men, and except for a few relatively chaste kisses and well-corseted embraces, had had no experience of the act of love. Still, she read a great deal, and was not entirely unaware of the way it was between a man and a woman.

She knew, from reading novels and from her mother's stern lectures, that men were uncontrollable when aroused, and that it was best not to stir them too far unless one was prepared to take the consequences.

Well, it would appear that this man, this Josh Rogan was aroused—if she was right about that pressure against her back—and she was alone with him here, at his mercy. What could she do? If she tried to flee, where could she go?

Josh mumbled something unintelligible, and again squeezed her breast. Despite her fear, the delicious tingle again radiated throughout her body, and she felt weak and drained of will. She could feel him moving behind her, but he was evidently still asleep. How could he be? Perhaps if she turned . . .

Carefully, she moved so that she was lying on her back.

His arm was now heavy across her chest, touching both breasts. This was certainly no better.

Then, with a suddenness that startled her, he threw one leg over her and pulled her upper body toward him.

Belinda struck out and attempted to sit up. As she did so, she touched something startling and strange—a large, firm, warm object that filled her hand as she unconsciously grasped at it, then pushed it away. My God! What was it? Her mind veered away from what she knew it must be.

Her cry seemed to fill the small tent, and evidently brought Josh to full consciousness.

Belinda became aware that she was crying in anger and confusion. For a moment the tent seemed to be full of flailing arms and legs, and again her hand came into contact with the throbbing protuberance that seemed to be attached to Josh's body.

She heard him cry out, "My God!"

He drew away from her as she pressed as close as possible to the cold canvas tent wall on her side. She could feel him moving, thrashing about, and then he was still.

The struggles had torn loose the nest of blankets, and she felt chilled and somehow guilty.

Finally Josh was still, but she could hear his breathing quite clearly; it was heavy and somehow threatening in the small, confined space.

He said tentatively, "Belinda?"

She did not answer.

"Belinda? Are you all right? Did I . . . did I hurt you?"

She swallowed convulsively. "No, I . . . I guess not." Her tone was accusatory.

He groaned. "God, I'm sorry, Belinda. Can you believe

that? I gave you my word, and I meant to keep it, I swear I did. I know it's no excuse; but I was asleep. I should have known . . . did I frighten you?"

"Yes," she said in a small voice.

"Oh, Christ! Here, give me one of the blankets."

She felt him pull away one of the coverings. He bumped her leg as he crawled out of the tent. His voice came low and hesitant from outside.

"I *am* sorry," he said, "I'll say it again. But you might as well know that a man has certain limitations, Belinda, and when the consciousness is asleep, the body sometimes acts on its own. I hope you can forgive me."

She heard the crunch of frozen snow as his footsteps moved away from the tent.

Feeling righteous, but strangely depressed, Belinda pulled the remaining blankets around her. Did Josh really have no control over what had happened? And that warm flesh— that live, pulsating part of him that she had touched—she could feel the heat of it still against her palm. Her body tingled and throbbed with the confusion of her emotions and the memory of the touch of his hand on her breast.

❦3❦

Lester Pugh, feet apart and planted firmly to support his great weight, carefully struck a lucifer and touched it to the end of the Turkish cigarette in the ivory holder.

Inhaling deeply, he held the smoke in his lungs as he peered through the grimy window of his office, out into the main street of Dyea. There was a smile upon his pink, rather full lips, but his small brown eyes were as hard as the wood of the ebony cane that leaned near him against the wall.

Dyea might not look like much right now, but it was growing minute by minute; and what there was of it, and what it would become, would belong to Lester Pugh.

Gently, he rocked back and forth on the balls of his feet. Yep, Dyea was his town—he owned it, or most of it, lock, stock and barrel.

His hard little eyes warmed at the thought. He had taken the town over, bit by bit—the gambling halls, the saloons, the bank. Everyone else was too busy running after gold to worry about who was ramrodding things. What they didn't see was the gold to be made right here, catering to the wants and needs of the vast hoard of stampeders. He would come away with more wealth than any of them, and without raising a callus on his well-manicured hands.

He chuckled softly, and his watch chain danced across the shining expanse of his vest. Soon the town would be entirely his, just like Skagway across the way belonged to Soapy Smith.

Now there was a man to admire, and emulate! Soapy Smith could dream up more schemes between bites of his breakfast ham and eggs than most men could in a month of Sundays.

Everyone was laughing at his latest scheme. A few weeks before he had opened a telegraph office in Skagway. Men had stormed the office to get off telegrams, at five dollars apiece, to their dear ones back home. The next day they could come in and receive an answer to their telegrams, again at five dollars a pop.

The thing was, there was no telegraph service. The messages went only as far as the back room of the office, where a drunken ex-newspaper reporter concocted answers to the wires.

The secret had gotten out a few days ago, and the whole territory was laughing fit to kill.

Sobering, Pugh's thoughts returned to his own plans. When he had Dyea sewn up tight and in his pocket, so to speak, he planned to expand. In expectation of this, he had already begun to acquire property in Dawson, his first acquisition being a saloon and gambling house. He had found that it was always best to start with a sure money-making property, for the profits from such an operation helped to provide the means to acquire other properties. He had put a good man in charge—Montana Leeds, a jovial, but cool-minded man, and an honest one, too.

Pugh chuckled again and exhaled one perfect smoke ring. He had no objection to honesty in other men, if it served *his* purpose, and Montana Leeds was serving his purpose very well.

A woman, shapeless in heavy skirt and parka, passed by on the opposite side of the street, and Pugh noted her passing. Not too many women were out here yet, and those who came were either tarts plying their trade or hard-bitten harridans who hoped to compete with the men in the search for gold. The occurrence yesterday had been unusual, those two girls with their pink cheeks and big eyes. In the days when his sexual appetites had been more pressing, and his size less of a hindrance to their consummation, Pugh would have directed his considerable energies toward seducing one, and possibly both, of them.

However, during the last few years, his carnal appetite had waned, and the energy he used to expend in pursuit of its satisfaction was now directed to the accumulation of power and wealth.

The Indians knew the secret, he thought. They knew that abstaining from sexual congress before battle and during ceremonial rites gave a man extra strength and power to use in other ways.

The girls had been pretty little things, all the same, and if his mind had not been occupied with other matters, he might still have tried to seduce them. But there was business afoot, important business, that required all of his interest at the moment. The matter of this damned government snoop must be settled!

He was just lucky that he had a couple of friends in Washington, who had sent along word that an undercover federal marshal was in the territory to look into the many charges of chicanery, thievery, and other forms of lawlessness, including murder, that had been made against Soapy Smith and himself.

When Pugh had informed Soapy of the presence of the marshal, he had laughed it off. "Let him investigate to his heart's content. I'm not worried."

Pugh wasn't greatly worried either, but he would rest easier once the snoop was out of his hair. He had a little more to be concerned about than Soapy. He was not yet as solidly entrenched as his friend; many of the residents of Skagway considered Soapy Smith a solid citizen.

At any rate, he had started a scheme in motion to handle the problem of the federal snoop.

He pulled out a great gold turnip of a watch, and clicked

open the carved case. Two o'clock. He made an impatient sound. By now it should have been done. Where was Harter?

Turning away from the window, he moved to his wide, carved oak desk. On top of it, in a silver frame, was a picture of a bearded man with his foot on a bar rail.

Pugh raised the picture and looked at the image of the man who was his goad to greatness. "Old Soapy," he murmured aloud. "I'm smarter than you, old friend, and a good deal more careful. I am going to have more than you even dreamed of. Nothing is going to get in my way!"

As Pugh spoke the last word, the outer door to his office swung inward. He turned, astonishingly swift for all his girth, as Chet Harter swaggered into the room, his hat aslant and his expression cocky.

Although Harter's attitude annoyed the hell out of Pugh, he did not change his expression, but only said mildly, "You know, I would appreciate it if you'd knock, Chet. If I remember correctly, I've spoken to you about this before."

Harter's eyes blinked lazily, and he rocked back on his heels, jamming his hands into his pockets. Today, he was dressed in the rough garb of a stampeder, and the clothing accentuated the dark threat of his features.

"Reckon you have, L.P., but you know how my memory is—plumb rotten."

Pugh carefully snubbed out the stub of his cigarette in a large, crystal ashtray on his desk. His tone was still bland, but his small, brown eyes held an expression that caused Harter to move back almost imperceptibly, and his eyes flickered with something that might have been anger, or fear.

Pugh said mildly, "I suggest that you work on that memory of yours, Chet. A bad memory can cause a man a lot of problems. Now, is your memory good enough to remember the events of this morning? If so, I would appreciate hearing about what has transpired. You know, Chet, I am not a particularly patient man."

Harter's black moustache twitched in what might have been an attempt at a smile. "Why, of course, L.P. I mean, that's why I broke in here without knocking, I was so anxious to tell you what happened. But it ain't good, L.P. I might as well tell you that right off."

Pugh's pink lips thinned. "Maybe you'd better sit down, Chet, and start from the beginning."

Harter, removing his hat and heavy coat, hung them carefully on the coat-rack, before sitting in the wide-bottomed chair on the visitor's side of the desk. Pugh, resting his ample haunches on the desk edge, stood in front of him. "Now!" he said.

He could see a faint film of sweat on the other man's forehead. That was all to the good. Harter was a good lieutenant, a good right-hand man, but he was inclined to arrogance, and had a mind of his own. It was necessary now and then to remind him who was boss, and it helped to keep him off-balance.

"Well, we got up to the Pass, me and Carl Doober," Harter began. "We left Dick Doober down below, and Carl and me went up the trail, stepping out about three-fourths of the way up, pretending to be tired. We planted the dynamite just under the overhang, which was covered with new snow, and waited for Dick's signal.

"Up to that point, everything went smooth as silk. Then,

I saw Dick's signal, and we set off the charge. It did the job, all right, wiped out the upper half of the trail, and buried, oh, maybe a hundred of the stampeders. Carl and me, we were safe off to the side, out of the way of the avalanche.

"I thought sure as hell that the job was done. We made our way down to the flat, acting like we wanted to help. We looked around for Dick and didn't see him at first. Then we spotted him off to one side, in a scuffle with some gent.

"We edged over closer, but I didn't think it would be too smart to interfere. Just then, Dick was knocked on his rump, and the other gent picked up some kind of camera and gear that was lying there in the snow. It was then that I saw the girl, the same girl who was in town yesterday taking pictures. The sharp one. You know, the two together?"

"Yes, yes, go on." Pugh's voice was tight, and his smooth hands were clenching and unclenching at his sides.

Harter's voice speeded up, as if to get the story over with. "Well, Dick got up and stumbled away, and we intercepted him and got his story. It seems that Dick, damn and blast his eyes, made a mistake. He mistook some other stampeder for this federal marshal, and signaled to us that he was near the top of the trail, but the marshal *wasn't* far enough up to get caught in the avalanche, and he got away without a scratch . . ."

"That fool!" Pugh spat the words out of his mouth with explosive force. "Now it's all to do over again!"

"You haven't heard it all yet, L.P." Harter leaned forward. "Dick fouled up, true, but he did try to make up for it. That's why he was fighting."

Pugh fixed Harter with his stare. "Yes? I'm waiting."

"Well, when the dynamite went off, Dick happened to

notice that this dame, the one with the camera, was taking pictures of the trail. She had the damned thing pointing right up there, right where me and Carl were, and chances are good that she got us in one of the pictures she took. Anyway, Dick figured that he had better get that camera and any pictures she might have made. He was doing just that, when this gent jumped him. So, I'm afraid that's where it stands, L.P." He spread his large, long-fingered hands. "We missed the marshal, and it's possible that the girl has our picture in that camera of hers."

Pugh struck the desk with his fist. "I'm surrounded by incompetents! Must I do everything myself?"

"Seems to me I'm the one who should be worried. I'm the guy in the picture, if there *is* a picture. It's my butt that's in a crack."

"And everybody knows you work for me."

Harter's eyes were wary. "It was just one of those things, L.P. It wasn't anybody's fault."

Pugh looked at him coldly. "When things go wrong, it is always *somebody's* fault! Always! And this time it would appear to be Dick Doober. What in hell's name possessed you to use those halfwit brothers on a job this important?"

Harter said defensively, "You think it's easy to get someone to do a job like this? Practically everybody in this damned town, except us, is chasing after gold. I took what I could get, and I ain't apologising."

Pugh sucked on his upper lip. His eyes were thoughtful, and when he spoke his voice was calm. "The situation is past now, and cannot be mended. You know, Chet, that I am not one to cry over spilt milk. However, in the future, you will be more careful whom you hire. Is that understood?"

Harter nodded, but his expression was sullen.

"Now," said Pugh, "we must prepare for a trip. You will line up bearers, supplies, and trail clothing. You and I, we are making the trip to Dawson."

Belinda did not sleep for the rest of the night. When Josh called to her in the morning, she came out of the tent reluctantly to find him silent and closed off behind the hood of his parka. She had not thought she could face him, but as he handed her some dried meat and a hard biscuit with a brief, "Good morning," she answered him in kind.

Her feelings were still in a turmoil, and she was both relieved and disappointed by his attitude. Together, they struck the tent and packed his belongings. Belinda could see that the trail was clear now, and that the inevitable line of men was again filing upward.

"Well, we'd better get going," Josh said briskly. And without further ado, he started toward the trail. With an effort, she put the events of the night behind her, and followed after him.

Their progress up the trail, geared as it was to the pace of the slowest man, was not speedy. Belinda, glad of the convenience of her trousers and in good physical condition, made it with relative ease, as Josh had insisted on taking the tripod, leaving her only the valise with the camera to carry.

The trail had been cleared all the way to the top, but they learned on the way that so far fifty bodies had been found—a depressing statistic. However, Belinda felt her spirits lift as they neared the summit. Somehow it seemed to her that last night would be washed away when she reached the top. She would be with Annabelle and Charlie, she would have her own things, and not be required to depend on the kindness of strangers. Josh Rogan would go his way, and they would never see one another again. She ignored the small flash of regret she experienced at this thought and trudged upward.

And then they were there. Exhilarated, she looked back down at the Scales and the ant-like line of men crawling upward.

She looked around, taking in her surroundings. To one side, away from the large tent before which flew the Canadian flag, she saw Annabelle, Charlie and the other two bearers. Behind them was their pile of gear.

Annabelle waved and Belinda started toward the figure of her sister, anticipating the pleasure of their reunion. Then she saw that Josh was looking at her and her gaze caught his . . . and held for a timeless moment.

Finally she lowered her head and looked away. "I want to thank you again, Josh," she said carefully. "You did a kind and good thing, when you saved my camera." Should she apologize for last night? No! She wasn't at fault.

His mouth twitched and. he looked away. "I wish you well on your journey to Dawson, Belinda," he said. "Maybe we'll meet again."

"I don't think so," she said too quickly. Then, to make up for it, she added, "But I do appreciate what you've done. Maybe someday I'll be able to do something for you in return."

Josh ducked his head slightly. "Maybe you can," he said, and held out his gloved hand. With only a moment's hesitation, Belinda took it and returned the brief pressure. Then she turned away and plodded through the snow toward her sister.

Annabelle's pink-cheeked face was petulant, and her pointed chin was stubbornly set, signs which Belinda knew all too well. Her heart sank. Was something really wrong, or was Annabelle simply piqued at having to spend the night up here?

Well, whichever, cheeriness seemed to be advisable. "Annabelle!" she cried, embracing her sister. "Were you worried about me?"

"Yes! And we have other things to worry about as well!" Annabelle's tone was aggrieved. "Tell her, Charlie!"

Charlie stepped up from where he had been seated on a heavy packing case. "Big trouble, Miss Belinda. We got big problem!"

"What? Whatever can be wrong?"

"Not enough supplies," Charlie said sadly, shaking his head. "They, the redcoats,"—he nodded toward the Northwest Mounted Police, vivid spots of color in their scarlet coats—"they say you not have enough supplies for year. They say you cannot go into Yukon, Miss Belinda!"

≈4≈

Belinda stared at her sister in disbelief. "What is he saying, Annabelle?"

Annabelle shrugged and pointed to the uniformed Mounties at their check-stand. "It's true, Bee. Ask them yourself. They claim we're supposed to have enough supplies to last both of us for a year, and we're underprovisioned! Why didn't you take care of everything, like you were supposed to, Bee?"

Belinda looked back at Charlie. "But we don't intend staying for a year! I only planned on a few months, at the most. Didn't you tell them that?"

Charlie shook his head. "They say it not matter. They say everyone swear that. They say one year's supplies, or you cannot go." He turned his hands palms upward. "So, what we do? Take things back down trail?"

Belinda did not answer for a moment, but her mind was busy. Then she said firmly, "No, Charlie. I'm not giving up that easy. Wait here for me. I'm going to talk to the person in charge."

Feeling the eyes of the others on her, she marched toward the checkstand, head held high. What if they wouldn't listen to her? What if they did have to go back? It must not happen!

The Mounties manning the checkstand seemed very young to Belinda. Still, they were very large young men, seemingly strong enough to handle any physical objections to their decisions, and their faces were stern with purpose.

Belinda approached the one who struck her as the least formidable; he had just finished stamping the papers of a middle-aged man in a bulky, plaid coat.

"Sir," she said tentatively. Then louder, as he did not seem to hear her, "*Sir!*"

He looked over at her and a startled expression crossed his face. After staring at her in open astonishment, his face flamed, and he touched the brim of his wide hat. "Ma'am . . . Miss, what can I do for you?"

"I'm with the party over there," she pointed to where

Charlie and Annabelle were standing, "and my sister tells me that you refuse to let us into Yukon Territory. I want to clear up this misunderstanding."

The red flush on his cheeks grew brighter. "I'm sorry, Miss, but I'm afraid there is no misunderstanding," he said firmly. "Your party does not have sufficient supplies to last the year, and the rules allow no one into the Yukon who does not satisfy this requirement."

Belinda kept a rein on her temper. "Didn't my sister tell you that we don't intend to stay in the area for that long a time? We only intend to remain a few months, at the most."

He shook his head, and while his eyes mirrored his distress at having to say no to her, his square jaw was set. "I'm sorry, Miss. Practically everyone who does not meet the requirements says that, and those *are* the rules. I don't make them. I just enforce them."

Belinda was slowly losing her grip on her temper. Showing anger and annoyance could only hurt her cause. Damn! For once she wished that she was like Annabelle, able to use her feminine wiles to coax and wheedle; but then, Annabelle had been here first, and had no doubt already used her considerable arsenal of weapons upon these men, obviously to no avail.

At any other time, Belinda would have been heartened by the sight of men who did not succumb to female blandishments, but at this moment, she could only wish that Annabelle's charms had produced their usual effect.

Swallowing her disappointment, she tried again. "But I'm a photographer, sir. I'm not here to hunt for gold, only to photograph the search. We're not going to become charity cases, you know, if that is what your government is afraid of."

The Mountie shook his head again. "Sorry, Miss. I have my orders."

Belinda's spirits plummeted. The icy wind stung her cheeks, for she had pushed back her parka, the better to converse with this obstinate man, and she felt that at any moment her eyes would spill the tears she could feel building up behind them.

She knew that she could take up no more of this officer's time; the men waiting behind her were growing impatient and beginning to grumble. Clutching at a last straw, she said, "May I talk to your commanding officer, please?"

The young man stuck his chin out even further. "Certainly, Miss. Just go to that big tent over there and ask for Sergeant Mackenzie."

Belinda marched over to the tent and ducked inside. The interior of the tent seemed very dark, but in a few minutes, her eyes became accustomed to the gloom.

Before her, behind a small desk, sat a tall, slender man with hair almost the same color as her own. He was busily writing, moving the pen with great speed, and it was only when the page he was working on was finished that he looked up at her.

His face was thin and intense, with large, hazel eyes of exceptional clarity. He looked, she thought, very bookish and academic for a Northwest Mounted Policeman.

Unlike the Mountie outside, this one did not seem surprised to see a young woman at the checkpoint. His expression was merely that of polite interest. "Yes?" he said. "What may I do for you?" His voice was deep and, she thought, kind.

Belinda, sternly reminding herself to remain poised and calm, again explained her situation. She finished with, "This trip is very important to me, Sergeant, and I believe it can be important to both our countries. The gold rush is an event of historical importance, and a record of what is happening should be preserved for posterity. I am here to do that. There are newspapers and magazines at home, waiting for my pictures. Will you turn me back, and disappoint thousands of Americans who are anxious to know what is transpiring here?"

She felt a bit guilty about the exaggeration, yet she told herself that it was only a small lie, and in a very good cause.

When she was finished, Belinda made an effort to clasp her hands and hold them still, as if her whole life did not hang in the balance of his answer.

He looked at her thoughtfully. "Exceptions *are* made, for instance, in the case of businessmen who must travel between Dyea or Skagway and Dawson. Does it seem to you that you might fit into the category of businesswoman?" A smile lightened his rather serious features.

Belinda answered with a beaming smile of her own. "Oh, yes! I should say that very definitely I am a businesswoman!"

"Well then, in that case, I believe that we can let you go into the Yukon, with the understanding, of course, that you will stay no longer than six months."

"Of course!"

Belinda's mind was ablaze with relief and joy. Despite her brave front, she had really feared that they would be sent back. "Thank you so very much," she said. "This means so much to me."

"I gathered that it did," he said seriously. And as she turned to go, "Miss Lee?"

She turned back. What was it now?

"You go to Dawson, you said?"

"Yes." He hesitated. "I am traveling to Dawson myself, in a few weeks. If you are still there then, may I have the privilege of calling on you?"

Startled by the unexpectedness of his request, Belinda couldn't answer for a long moment. Somehow, in this raw, primitive land, she had not expected the amenities of male-female courtship. But he *was* attractive, and seemingly a gentleman.

"I would be delighted," she said honestly. I shall look forward to seeing you in Dawson."

Then she put the matter out of her mind. Bursting with excitement, she hurried back to where Annabelle and Charlie were waiting.

The first leg of the descent from the summit of Chilkoot Pass was a pleasant contrast to the upward climb. There was a packed, well-traveled trail leading down a comfortable incline all the way to Crater Lake, and the Chilkats took advantage of this to make good time.

Belinda, with another obstacle overcome, was in excellent spirits, and even Annabelle, pleased by the easier going, seemed more cheerful.

The first sight of Crater Lake was impressive—an expanse of clear ice, cupped in a volcanic crater. Belinda stopped and took a picture of the lake and the ice-boats that skimmed across the frozen lake bed.

It made a strange picture—the vastness of white; the dark, moving figures of men; and their bulky bundles, with square sails, that moved slowly across the lake.

As Belinda put the exposed plate into her storage bag, she wished that she had time to develop her prints; that, however, would have to wait until they made camp at Lake Linderman, where she meant to set up a temporary darkroom.

On reaching the shores of Crater Lake, Charlie called a halt. They made camp for the night, and in the morning, Belinda and Annabelle were awakened by the sounds of activity outside their tent.

Belinda forced herself out of the warm cocoon of her sleeping bag, and poked her head through the tent flap. Charlie and the other two bearers were busily piling the gear and supplies aboard two sleds constructed of poles. Each of these odd vehicles had a central pole or mast, with a crossbar, around which the trunks and crates were packed. As she watched, Charlie efficiently attached a large, brown blanket to each mast, thus making a square sail.

All around them, Belinda saw, other men were likewise engaged. Some of them had steel-runnered sleds, which they had packed over the Pass; and some, like the Chilkats, were building their own sleds with poles and ropes.

After a quick but hearty breakfast prepared on the spirit stove, the men pulled the sleds onto the snow-covered ice, and the trek across the lake began. Belinda knew that beyond Crater Lake lay Lake Linderman, where Charlie and the other Chilkats were supposed to leave them. She had already decided that she would ask the sturdy little men to stay with them.

Before the trip began, she had had visions of herself and

Annabelle alone, bravely coping with the rigors of the trail, but now she admitted that Annabelle was next to useless. It would be a great help if Charlie and the others would stay with them, although she was a bit concerned about the expense involved.

Annabelle had awakened in a cranky mood, and seemed to feel none of the excitement that buoyed Belinda. Annabelle was hardly out of the tent before she began a long litany of complaints.

For this reason Belinda decided to let her sister ride on the first sled, handled by Charlie and one of the bearers, while Belinda followed in the second sled, which would be guided by the third bearer.

The wind across the flat lake was brisk and steady, and the makeshift ice-boats, with some initial pushing by the Chilkats, soon moved out at a slow but strong speed that increased steadily as they moved farther out onto the ice.

Belinda, relatively snug in her parka, woolen trousers and heavy boots, found the experience exhilarating. Now and then, over the distance separating the two sleds, came the sound of Annabelle's voice, still raised in complaint. Belinda could not help but smile. Poor Charlie, his ears would be quite worn out by the end of the lake crossing.

She smiled at the young Chilkat, who ran tirelessly alongside her sled, and his brown face split in a white-toothed grin.

Nearby, a steel-runnered sled, lightly loaded and with a man clinging to the rear, overtook them and slowly drew ahead.

As they reached the main body of the lake, the traffic was heavier. Belinda, fascinated by the colorful spectacle of the lake crossing, knew that she must have pictures taken at close hand.

She motioned for the Chilkat to stop the sled, and explained as best she could what she wanted to do and that he must wait for her.

The Chilkat's English was limited, but he seemed to understand, and did not seem happy about her decision.

As she prepared the camera and inserted the film in its holder, a few snowflakes drifted down onto the Graflex.

The Chilkat said something that Belinda did not understand, and motioned for her to get back onto the sled, but she shook her head. "Just a minute," she said. "Just a few minutes."

Looking out onto the lake, she saw several sail-sleds close together. They had, for some reason, stopped on the ice, as if waiting for Belinda and her camera. Picking up the Graflex, she moved toward them, not even hearing the worried voice of the Chilkat behind her.

Lester Pugh was very uncomfortable. Despite his heavy overcoat and high boots, despite his ear muffs and woolen muffler, he felt the brutal teeth of the cold, and the stiff harness that encircled his body bit into the soft flesh under his arms.

He and Chat Harter stood at the base of Chilkoot Pass, looking upward at the narrow line of stampeders, and the cables that swung overhead like a great spider's web.

The cables, hanging from their high supports, belonged to a freight company from Tacoma, and were used—by those who could pay the price—to haul material up the Pass. Unfortunately, most of the people negotiating the

Pass did not have the funds to pay the exorbitant rate charged by the freight company. The majority of the gold seekers carted their own supplies, making as many trips as necessary to get it all to the top, and those who did have funds to spare generally found it more practical to hire the Chilkat bearers to take their goods as far as Lake Linderman.

However, for Lester Pugh, the freight cable was a godsend. Without it, he would never have been able to negotiate the steep incline.

Now, with the harness securely under his arms and buttocks, he sat in the improvised bosun's chair, waiting to be hoisted up the mountain.

Beside him, Harter pulled down the fur flaps of his cap. "Well, I guess I'd better get going, L.P. Meet you at the top."

Pugh nodded somewhat coolly. He would reach the summit considerably before Harter, and would thus be forced to wait, yet nothing he could say would convince Harter to ride the cable with him. The other man had told him he was afraid of heights, but Pugh knew that the real reason was that Harter did not want to be seen riding the cable. It was important to his ego that it be known that he climbed the trail just like any of the other men.

Pugh sneered. Let the idiot protect his ego then. Power gave one certain privileges, and there was not a soul in Dyea who would dare laugh at Lester Pugh, no matter *how* he traveled.

The cable grew taut, creaking, and Pugh felt his feet leave the ground. The leather of his harness settled and strained, and then he was aloft, moving slowly over the heads of the laboring climbers. Beneath him, he could see the whole panorama of the Pass and the men who struggled to cross it.

Despite the majesty of the scene, Pugh did not see it, for his mind was turned inward. Slowly, like a great, airborne whale, he soared over the heads of the climbers in his mind, he mapped out the moves he would make to put his plans into effect, once he had reached Dawson.

At the summit, the cable squealed to a halt, causing Pugh to swing back and forth until he feared he would become sick with the movement. At last someone stopped him by grabbing the leather harness, and he was helped out of the contraption and onto the ground.

Gingerly, he flexed his arms and knees, restoring circulation to his stiffened limbs. He watched passively as the team of sled dogs was brought up and unloaded from the cable. A good dog team was worth its weight in gold up here in the Yukon. Transportation was so difficult to obtain that not only Huskies and malamutes were pressed into service, but any dog large enough to help pull a sled, no matter what his antecedents. Pugh's matched team, healthy and strong, was a matter of great pride to him, and another symbol of his power and wealth. He instructed the freight handler to harness them to the sled. Pugh gave them the order to stay, then he went to take care of the paperwork for his journey into Canada, consulting with the bright-jacketed young Mountie at the checkpoint.

By the time Harter, breathing heavily, had reached the top of the trail, Pugh had imbibed three cups of heavily sweetened tea and eaten a half plate of biscuits, thanks to the courtesy of Sergeant Mackenzie, and was feeling rather mellow.

While Harter loaded the sled in preparation for their departure, Pugh sat on in Mackenzie's relatively warm tent and digested his snack. Only when everything was ready for their departure did he take his place on the back of the sled, where, swathed in fur blankets, he rested in comparative ease.

They would make good time—the team was fast, and the sled, except for Pugh's weight, was lightly loaded. Pugh rammed his hand into a side pocket and removed a large bar of German chocolate, from which he began to take small, nibbling bites. His mind was busy. The fact that Harter had failed in his task to eliminate the federal snoop was only a minor setback, and should be easily remedied in Dawson, if it was still necessary. After all, the marshal had no legal standing in Canada. But mostly on his mind was the expansion of his business interests in Dawson—a delightful prospect.

He wriggled slightly in his nest of furs, and as his mouth began to move rapidly, the chocolate disappeared in larger and larger bites, until the only trace left were the dark smears in the corners of his pink-lipped mouth.

Chet Harter, balanced easily on the back of the bouncing sled, cast a quick eye downward at the vast bulk of his employer.

The great pile of furs was still, and Harter knew that the other man was either sleeping or thinking—plotting new plots, planning new plans, plans which would inevitably succeed.

A wry smile arched Harter's dark moustache upward. He had to hand it to the fat bastard, he had a good mind in that round, pink-cheeked head of his. A mind so devious and quick that there were few who could match it.

Yep, old L.P. had done a world of good for himself and for one Chet Harter. Harter would be the first to admit it. But that didn't mean that he trusted the man, or that he didn't have his own dreams of success, dreams that did not include the fat man.

He knew that Pugh looked down on him to some extent, but then Lester Pugh looked down on everybody, and Harter considered that one of Pugh's few weaknesses. Harter had learned, through experience, that you could get yourself in a whole mess of trouble by underestimating your opponent, and he tried never to make that mistake.

For instance, Pugh underestimated him, Harter; which was just fine as far as Harter was concerned. Someday, when things were just right and Harter was ready, he planned to get rid of the fat man and take over Pugh's little empire. Just how this would be accomplished, he had not yet decided, but it could only be a help to have Pugh not really knowing what he was facing.

Harter's smile thinned. Yep, old L.P. was in for a grand surprise one of these days. But until then, Harter figured he would bide his time, doing what he was told, and stashing away his share of the loot, which was considerable. Whatever else Pugh might be, he was not stingy.

Harter cracked his whip over the backs of the dogs, and the sled picked up speed. They were making very good time, passing the overladen stampeders, like a clipper ship passing a flock of rowboats.

At Crater Lake, where many of the stampeders stopped to rig makeshift sails, the dog team traveled even faster, aided by the smooth ice and the even footing.

They were almost to the center of the lake when Harter saw the woman. Even at a distance he knew it was the one he had seen back in Dyea, because she had the camera apparatus with her, evidently taking pictures of some of the ice-boats.

Reluctantly, he reined the team to a halt. He hated to lose the time and the momentum of the sled, but he sensed that this might be a chance too good to miss.

As the sled slowed, he looked around and saw a young Chilkat standing by an ice-boat, loaded with goods. He seemed to be waiting and Harter guessed that he was waiting for the young woman.

"Chet? Why in hell, may I ask, have we stopped?"

Harter stepped down from the back of the sled and leaned down toward the spot where Pugh's face shone through the nest of fur.

"Over there!" He pointed. "See her? It's that camera girl!"

Pugh poked his head up, looked, and nodded. "So it is! Isn't anyone with her?"

Harter indicated the ice-boat and the Indian. "I think just the bearer with the ice-boat."

"Hmmmm." Pugh's tone was thoughtful. "I wonder where the rest of her party is? But no matter. It does seem providential that we have come upon her alone."

Harter grinned. "Doesn't it, though!"

Pugh's brown eyes twinkled up at him. "Now, I know little of cameras, but I don't suppose that the picture she took of the avalanche would be in her camera now, would it?"

Harter shook his head. "I don't think so, either."

"But it would seem likely that the plates for the pictures already taken would be among her things. Perhaps on the ice-boat?"

Harter gave him a mock salute. "I'll be back in a few minutes, L.P. You just remain comfortable now."

Pugh settled himself deeper within the furs. "I have every intention of doing so. Just don't be gone too long."

While they had been talking, the light drift of falling snow had grown heavier, reducing visibility and increasing the cold.

The Lee woman had her back to Harter, involved with her equipment, and the other ice-boats were too far away for their occupants to see him clearly enough for later identification.

The bearer was young and small, but Harter respected the legendary Chilkat strength. For this reason he circled around behind the youth, who seemed to be dozing on his feet, leaning against the ice-boat.

It took only a moment. The young Chilkat fell like a sack of meal, as Harter's gun barrel smacked him just behind the ear. The search of the trunks and crates took longer; but within a short time, Harter knew that there were no films, or prints, on the ice-boat. Angrily, he released the crude brake and loosed the blanket sail. Giving the vehicle a push with his foot, he watched it move away through the thickening curtain of snow. Damn! The picture must be with the rest of her gear!

Well, with any luck, they might be rid of the woman. The snow was now falling heavily, and she was a tenderfoot. For a moment Harter felt a twinge of regret. Too bad, in a way; she was young and pretty, although not nearly as pretty, in Harter's estimation, as her sister, the blue-eyed one. If it had been the sister now—well, that might be a different matter. But this one was a snotty piece, the kind of a woman who thought she was as good as a man. Well, let her prove it. Let her get out of this!

Quickly, he trotted back to the sled, and took his place on the back.

"Well?" Pugh's voice came faintly through the falling snow.

"No luck finding any picture," said Harter. "But we just might be rid of the woman. I think she's going to be lost in this storm, and I sent her ice-boat sailing off without her."

The bundle of furs quivered as Pugh shook with laughter. "Sad, really. She *is* a pretty thing. But perhaps that would solve our problem as well, or better, than the destruction of her pictures."

Harter raised his whip and sent it curling out over the backs of the sled dogs, making a sound like a pistol shot. In a moment the sled was gliding swiftly across the frozen lake bed.

As Belinda put her exposed film into her storage bag, she became conscious of the biting cold.

Shivering, she closed up the Graflex, and turned away from the vista of three ice-boats, which were becoming obscured by the increasingly heavy snowfall that had begun to swirl about them.

The falling snow made vision very difficult. Where was the ice-boat, and the Chilkat? They should have been right behind her. Belinda brushed the flakes from her face and pulled her parka forward. Fear, as insidious as the cold, began to creep into her bones.

"Halooo!" she cried out into the thickening curtain, but the sound seemed to be swallowed by the snow, and there was no answering hail.

She kept moving forward, trying to move in a straight line. He *must* be here. Surely he would not have gone off without her!

She called again, and as if in derisive response to her call, the snow began to fall thicker and faster.

The world around her now was completely white. The wind was rising, and the cold dug through her clothing with fingers of ice until she was shivering uncontrollably. She was alone and unprotected in an alien and hostile environment. This knowledge, and the fear it brought, came upon her in a rush, leaving her devastated and shaken. And she realized that, for her, this might well be the end of the journey.

T he wind had risen, and Josh's steel-runnered sled, powered by the canvas sail, picked up momentum despite the heavy load of supplies. The remainder of his stores were cached near the top of the pass, and he would cache more at Lake Linderman. The sled he had bought from a stampeder, who had given up in disgust when his sled dogs were stolen.

Clinging to the back of the sled, shifting his weight from time to time for balance, Josh felt a rush of sheer pleasure as he sped past the slower sleds and ice-boats.

Such moments had been few on this trip, he thought. It had been a cold, rough trek, providing little in the way of amusement. Except for the girl, of course—Belinda Lee, with her stormy, gray eyes and tender mouth—and he wasn't sure that meeting her had exactly been a pleasure. If so, it certainly had been mixed with pain.

He shrugged the memory away. There was no use thinking of her. Even if he had the time to seek her out, and he didn't, she had made it clear she wished nothing more to do with him. At any rate, he was not here to enjoy himself. He had a job to do, an important job, that would demand all of his attention and skill.

A sudden gust of wind blew a flurry of snowflakes into his face, but he did not dare release a hand to wipe them away.

The snow, which had been coming in a few delicate flakes, now suddenly began to fall heavily. Visibility was growing worse, and at its present speed, the sled could easily capsize. Josh raised his boot and pressed down on the brake lever.

The sled slowed, with a whine of steel on ice, and the vehicle slewed sideways, almost tilting over, but finally remained upright. Josh reached up a gloved hand to wipe the snowflakes from his eyes.

Through the veil of snow, he caught a glimpse of something dark on the ice ahead. It appeared to be an ice-boat, and it was coming straight toward him from his left side!

He leaned hurriedly to the right, and his own vehicle changed direction slightly. Still, the other boat came on toward him.

"Hey!" he shouted. "Veer off!"

Evidently the other driver did not hear him. Josh had only time to mutter an expletive under his breath, before the ice-boat was upon him. He slammed on the sled brake again and the vehicle shuddered to a halt, just as the other craft hit him broadside and stopped.

Quickly, Josh yanked down his sail and let it drop, then turned to look at the ice-boat, ready to give the operator a tongue-lashing.

It took several seconds before he could believe that there was no driver. All of the bundles on the ice-boat had been torn open, and some of the gear hung half off the vehicle.

Thoughtfully, Josh dropped the blanket sail on the ice-boat. The owner of the sled must have met with an accident, and was probably lying on the ice somewhere slowly freezing to death. Josh shivered in sympathy.

Time was of the essence. He needed to push on with as great a speed as possible and get off the ice before the storm got much worse, but he couldn't leave another human being out there to die.

His mind made up, Josh lashed the two vehicles together, and covered the contents as much as possible with the sails. Then he removed a small compass from his inner pocket and took his bearings. The snowfall seemed to be lessening a bit, but he wanted to take no chance of losing his gear, or of winding up in the possible condition of the man he was seeking.

He set out briskly in the direction from which the ice-boat had come. Since the boat's sail had been set at a certain angle, it should have traveled in a more or less straight line.

It soon became apparent that he was on the right track,

for he began to come across scattered packets and bundles on the ice. For the moment, he let them lie, and quickened his pace. He had been traveling for perhaps fifteen minutes when he saw the dark form against the white.

It was a young Chilkat. He had received a wicked blow on the back of the head, but he was alive. Josh hoisted the boy over his shoulder, and, consulting the compass, headed back the way he had come. The wind had definitely lessened now, and the snow fell steadily, but no longer quite so heavily.

Josh propped the young man against the sheltered side of the vehicles, and after digging into his own supplies, got a few drops of brandy down the Indian's throat.

The blankets and the brandy seemed to help. The Chilkat at last opened his eyes. They widened with fright at the sight of a strange man bending over him.

"It's all right," said Josh quickly. "You're safe. Whoever hit you is gone."

The fear in the young man's eyes abated, and he touched his head and moaned.

"You were hit on the head," Josh said, "and it looks like your ice-boat was searched. Do you know why?"

The Chilkat shook his head, then a sudden thought caused him to widen his eyes. "Missy!" he said. "Where Missy!"

Josh felt the cold touch of premonition. "What Missy? What do you mean?"

"Missy," repeated the youth. "Missy Lee. I been waiting. Where Missy?"

Josh tried to speak slowly. "You have a young woman with you, a Miss Lee?"

The Chilkat made motions with his hands. "Box," he said. "She have box!"

Oh, hell! It *was* her. Somehow it did not surprise him greatly. He thought briefly of the time he was losing, and sighed with resignation. "Can you get up?" he asked the youth.

The Chilkat nodded, and rose unsteadily to his feet. "Chilkat strong!" he said, with a flash of teeth.

"Good." Josh patted his shoulder. "I'll help you to retrieve your things, and repack the ice-boat. Then you continue on to the other side of the lake. I suppose that the rest of your party is there. Tell them what has happened. I'll look for Miss Lee. Can you do that?"

The Indian nodded. "Will tell Charlie. Charlie understand."

By the time the supplies had been collected and the ice-boat repacked, the falling snow had dwindled. Visibility was still limited, but the wind had lessened, although it still blew with enough strength to move the ice-boat.

When the Chilkat was on his way, Josh took the flask of brandy, and some biscuits and dried meat from his supplies, stowing the items in the deep pockets of his parka.

He had no idea just where to begin his search, as the Chilkat had only been able to tell him that the incident had occurred near the middle of the lake. Belinda could have wandered quite a distance in any direction by this time. In the storm, she would not have been able to see the lake shore, and would have had no sense of direction.

He refused to even consider the possibility that she was no longer alive. The storm was not that severe, and she was a strong woman. True, it was not unusual for a tenderfoot,

70

lost and confused, to succumb to the treacherous sleep brought on by the cold. Josh had experienced that temptation himself—the stopping, from weariness; the feeling of languorous warmth that began to overtake you; the insistent pressure of the need to sleep, just for a moment, a moment from which you would never waken.

Josh took his bearings and began to travel in a small circle, widening his range each time he completed an orbit. A half-hour went by, and then an hour. He was growing cold and tired.

What on earth had happened to Belinda Lee? Where had she gotten to?

Wearily, Josh checked his bearings. One more pass, and then he would have to give up the search. There would barely be time to get back to his sled before darkness fell. As it was, he would have to spend the night on the ice. Although cold and fatigue made his feet and legs feel heavy, he trudged forward, eyes straining through the lazy swirl of snowflakes.

Suddenly, he blinked, unable to be certain of his vision. Was something there, on the ice?

Almost afraid to hope, he moved forward. As he approached what had caught his eye, he sighed in discouragement, sure that it was only another drift of snow . . . no! There was something dark, a bulky object.

Adrenalin gave renewed strength to his limbs, and he raced toward whatever it was, falling to his knees beside it.

His hands brushed away the snow, and came to rest on something soft. Frantically, he brushed the rest of the snow away. It was Belinda Lee, all right, still and almost as cold as the ice on which she lay.

Josh jerked off his right-hand glove and touched her face with his fingertips. It was chilly, but not frozen, not yet; the parka had protected it from the ice, and most of the falling snow. He felt for the pulse in her throat. The beat was faint but steady. Thank God!

Putting his arm behind her, he helped her to a sitting position. She slumped lifelessly against his arm. He opened the flask of brandy, and gently pressed the mouth of the flask to her lips.

Much of the liquid trickled down her chin, and she made no effort to swallow. He tried again, and this time her throat worked, as the brandy went down, and she coughed feebly.

He tried the brandy yet a third time. This time he got enough down to do some good; then, raising her in his arms, he set out in the direction of the sled. He had to get her into some kind of shelter, and he needed to check her hands and feet for frostbite.

Even in his fatigue, Josh was surprised at how light she felt in his arms.

Belinda opened her eyes to the bright flicker of flame. For an instant panic rose in her throat, stopping her breathing, and she gasped aloud. Where was she? The last thing she remembered was being alone in the storm; the terrible fear and despair; the certain knowledge that she faced death.

Opening her eyes to the glow of flame against darkness had conjured up a sudden vision of hell, and then she became aware that someone was with her. A firm grip held her hand. With a cry, she turned her head, hoping and yet afraid to see a face.

"Shhh, it's all right." The voice was familiar, and gradually her eyes adjusted to the flickering light.

"It's me, Josh Rogan."

Now Belinda could see his face, pale in the semidarkness, and the gleam of his hair. The ice-blue eyes were looking tenderly down into hers, and the fear left her as quickly as it had come.

"Josh?" She repeated his name foolishly, but it comforted her to say it. Back there, in the storm, she had thought she was going to die, but now she was alive, and somehow, he must be responsible. "How did I get here? What happened to my bearer and the ice-boat?"

"The Chilkat met with an accident, and your sled had been sent sailing across the lake, after being searched. I stumbled onto it, or I should say it *ran* into me, and a short time later I found your bearer on the ice. He told me that you had been with him, and so I searched for you, and found you, thank heaven!"

She tried to sit up, but she felt weak and listless, like a convalescent. "Where is he now? The Chilkat, I mean?"

"I sent him on to join the others of your party, and to tell them that I was looking for you. With any luck at all, he should have reached them several hours ago."

The flames, Belinda could see now, came from a spirit stove in the middle of a small tent. The fire was modest, but it gave off enough heat to warm the tent somewhat.

Josh reached out to pick up a cup of steaming liquid from the stove; it smelled delicious. "Here, here's some broth. It'll warm you up."

Gratefully, she accepted the tin cup, warming her mittened hands around it. The broth tasted rich and satisfying, and she drained it to the last drop.

"Where are we?" she asked.

He smiled crookedly. "Right smack in the middle of the lake. It was almost dark when I found you. I barely had time to get you to my sled and put up the tent."

She wiggled her feet inside her boots and flexed her fingers. "My hands and feet still seem to be working. No frostbite?"

He shook his head. "You were very lucky. I must have found you shortly after you passed out." He smiled wryly. "You know, you gave me a bad couple of hours."

She could feel heat touch her face, and it was not from the fire. "You mean you cared about what happened to me?"

His expression changed, becoming unreadable. "Of course not. I spent all that time mushing through the snow and ice, looking for you, simply for the hell of it," he said testily. "Now I am going to spend a sleepless night, for the same reason!"

She flushed again. She simply couldn't seem to get off on the right foot with this man. What made her say such stupid things?

"Why a sleepless night?" she asked, hoping to change the subject.

His smile was strained. "Because, considering what happened the last time you shared my tent, I daren't go to sleep. I wouldn't want to send you screaming out into the night!"

This time the heat not only touched her cheeks, but washed over her whole body in a flush. She did not answer because she was totally unable to do so. What could she say?

Josh was staring at her strangely. At last he broke the

awkward silence. "Well, at any rate, you'd better try to get some sleep. As soon as it's light, we'll get started for the other side of the lake."

Belinda, without speaking, sat obediently, while Josh arranged the blankets. She noticed that he had insulated the bottom of the tent with waterproof canvas sheeting and furs.

In a short while she was stretched out in the makeshift bed, feeling reasonably comfortable and warm. The spirit stove had been extinguished, and she could no longer see Josh, but she knew he was there.

Her own body heat was warming her in the blanket cocoon, and she began to feel drowsy; however, guilt over Josh, sitting there with only one thin blanket around his shoulders, kept her from sleeping. It didn't seem fair that he, after searching for her, finding her, and rescuing her, should have to spend a sleepless night, while she dozed in comfort.

Stealthily, across the back of her mind, slipped the memory of that other night they had spent together. Of his body, hard and insistent, against her; his hands, warm upon her breasts; of the way she had felt before she had become frightened. Hastily, she put such thoughts out of her mind. That need not happen again, and it was cruel to make him spend the remainder of the night uncomfortable and cold.

"Josh?" she whispered softly.

He grunted.

"Josh, I . . . well, I'm sorry about the way I acted the last time. I really do think you'd better get under the covers. You won't be any good tomorrow to either of us, if you don't get some sleep!"

There was a lengthy silence, and she was thinking that perhaps he hadn't heard her. Then his voice came, low and husky, "Despite what happened last time?"

Belinda hesitated, her mind tumbling with confusing thoughts and feelings. Her body was tingling. She felt both excited and afraid. Her throat was dry and she swallowed hard. "Yes, despite what happened."

Why had she said that? It sounded like . . . oh, my God! She wanted him—at least some part of her did. Feeling divided and miserable, she waited for his answer.

It came with action, not words.

She felt him moving, and then the blankets were lifted, and his body slipped under them, next to hers.

When the blankets were raised, there was a momentary escape of heat, and an influx of frigid air, but then the cocoon was tight again. She could hear the sound of his breathing close to her ear. She was lying partially on her left side, and he was lying on his back. For a long moment neither of them moved, and then, with a groan, he turned to her.

As he turned, her heart began to hammer until she felt that it would burst free of her breast. Now his lips were upon hers, sweet and insistent and warm. Without thinking, she strained toward him through the layers of clothing they both wore.

She had never known that it could be like this, so wild and sweet, tinged with the thrill of the forbidden.

Josh pulled his mouth away and put his cheek next to hers. His lips, near her ear, whispered endearments, and each word kindled further the excitement that was rising within her.

"Belinda, my sweet Belinda! I want you! Oh, God, I want to feel your body next to mine. Oh, Belinda!"

Then his lips were again upon hers, and his hands were

exploring under her parka and shirt, seeking for and finding the warm mounds of her breasts. As his fingers touched and fondled a nipple, a feeling which she had never before experienced spread quickly along the nerves of her loins, setting the bud between her legs to throbbing in a sweet mixture of shattering pleasure and pain.

She pulled her mouth free from his, and moaned. Oh, God, she wanted! She wanted! So this was what love was, this was the powerful and mysterious secret that bound men and women together. But there must be more! The strange hunger rising inside her needed to be satisfied. Instinctively, she began pulling at her clothes, wanting to be closer to him, wanting to feel his body against hers. He gave a sobbing laugh, and began to help her, his hands clumsy in his eagerness.

In a moment the barriers of clothing were gone, and flesh was against flesh. As his strongly muscled arms enclosed her, drawing her to him, Belinda almost cried aloud with pleasure. Never in her life had she touched another naked body. The feel of him, warm and solid against her, was both exciting and comforting. Her breasts were pressed against his chest, and his manhood, disturbingly large and hard, touched her private parts. She could feel the pressure against her, and against the bud of her inner place, and this pressure was so pleasant that she began to move against him, thereby increasing the pressure and the excitement.

"Belinda!" he said in an anguished voice. "I can't wait!"

Almost roughly he pulled away from her, and pushed her down upon her back; he moved over her, his head face down beside her cheek, his breath warm against her ear.

"Open for me," he whispered.

She did so without question. It seemed natural and good to do so.

As her thighs parted, she felt him, the soft-skinned hardness of him, touch her where she lay open and exposed.

As his organ touched her bud, a shock of pure ecstasy flamed through her body, and then he moved forward abruptly, and a sharp, tearing pain made her flinch. Oh! Oh! He was inside her . . .

For a brief moment Belinda felt fear, cold and sobering as a chill ocean wave, threaten to drown her desire; but now he was moving rapidly, in and out, and with each forward thrust, there was the delicious pressure.

Oh, heaven, she thought, please don't let him stop! Let it go on forever!

She strained toward him, the brief pain forgotten, and then, with a protracted shudder, he slowed and stopped, his body contracting, as he cried out in her ear, "Belinda! Oh, Belinda!"

Her own body still throbbing, Belinda lay in puzzled silence, unable to voice the plea that was crying in her. Why had he stopped? He must go on. She moved restlessly, feeling the weight of his body heavy upon her.

He took a shuddering breath. "I'm sorry," he said in a low voice. "I was so . . . so excited, I finished too quickly." He kissed her cheek and raised himself off her. His once aggressive male organ trailed softly across her thighs as he moved to stretch out beside her.

Gently, his arms still around her, he kissed her on the mouth. She returned it eagerly, her body still aching with desire.

"Darling," he whispered, "it will be better for you the next time, I promise."

His hands began to stroke her body. He knows, he knows, she thought, although she was not sure what it was that she meant. But it didn't matter, because his hands were busy now. Wing-soft and knowing, they caressed and touched. First the nipples . . . why did his touching her nipples cause thrills of sensation to run down her body to her abdomen? And then her secret place, the place he had just filled with his maleness—touching, fondling, until she writhed and moaned in a torment of sensation. The sensation built, growing, a wild momentum rising within her, and his movements became stronger and more agitated.

Belinda could hear her own breath sobbing, and then she heard his too, louder and wilder than her own, as once more he raised himself atop her and parted her thighs with the strong prod of his manhood. This time there was no stopping. Again and again he thrust and prodded, as her tension mounted to an almost unbearable pitch.

Crying aloud now, clutching his shoulders with wild hands, and moving her body frantically beneath his, she labored toward something she had never even imagined, until at last, almost swooning with ecstasy, the tension shattered in a soundless explosion of nerves and organs. Her body spasmed again and again, contracting automatically as he moved within her, and within a few seconds, as her own body relaxed slowly, he again cried out his own completion, and she was filled with a warm feeling of gratitude and love.

Belinda fell asleep with her head on his shoulder, feeling warm and safe, relaxed by a pleasant lassitude she had never before known. . . .

It seemed like too short a time before he woke her with a tender touch on the shoulder.

As she looked up into those blue eyes she had once thought cold, an exquisite embarrassment flooded her body, and she lowered her eyes.

Laughing, he bent down and touched his lips to her forehead. "It's all right, my love. It really is. In fact, everything in the world is all right, at this moment. Don't you feel it, too?"

Smiling despite herself, she murmured a soft yes against the hair of his chest, wondering at the strange man-smell of him, and at her own tumultuous feelings.

"Now," he said briskly, "we'd better get moving. Your sister is probably worried, and we want to let her know you're all right."

Belinda nodded, although at that moment, she would have been just as happy to stay here forever, snug in this little nest of happiness. How strange of me, she thought. Is this all it takes to turn a woman into a domesticated creature? For the first time, she considered the possibility that it might be worth it, being an ordinary woman, cozy with her own home and fireside, waiting for her man.

She grimaced. There was the rub—waiting for her man. Waiting patiently in the background, while her husband went out into the world, doing the exciting things, visiting the exciting places. No, no . . .

Suddenly, beneath her, the surface shifted slightly, and a harsh, grating sound seemed to come from everywhere at once.

"Dear God!" she exclaimed. "What was that?"

Josh's eyes were pale in the tan of his face. "Just a slight warning from the lake ice. The thaw is beginning."

"Then let's get off the lake!" She reached for her clothes, awkward in her haste.

Josh touched her arm. "Relax, Belinda. It won't go for a day or two, maybe even longer. This is just a warning. We'll have plenty of time to get to shore. It should only take an hour or so, if the wind is right."

She nodded, but still continued to dress herself in haste. The sound of the breaking ice had been the voice of reality intruding into their little private world, letting in the other voices that spoke of responsibility and purpose, and ripping away the feeling of timeless pleasure.

When the sled was packed and they had finished a quick breakfast, Josh made a seat for her among the bundles. Heavily loaded, the sled moved out slowly at first under the canvas sail, but soon picked up speed, so that Josh had to trot briskly alongside.

As the last traces of darkness faded, Belinda could see that the day was going to be clear. On either side of them, across the lake in a long, widely scattered band, other vehicles and men plodded or sailed toward the far side of the lake.

Belinda wondered how Annabelle was taking her disappearance. Was she bearing up, or was she being sulky and mean to Charlie? Belinda didn't want her sister to alienate the Chilkat. If she did, Charlie probably wouldn't agree to accompany them farther.

In what seemed a very short time, the edge of the lake appeared before them. Along the shore were scattered many ice-boats, their owners taking down the makeshift sails, readying them for the trek to Lake Linderman.

Eagerly, Belinda searched among them for her sister, and at last caught sight of her, a distance back from the lake shore against a low snowbank.

While Josh pulled his sled off the ice and onto the snow-covered shore, Belinda, calling Annabelle's name, hurried toward her. She could not see Charlie and the other bearers.

Then Annabelle saw her and ran to meet her, until the two sisters met in a joyful embrace. Belinda stepped back first, and noticed with astonishment that there were tears on Annabelle's cheeks. She found herself greatly touched.

"Oh, Bee! I thought sure you were dead. It was so awful! All night I kept thinking of you, frozen and alone some-where out there. Oh, I'm so glad to see you safe and sound!"

No gladder than I am to see *you*." Belinda kissed her cheek. "Did the other bearer get back?"

Annabelle nodded. "He's around there," she pointed to the snowbank, "with the others. They're playing some kind of silly card game." She sniffled, then giggled. "But you're all right! What happened?"

Belinda felt her face grow warm as she started guiltily. If Annabelle only knew! For the first time, Belinda felt sexu-ally superior to her sister. Annabelle, she was fairly certain, despite her coquettish ways, was still virgin, while Belinda, the proper one, could no longer make that claim. How oddly things turned out!

Carefully keeping any emotion out of her voice, Belinda told Annabelle an edited version of the night's happenings, but Annabelle, ever aware of romantic opportunity, smiled slyly. "And so he has come to your rescue twice! How romantic! And is he handsome, this rescuer of yours?"

Belinda could not control her blush. "Yes, I suppose," she answered lightly, "but things were so hectic that I really didn't notice."

"You suppose!" Annabelle pouted. "Bee, you really are impossible! Here you have a marvelous opportunity to make an impression on an attractive man, and you don't seem to realize it. How do you ever expect to catch a husband?" Her tone was teasing now.

'Well, first of all," Belinda said in annoyance, "I don't expect to 'catch' a husband, as you so nicely put it. I hate that phrase. It makes a man sound like some kind of game animal, or something, and makes the woman sound like the most awful, calculating creature, using her femininity as bait. It's dreadful!"

Annabelle pouted again. "I was only teasing, Bee. And besides, that's the way it really is, you know."

Belinda was saved from replying by the appearance of Josh, striding toward them over the snow, his shoulders broad against the white background and his red hair flaming in the sun.

"My goodness!" Annabelle sucked in her breath. "He's ever so nice-looking, Bee. Much handsomer than I would have thought."

Belinda experienced a stab of jealousy. Annabelle was much prettier, and far more skilled in the games that men and women play. What if Josh should like Annabelle more than her?

He was in front of them now, smiling and breathing out great puffs of white air. "I see you found her," he said, nodding at Annabelle.

"Yes, thank goodness. The bearers are over behind that snowbank, there, so I guess everything is in order."

"Good." He turned toward Annabelle. "And this, I gather, is your charming sister?"

Flustered, Belinda said, "Yes. This is my sister, Annabelle. Annabelle, this is Josh Rogan."

Annabelle, smiling and fluttering her thick lashes, gave a mock curtsy. "Pleased to meet you, Mr. Rogan. After all, it's not every day that a girl gets to meet a man who has been twice a hero."

Josh grinned. "Well, I'm glad that you appreciate my virtues, Miss Lee. I hope that you will remind your sister of this from time to time. I'm afraid that she thinks that my manner lacks something in the way of polish."

He gave Belinda a keen look and she looked away, but she felt greatly relieved. He was being polite to Annabelle, yet he did not seem particularly impressed.

"Well, ladies. The days are still short, so if we're going to make any distance today, I imagine we should get started. If you will excuse us, Miss Lee," he nodded to Annabelle, "I would like a few words with your sister alone."

Annabelle smiled and waved her hand. "My permission is granted, sir. Only don't keep her too long. After all, she is my younger sister, and I must look after her."

Josh took Belinda's hand and led her to a spot a few yards distant, where they could speak without being overheard. He took both her hands in his. "Belinda," he said earnestly, "I want to tell you that last night was the most beautiful night in my experience, and I will cherish and remember it always."

She looked at him in sudden alarm. Why was he talking like this, taking this tack?

"It was . . ." She hesitated, searching for the right words. "It was beautiful for me, too, Josh, but why are you speaking as if we won't be seeing one another again?"

"We won't, not for awhile," His features tightened, and his lips compressed, then relaxed. "Belinda, as much as I want to, I can't stay with you. I must go on to Dawson alone."

"But . . ." Suddenly the pale sunlight was gone, and the cold pierced through her parka, touching her skin, then creeping inside, into her chest and vitals. "But I thought . . . I mean, last night. . . . I thought it meant something to you!"

She tried to pull her hands away, but he held them tightly, groaning slightly. "It did! How can I make you understand? I have no choice, Belinda. Believe me. If I did, I would travel with you to Dawson, and we would be married there, and I would never leave your side. But right now, that's impossible. I must go on to Dawson alone, and at the moment, I cannot make any commitments."

"But why?" The question was a cry of pain.

Josh winced. "I can't tell you that, Belinda. I can only ask you to trust me."

"Trust you? You can ask that, *now?*" she cried, wrenching her hands away. "From this moment, I will never trust any man again!"

Resolutely, swallowing the tears that threatened to engulf her, Belinda trudged across the snow to where Annabelle waited.

≈6≋

Lester Pugh drew back the plush drapes across the window of his quarters above his saloon, the Golden Poke, and gazed down onto the main street of Dawson—the Golden City, or as some referred to it, "a rectangle in a bog."

Although a visitor might see the growing city as a motley collection of jerry-built, sawboard buildings and now-dusty troughs that passed for streets, Pugh saw something quite different—he saw opportunity. Dawson was growing at a rate that was unbelievable, and those who got in on the ground floor were certain to be millionaires almost overnight, if they played their cards right.

He smiled as he studied the scene below. Although the hour was early, the street was busy with both foot and horse traffic. Yes, it was good that he had decided to come to Dawson now instead of waiting. Perhaps the federal snoop had done him a good turn, jolting him out of his complacency.

He let the drape fall back into place, and returned to his chair, which was pulled up to a small table by the window.

Half of the second floor of the building had been turned into living quarters for Pugh to use during his infrequent visits to Dawson. They were quite comfortable rooms, even luxurious by north country standards, and now Pugh reached a decision that had been coming on him for some time—he was going to spend more time here in the future.

The dishes that covered the table had earlier held a variety of items that had comprised his breakfast, but they were empty now, and Pugh pushed them aside, as he reached for the coffee pot. It was almost empty and he frowned.

A heavy-handed knock, roused him from his thoughts, and he called out, "Come in!"

The door opened to admit Chet Harter. Harter's smile was tight, and his eyes glittered brightly. He took off his hat and tossed it onto the sofa. "I've got news for you, L.P. Some good news, some bad."

"Oh?" Pugh took out his gold cigarette case and extracted a cigarette. He put it carefully into the holder, and took his time lighting it. It would never do to let Harter think that he was anxious. "And what is this news?"

Harter strode over to the breakfast table, hefted the coffee pot, and finding it empty, put it back down. Pugh made a mental note of the other man's manner. Harter was getting carried away with his own importance again. It was about time to bring him down a little. "I asked you a question, Chet," he said softly.

Harter gave him a slit-eyed glance. "Sure, I know you did, L.P. I was just seeing if there was a cup of coffee left, but I should have guessed there wouldn't be."

Although he was smiling slightly, his tone of voice was insolent and Pugh frowned blackly, examining the glowing end of his cigarette. Yes, he would have to do something about Harter's attitude.

Thoughtfully, he reached over for his cane and balanced it lightly in his hand. Harter watched, still smiling. Then, with a movement of cat-like swiftness that belied his great bulk, Pugh surged to his feet, swinging the cane up and out. There was a snicking sound as he pressed a button.

Harter's eyes bulged, and his face paled as he felt the ice-pick-sharp point of the blade at his throat. As Pugh increased the pressure, small beads of sweat broke out on Harter's forehead. "What the hell, L.P.!" Harter forced the words out through stiff lips. "That goddamned thing's sharp!"

Pugh held the cane steady, his smile benign. "Yes, it is, isn't it? A little thing I picked up from a passing trader, who got it in France. A sword-cane, they call it. I consider it the ideal weapon for a gentleman."

Harter swallowed noisily. "But what the hell's the idea?"

Pugh's smile widened, and he moved the cane ever so slightly, causing Harter's face to blanche further. "The idea, my fine friend, was to catch your interest. I seem to be having a bit of trouble doing that of late. As I have told you so many times, Chesley, I am not a patient man, and you should not try that patience. Agreed?"

Harter nodded carefully. He hated to be called by the name given him by his parents, and Pugh knew it. Slowly, the fat man lowered the cane and pressed the button that retracted the stiletto-like blade. "Now, where were we?"

Harter pulled a copious handkerchief from his pocket, and wiped his brow, concealing his face for a moment in the cotton folds. One of these days, he thought viciously, this fat bastard is going too far with me, and I'm going to split his plump carcass like a Christmas goose!

But when he put the handkerchief away, his expression was carefully blank.

"I asked where we were?" Pugh sat back down in his chair, and laced his fingers together over the mound of his belly. "Ah, yes, your news." He looked up at Harter expectantly.

"The marshal, he's in town. The son of a bitch got here before we did, I understand. He's camping out on a claim over near Small Creek. Are you sure this gent's a federal? I mean, it seems pretty silly for him to go through all that trouble if he's not really going to dig for gold."

Pugh raised his hands until his chin touched his fingers. "I'm quite sure, Chet. Quite sure. However, it would seem that he is cleverer than I had thought, a worthy opponent. Be that as it may, I still can't waste too much time on him. He will have to be disposed of. Now, that is the *good* news, I presume. What is the bad?"

"That Lee bitch, the photographer, is here, too. How she ever managed to get out of that storm alive, I'll never know. She's set up business, down at the end of the street in tent town. Should I make another try for the picture?"

Pugh pursed his lips. "I suppose so. But do it subtly this time. We're in Canadian territory now, and I don't wish to call undue attention to ourselves." He heaved a windy sigh. "Now, is that all?"

"Yeah, except that I ran into Montana downstairs, and he says to tell you that the books are ready for you to examine."

"Excellent." Pugh rose to his feet, with a smooth motion that set his belly to jiggling. "We'll go down right now."

Downstairs, in the small office in the rear, Montana Leeds spread the large ledger out on the desk top and smoothed the pages.

Everything was in order, he knew, and he had nothing to hide, yet he felt nervous as the devil; for some reason

Lester Pugh always made him feel that way. The man had a cold ruthlessness about him that, for Montana at least, was not hidden by the bland, oily good manners of his surface personality. He suspected that Pugh was engaged in any number of shady activities, but so long as he, Montana, was allowed to operate the Poke legitimately, what Pugh did outside the saloon was his own affair.

Certainly, Montana did not doubt that Pugh was a dangerous man, and he had no illusions as to how he would fare if he ever made a gross error, or cheated him, or otherwise crossed the man. However, he had no intention of doing any of these things, and since Pugh paid him very well, it seemed relatively safe to continue in his employ, at least for the time being.

Montana sighed as he finished preparing the books for inspection. In his late fifties, he was an elegant, still handsome man, with a shock of theatrically white hair, a ready wit and booming laugh. He was far too capable a man to be working for another, particularly someone of Pugh's type; but a man had to live. If things hadn't gone wrong for him . . .

He smiled wryly. But then things always *did* seem to go wrong for him, didn't they? It was the story of his life. One glowing dream after another, each one promising success and riches, and in the end all coming to the same thing— failure.

This last dream, of striking it rich in the Klondike, had at first seemed as if it might come true. Montana and his partner had found a rich claim and staked it. They had drawn lots to see who would hasten into Dawson to file the papers, and Jackson, his partner, had drawn the long straw.

Montana had stayed behind at the claim, working the mine.

A week later, Jackson had returned. Waving a gun, he ordered Montana off the property. Jackson had filed the claim in his own name. Only the fact that Jackson had the foresight to provide himself with the gun saved his life. Montana filed a protest with the Mounties in Dawson, but there were so many like complaints, so many cases on file—and it was only his word against his partner's—that Montana knew he had little chance of ever seeing any of the wealth that began to pour out of the mine. All he had was the gold he had taken out while Jackson was absent in Dawson.

He had even been cheated out of any revenge, for Jackson had sold the claim shortly thereafter, and was gone from the territory.

A lesser man, Montana thought, might consider himself a failure with such a record, might have given up trying, and settled into being an ordinary man with ordinary dreams; but Montana was already working on a new plan. This time, however, it was a practical plan—at least, it seemed so to him. This time, it wasn't a dream of glory or fame he was after, but something that he should have done long ago. For once he wasn't after the pie-in-the-sky money. He was going to stay right here, running the Poke, saving his money, until he had enough, enough to . . .

His thoughts were interrupted by the sound of heavy footsteps outside. He leaned back in his chair, and arranged his features in an expression he hoped befitted a valued employee, as Lester Pugh and his cohort, Harter, entered the room.

The things a man has to do to get ahead, Montana thought.

Belinda stood looking down at the prints spread out on the makeshift table set up against the back of the tent. She smiled approvingly. They were good; she knew they were.

Many of them had been developed at the temporary camp set up at Lake Bennett, where they had been forced to wait for the thaw before making their way on to Dawson.

She shuddered slightly, as she thought of the trip here. Thank heaven for Charlie, who had stayed on, even though the other bearers had returned to their families in Dyea. Without the little Chilkat's knowledge and strength, the rest of the trip would have been impossible.

First, a boat had to be built, which meant that trees had to be chopped down and cut into lumber. Then the treacherous waters of the Yukon had to be navigated. First was Lake Bennett itself, twenty-five miles long, with a strong headwind that made every mile gained a stubborn battle to keep from being dashed onto the shore. After Lake Bennett came Tagish Lake, a necklace of wind-blown inlets that in certain parts had claimed more victims than White Horse Rapids. It was a miracle that they had made it through unharmed—a miracle named Charlie. In Belinda's opinion, she and Annabelle owed their lives to Charlie.

Now, she sorted through the pictures, holding them up one at a time to examine them. There were exciting shots of Miles Canyon, and the cloth flag that warned of danger, as well as the painted plank sign that said: CANNON. How she had yearned to get a picture of the huge whirlpool that made navigation through the canyon so dangerous, but all her energies had been directed toward keeping the boat and its cargo intact.

She studied one of the earlier pictures, the one she had taken of the pass at Chilkoot just as the avalanche struck. Despite the rough treatment at the hands of her attacker, the film in the camera had not been damaged, and she had developed it at Lake Bennett.

Belinda held this one up to the light coming through the tent window. She was pleased with the composition—the thin line of men moving upward; the freight cables overhead, like pencil strokes. She leaned forward to examine a small dot at the top and to one side of the picture. Strange, she hadn't noticed that before. It looked like a man, but what would he be doing off the trail and to one side like that?

Well, it didn't really matter, as it did nothing to spoil the composition of the picture.

As she set that picture aside, the tent flap lifted, and Annabelle came inside. She was wearing a pink muslin dress and bonnet that enhanced her vivid coloring; and Belinda smiled, thinking what a lovely picture she would make if only there was some way of capturing color on film.

"Did you have a good time?" she asked.

Annabelle shrugged. "How could anyone have a good time in this godforsaken place? It's awful, dusty and ugly, and the mosquitoes eat you alive! She threw her gloves onto her cot, and dropped down beside them. "Bee, when are we going to move into a decent place? I'm sick and tired of living in this tent!"

Belinda sighed, frowning. It seemed to her that all she heard from Annabelle were complaints about one thing or another. "We'll move when we get enough money ahead to put up a building," she said curtly. "I'm starting to take in some money now. It shouldn't take too long. These miners are hungry for recognition of some kind. They're anxious to have their pictures taken so that they can send them home to their families. More and more of them are coming in every day."

Annabelle pouted. "I don't see why we have to wait. There are hotels, you know. I realize they aren't much, but at least they have real walls and *real* beds." She thumped the canvas of the cot.

Belinda shook her head. "Their prices are outrageous, and there are no business buildings for rent, they are all taken. So, we would still need the tent. No, it's out of the question, Annabelle. You'll just have to be patient!"

She could feel herself losing control of her temper, something that seemed to be happening more and more nowadays, and this realization made her crankier than ever. It was on the tip of her tongue to say that it was Annabelle who had insisted upon coming, but she held back the words—she had said them too often. Anyway, they had no effect on Annabelle, who heard only what she wanted to hear. Besides, Belinda just didn't feel like arguing right now.

She looked at the watch that hung on the long chain around her neck. "I have to get to work now. It's almost one o'clock. We'll talk about this later."

Annabelle pouted, and sprawled back upon the cot. "I know what *that* means. It means that we won't talk at all. You know, Belinda, I'm the older sister, not you. I should have *some* say about how we live!"

Belinda picked up her warm shawl and turned away

without answering. Annabelle seemed to forget that it was Belinda's earnings that supported them; and, as far as Belinda was concerned, this gave *her* the right to make the decisions. She wrapped the shawl around her shoulders.

"You might clean up around here a little while I'm working," she said pointedly. "This tent looks like a pigsty!"

She left the tent before Annabelle could reply and walked next door to the second tent, which contained her camera and darkroom equipment. Before this tent was a low platform with a painted backdrop of mountains, a stream bed, and figures of miners bent over gold pans and sluices. Bits of rock and brush were artistically situated so that the foreground would look natural.

Belinda was quite proud of her set. An itinerant sign painter had done the backdrop, and she herself had arranged the foreground.

If left to her own inclinations, she would have photographed the miners against a natural background, but they all desired a "studio portrait," while at the same time wanting to be shown in pursuit of their trade. The set was Belinda's answer to these conflicting desires, and she had almost more business than she could handle.

Belinda was anxious to be about what she considered her "real" work, and spent her mornings doing shots that interested her—recording the busy life of the boomtown of Dawson, and the men who had come here seeking their fortunes. But they had to have money, and so her afternoons from one to four she devoted to doing portraits, for which the miners were willing to pay very well. Right now, there were more than a dozen men awaiting her, lined up beside the wooden sign that proclaimed, in large, black letters: B. LEE, PHOTOGRAPHER, PORTRAITS AND KLONDIKE VIEWS.

The sight of the sign cheered her briefly, and putting her personal problems out of her mind, she set about the business of earning a living.

Annabelle stared balefully at the dull, green canvas over her head. She felt, hot, sulky, depressed, and worst of all, terribly, terribly bored.

Again, as she had so often done during the past two months, she castigated herself for insisting on this—as far as she was concerned—ill-fated trip.

Originally, it had sounded exciting—the far Yukon, fabled and mysterious; the high adventure of it all; men seeking their fortunes; and according to the reports, many of them finding wealth beyond their dreams.

She sighed soulfully. Who would have thought that it would be so cold and uncomfortable, and the promised excitement missing? Somehow she had not imagined that it would be like this.

And Belinda. Well, Belinda was getting to be quite impossible!

At home, back in New York, she had been bad enough, heaven forbid—bossy, opinionated, and smart. At social gatherings, she stuck out like a sore thumb, always debating with the men on serious matters. She simply didn't act like a young woman was supposed to act.

One of their mutual male friends had once told Belinda, in Annabelle's hearing, that "she thought like a man!" He meant it as a compliment, and Annabelle confessed to herself that she had been impressed, but Belinda had given a rather superior smile and retorted, "Although men don't seem to realize it, they do *not* have a corner on intelligence!"

Annabelle sighed again. And now, here in this godforsaken wilderness, Belinda had grown worse, even more bossy and unreasonable. And recently, she had a habit of falling into gloomy moods, becoming as thorny as a porcupine. It was simply impossible to talk to her!

"Is anybody here?"

The sound of a man's voice at the tent flap brought her to her feet in one startled movement. "Yes?" she called out tentatively. "Who is it?"

"Chet Harter, ma'am. Can I come in?"

Chet Harter? Oh, yes! The dashing fellow with the sinister, pitted face she had seen in Dyea.

Annabelle raised her hand to her hair. She must look a sight, but then the light in the tent was dim. Should she let him come in? With her alone? Why on earth not? She was bored near to tears.

"Come in, Mr. Harter," she said sweetly, then seated herself quickly on the edge of the cot, arranging her skirt gracefully around her.

The tent flap was pushed aside, and Harter's tall figure stooped to enter the tent. He stood blinking his eyes to adjust to the change in light. As he removed his hat, Annabelle studied him. Yes, he was attractive in a fascinatingly sinister fashion, a bit like the lead villain in a play—both attractive and a little frightening. Just enough, she thought, to make being in here alone with him exciting. Her heart began to beat faster.

She stood, keeping her head down a bit and raising her

eyes to meet his, a trick she had always found very effective in gaining the interest of the male sex. "Mr. Harter, this is a pleasant surprise. What brings you to Dawson?"

He leaned toward her, standing perhaps a trifle too close, and a pleasant prickle of fear tickled Annabelle's spine. Oh, he was daring!

"I'm here on business, and just happened to see your sister's sign. I figured that it wasn't likely there was another photographer in the territory by the name of Lee, so I thought I'd see if it was your sister and you. Mighty glad to see that it is."

"Well, I'm glad to see you, too," she said pertly. "It's been awfully dull here, I can tell you, and it's a pleasant relief to see a friendly face. Are you staying in Dawson long?"

"Probably for quite a spell, but I hope that I'm not interrupting anything. I mean, I see that you are all dressed up to go out."

Annabelle laughed lightly, and shook her head so that the curls bounced. "I've *been* out. In fact, I just now came in. I've been looking over the town, so to speak. What there is of it."

He smiled, showing even, white teeth. He did have a nice smile.

"Well, I know that it's not the proper place for a lady, Miss Lee," he said, "yet Dawson has a lot of possibilities for a man looking to make his fortune, and it's growing. There's even a couple of dressmakers in town now, and a candy shop. You might say Dawson's practically on the edge of becoming civilized."

Annabelle echoed his laugh, feeling quite giddy. This

was the best time she had had since this miserable trip had begun. She had not realized how much she missed the game of flirtation, the light male-female banter that had made up so much of her social life back in New York.

She noticed that he was staring at her intently, and she lowered her gaze. He did make her a little nervous, being somewhat bolder and more forceful than the young men she had known back home, but that was probably because he was older; and then the men in this country seemed to lose some of their gentlemanly manner. It was the boom-town atmosphere, she supposed.

"I just had an idea," he said. "Since you're still dressed up to go out, what do you say we go down to the Aurora and have us a good dinner? The food there's not bad, even if they do charge you an arm and a leg for it."

Annabelle felt jittery with excitement. Did she dare? Belinda would be furious if she went off and left all the work undone.

"I just don't know." She gave her curls a bounce, looking down and then up, so that he could see how long her lashes were, and how prettily they lay against her cheek. "I do have some work to do here . . ."

"Oh, I'm sure the work can wait. Besides, a pretty lady like you shouldn't have to be working on a nice day like this. Come on, what do you say? It would pleasure me a great deal to have your company."

"Well, for goodness sake, I don't see why not!" She tossed her head. "It would certainly brighten my day to be able to have some conversation with a civilized man for a change, and I'll admit that I could eat a bite, too. All that walking stirred up my appetite."

"Great! Let's be on our way then."

"I'd better leave a note for Belinda."

Annabelle rummaged through her writing box for a scrap of paper. While she did so, Harter wandered to the back of the tent, and stood looking down at the prints spread across the rough table.

"These your sister's pictures?"

Annabelle, busy with the note, only half-heard him. "Yes, they're Belinda's pictures."

"They're mighty good," Harter said musingly.

"I thought she was just, you know, playing around with this photography business, but she knows what she's doing." He picked one up and looked at it closely. "I've never seen pictures any better'n these, even taken by a man."

Annabelle folded the note and laughed. "You'd better not tell Bee that. She thinks men are vastly overrated."

"Does she now?" He turned away from the pictures. "Well, are you ready? Shall we go?"

She nodded happily, feeling really alive for the first time in weeks. This was exciting! "Ready as I'll ever be," she said.

He held the tent flap open for her, and then closed it behind them. In the light, she could better see his clothes. He was wearing a tan suit and hat, and looked the proper gentleman among these roughly clothed stampeders. Happily, she took his arm when it was offered. It was nice to be treated like a lady again, and Belinda could just carry on all she wanted. It was going to be worth it, Annabelle knew.

A glance at the other tent showed her that Belinda was busy taking pictures, and didn't notice their departure. It was just as well, Annabelle thought; she would probably cause an embarrassing scene if she saw her sister strolling off on the arm of a strange man.

At the Aurora Café, Chet Harter ordered a private room, and Annabelle, belatedly thinking of her reputation, made a small sound of protest.

Harter turned toward her, his expression bland. "Yes, Miss Annabelle, what is it?"

Annabelle felt a bit ill-at-ease. Was she being silly, acting like a naive girl? But at home it wasn't considered proper to have dinner alone with a man in such a room. There were stories . . .

"Oh, I see. It's the private room you're worried about. It's just that I wanted to shelter you from the rough company we might meet in the public dining room, you see. But if you'd rather not?"

"Oh, no. It's quite all right," she said hastily.

Harter nodded over her head at the waiter. "We'll take the room."

Annabelle, feeling gauche, a feeling that she was not used to and did not like, felt her cheeks burning. For just a moment, she questioned the wisdom of coming here with this man, and something warned her that he might not be quite as easy to handle as her suitors back home, but as they were shown into the small room, with the red velvet draperies and the linen-covered table, the thought slipped away. Why, this was so elegant—the first really civilized room she had seen since leaving New York. She crowed with delight and plopped down onto the sofa, the red velvet covering of which matched the drapes. "It's lovely!" she cried.

Harter smiled expansively, and reached for the bottle of wine that the waiter had left in the silver bucket. "I'm real glad you like it," he said, pouring a glass of the deep, red liquid. "Now, let's have a little glass of wine while they bring the food."

The meal was well-prepared, much better than that which was served in most eating places in Dawson, but although Harter ate heartily enough his mind was not on the food.

He was in a very good mood as he surreptitiously examined the young woman opposite him. Who would ever have thought that he would have an opportunity such as this? And in this frontier town? It was an unexpected bonanza.

He poured the remaining wine into Annabelle's glass, and watched smilingly as she sipped it. Her cheeks were flushed, and her eyes glittered from the wine. As he had suspected, she was not an experienced drinker, and the few glasses of wine had gone to her head, making her giddy and flirtatious. Another glass or so and she would be on the verge of drowsiness, at that stage where liberties taken were not noticed, and a man could slip past a woman's defenses and lay siege to that inner sanctuary which they kept so well concealed.

He gave the bell at his side a tug, and when the waiter discreetly tapped at the door, Harter called for another bottle of port. He smiled at Annabelle's pretty confusion.

Yep, this was really his lucky day. Aside from Annabelle falling into his clutches so easily, he had something else to be pleased about. He had been hoping to find the Lee tent empty, and had been a little disappointed when a voice had answered his hail, but that had worked out fine, too. After finding the picture that Belinda had taken at the Pass, it had been no trick at all to slip it into his pocket. Although he hadn't had time to examine it properly, so far as he could tell, there was nothing on it to incriminate him. That was a real load off his mind. And then finding that the sister responded to him, and that she was even prettier than he had remembered—things were really going his way!

The waiter returned with the wine. Harter took the bottle and turned to Annabelle. "Ready for some more?"

By God, she was a juicy piece—that soft swell of breasts; the tiny waist. Most of the women up here looked like work horses, or were so shop-worn that there was little pleasure in seducing them.

He could feel the pressure of his mounting lust, and took a steadying breath in an attempt to hold it back. There was no great hurry. Harter liked to take his time with women—none of this rush to get it over with. He fancied himself a connoisseur. It was like a good meal; if you hurried through it, you couldn't properly enjoy it, and he surely liked to savor both his women and his food.

Annabelle giggled, and hiccuped charmingly; she was almost ready. "Do you think I should?" she said in answer to his question. "I mean, I do believe I'm getting quite tipsy."

"Of course you're not tipsy," he said soothingly, filling her glass to the brim. "Just a little more to keep the glow in your cheeks, and pretty cheeks they are, too." He reached over and stroked her face. She giggled again, and flushed.

"Oh, you're such a . . . such a flat . . . flatterer!" she hiccuped. "Oh, my!" She dissolved in laughter, and he joined her.

"Let's move over to the sofa where it's more comfortable."

"Oh, I'm comfortable."

But his hand was under her elbow, and he was helping her over to the velvet sofa. He sat down beside her.

The mounting anticipation was exciting his lust now. He already knew far more about Annabelle than she knew about him. He knew, for instance, that despite her flirting ways, she was inexperienced. And that, although she clearly thought herself an authority on the male animal and prided herself on her ability to handle men, Harter was confident all her experience had been limited to boys her own age, unsure of themselves and easy to control. The fact that she had no inkling of what was in store for her only added to his pleasure. He surely did like to take a virgin. He liked being first, liked dominating and controlling his women, and firmly believed that that was how the Good Lord intended it to be—man, the master, and woman there to serve his needs.

The last glass of wine was doing its work now, and Annabelle's beautiful eyes were growing glassy. He put down his own glass and took hers away.

"I feel a little . . . funny," she said weakly.

"It's just too much excitement, that's all. You'll be fine, just lay back now. Here, I'll just unbutton the top of your bodice so you can breathe better.

"I . . . I . . ."

Her hand came up hesitantly to fend him off, but Harter murmured reassuringly, and continued to work on the row of buttons. As each one slipped from the catch, his desire mounted. Her eyes were closed, and she seemed unaware of what he was doing; then her bodice was undone, and he could see the smooth, white flesh swelling over the top of the ruffles and ribbons that made up her undergarments. Carefully, he pushed these aside and found the laces of her corset. Lord, how did women ever get themselves into all this stuff? Still, it was enjoyable stripping it away. He was reminded of a sweet, ripe peach, luscious and juicy, when the skin was removed.

And then there they were, those two soft, womanly mounds. These were something special, too; full and firm with the bloom of girlhood still on them. He gazed at them for several moments before he placed one hand on her right breast, feeling the satin smoothness beneath the rough skin of his fingers, savoring the warmth. Then, as his lust became almost uncontrollable, he squeezed roughly, causing Annabelle to cry out.

Her eyes opened, and the sight of the terror he saw there fueled his passion. "No, no!" she cried out through the dizziness brought on by the wine. She was groggy, but still knew what was going on. That was fine with him, just the way he liked it.

Brutally, he pulled away her skirt, ripping the fasteners, then tugged at her petticoats and lacy bloomers, exposing plump legs with full thighs and narrow ankles.

His eyes fastened greedily on the triangle of curly hair at the juncture of her thighs. Annabelle was weeping now, and struggling weakly, but Harter felt strong as a bull, as a lion.

He was laughing as he forced her thighs apart and gazed at the forbidden center of her, one hand fumbling his trousers open.

Yes, this was really his lucky day!

$$\approx 7 \approx$$

With easy efficiency, Belinda slid the film, in its holder, into the camera.

The man posing on the small platform was a typical miner. Of medium height and about thirty years of age, he sported a full beard and wore work clothes—heavy trousers stuffed into knee-high boots, a faded blue shirt, galluses, and a weathered, wide-brimmed black hat. He leaned on his pick, handle up, as he assumed a pose—one leg bent, right hand on the pick, the left holding his poke toward the camera.

His expression was proud, although his face had weary lines. Belinda speculated upon his family at home, and how they would react to the picture of their distant head of household. She hoped that he would get home with all his gold intact, a conquering hero.

Gently, she depressed the camera lever. "All right, Mr. Johnson. The prints will be ready on Monday."

The miner nodded. "See you then, Miss Lee."

He stepped down from the platform, and another immediately took his place. The new miner said shyly, "I'd like to be pictured with my gold pan."

"Right over there then, by the stream." She pointed to the painted stream in the backdrop, and the man squatted self-consciously, pretending to be engaged in panning.

Before inserting the film, Belinda looked skyward. Because of the fact that the sun hardly could be said to set during the summer months here, you could not judge the time from the sun's position, but she was growing tired. She decided that this would be the last picture for the day.

"All right now," she said, "hold as still as you can."

There were still men waiting to be photographed when she closed up shop. She told them to return on Monday, promising they would be first.

She felt very weary, more so than her day should have warranted, and this knowledge depressed her. Slowly, she gathered up her gear. Maybe she should hire an assistant. Of course there was always Annabelle, but knowing her sister's aversion to work of any kind, and thinking of her incessant chatter, made the idea unappealing. Perhaps she could use Charlie; he was quick and bright, and he could learn quickly. She decided to ask him when he returned from his visit to a nearby village, where he had gone to see some relatives.

Belinda opened the flap to the darkroom tent and carried her equipment inside, placing the case with the exposed film carefully on the workbench. She would have to develop these in the morning if she wanted to have the weekend free to go about her own work.

She was perspiring by the time she left the work tent. Vainly, she lifted her face, seeking a breath of air. A few high clouds were moving across the darkening blue of the sky, which seemed much higher here than it did at home.

Behind the town, the hills and mountains rose, the higher slopes still bearing a white brush of snow. The vista, except for the sprawl of the town, was beautiful, and she thought of a line of a hymn they sang in church back home: "Though every prospect pleases, and only man is vile." Did the presence of man always ruin things? Unhappily it often seemed so.

She pushed up the flap of the living tent reluctantly. She did not feel up to facing Annabelle and her complaints, yet she had little choice. Unconsciously, she straightened her shoulders, and lifted her head as she ducked into the tent.

The interior was very dim, and there was no sound. Had Annabelle gone out?

In the faint lights admitted by the glassine window, Belinda saw the form under the blankets of her sister's cot. Was she sleeping?

A hot flash of anger seared her. It was just like Annabelle. The tent was still a mess, and here she was napping, and after doing nothing all day.

Angrily, Belinda strode to the cot, grabbed the covers, and threw them back.

A mewling sound came from Annabelle. As the light struck her prone figure, Belinda gasped in shock. The full skirt of Annabelle's dress was ripped, and the bodice was completely torn away from one shoulder.

"Annabelle!" Belinda cried. "What happened to you?"

Slowly, Annabelle turned toward her, exposing a face swollen with tears. Their eyes met, and Belinda gasped again, frightened by the look in her sister's eyes, a look so alien to Annabelle's nature as to be appalling.

Without another word, Belinda gathered her sister into her arms. Her mind was a riot of questions, but she only murmured soothingly. What on earth could have happened? It was plain that Annabelle had been assaulted, but by whom, and more importantly, to what extent?

For a long time, Annabelle sobbed against Belinda's shoulder, while the tent grew cold. A hard purpose filled

Belinda's mind. Whoever had done this would pay. Now, she must find out what had happened.

"Annabelle," she said softly. "Annabelle, you've got to tell me what happened. I *must* know."

Annabelle knuckled her eyes, her body still heaving with sobs. "It . . . it was Chet Harter. He . . ."

"Who? Chet Harter?" Belinda could not remember anyone by that name.

"The man in . . . Dyea. In the street, remember?"

Belinda remembered, and her lips tightened. "He came here?"

Annabelle nodded. "This . . . this afternoon, just after you went out. He . . . he asked me out to supper."

Belinda's heart sank. Oh, God! She felt an awkward mixture of annoyance and compassion. It was at least partially Annabelle's fault then, if she went out to dinner with the man. "And you went?" She tried to say it gently.

Annabelle nodded miserably. "We went to the Aurora Café. He asked for a . . ." she turned her face away, "for a private room."

Belinda groaned. "Oh, Annabelle! How could you be so stupid?"

Annabelle looked up, her lips trembling. "I know I shouldn't have, but he explained it. There were several rough types, he said, in the public room. So I . . . I went."

Belinda took a deep breath. "And after dinner he . . ."

Annabelle was silent for a moment, then nodded almost imperceptibly. "He gave me wine. I drank quite a bit. Too much, I realize now. I felt all . . . all tipsy . . ." She glanced up, her eyes like wounds. "Oh, Bee! It was awful! It wasn't like you read about. He . . . he hurt me!"

"Shhh, shhh! There now." Belinda held her close again. She knew that, up until now, Annabelle had thought she was in control of the world, particularly that part of it which consisted of the male gender. She had been wooed, courted, treated like a princess on a pedestal; and now a man had toppled that pedestal, bringing her down into the dirt, and Belinda sensed that her sister would never be quite the same.

For an instant, her experience with Josh sprang vividly to mind, and she was grateful that it had been so different; but then what did that really matter when the end result was the same? She had given herself willingly, and Annabelle had been raped, but in a sense they were both victims of men.

"When I fought him, he hit me . . ." Annabelle pointed a trembling finger at the dark bruise on her cheek. "And . . . and he laughed when he . . . when he . . ."

Sobs drowned out the rest of Annabelle's words, and Belinda, in pity, felt tears come to her own eyes. Whatever Annabelle was or was not, she *was* her sister, and although she might be thoughtless and vain, there was no real harm in her. She had never, insofar as Belinda knew, done a consciously cruel thing; and now this man Harter, this animal, had hurt her terribly, Belinda vowed that he would pay for what he had done. She didn't know how, not yet, but she would think of a way.

Josh Rogan gazed around his camp with a feeling of satisfaction. It looked like the camp of any other gold seeker. His claim, which included a section of the bank of a small stream, had been chosen for convenience and effect, and not for any possibility of gold discovery. To those who had told him that he was foolish for selecting this particular site, he just looked mysterious, and said that he had a hunch about the location. The fact that no other miners had seen fit to lay claim to this spot was all to the good as far as he was concerned, since he intended to spend little time there and did not want this fact to attract notice.

Next to his tent lay his pick, gold pan and shovel. Josh thought the whole setup looked authentic enough—he had compared it carefully to the camps of other miners—and now he could go about his real business.

Josh had his work cut out for him, he knew that. He was working alone. The gray man in the spartan office in Washington had made that plain enough. "I can't spare any more marshals, Rogan. Another man would probably be in the way, anyhow. This office has been flooded by complaints from these damned gold seekers, complaints about being conned, robbed, all kinds of skullduggery, even murder. I think they're all damned fools, for being up there in the first place, and deserve most of what happens to them. But not murder! This office cannot overlook murder. The complaints are coming out of Skagway and Dyea, and Dawson City. Dawson is Canada's problem, but if you have to go there to get proof of murder, do it.

"One man we know about, the jasper operating in Skagway, Soapy Smith, he calls himself. I understand there's another in Dyea. They're both unscrupulous jaspers, so watch yourself. Watch your back, I don't want to have to send another marshal in there to investigate *your* death!"

"Nice of you to be concerned about me, sir."

"It's not you I'm concerned about so much. We're short-handed enough as it is."

Recalling the conversation, Josh chuckled to himself. He

had trained himself not to spend too much time thinking about the less pleasant aspects of his job. He knew that he lived with the ever-present threat of physical harm and death and normally this didn't worry him; but ever since meeting Belinda Lee, the subject had been much on his mind.

The undreamed-of sweetness and fulfillment he had experienced that night in the tent on the ice was never far from his thoughts, and he had to fight to keep it in the background. Still, when he was not on guard, the thought crept in; if he were to die, he would never know that sweetness again.

He wrenched his thoughts away from her and back to the task at hand. It was both dangerous and futile for a man in his line of work to think of a lasting relationship. He had seen what it had done to others, to his friends. Worrying about a wife and family tended to make a man over-cautious, made him hesitate when he should be bold, and that cut down on his chances of survival.

No, he would have to forget Belinda Lee, at least for the time being. Perhaps when this was all over . . . well, he had been thinking of retiring from the field, for some time. Maybe this could be the time to do it. The job had lost its glamor long ago, and the enthusiasm he had once felt was ebbing.

Josh only hoped that Belinda would wait, would not do something foolish—like take up with another man. He knew that she had been hurt and angered by his seeming abandonment of her, and he understood her feelings, and ached to tell her the truth, but he could not. He had asked her to trust him, yet that was probably an unreasonable request in the face of his behavior.

He sighed and said a silent prayer that she would still be there, unattached, when he was finally able to tell her the reason for his actions.

Sergeant Douglas Mackenzie looked around his new office with some satisfaction. It might not be as elaborate as he would like, but it was certainly larger, better appointed, and more comfortable than the tent at the check-stand on Chilkoot Pass.

Also, his transfer had been by the way of a promotion. Although his rank had not changed, the post here was considered more important, and he would have more men under his command. He was determined to do well.

Outside, he could hear the creak of wagons, the babble of many voices, and the myriad sounds that made up the daily hustle and bustle of Dawson. He listened idly. It wasn't all going to be tea and crumpets by any means, he knew that. Dawson was a frontier town, and like all frontier towns, it could be rough, bawdy, and violent.

Then there were the disputed mining claims, which brought about claim-jumping; arguments over rights, which often led to mayhem; theft, and the danger of theft—wherever there was gold, there was the ever-present threat that one person would try to take it away from another. There were drunken brawls, knifings, and despite the fact that the Canadian government had a law against the stampeders bringing guns into the territory, an occasional shooting. No, keeping order in Dawson would not be an easy job. However, he would do it, and would do it to the best of his ability!

He smiled. There was a bonus attached to this transfer.

His mind filled again, as it had so often recently, with the image of the beautiful, young woman, Belinda Lee, who had asked a favor of him at Chilkoot Pass.

His smile broadened. He wondered if his superiors would consider her promise to go to dinner with him a bribe for his letting her into Canada without the required provisions?

Be that as it may, he had never met a girl, or woman, who attracted him more. It was not just her form and figure—although both were outstanding—but also the intelligence that shone out from those luminous, dark-lashed gray eyes. There was a certain nobility of spirit about her that somehow touched him deeply, and he wanted very much to see her again. As soon as he was set-tled in here, and had made the acquaintance of his men, he would seek her out.

But several days passed before Douglas could carry out his resolution to look for Belinda Lee. There had been a fatal knifing in the Golden Poke, one of the larger saloons in town, and the incident had stirred up considerable con-troversy.

The victim, a young prospector from New England, had, before his untimely demise, been complaining loudly that he had been cheated. The man who had done the knifing, an employee of the owner of the Poke, had insisted that the act was committed in self-defense, and when Douglas arrived, indeed there was a heavy-bladed Bowie knife on the floor by the dead man's hand. There were others pre-sent however, who made a point of telling the Mountie that there had been no knife in the victim's hand at the time of the stabbing; it had only appeared after he sprawled on the floor in death.

Douglas talked with Lester Pugh, the owner of the Poke, in an effort to ascertain exactly what had occurred, but although Pugh deplored the incident and expressed his concern and desire to help, Douglas had a bad feeling about the man.

Pugh was a bit too slick, his manners too perfect, his voice *too* respectful. Yes, there was more to Lester Pugh than met the eye—although *that* was certainly consider-able. He was the biggest man Douglas had ever seen!

Douglas also didn't care much for Pugh's underling, Chet Harter. He didn't need to look too far beneath the sur-face there to know that this one needed watching. In fact, the whole crew at the Poke was a bit less than savory, except possibly for the manager, Montana Leeds, who seemed to be a straight enough chap. Douglas wondered how he had gotten himself mixed up with a pair like Pugh and Harter. Unfortunately, Leeds had not been present at the time of the stabbing, and knew nothing about it.

At any rate, Douglas made a mental note to keep his eye on the Poke, and Mr. Lester Pugh. Dawson, for all its roughness, had comparatively little heavy crime because of the presence of the Northwest Mounted Police, and Dou-glas intended to see that it did not change.

The attacker was not brought to trial. Strangely, those willing to swear that the victim had possessed no knife, and had not started the brawl, were not willing to swear to this in front of a judge. Resignedly, Douglas washed his hands of the affair, and began to look for Belinda Lee and her sister.

Finding them wasn't at all difficult. Despite the flow of

people in and out of Dawson, there was a well-developed grapevine that spread gossip and news faster than the local newspaper, so two young women as pretty as the Lee girls did not go unnoticed. The fact that Belinda had set up as a photographer—the first woman photographer that many of them had ever seen—also engendered considerable gossip and speculation.

As Douglas stopped in front of the two large tents adjacent to the wooden stage, he felt a nervousness that was unusual for him. Would Belinda Lee remember him? More importantly, would she still be interested? The men here were hungry for women, and a nice woman, young and beautiful to boot, would be besieged by suitors. The thought gave him a real pang.

Since there was no door in the real sense, he called out, "Hello! Miss Lee? Is anybody home?"

He heard shuffling sounds from inside, and the tent flap opened to show the round, brown face of a Chilkat. The dark eyes that regarded him were intelligent, and after a cursory examination of Douglas, almost disappeared as the man smiled.

"Yes," the Indian said. "This Lee tent. I am Charlie, Miss Lee helper. What do for you?"

Douglas found himself returning the friendly grin. "I'd like to see Miss Lee, Miss Belinda Lee, that is. Is she in?"

Charlie shook his head until the straight, black hair bounced. "Miss Belinda not in. Out making pictures." He mimed the act of using a camera. "Be back soon. You wait? Can give tea. Miss Belinda show me how to make."

Douglas hesitated. He had work to do back at the station, but now that he was here, so close to seeing her . . .

"I'll stay," he said, "and tea would be fine. Thank you, Charlie."

As she and Annabelle approached their tent, Belinda could hear the sound of male voices inside. One she recognized as belonging to Charlie. The other . . . for an instant, a wild hope filled her, and then was quickly pushed away. It wouldn't be Josh, and even if it was, it would mean nothing to her. He had made his feelings quite clear back at Crater Lake. So why should she keep thinking of him?

She turned to Annabelle, who was following close behind her. "It would seem that we have company."

Annabelle, cheeks pink from the brisk walk, only nodded, and Belinda experienced both annoyance and sadness. Part of her felt great sorrow at the change in her usually perky sister, and part of her was impatient at Annabelle's inability, or unwillingness, to bounce back from her ordeal with Chet Harter. Physically she was fine. Belinda had called in a doctor, who had examined Annabelle and pronounced her fit. She had just had her monthly, and so, thank God, she was not carrying that man's child . . . but it was as if something had broken in Annabelle that night, shattering her spirit.

Still, Belinda thought, what could she do but try to act normally, try to bring Annabelle out of herself? So, Belinda smiled at her sister, and took her arm. "We'll go in and have a nice cup of tea, and some of those cakes Charlie got at the new bakery."

"That will be nice." Annabelle's voice was listless, but she did attempt a smile.

Well, that was *something!*

As it did so often now, rage at Harter rose like vomit in Belinda's throat. Two weeks had passed, and still Harter went unpunished, and probably untroubled, by what he had done to Annabelle.

At first Belinda had considered going to the authorities and pressing charges, but Annabelle had gone with the man willingly—even agreed to the private room. There would be embarrassing questions, and the matter would be bruited all over Dawson.

Belinda had fantasized various scenes in which she confronted Harter and his employer, but that was all they were, fantasies. In the end she had realized there was little they could do, at least legally, but she was still determined that at some point, Chet Harter would pay for what he had done!

They went into the tent.

"Oh, Miss Lee, I've been waiting to see you!"

In the dim light of the tent's interior, Belinda had difficulty in recognizing the tall figure that quickly rose to greet her. If it had not been for the scarlet uniform, she might not have remembered the young Mountie from the checkpoint at Chilkoot Pass.

"Oh, yes, Mr. . . . ." She could not remember his name.

"Sergeant Mackenzie, Douglas Mackenzie. You came through my station at the Pass."

"Of course! Sergeant Mackenzie!" She was embarrassed that she had not remembered his name, particularly since he had been so nice to her. If not for his kindness, she would not be here now. "It's so dim in here after being outdoors . . ."

"I understand," he said politely, his gaze fixed on her face.

Belinda did wish that he wouldn't stare so, it made her uncomfortable. "Please sit back down, Sergeant. Annabelle and I will just get rid of our things, and be right with you. Charlie, get the cakes out, will you? We're hungry after our walk. If you'll excuse us, Sergeant?"

"But, of course."

Belinda and Annabelle retired behind the curtain, which Belinda had hung to provide a dressing room in the rear of the tent. In the small mirror that hung from the tent post, Belinda examined her face and straightened her hair. Annabelle, who usually would have spent a long period of time primping for the presence of any male, did not even bother to look into the mirror.

By the time they came round from behind the curtain, Charlie had set out plates of cakes, and was brewing a fresh pot of tea.

Belinda sat on one of the cots, and Annabelle took the other. The tea table was only a square board set atop a small barrel, yet the atmosphere took on a cozy air, as Belinda poured tea for herself and her sister, and refilled Sergeant Mackenzie's cup. He sat quite near her on a small canvas chair, and Belinda could see what she really had not had time to notice on their previous brief meeting—he was very attractive, quite masculine, with a strong presence.

"I've been transferred to Dawson, as I told you I might be," he said, "and I've just been settling in. As soon as things were brought under control, I began to look for you."

Belinda felt color rise to her face. He made the statement without any attempt at flattery, but the bald words were in themselves a compliment, and demanded some kind of a response. "I'm very pleased," she said slowly, "that you took the time and trouble to look us up, Sergeant. It will be nice to have a . . . friend here in town. So many of the people are just passing through, and it's difficult to make lasting friendships."

"Please." He held up his hand. "Sergeant sounds so formal, so *official.* Would you please call me Douglas?"

"All right . . . Douglas."

He took a sip of tea. "I do hope that you will consider me your friend, and will allow me to call on you. If you don't mind my saying so, this is a forbidding town for two women alone. I'm glad to see that you seem to be in good hands." He nodded at Charlie, whose wide smile threatened to split his cheeks. "However, if you ever have any trouble, or encounter something Charlie can't handle, please don't hesitate to call me. I would be happy to help." He appeared embarrassed by his earnestness, and Belinda was touched.

After her experience with Josh Rogan, she was reluctant to become involved in any sort of romantic attachment; but one did need friends, and there would be no advantage in turning this kind, attractive man away. Besides, there was the practical side—having the commander of Dawson's detachment of the Northwest Mounted Police at her beck and call certainly could do no harm. She smiled charmingly. "Thank you, Douglas. We appreciate your offer, don't we, Annabelle?"

Annabelle, her eyes on the cup in her hand, gave a start and murmured softly, "Yes, yes, of course," and lapsed back into silence.

For another half-hour, they nibbled cakes, drank tea, and chatted, and for the first time since leaving New York,

Belinda relaxed into an approximation of the normal social life she had enjoyed at home. It *was* nice to have someone well-bred and intelligent to talk to—it made her feel civilized again. Until now, she had not realized how primitive their lives had become, concerned only with the basics of life. Perhaps Annabelle was right; Belinda decided that she would count her growing hoard of gold, paid her by picture-seeking prospectors, and see if she had enough to start construction on a permanent building so they could live like real people once again. And that thought made her realize that it was time to start work. There had been a line already forming when she and Annabelle came up, and she did not want to keep the men waiting.

She checked the watch hanging around her neck. "I'm sorry, Douglas, but I must get to work. It's almost one, and there are customers waiting."

Nodding, Douglas set down his cup and rose to his feet. "May I see you over to your, er, stage? Is that what you call it?"

She laughed. "That's as good a word as any." She also got to her feet. "I'll even let you carry some equipment, if you'd be so kind."

"I would be delighted." He smiled, and for a moment, his usually serious face looked younger and more vulnerable. For the first time Belinda realized that he probably was not a great deal older than herself, and for an instant the thought made her feel close to him.

As they crossed over to the second tent, with Charlie trotting after them, Douglas leaned down and spoke close to her ear. "Belinda, I hope that you will do me the honor of letting me call on you again. Perhaps one evening you might even let me take you to supper?" His face was very earnest and sincere, and Belinda, sensitive to the feelings of others, knew that he considered her answer very important.

How strange, she thought, that he should care so much, be so interested in me, after knowing me such a short time. She could almost see what it was about, the man-woman game that captivated Annabelle so. Belinda supposed that it could give you a feeling of power, this ability to so turn a man's head, this strange influence that women seemed to have over men. Yet, it was a troublesome thing, as well. It got in the way of a simple give-and-take relationship between people as people. Oh, there was certainly a difference between men and women—she would be the first to agree to that, and to appreciate it, too—but sometimes she wished that she could simply be friends with men, just person to person, human to human, so to speak, and not male sex to female sex.

"Belinda?"

She realized that she had not replied to his question. "Oh! Yes, Douglas, I would be happy to have you call, and supper some evening would be nice." Her mind touched the memory of Annabelle on the night after her "evening" with Chet Harter, and winced away.

He gave her one of his rare smiles, and again it puzzled her that such a small thing could make a man happy.

The line that afternoon was a long one, and when she had shut down operations, Belinda looked with satisfaction at the bag of gold dust and nuggets in her hand. Yes, they would have to see about getting a real building. Annabelle should like that.

Charlie had already gathered up the equipment and now trudged ahead of her on strong, bandy legs, toward the darkroom tent.

It was still daylight—as far as the light went, she could take pictures almost twenty-four hours a day now, if she had the stamina—and she still wondered at the phenomenon of days that lasted twenty hours or more. At first she had found it difficult to sleep, but now she was able to get sufficient rest. Annabelle, however, seemed to be sleeping little, if at all.

As Charlie carried the equipment into the darkroom tent, Belinda went on into their sleeping tent. She was hungry and wondered if Annabelle had started supper, as she occasionally did, or was still sitting listlessly on her cot, which was more often the case, staring into space or crying. "Annabelle?" she called out, as she entered.

There was no answer. The tent was empty.

A feeling of foreboding crept like a chill over Belinda. "Annabelle!" she called again. She hurriedly pushed aside the blanket that formed a clothes closet and dressing room, and shock made her numb. Annabelle's clothing was not there.

Annabelle was gone!

≈8≈

Lester Pugh closed the top of the humidor with exaggerated care. When anger raged in him he was particularly careful to exercise full control, so that it would not show—and he was *very* angry now.

Why was it so difficult to find competent people to work for him? Perhaps it was the curse of genius, that the man at the top must ever be served by dolts and imbeciles.

He relaxed his clenched fist, and forced himself to draw gently on the cigarette in the holder. That fool, Harter! First there had been the incident of the knifing—the dealer who had stabbed the tenderfoot prospector had been hired by Harter—and now this thing with the girl. Women, it had to be said, were at the bottom of a good many of the world's problems.

Pugh paced back and forth across the room with heavy and measured steps, a sign of his great agitation. And the fool couldn't have chosen a girl from one of the cribs, or even from the saloons. Oh, no, he had to choose a *nice* woman, a girl who had a sister who might very well make trouble. And trouble was the last thing Pugh wanted at this time.

He was right in the middle of closing a deal, a very lucrative deal, wherein he would take over Dawson's biggest hotel, a mining supply house, and another saloon—all legitimate concerns, or nearly so. He was also involved in setting up an excellent connection with a supplier of first-class tarts for the houses. Now all of these enterprises could be in jeopardy because Chet Harter hadn't the brains of a mosquito!

So far, the inhabitants of Dawson had been too blinded by gold fever, too busy going their individual ways, to care much about what went on in the town. But there would come a time, as Dawson grew larger, when the entire population *would* begin to take an interest. After that, it would be a good deal more difficult to establish the sort of business syndicate that Pugh had in mind, and he intended to make sure before that happened, he would be well established and disguised as a honest businessman, his steps so well-covered, and his operations such an integral part of the community, that they would not be questioned.

And now Harter's stupidity threatened all this. The man would have to be taught a lesson!

The incident in the saloon had caused a lot of talk, and a worrisome number of miners had been ready to swear the young prospector had had no knife on him, and that the dealer had initiated the violence. Well, it had been taken care of, smoothed over, but the Mounties would be watching the Poke more closely now, and Pugh certainly did not want them to notice anything out of the ordinary—such as a young woman being raped and lured away from her sister.

The cigarette had burned down to an ash, and he stubbed out the smouldering butt in the crystal ashtray. The time had come to pay his respects to the happy couple. With a sour expression on his face, Pugh left his quarters and made his way down the hall to Harter's room, where he knocked briskly on the door, calling out Harter's name.

"Just a minute, L.P." Harter's voice sounded hoarse and Pugh wondered, with distaste, if he had caught them at an inopportune moment. If he had, it was just too damned bad! They could put off their rutting until he had his say. He knocked again, harder.

In a moment the door opened, and Harter, in his shirtsleeves, face flushed and eyes bright, answered the door. He had a half-filled glass of liquor in his hand, and by the swollen condition of the front of his trousers, he had indeed been caught either beginning, or in the midst of, enjoying his female companion.

Pugh scornfully averted his gaze, then fixed Harter with a cold stare. "Harter, I have some things to say to you and your . . . your lady friend, and then I shall leave you to finish whatever it was you were doing."

"Sure thing, L.P.," Harter said blandly. "I've just been telling Annabelle here how I owe everything to you. Haven't I, baby?" He directed an intimidating look at the young woman seated on the bed, and she nodded listlessly. Her clothing was in disarray, and she looked cowed.

Well, Pugh thought; it looks as though Harter has broken her spirit already. A pity, really, for it had taken something out of her. Pugh briefly recalled her appearance during their short meeting in Dyea. Yes, a great pity, but that was none of his affair. All he was concerned with was that they should come to no trouble through her presence here.

"Would you like something to drink, L.P.?" Harter held up an almost-empty bottle.

"No, thank you, Chesley," Pugh said coldly. "I'll just say what I came to say . . . Miss," he glanced over at the woman on the bed, "are you here of your own free will? Has Mr. Harter coerced you in any way, or threatened you, to get you here?"

The woman shook her head. "No, I came here of my own free will."

"Why, L.P., would I do a thing like that?" Harter said, smiling.

Pugh silenced him with a savage gesture. "Then would you be prepared to swear this to your sister, or to the Mounties, if it became necessary?"

She hesitated, lowering her head before she spoke in a

whisper, "Yes."

Pugh shrugged, satisfied. "Very well then. I don't see that any real difficulty will arise. Harter?"

He motioned with his head toward the hallway and Harter reluctantly followed him out of the room, shutting the door behind him. "What is it, L.P.?"

Pugh looked him steadily in the eye and Harter began to fidget. "Come on now, L.P. What's bothering you? Spit it out so I can get back to that pretty little dolly in there."

Pugh spoke coldly and distinctly, "That pretty little dolly in there had better not get us into any trouble, Harter. I hope, for your sake, that she's telling the truth when she says that she is here of her own free will. I'd hate to find out differently!"

Harter began to bluster, a sure sign that he was concealing something. "Why, hell, L.P.! You heard the girl. I didn't even know she was coming. She just showed up here last night with her suitcase in her hand. Now you know I couldn't turn away a pretty thing like her, could I? I figure that in a week or two I'll break her in to helping out in the saloon. These randy sourdoughs should be willing to part with a few nuggets, or some dust just to be around someone as fresh and pretty as she is."

Pugh nodded, but his expression did not ease. "Perhaps that is a good idea. We'll see. In the meantime, keep a tight rein on her, and keep her out of sight. I don't want *any* trouble from the sister, or the Mounties. Understand?"

"Sure thing, L.P.," Harter said carelessly. "There won't be any fuss. You can depend on me."

"I surely hope so," said Pugh, turning away. "I hope so for your sake, Harter. I really hate breaking in a new right-hand man, I surely do!"

Pugh walked back to his quarters, wondering if Soapy Smith was having as much trouble in Skagway as he was in Dawson. As he reached the door of his rooms, he paused, one hand on the knob, and chuckled. Thinking of Soapy always brought a smile to his lips. Of course Soapy's methods were very different from Pugh's own. Soapy leaned more toward the unlikely, haphazard scams that couldn't possibly work, and yet did—for Soapy. That was his genius.

Pugh went inside and picked up the silver-framed picture of his friend from his desk. Yes, Soapy was an original.

He put down the picture and picked up the letter that had arrived yesterday afternoon, weighing it thoughtfully in his hand. Soapy was no great hand at letter writing, yet the message was clear—Soapy was in trouble, and it was plain to Pugh that his friend had no idea how much.

According to the letter, the better elements in Skagway felt that Jefferson "Soapy" Smith was dirtying the name of Skagway and the White Pass, and would make this route unattractive to the gold seekers. The railway entrepreneurs were siding with influential townspeople, and though in the letter Soapy scoffed at their chances of accomplishing this, Pugh felt in his gut that Soapy was whistling in the wind. It was the same kind of thing that could happen here, and in Dyea, if he, Lester Pugh, wasn't careful—but then he *was* careful. That was another way in which he and Soapy differed.

Of course Soapy's way was showier, and at least one of his practices had been incorporated into sourdough slang—"seeing the eagle."

Soapy had a saloon in Skagway, called Jeff's Place, which was the center of his operation. In the courtyard back of the saloon, there was a large eagle chained to a perch, and since there were no "facilities" in the saloon, this area also served as a urinal for the customers. Given to colorful turns of phrase, the locals soon came to refer to their visits to the courtyard as "seeing the eagle," a phrase which was quickly adopted into the local jargon.

Some of the customers who proved resistant to the enticements of the saloon girls, or the gaming tables, found the visit to the eagle very unpleasant, for the courtyard was the perfect place for sandbagging, and many a greenhorn who went out back "to see the eagle," returned with an aching head and empty pockets. So the term had also come to mean getting slugged and rolled.

Pugh chuckled. Yes, old Soapy was a real pistol. It was amazing how much he reminded Pugh of his brother, Wendell.

Pugh sighed. Poor Wendell. Was he alive somewhere? Or was he dead?

There had been just the two of them, Wendell and Lester Pugh, after their parents had died in a boating accident; two small boys left alone in the world, with no one to care about them.

Pugh sniffed. The one thing in the world that could make him feel sentimental was the thought of his early childhood back in Michigan. Poor little tykes they were, seven and ten years old. Their only relative was an elderly aunt, Penelope Pugh, their father's sister. She had not wanted them, but took them in out of a sense of duty, and was careful not to let them ever forget what they owed her.

She had been a mean, cold woman, Aunt Penelope, although she had seemed to feel some fondness for Wendell. She had not liked Lester; he knew it, but did not resent it, or the fact that she favored Wendell, who was the elder. It was hard not to like Wendell, with his gentle voice and soft, dark hair and winning ways. Lester had looked up to him and admired him, as only a younger brother can.

And then came that awful day at the lake. They had been out in the little punt—they were both good sailors, as their parents had been—and a sudden wind came up. In a flash, Wendell was overboard and out of sight beneath the chop. Lester had searched and searched. After a time, he had finally found his brother, cold and almost unconscious. Although he was only seven, Lester had pulled Wendell aboard, and gotten the punt to shore. It was the last time he saw his brother. The next day a visiting couple, the Brewsters, had departed from his aunt's home and had taken Wendell with them. It seemed they were adopting Wendell, but not Lester, as they did not have room for more than one boy.

And Lester, bewildered lad that he had been, had not understood; he had only known that his beloved brother was gone, taken from him arbitrarily.

He remembered the anger, the crying, the screaming at his aunt, the anguished cries of why? She had no real answer for him; except that it was for the best, that Wendell would have a good home, and Lester would simply have to adjust to the change of circumstances.

He had been lonely after that, for Aunt Penelope and he had stayed on at the lake after the season was over. A tutor had been brought in for him, and although Lester occasionally missed the activity and the friends of the public school, he had adjusted. He had recognized, even then, that he was a superior individual, and as such, was not meant to mingle with the common herd.

At any rate, that was probably why he had become friends with Jefferson Smith, who looked a great deal like Wendell might have looked when full-grown. Soapy even had the same soft-spoken ways, although in Soapy's case, this deceptive manner concealed a streak of ruthlessness.

But enough of this maudlin reminiscing! There were things to be done, deals to be consummated.

Pugh settled himself behind the big desk and drew a large stack of papers toward him.

The stranger ambling in a lopsided gait toward Josh's claim was one of the strangest-looking men Josh had ever seen.

Gnome-small, wearing an oversized, checked work shirt that hung almost to his knees, and a drooping, wide-brimmed hat that all but covered his face, the man came steadily on with his peculiar, hitching gait. Shoulder-length gray hair, and a full, gray beard, added to the gnome-like appearance, and Josh could only stare, bemused and intrigued, as the man came toward him.

When he was within hailing distance, the man slowed, pushing his hat back on his head to show a wizened, red-cheeked countenance with blue eyes sharp as diamonds.

"Howdy!" The little man's voice was full and deep, and comically incongruous coming out of so small a frame.

"Howdy," Josh answered seriously. Somehow he realized that this strange person was not to be laughed at—perhaps it was the eyes, clear, direct, and intelligent.

"This yere yore digs?"

Josh nodded and the small man came closer. He removed his hat, revealing a rosy circle of flesh on the crown of his head.

"I'm Two-Step Sam. Smelled yore beans a-cookin' as I came up the stream. Wondered if ya might have a plateful to spare for a hongry man."

Josh, amused by the old man's dialect, nevertheless maintained a sober countenance. I think I have enough for two. Have a seat, Two-Step Sam."

"Much obliged. Been walkin' all mornin', and my feet have been hollerin' for a rest, while my stomach feels like my throat's been cut."

He sank down onto the piece of log, near the fire over which Josh had been heating a pan of beans and a pot of coffee.

As Josh ladled the beans onto two tin plates, the old man lifted first one foot and then the other, to examine the soles of his heavy boots. Josh could not help noticing that his dinner companion had the feet of a much larger man. The boots must have been at least a size twelve. Both soles were worn thin, and the right one had a deep hole the size of a quarter in the middle of the ball of the foot.

"Gone through, it has," said Two-Step, sadly. "Knew it would one of these days." He sighed. "I tell you, younker, it gets harder and harder to keep body and soul together these days."

The twinkle in Two-Step's eye told Josh that the old man had made the pun intentionally, and he grinned in appreciation, as he handed him the plate of beans and a cup of the strong coffee, laced with canned milk.

Two-Step Sam took the plate and cup with alacrity, and had cleaned the plate before Josh was even half done with his own. Two-Step burped mightily, and took a swallow of the steaming coffee.

"That tasted mighty good, younker. You may have saved an old man's life for one more day." He grinned, showing tobacco-stained stubs of teeth. "You're a Cheechako, ain't ya?"

Josh, familiar with the Klondike word for newcomer, nodded. "Yep. How about yourself?" He asked this last knowing that it would get a rise out of the old man.

"Myself!" The old man snorted and sat up straighter. "I'm a sourdough, friend, been one man and boy. Why, there ain't nobody been up here longer than Two-Step Sam. Why, I been prospectin' this country for twenty-some years, and there ain't *nothin'* I don't know about findin' the heavy yaller. Jest ask around, any of the old timers'll tell you about Two-Step Sam."

The obvious question went through Josh's mind. If the old man had been around that long, and if he knew anything at all about prospecting for gold, he should be rich by now. However, it seemed unkind to bring this up, and Josh held his tongue.

Two-Step amused and delighted him, and yet there was also something about him that aroused respect.

"I know, you're asking yourself that if this old bastard has been here so long, and knows so much, why ain't he rich?" He cackled gleefully, a cracked, piercing squall that made Josh wince. "Well, ya see, younker, I *have* been rich, yep, rich as Croesus, and poor as a black slave. I've made and lost my fortune a lot more'n once, but I don't blame nobody but myself, cause it all came about through my habit. Ya see, I'm a little overfond of the bottle, ya might say, and on top of that, I can't seem to hang onto money, gold dust, whatever, when I get it. Seems like there is a veritable devil in me that drives me to wild spendin', and loose livin', and before ya know it, I've spent the whole caboodle on strong drink and weak women, and the gamin' tables, and there I be, back prospectin' again." He shook his head dolefully. "Somehow, I don't learn."

Josh nodded. What could you say to a story like that? He wanted to keep Two-Step talking. "That's an interesting name, old-timer," he said. "How did you come by it?"

Two-Step cackled again, striking his knee with a gnarled hand the size of a small ham. "It's my locomotion," he said, still laughing. "I 'spect ya noticed that I have what ya might call, if ya was bein' generous, a highly individual locomotion?"

Josh nodded, keeping a sober face. "Very distinctive."

The old man's eyes twinkled at him over the mass of beard. "Well now, it's right kind of ya to say that. Yep, distinctive, that's what she is. Well, a bear gave me that walk. A big brown, one summer over near Crater Lake, got me with his front paw, just back of the knee." He mimed a great swipe with his hand. "Been walkin' that way ever since. Some of the boys thought it looked like I was dancin'. Still and all, I've covered a lot of miles that way." He grinned. "Say, ya got any more of that moose piss ya call coffee?"

Laughing, Josh lifted the pot and filled Two-Step's cup.

An idea was growing in his head. It was clear that Two-Step Sam, whatever his past glories, was now only two steps from being down and out. Josh could only speculate, but from the man's conversation it would seem that, at the moment, it was very possible Two-Step had no claim of his own, and no gear or supplies. If this was the case, he might be just what Josh was looking for.

"Tell me, old-timer," he said, handing the man the canned milk. "Do you have a claim to work?"

Two-Step looked at him sharply. "Did. Over on Stoney Creek, but I ain't got it now. Lost it in a crap game. A week ago today, that was. All that was left of my gear, too."

For a moment Josh glimpsed the very real sorrow that welled into the man's eyes, then Two-Step managed a smile and a cackle. "But what the hell, that durn claim weren't no good, anyways. Never took out nothin' but a few shavin's."

"Where you staying now?"

Two-Step shrugged. "Oh, here and there. Got me a few friends yet, who still care what happens to old Two-Step, though sometimes I wonder what for. Mrs. Billis, widow lady what runs a restaurant in Dawson, feeds me now and again, but I think her patience is wearin' thin."

"Two-Step, about this drinking of yours . . . just how bad is it? I mean, how does it take you? All the time, or a big binge once in a while?"

Two-Step's eyes turned sad. "I'm a binger. I'll go for weeks or months at a time, with only a nip now and then to wet my whistle, and then somethin'll set me off . . . havin' a full poke, usually. It seems like I just can't stand havin' money in my pocket. It's a strange thing, that it is, and I ain't the only one by a long shot. There's many a man along the Yukon that works and struggles all year to collect his pile, then blows it in a few nights in town. A mighty peculiar thing. I've pondered on it more'n once!"

"You're quite a philosopher, Two-Step."

"Yeah, well, livin' out here in the lonelies will do that to a man, a thinkin' man, that is. Durin' those long, dark, winter nights, there ain't much else to do but think."

"Tell me . . . do you think you could swear off the booze for a time?"

"I could, but a promise like that from me wouldn't mean a dad-burned thing." He narrowed his eyes in suspicion. "Why ya askin'?"

Josh, his mind made up, leaned forward. "Tell me, how would you like to be my partner? Maybe I'll never strike it rich here. There are those who say this is a bad site. But at least you'll have a roof over your head, and something hot for your belly."

Two-Step squinted at him thoughtfully. "In my present condition, I'd be a pure-D fool to say no, but why are ya askin' me? I just told ya that I'm a drunk and a certified wild man. What do ya want with a worthless old coot like me?"

Josh shrugged, smiling. "Well, first of all, I'm going to have to be gone quite a bit. I have other business here, in Dawson, and I don't want to be leaving the diggings unattended too much. Second, despite your bad habits, which you've been frank enough to tell me about, you've got something that I need, experience. Like you pointed out, I'm a Cheechako, and I've yet to spend a winter up here. I think you would more than pay your way."

Two-Step studied him shrewdly. "It sounds great to me, and I was never one for lookin' a gift horse in the mouth, as the sayin' goes. I got me a few things in town, at Mrs. Billis's. I'll pick 'em up, and be back tomorrow mornin'."

"Fine." Josh stuck out his hand, and it was almost swallowed in the huge palm of the older man. "See you tomorrow morning then . . . *partner.*"

"Yeah, right!"

Two-Step got to his feet with surprising agility and started off, with his strange, rolling walk, toward Dawson. He was shaking his head as he went, and Josh could not help but smile. The old bastard was sharp and he might eventually tumble to what Josh's real purpose up here was, but somehow Josh felt sure if this happened, his secret would be safe with Two-Step.

The man was a godsend, in a way. Alone, it would have been difficult to keep up the pretense of working the claim, while performing the job he had come here to do. This way, the claim would be kept active, the camp would be safe, and Josh could come and go as he pleased. The only problem might lie with Two-Step's drinking. But, if it was as he said and he only went on a bender when he was flush, there should be no problem. This claim was not likely to yield any great amount of gold, and Josh intended to furnish Two-Step only enough money for the necessities.

Yes, the man was almost perfect for his purpose, and in turn, he would be keeping Two-Step Sam fed and sheltered. It looked as if it would be a good bargain for both of them.

Belinda opened her eyes with an effort. She had not slept the whole night long, but about five A.M. she had fallen into a restless slumber, only to be awakened about an hour later as the town stirred into noisy life.

She sat up and looked at the empty cot across the way. There had been a hope, lurking in the back of her mind, that during the night Annabelle would come home. Despair turned her thoughts bleak. Where could her sister be? Why had she gone?

Feeling stiff and much older than her twenty-two years, Belinda got up from the cot and dressed herself, not even caring what she put on. Annabelle had been a nuisance and a trial, and she knew her sister's faults as well as anyone; yet Annabelle *was* her sister and she cared for her.

The fact that Annabelle had taken all her belongings made it clear that her leaving was a well-thought-out action, done deliberately. Annabelle had to have some sort of plan, but what could it be?

Belinda lit the camp stove, and put a kettle of water on for tea. She felt pretty certain that Annabelle had not left Dawson. If her intent had been to return to New York, Belinda was certain that her sister would have first tried to convince her that they should both return. No, she was probably here in town, perhaps at one of the hotels. The one drawback to that was that Annabelle had no money.

The kettle piped its readiness and Belinda poured the boiling water into the pot. There was a thought in the back of her mind, an unpleasant one. Was it possible that

Annabelle had gone to Chet Harter? No, it couldn't be, not after what he had done to her! Still, the thought would not go away, and Belinda paced restlessly as she drank the hot, sweet tea.

She had just finished the cup, when Charlie called through the tent flap, "You up, Miss Belinda? Charlie here."

"Yes. Come in, Charlie."

Charlie entered the tent, eyes bright and teeth gleaming in his dark face. "What we do this morning, Miss Belinda? Want Charlie to take you out to the fields to photograph miners, or want to photograph in town?"

She shook her head. "Neither, I'm afraid. Charlie, something has . . . well, something has gone wrong. Miss Annabelle is gone. She hasn't been home all night!"

Charlie shook his head, and his grin widened. "Miss Annabelle not like you. She . . ." He hesitated. "She maybe just out having good time. She be back. You not fret, Miss Belinda."

Belinda, despite her low spirits, had to smile. In Charlie's uncomplicated existence it was probably not unusual for a man, or a woman, to stay out all night having a "good time." She did wonder, though, at the implication that *she* was different. Did Charlie think that she was incapable of enjoying herself? Did she seem that rigid and uncompromising? The thought disturbed her.

"No, Charlie. I'm afraid that it's more than that. I'm going to have to ask your help in finding her."

Charlie shrugged. "Sure, Miss Belinda. I do whatever you ask. You know that. Where could Charlie look?"

Belinda took a deep breath. "At the Golden Poke Saloon,

for one. You have friends in town, you know your way around. Do you think you can find out if Annabelle is staying there?"

His eyes had widened and he stared at her in astonishment. "At Poke Saloon? You think . . .?" Then his expression became veiled and he nodded. "Sure. I be back in little while." He started to leave the tent, then turned back, his eyes kind. "You not worry, Miss Belinda. Charlie find out, you bet boots on that."

"Don't do or say anything, Charlie. Just find out if she's there, and let me know. That's all you need to do right now."

"Sure, Charlie understand. You not worry. Drink more tea. Be cheerful."

Again, she had to smile. "Thank you, Charlie. I'll try to do that."

Belinda was far too nervous to work, so she took Charlie's advice, finishing the pot of tea and nibbling on some biscuits, as she tried to read the latest issue of a Dawson newspaper.

Although the time dragged, Charlie had only been gone about an hour when she heard him at the tent flap, scraping his feet. He looked very pleased with himself when he came in.

Belinda knew at once what he had learned. Her heart sank. "You found Annabelle?"

Charlie bobbed his head. "You betcha! Right where you say. In the Poke Saloon! Friend say she came in there yesterday afternoon. To see Mr. Chet Harter. Friend say she look fine. Healthy. So Miss Annabelle all right. You think?" He looked anxious.

Belinda sat back, feeling drained. She didn't know whether to be happy or disappointed. She now knew where Annabelle was, but the fact that she had gone, willingly it appeared, to join Harter was a terrible, shameful thing. And why? She had to know why!

For a few minutes she sat slumped in discouragement; then she straightened her spine and pulled herself upright as the image of the little harlequin clown got up from the floor of her mind.

"Charlie, you stay here and watch the tents. I am going to the Poke and talk with my sister!"

An hour later, her cheeks flaming, head held high, Belinda marched down the dusty street. She had never been so mortified in her whole life! The nerve of Chet Harter! The unmitigated gall!

Ahead of her, she could see the clapboard building that housed the offices of the Northwest Mounted Police, and she headed toward it.

When she had arrived at the Poke, the place had been quiet and almost empty. The single bartender behind the long bar had been evasive when she had asked him if Annabelle Lee was there. Finally, Belinda had demanded to talk to Chet Harter.

Harter had slouched into the barroom. In an arrogant, condescending voice, he had said that Annabelle did not wish to talk to her. When Belinda persisted, he had told her bluntly to be on her way.

Well, Belinda thought, we'll see about that!

But once inside the office of the Northwest Mounted

Police, she began to have misgivings. Should she bring this problem to the Mounties? Was it the kind of thing they were concerned with?

She was close to tears, in her frustration and helplessness, and she realized that she had come here seeking words of comfort from Douglas Mackenzie as much as for any official help.

That realization almost drove her away, then her resolution stiffened. The Mounted Police represented the only law in Dawson, and *somebody* should be able to help her.

The office was extremely neat, if sparsely furnished. There were a few straight-back chairs for visitors, and a long, wooden counter that ran the width of the room. Behind the counter sat two plain desks, and behind the desk was a partition with a door that must lead to the senior officer's office.

At one of the desks behind the counter sat a young man. He looked up as she entered and came to the counter. "Yes? May I help you?"

"Yes, may I see Sergeant Mackenzie, please?"

The Mountie nodded. "I'll tell him you're here." He went through the door in the partition.

Belinda, now that she was doing something, taking some action, felt some of the tension leave her and she took a seat in one of the wooden chairs.

The Mountie was gone for a few minutes, and Belinda used the time to compose herself, to rehearse what she was going to say. Again, doubts beset her. Was she doing the right thing?

She didn't have time to ponder further, for a smiling Douglas Mackenzie was striding through the door.

"Belinda, what a pleasant surprise! I've been hoping that you would do me the honor of calling on our offices."

He certainly was a nice-looking man, and kind, too. Please God, she prayed silently, let him be able to help me!

"May I talk to you alone, Sergeant?"

He looked a bit surprised, but maintained his aplomb. "Why, of course. Come into my office."

Douglas escorted Belinda through the door into a small, even more sparsely furnished office. "Here, sit down. Do you have a problem, Belinda?"

His solicitude almost undid her. She had to struggle not to cry. After a moment, she regained her composure, and said, "I suppose you might say that. I . . . I don't know if this comes under your jurisdiction, if it's the sort of thing you handle, but . . ."

He leaned across his desk, and smiled gently. "Suppose I be the judge of that, Belinda. You were quite right in coming to me. If it is something that cannot be officially handled, well, I hope that you consider me your friend, and we will proceed on that basis. Now, tell me . . . what's the matter?"

Belinda took a quivering breath, and began her story. At first she had intended to tell him only of the events that had transpired since Annabelle's leaving, but then her instinctive honesty, and her thought that he should know the whole sorry situation if he was to help her, prompted her to relate it all, beginning with the afternoon that Annabelle had been attacked by Chet Harter.

When she was finished, there was a silence, as Douglas leaned back, considering her story. Then he stood up, came around the desk, and took both of her hands in his.

"Belinda, there are some men who make me ashamed to be called a man, and this Chet Harter is one of them. I have already encountered Mr. Harter. A brief meeting, but he didn't make a very good impression on me. Now, I can understand why." He shook his head and released her hands rather self-consciously, as if embarrassed by the spontaneous action. "Now, let me be sure I have this right. You didn't make a complaint against this Harter at the time of your sister's . . . uh, violation?"

"That's right." She shook her head. "I thought about it, but you see, it seemed to me that since she had gone with him willingly, it might be difficult. It might look as if . . ." She stopped, unable to frame her thoughts into the proper words.

Douglas was nodding. "You were quite right. At the time, it was the only thing to do. But now, now that this has happened, it makes it difficult to file charges against this Harter chap. You said that your Chilkat, Charlie, was informed that your sister went willingly to the Golden Poke, am I correct? That would rule out kidnapping, or coercion."

Belinda raised her face to him. "There are other kinds of coercion than the obvious."

"I am aware of that." His voice was gentle. "But unfortunately, the fact remains that your sister is an adult. Legally, I am afraid I can do nothing. Wait, wait!" He held up his hands as she started to protest. "As your friend, I will offer my services. The majority of the businessmen in Dawson prefer to stay on the right side of the law, if for no other reason than that it is more convenient. It's possible that if I accompany you to the Poke, and exert a little unofficial pressure, I can at least make sure you see your sister. However, I must tell you now, that if she doesn't wish to leave, I have no power to force her."

Belinda's spirits rose. At least it was something—a foot in the door, so to speak. "Thank you, Douglas. That's all I want, really . . . a chance to talk to her and find out *why* she has done this. Of course, I hope that she will come away with me, but . . . well, if I can at least see her, find out if she is all right . . ."

It was late afternoon now, and business in the Poke had picked up to a feverish tempo. The sound of an out-of-tune piano poured onto the street, along with raucous shouts and rough laughter. Those prospectors who had accumulated a bit of gold were already well launched into a celebration, which would undoubtedly last until their gold ran out.

This time, the bartender was intimidated by the sight of Douglas's scarlet uniform and fetched Chet Harter at once.

As she had that day on the street in Dyea, Belinda found Harter a repulsive, rather frightening man. How on earth could Annabelle find him appealing?

"Yes?" Harter's tone was wary, and his eyes veiled.

"Mr. Harter, I am Sergeant Mackenzie of the Northwest Mounted. We have met before, I believe. We would like a word with you."

"We?" Harter's cold eyes moved to Belinda. Then he glanced toward the narrow stairway in the rear of the bar-room and gestured for them to follow him. He led them to an empty table in the back, a relatively quiet place. He sat down across from them, pockmarked face unreadable. "Now . . . what is this all about?"

Douglas said, "Miss Lee has come to me with a rather delicate problem. It seems that her sister has been acting rather strange lately. She's been ill, you might say, and not herself. Last night, Annabelle Lee disappeared, and it has been reported that she is here, in the Golden Poke. Now, Miss Lee would like very much to see her sister, to assure herself of her safety and good health. I understand that Miss Lee was turned away from here this morning, was not allowed to see her."

Harter said calmly, "I hate to say this, Sergeant, but the hard fact is Miss Annabelle Lee doesn't want to see her sister."

'That may very well be the case, Mr. Harter, but Miss Lee would like to hear those words from her sister's own mouth. My pardon if my words sound accusatory, but we have only your word for this."

Harter blustered, "You mean to say you think that I'm lying?"

Douglas Mackenzie sat ramrod straight, the stern figure of authority, and Belinda was impressed with his demeanor while confronting a man who was obviously dangerous.

"Now, I didn't say that, sir, but I'm sure you can understand Miss Lee's desire to hear such words directly from her sister. So, we would appreciate it if you would let Belinda visit Miss Annabelle Lee. Just a short while, a few minutes, and then she will leave. If all is as you say, and her sister does not wish to leave this place, we shall be on our way."

Harter's gaze dropped away. "Well, I suppose that's all right. Come on, I'll take you upstairs."

As they climbed the narrow, wooden stairs, Belinda was

tense and distraught. She had gotten what she wanted. She would see Annabelle; but what if what Harter said was true? What if Annabelle did not really want to see her, or speak with her? How could she convince her to come away from this place?

Belinda noticed that Harter glanced apprehensively at the first closed door they passed at the head of the stairs, and gave the strange impression of walking on tiptoe. He led them to a plain wooden door down at the end of the narrow corridor, and jerked his thumb. "She's in there. Go on in, but don't stay too long. She and I have some business to attend to this afternoon."

Belinda would not look at him, wondering about his remark. What kind of "business" was he talking about?

Douglas touched her arm. "I'll wait here in the hallway, Belinda. Call if you need me."

Harter scowled. "She won't need you. Once she hears with her own ears that her sister doesn't want to go with her, and doesn't even care to talk with her, that'll be all she wrote. And as I said, I'd thank you kindly if you'd hurry it up." He glanced ostentatiously at his pocket watch, then strode toward the head of the stairs.

Belinda gave Douglas a wan smile, turned the knob on the door, and went in without knocking.

The room wasn't at all what she had expected. Somehow, she had been envisioning it as drab and plain, as a frame for a pale and remorseful Annabelle. The reality could not have been further from this concept.

The room was heavily draped with red velvet, and the walls were covered with what looked to be expensive paper. The main item of furniture was a large, four-poster bed—how on earth did they ever get *that* over Chilkoot Pass?—and in the center of the bed, wearing a red, velvet dressing gown that Belinda had never seen before, was Annabelle. She was buffing her nails vigorously.

Belinda knew that she must be gaping like an idiot. Annabelle, perfectly groomed and apparently in the best of health, glanced up, her eyes guarded, and her expression became sulky when she recognized Belinda. She seemed to be unwilling to speak first, for she only stared challengingly.

As for herself, Belinda was at a loss for words. Was this the same Annabelle that had been dragging herself around the tent these past two weeks?

"Annabelle?" she finally said. "Why? Why have you come here like this?"

Annabelle shrugged, then gave all her attention to her nails. "I should think that would be perfectly obvious to such a clever girl as you."

Belinda felt her temper began to boil, but she determined to hold it under control. Losing her poise would get her nowhere, she well knew.

"I was worried about you, Annabelle. You didn't even leave a note."

Annabelle refused to look up. "You know I don't like writing letters. I can never think of what to say."

"You could have told me you were leaving. You owed me that much!"

Annabelle's attention was focused on the buffer, which she applied to her nails with renewed energy. "I knew you would try to stop me, and I had made up my mind."

Holding a rein on her anger, Belinda forced herself to

speak calmly. "What was it you had made up your mind to do?"

"Why, to come here, of course. You see, after . . . what happened, well, I felt pretty low, I'll admit. And hanging around that tent with nothing to do made me feel even worse. It finally came to me that since I was a . . . well, a," her mouth twisted, "a soiled dove, you might say, I might as well use it to my advantage."

"What on earth do you mean?" The words came out sharper than Belinda had intended them to.

Annabelle stopped buffing, and pouted. "See, there you go! That's why I told Chet that I didn't want to talk to you. I knew you'd make a scene. You never understand how *I* feel!"

Belinda took a deep breath. "I do want to try and understand," she said in a calmer tone. "I don't wish to fight with you, Annabelle, believe me, I don't. But please help me to understand."

"All right then, if you promise not to get angry. You know how I hate scenes. Anyway, what I decided was, since I *am* a fallen woman . . . and I've suffered because of it, haven't I? Well, since I *have* suffered, why shouldn't I enjoy some of the pleasant things that go along with it? I mean, there *are* some nice things about it, you know. Chet, Mr. Harter, had told me that I could stay here with him, if I wanted, but at the time, you know, I was upset . . ."

Her voice drifted off and Belinda, keeping her mouth shut with an effort, could scarcely credit what she was hearing. She was astounded at Annabelle's naivete. She was like a child, a spoiled child, and this rambling narrative made that glaringly apparent.

"Anyway, I thought it over," Annabelle went on, "and I finally decided there was no reason to remain in that tent, wearing what you call practical clothes, ruining my hands and my complexion, when I could have a lovely room here, and have some good times as well." She gestured around the room, and Belinda could see that she was perfectly sincere, and evidently content with her bargain.

"You want to stay then," Belinda said.

Annabelle looked up, for the first time meeting Belinda's eyes fully. "I intend to stay, Belinda. You might as well realize that I am a grown woman, older than you, for heaven's sake! You can't look after me forever, you know, and anyway, what makes you think that *you* know what's right for *me?* I'm a real woman now." For an instant she looked unbearably smug. "When it happens to you, then maybe you'll understand."

Oh, God, Belinda thought despairingly, what she's saying makes no sense at all! And yet one thing did. She, Belinda, really didn't have any right to try to live her sister's life. It was time to sever the emotional cord that bound them together, but it was hard. Briefly, she wondered what Annabelle would think if she knew that Belinda too had experienced that ultimate closeness between a man and a woman, but that wasn't important now. What was important was that she and Annabelle remain friends, no matter what kind of life Annabelle had chosen for herself. If they became estranged now, it might open a breach between them that would never heal.

She put her hand almost shyly on her sister's hand and sat down beside her on the bed. "All right, Annabelle. I'm trying to see your side. You must make your own life and your own decisions, but are you sure this is what you want? I mean you and Chet Harter . . . I mean . . ." Belinda almost choked on the words. The thought of Annabelle in this bed, in that man's arms, almost made her gag.

Annabelle was smiling. She reached across to touch Belinda's cheek. "Oh, Chet's not so bad, you know. Rather exciting really and, well, all that, you know, isn't so bad either, once you get used to it. I'll have to admit that I enjoy all the attention. And he gives me everything I want. He's a very generous man, and seems to have plenty of money."

Yes, Belinda thought, wondering where, or how, he got it.

She kissed Annabelle's cheek. "I wish you the best, Annabelle, and I do hope you'll be happy. But keep in touch with me, please. Come to see me, and I'll come to see you. I'll meet you for luncheon, things like that. All right?"

Annabelle nodded, her face radiant now. "Oh, Belinda, I wouldn't have sneaked away like that if I'd known you were going to be this understanding. And don't worry, I'll be happy here. You know how I love to sing? Well, Chet has arranged for me to sing here, downstairs in the bar-room. He's having a wonderful costume made for me."

Belinda swallowed. Annabelle, the society belle, singing in a saloon? What if their friends back home learned of this?

Her face must have shown something of what she was thinking, because Annabelle patted her arm comfortingly, if somewhat condescendingly. "Oh, I know, it sounds shocking, doesn't it? But Chet has assured me that I will be treated with respect. He says that real ladies are scarce up here, and the men will pay to see and hear me. I feel so, so, *naughty!*" She giggled. "And you needn't worry about the family name. I wouldn't do that to you, Bee. I'm going to use another name, we're making one up now. So, no one in Dawson will know that your big sister is singing in a saloon." She giggled again. "Now, don't frown so, Bee. It *is* exciting, and I've decided that it's what I want, under the circumstances."

"Well, that's the important thing." Belinda forced herself to smile and kiss her sister's cheek. "I guess I'll be going now."

"Yes, you must. I have to get dressed and go downstairs so that I can practice my numbers with the piano player. But I'll see you soon, Bee."

Belinda got up from the bed. "Yes, Annabelle. Soon."

She kept the false smile on her face until the door was between her and Annabelle. Then her shoulders slumped, and her eyes grew moist with unshed tears.

"Belinda?"

At the sight of Douglas's concerned face, Belinda fell into his arms, and let the tears come.

≈10≈

When Two-Step Sam returned the next morning, Josh was busy down by the stream, building a rocker. He didn't even hear the old man approaching—he was as quiet on his big feet as an Indian—and the first he knew of his presence was the sound of Two-Step clearing his throat.

"Well, younker, here I am, kit and caboodle, ya might say."

Josh turned, startled, to see Two-Step standing not three feet from him, holding a large, bearskin-wrapped bundle. At his feet crouched the strangest-looking animal that Josh had ever seen.

It was a cat, he surmised, but like no cat he had ever laid eyes on. Extremely large, with short, dark-brown fur and yellow-green eyes, it stared back at Josh unwinkingly.

A long scar traversed its face, giving it a raffish look, but the most bizarre thing was its ears—or lack of ears, because the cat had none. Oh, the holes were there, looking strange and pale atop the animal's head, but the upright portion was gone. Only two pale lines marked the place from which they had been growing.

"What in the hell is *that?*"

"What?" Two-Step looked around innocently, then he cackled laughter, and slapped his leg. "That there is No-Ears Riley, my friend and bosom companion. Riley, this here is Josh Rogan, and you'd better get to know him, 'cause he's the man who'll be furnishin' your victuals from now on."

"Uh, his ears? What happened to his ears, Two-Step?"

"Funny ya should ask that." Two-Step shook his head mournfully. "Durned shame, ain't it? They froze off, is what happened. A cat's ears don't have much hair, you see, and when it gets real cold, oh, around forty or so below, well, all a cat has to do is step out the door, and wham, they freeze right up. Then ya can knock 'em off with the tip of your finger." He flicked his middle finger with his thumb. "It's a shame, too. They lose a lot of their hearing, with nothin' up there to catch the sound. But Riley's okay, for all that. He'll keep the rats and other varmints outta the stores, and he forages for hisself most of the time. Ya two will get along."

Josh shook his head, and the cat glared at him balefully. "I'm sure we will. Well, put your stuff in the tent, and you can help me with this rocker. I'm sure you know more about building one than I do."

"Reckon that's so. Come on, Riley, we can start earnin' our keep."

It didn't take long for Two-Step Sam and No-Ears Riley to settle in. Two-Step threw his bundle in one corner of the tent, and Riley, stepping fastidiously and waving his tail, thoroughly examined everything on the premises before settling himself comfortably on Josh's cot to take a lengthy, noisy wash.

Satisfied that the camp was in good hands, Josh set out to do the job he had come to do.

In the time that he had been up here, Josh had learned that everything the gray man back in Washington had told him was true—Alaska, and the Yukon Territory, was in the grip of a crime wave. Many of the crimes were perpetrated by individuals, yet a large number of the outrages against the gold seekers were committed by the minions of two men-Soapy Smith in Skagway, and one Lester Pugh, of Dyea and Dawson City. Josh had learned that Soapy Smith had recently been killed, which would likely result in his organization being disbanded.

But that left Lester Pugh.

Pugh had originally come to the attention of the authorities in the Puget Sound area in Washington state. He had operated a saloon and other enterprises. His criminal operations came to light when a young undercover agent had been found dead in an alley behind Pugh's saloon. When the agent's death was investigated, a number of other unsavory activities were uncovered, and they all involved Pugh. He had been engaged in white slavery, opium smuggling, the selling of denatured whiskey that had caused countless illnesses and a number of deaths, crooked gambling, robbery, and murder.

However, all of this had been difficult to prove, and while the officer in charge of the case was attempting to amass enough evidence to bring Pugh to justice, Pugh had sold his holdings in Washington and vanished.

Eventually he had showed up in Dyea, where he had set himself up in business again, and that was where Josh had come into it. Josh had found Dyea to be a transient town, used mostly as a stopover point for those heading for the gold fields. At first he had been puzzled at Pugh's picking it as a base for his operations. After a brief investigation, he had concluded that Dyea was evidently only a stopping point for Pugh as well. The information he had gathered disclosed that Pugh already owned several businesses in Dawson, and had been making overtures to purchase more.

It had seemed clear to Josh that Lester Pugh intended soon to move on to Dawson, where the pickings were easier and richer. Of course, Dawson was in Canadian territory and under the jurisdiction of the Northwest Mounted Police, so Pugh would have to watch his step there. And that meant it would be more difficult to obtain evidence against him, so Josh had decided to get to Dawson before

Pugh. In that way, he could investigate Pugh's operations while the fat man was still in Dyea, and also, hopefully, talk to some of the victims of Pugh's shenanigans in Dyea—for no one stayed long in Dyea except those who ran the businesses there. They all went on to the gold fields as quickly as possible.

So, after giving Pugh's operation in Dyea a cursory investigation, Josh had set off for Dawson. Just another stampeder. Hopefully, he would be settled in Dawson with a good cover by the time Pugh arrived. That hope was dashed only days after his arrival, when he learned that Lester Pugh was now in Dawson. Josh still planned to uncover some of Pugh's victims; he would just have to be more circumspect about it.

Now, leaving the camp, he looked at his pocket watch. It was too early to go into Dawson yet. Although it was possible always to find someone in the saloons, no matter how early it was, Josh preferred the protective cover of a crowd so he decided to hit the Golden Poke sometime after noon.

In the meantime, he might as well take a look at the different mining operations that were going on along the streams. Claim watching was a popular pastime, and it was not an unusual sight to see several observers standing around watching while the owner of a particular claim went about his work. If you couldn't make it yourself, the next best thing was to be present when someone else made a rich strike.

In this way, Josh hoped he could become acquainted with some of the other men, and sound them out about what went on in Dawson. A lot of very useful information was bandied about in the guise of small talk, and Josh was an expert at eliciting this information, putting the bits and pieces together to build a solid case against evildoers. It had worked for him before; no reason why it shouldn't this time.

A stabbing pain in the back of his neck caused him to slap at the offending area with some force. Damn those pesky mosquitoes! Tiny they might be, but they had stingers as big as knitting needles!

Another one bore into his throat, and he quickly-buttoned his shirt to the neck, despite the heat. What a contrary country! Beautiful as anything a man could ever wish to see, but frozen stiff as a cod in winter; and in the summer plagued so badly by mosquitoes and no-see-'ums that it seemed winter would never return.

Ahead of him, Josh could see a log-and-sod cabin, set well back in a small box canyon. Sounds of activity came from that direction, and he headed toward the sounds.

A small but deep stream ran near the cabin, and by the water's edge two men, one large and bulky, the other small and slim, struggled to put together a sluice box.

As Josh approached, making as much noise as he could—it was not prudent to come upon a man quietly in the Yukon—the larger man straightened up, and pushed his hat to the back of his head.

"Hello," said Josh. "Just passing by and saw your place, and thought I'd look in. If you don't mind, that is."

The big man grinned amiably. He was clean-shaven, with wide, square-cut cheeks, and bland-looking, pale eyes. A red button of a nose, and a wide mouth, gave his face a boyish cast, despite the fact that he must be pushing fifty.

"Howdy. You're more than welcome. Maybe I can get you to help us with this damn-fool thing. Can't seem to get it set right. I'm Carl Henly. This is my wife, Edna. Least-ways, that's the squaw name I gave her. Can't speak her Indian name."

The smaller figure stood up, and Josh had his first good look at what he had assumed was a young boy. A roundish, merry brown face, set with two black eyes, looked up at him, and the young woman smiled. In some embarrass-ment, Josh introduced himself and turned to help Henly with the stubborn sluice box. Within a few minutes, they had it set in place, and the braces pounded in.

Henly stood back and stared at it. "Well, there she is, ready to go. Thanks, Rogan. What say we have a sip of something cooling, in honor of the occasion?"

Josh had to smile. The older man's enthusiasm was con-tagious. "That sounds good to me."

At his words, Edna skipped ahead of them toward the small cabin. Henly shook his head in wonder, as he watched her. "Pretty little thing, ain't she? Some of these Indian gals are, you know. And she's smart, too. Bright as a new penny. I'll never understand how come she agreed to hitch up with a stuffy old buzzard like me."

Josh grinned. "Well, whatever you are, it's sure not stuffy. I saw that right off."

Henly's eyes twinkled. "Is that a fact now? And here I always thought I was a real serious type. Just goes to show how little a man knows about his own self."

As the two men seated themselves at the rough wooden table in the cabin, Edna put two corked, brown bottles, beaded with moisture, in front of them.

"Homemade beer," Henly said, popping the cork off his bottle. "Made it my own self, and keep it cooling in the creek. Tastes pretty damn good on a hot day like this."

He tilted the bottle up and took a large swallow, and Josh followed suit. The beer was bitter, but cool and tingly on the tongue, and he drank it gratefully.

"How long have you been up here?" he asked Henly.

The big man plunked the bottle down and pursed his lips. "Let's see. Been a little over a year now."

"Are you doing any good?"

Henly shrugged. "Making a living. Finding a little color. Things should be better this winter, now that I've got me a cabin and a wife." He grinned at the Indian woman, who giggled and ducked her head. "You know, the winters here are almighty long and cold, and the ever-lasting darkness can scramble a man's brains. A man needs company and some recreation. And Edna's a lot of help on the claim. She's strong, for all her size, and she ain't afraid of work. Yep, we'll try it for one more year, then if the mine don't come through better than it has, I reckon I'll pull stakes and head back home."

Josh couldn't help but wonder if Henly would be taking his Indian bride with him, but did not think it would be diplomatic to voice the question. Instead he said, "If your claim's no good, why don't you stake another?"

Henly shrugged again. "Hell, you *are* a tenderfoot, ain't you? I'm lucky to have this one. All the good claims are already staked. If you make a bad choice the first time around, it's plain tough luck. Why, hundreds of men are going home every day, and hundreds more, just coming in, are turning right around and heading back home. You know, the gold fields here ain't that big. They cover, oh, maybe twenty or thirty square miles is all, and right now, man and boy, there's about twenty thousand people milling around down there in Dawson, trying to find a piece of action for themselves. Now, what about you, Rogan? How are you doing for yourself?" Henly took another gulp of the beer.

Josh leaned back. "Well, as you pointed out, I am a newcomer. But I did manage to find a claim."

Henly reared back, blinking. "You did? Where?"

"Out near Bear-Toe Creek."

Henly put his beer bottle down. "Hell, there's nothing along there. As far as I know, nobody's ever turned up any color in that area. I hate to tell you this, but I'm afraid you're wasting your time."

Josh grinned. "So I've been told, several times. But you see, I have this feeling about the place. I think something will turn up."

Henly shook his head. "Well, I wish you luck, friend, because you're sure as hell going to be needing it."

Josh accepted another bottle of the beer from Edna, who also offered him a stick of jerky. He took it.

"Tell me, Carl, since you've been around here awhile . . . what's Dawson like? I mean, do the Mounties manage to keep it pretty clean, or is a green horn like me in danger of losing his poke there?"

Henly slapped down his bottle and rocked back, roaring with laughter. "By hell, friend, you do have a gift for innocence!" When his laughter had subsided and he had wiped his eyes on his shirt tail, he leaned toward Josh, putting his elbows on the table. "But to answer your question . . . yep, the Mounties keep it pretty clean, on the surface. But there's only so much they can do in a frontier town, with thousands of people coming and going at all times of the day and night. There're several decent saloons, but I'd advise you to stay away from one in particular."

"Which one is that?"

"The Golden Poke. Lately, it's been getting a bad reputation."

"In what way?"

Henly looked at him curiously. "Hell, friend, in every way. The Poke used to be a pretty good place, but since a new man bought it, there have been some funny stories going around the camps. Montana Leeds, the manager, is pretty straight, I hear, but some of the other characters working there ain't."

Josh, knowing that the Poke was the saloon owned by Pugh, persisted. "What kind of stories?"

Henly shrugged. "All the saloons have card sharks, quick-change artists, plain thieves, and painted women who'll relieve you of your gold dust, if you give 'em a chance; but some people think it's getting plumb dangerous to frequent the Poke. I've even heard stories that the scales there are rigged in favor of the house. Guess you already know that few up here have cash money, but pay for everything with dust or nuggets."

"You said dangerous. In what way?"

"Well, not long ago a prospector was knifed to death in there. Just a lad, too."

"Was his killer arrested?"

"Hell, no. A bunch of people swore that the kid had a knife on him, and had threatened the blackjack dealer with it. But I've heard a lot of other people are saying that the lad had no knife a-tall, and that the dealer provoked the fight."

"Then why didn't those people come forward and testify to that?"

Henly raised his eyebrows. "Who knows? Some of them don't want to be away from their claims, maybe. Others were already on their way back to the States. The rest . . . well, my hunch is they were well paid to keep their mouths shut. Anyway, the case was dropped. But it's not forgotten, I can tell you, not by the few up here with any brains. At any rate, stay away from the Poke, that's my advice to you.

"And look out for the girls in the cribs. A bunch of new ones just came in, and I hear that most of them have the pox. If you're lonely for female companionship, try the girls at Gertie's Parlor, or Madam X's Place. That's where I used to go before I got hitched. The madams there see that you get your money's worth, and they run a clean house. O'course, you could do like me, get yourself a pretty little squaw to keep house for you." He beckoned with a bear-paw hand, and Edna, giggling, ran into the crook of his arm. They seemed like a devoted and happy couple, despite Henly's rather patronizing air of possession, and Josh hoped that when the big miner left he would take his Indian wife with him.

"Anything else I should look out for in town?" he asked.

"Yep." The big man gave his wife a squeeze. "The merchants will all ask for an arm and a leg for anything you buy, so you'd best be prepared for that. And there's a bunch of fake stampeders walking the trails, working all kinds of shell games and trickeries."

"*Fake* stampeders?" Josh was puzzled.

"Yep. Packs on their backs and everything, but the packs are usually full of nothing but feathers, and their business is fleecing the foolish and the greenhorns." He shook his head dolefully. "Never had nothing like this before. The place is getting too damned many people. Yep, if I don't strike it big before winter of next year, I'm getting out. This territory is getting more crowded than downtown New York, and without any of the comforts."

Josh finished the last of his beer and placed the empty bottle on the table. "Thanks for the beer, Carl. Look in on me if you find yourself with a bit of free time."

Henly pushed back from the table, and reached over to shake Josh's hand. "Don't be expecting to have much of that, but if I'm over your way, I'll sure drop in. Now remember what I said about town. Stay away from the Poke."

Josh nodded. "I'll remember. Thanks for the beer, Carl."

If Carl Henly had been in Dawson later that afternoon, he would have snorted in disgust, for Josh was about to enter the Golden Poke.

As he started to shoulder through the wooden swinging doors, he was almost bowled over by a large man in red galluses, who was being propelled outward with considerable force.

Josh stepped quickly aside, and the man stumbled past, sprawling on his face in the dust of the street, cursing viciously all the while.

Grinning, Josh again tried the doors, and this time managed to enter without trouble. He saw a tall, wide-shoul-

163

dered man in a white bartender's apron just turning away, dusting his hands together—no doubt the force behind the violent eviction of Red-Galluses.

The large room with its long mahogany bar was noisy beyond belief. Men laughed, shouted and cursed. Glassware clinked, chips rattled, women shrieked, and over it all, the sounds of a piano, playing one of the new ragtime tunes, struggled to be heard.

Josh, after a brief look around, began to try to push his way up to the bar. It took some time, but finally he made a place for himself, and ordered a shot of whiskey.

When he received the drink, he turned, back to the bar, to face the room. Lord, what a lot of people! It occurred to him that Pugh could make enough money in legal ways from a crowd like this, without having to resort to crime. However, he had learned during his career as a law enforcement officer that to many men crime was a way of life. He supposed that Lester Pugh was such a man.

He sipped the whiskey gingerly, not wanting to fuzz his mind. His location, near the end of the bar, kept him somewhat out of the way of the largest part of the crowd, and it was a good spot from which to observe. He looked around carefully, trying to spot Pugh, or his second-in-command, Harter, but so far as he could see they were nowhere around.

At the moment, nothing unusual seemed to be going on—at least nothing that didn't go on in any saloon—but with this mob of people who could tell.

And then, just as Josh was finishing his drink, the big bartender who had tossed out the customer wearing red suspenders stepped up on the lip of the wooden stage at the far end of the room. He waved his arms and shouted for silence, and after only a few moments, the crowd quieted enough so that Josh could hear what the bartender was saying.

"And so, it is with great pleasure that the Poke presents a new entertainer. A lady of rare quality and charm, whose beauty alone is worth a man's gold, but who also has a voice to match her lovely face. Direct from New York State, Miss Alabaster White!"

Before the crowd could grow noisy again, the curtains of the stage parted, the pianist struck up the opening chords of a ballad, and a young woman walked delicately on stage. She was tall, slender, and dark-haired, with a lovely bosom—the curves of which were exposed by the deep-blue satin gown she wore. The dress was trimmed with black and she held a huge, black, feathered fan, sparkling with rhinestones, in her right hand.

Before she even began to sing, the men nearest the stage started to applaud wildly. The girl was really a beauty, and it was unusual, Josh knew, to see anyone so young and fresh on the stage in a place like Dawson.

She bowed gracefully in acknowledgment of the applause, which grew even louder as her curtsy exposed more of her beautiful cleavage, then she stood erect and began to sing.

Not immediately, but slowly, little by little, the saloon quieted as her clear, sweet voice filled the room. Her voice was of exceptional clarity and sweetness, and the song was one Josh was familiar with, "I'll Marry the Man I Love," a song calculated to melt the hardest heart—particularly when sung by a beautiful young girl.

She finished the first verse before Josh recognized her as Annabelle Lee, Belinda's sister.

This discovery had a devastating effect on Josh, setting up a conflict of emotions that he was ill-prepared for. At first he told himself that he must be in error. He had only met Annabelle briefly, but she had seemed to him a young woman who held a very high opinion of herself—far too high, he had thought at the time—and certainly not the sort to be found singing in a place like this.

But as she began the second verse, he knew that he was *not* mistaken. It was Annabelle, and the only reasons he could think of for her being in the Golden Poke were all bad.

Had they lost all their money? Had something bad happened to Belinda, leaving Annabelle all alone and forced to take a job like this?

Josh found his throat was dry, and he motioned for another whiskey, which the bartender set before him. Josh drank it down quickly, hoping it would ease the dismay he felt rising in him. He had tried, without much success, to put Belinda Lee and what had happened between them out of his mind—at least until his job here was done. But now it was impossible not to think about her, and to worry. He had to find out if she was all right, at least that. If she was, then his mind would be at ease . . . well, more or less.

Alabaster, or Annabelle, had finished her song now, to a great thunder of applause. Her cheeks were pink with pleasure, and she looked a rare beauty all right—better than these men had seen in months. They were stomping and calling out her name. She waved to them and motioned with her fan at the piano player to begin another tune.

Josh attempted to get his thoughts in order. He'd try to see her after the performance. She certainly should remember him, since he had rescued her sister, not once but twice.

The man next to Josh was watching the stage avidly, a yearning expression on his face. Josh shook his head. She's got them in the palm of her hand, he thought. But as far as he was concerned she wasn't the beauty that Belinda was. Belinda had more than surface prettiness; she had real, bone-deep beauty, and at the thought that something might have happened to her, Josh felt such a sweep of sorrow that he had to clench his teeth to keep from groaning aloud.

≈11≈

Annabelle sang three songs in all, each more wildly received than the last, and at the finish of her last number, she left the stage to a shower of coins, and even a few nuggets.

As the curtains swished shut, she squealed and stooped to gather up the largest nuggets. When Chet Harter met her in the wings, she held them out to him, smiling in delight.

"Look!" she cried. "They really liked me!"

Harter smiled down at her, his expression smug. "Told you they would, didn't I?"

Annabelle—she still couldn't get used to thinking of herself as Alabaster, although she adored the name—pulled a face, and tapped him with her folded fan. "I know you did, Chet. But how could I be sure? I've never sung before an audience before."

"Next time, maybe you'll believe me when I tell you something." He pulled her close and kissed her full on the lips, while with his free hand he caressed her half-bared breasts.

Annabelle was willing enough. She was finding, as the days went by, that going to bed with Chet was enjoyable. Sensuous by nature, she enjoyed the stroking and closeness that accompanied the act, and she rather liked the feeling of yielding to a man's violent passions. There was something very flattering in being desired. One thing about Chet did trouble her a little. Sometimes, especially when he'd had too much to drink, he became rough, hurtful, almost brutal.

The men in the saloon were still clapping, stamping their feet, and calling out her name. Annabelle pulled back slightly from Harter's arms. She cocked her head. "Chet, should I sing another? They want me back out there."

Harter's breath was coming faster. Annabelle knew the signs well by now, and she smiled to herself. Yes, it was nice to know that you were capable of arousing a man's passion.

Harter's mouth was close to her ear. "Nah," he said huskily. "You've got to learn to always leave them wanting more. Come on. Let's you and me go upstairs."

She pulled away and smiled up at him demurely. "But you just said that I should leave them wanting more, and we've already . . ."

He grinned back at her, and began to lead her toward the stairway. "That only applies to them, baby, to other people, not me. You just keep me happy, and I'll treat you right."

"Yes, Chet." She followed him, smiling. She was smiling not so much in anticipation of what was to come, as in memory of the ovation she had just received.

"Tonight, you can give 'em another show," Harter said, as they mounted the stairs. "Word will have spread, and we should have a packed house. You're going to be good for business, honey, damned if you ain't. In a few days, your name'll be all over Dawson. Alabaster White. Canary of the Yukon!"

Montana Leeds was behind the bar, spelling one of the regular bartenders, and he watched as Chet Harter and the pretty new girl called Alabaster White left the stage and headed toward the stairs. It was beyond him how a seemingly nice girl like that had ever gotten mixed up with a hardcase like Chet Harter.

Montana shook his head. It was really a shame. It was clear that the girl was not used to this kind of life—she was obviously meant for better things. What could have brought her to this place?

His thoughts strayed briefly to his own family, whom he had not seen in years. He had meant to go back, he always meant to go back. But something wonderful always seemed to be beckoning him over the next hill, down the next road; the years drifted by with frightening speed. And here he was, managing a saloon in a godforsaken town in the wilderness! There must be something wrong with men like him. Maybe it was a disease. Maybe at birth some kind of little creature flew by and took a bite out of certain men, infecting them with wanderlust. He grinned at his own fancy. Well, if that was so, he certainly had a bad case.

"Hey, Montana! You asleep back there? Willie here wants a drink, and he's buying one for me."

Montana looked around into the mismatched eyes of Slew-Eyed Sue, one of the saloon girls. She was a short, muscular woman of indeterminate age, with a frizzy mop of faded yellow hair and an aggressively turned-up nose.

He poured the drinks, whiskey for Willie and colored water for Sue, then pushed them across the bar and looked at her companion, who was a very drunk young miner.

Sue good-naturedly poked the young man in the ribs. He seemed about to fall asleep on his feet. "Hey, Willie, pay up! This ain't no free lunch counter, you know."

Willie grinned and fumbled in his pocket for the necessary money.

Montana watched with amusement as the oddly matched couple took the drinks and wandered away. Slew-Eyed Sue. Could you beat that name?

Montana, who fancied himself a man of letters, had been keeping a journal of his wanderings ever since he had set out. He was fascinated by the nicknames and appellations used in the mining towns he had been in, particularly the names of the dancehall girls. He would have been willing to wager a month's wages that the newest addition to the Poke was using an assumed name. *Alabaster* White? But at least it wasn't as farfetched as some others. Why, in the barroom right now he could see Gap-Tooth Gertie, Broken-Nose Kate, Siwash Sal, and Fat Peggy!

He had wondered more than once why the names were so often insulting, calling attention to the flaws and defects of the ladies in question. True, most of them had seen better days, and some of them showed unmistakable signs of wear and tear; still, it seemed to him a bit ungallant, to say the least. And what was even more unusual, it seemed to

Montana, was the fact that the women didn't seem to mind the names!

The men, too, had nicknames, but they were usually less derogatory, and consequently less colorful. There was, for instance, just to take the Smiths—Big Smith, Little Smith, Brainy Smith, and Muscles Smith. There were also a plethora of kids—the Siwash Kid; the Skinny Kid; Cheechako Kid; and confusingly, Old Kid.

The man directly across the bar plunked down money for another drink, and Montana filled his glass. The man was a stranger to Montana, but he was the kind of man who attracted notice—heavy-shouldered, with a sure-of-him-self manner that bespoke self-confidence. He had sharp, pale blue eyes that seemed to miss nothing, and he was studying the barroom thoroughly. Well, maybe he was just curious; a lot of newcomers were.

Montana shrugged away a nagging feeling of unease and began refilling glasses. Now that the entertainment was over, the tempo of the room was building, and it would be busy as hell on ice skates until the Poke closed.

The thought depressed him. It was not that he minded hard work, he was accustomed to that; but it was getting more and more difficult to maintain order in the Poke during the busiest hours. Also, there were undercurrents—things going on which he did not approve; too many accidents; too many brawls; too many men complaining that their pokes had been stolen, or that they had been cheated. The atmosphere of the place was changing, and certainly not for the better.

Montana had, in fact, been wondering if he should get out, take what money he had accumulated—precious little!—and leave, go back to the States. Maybe, at long last, go back to his wife and children. But then he would realize that he couldn't go back this way, a failure, with nothing to show for his twenty years of absence. No, he would have to stick it out here, keep stashing his money away, and hope that the Mounties didn't close the Poke, or that Pugh or Harter did not do something so heinous that he would be forced to leave out of good conscience. Damnit, he thought, I'm really caught between a rock and a hard place.

"Hey, Montana! What does a man have to do around here to get a drink?"

Montana sighed, and reached for the bottle, putting a smile on his face.

Josh left his fresh drink on the bar, and looked around the barroom again. In his agitation at recognizing Annabelle Lee, he had bolted the last drink, and it was now registering on his all-too-empty stomach. He felt a little lightheaded.

He couldn't stand here without a drink in his hand, or he would look suspicious. At the same time, he had to keep his wits about him if he was to operate efficiently. He should get something in his stomach, but he was pretty certain there was no chance of getting any food here. Also, he wanted to talk to Annabelle. Yet he had seen Chet Harter with her as she went up the stairs, and Josh knew that talking to her with Harter around would be difficult, if not impossible.

The room was getting even more crowded now as the afternoon waned, and voices and tempers seemed to be rising. At one table, a fist-fight broke out, but as far as Josh could tell the argument was between miners, and no employees of the Poke were involved.

He was just about to call it a day and go next door to the hotel restaurant for a meal, when he saw Harter jauntily descending the stairs. As soon as the man disappeared in the crowd, Josh walked quickly away from the bar, leaving his drink and heading for the stairs.

At the top of the stairway was a long hall, with several doors opening off it. The doors were closed, and all pretty much alike. Which room was Annabelle Lee in? If he asked downstairs, Josh knew they wouldn't tell him unless he could convince them he was a friend of the young lady, and that might be difficult, as well as dangerous, to do.

With a shrug, he started at the first door, knocking softly, and calling out, "Miss Lee? Miss Annabelle Lee?"

He had worked his way about halfway-down the hall before he received a response. Just as he was about to turn away from one door, he heard a voice from within, "Yes? Who is it?"

Josh put his face close to the door. "Miss Lee, it's Josh Rogan, the man who rescued your sister. We met at Crater Lake, do you remember?"

There was a moment's silence, then he heard footsteps, and the door opened cautiously. He could see a blue eye studying him carefully. Then the door swung open.

Annabelle Lee looked quite different than she had when he had last seen her. Dressed in a blue satin dressing gown, with her hair in ringlets and rouge on her face, she looked like a fancy, overdressed doll—beautiful, but a touch unreal.

"Come in," she said quickly, and shut the door behind

him as he did so. She seemed a little nervous, and Josh, attributing this to the fact that she might be expecting Harter back any moment, hurried into what he had to say.

"I suppose you're wondering why I'm here?"

Annabelle shrugged, and Josh realized that she was probably the kind of woman who was used to having men come to call for no other reason than her beauty. He struggled to think of a way to phrase his question in a diplomatic manner. "I saw you perform downstairs. I was . . . well, I was surprised to see you here. I mean, it didn't seem the kind of place . . ." He stumbled to a halt. Hell, he was making a botch of it! It seemed that he couldn't say the right thing to *either* of the Lee sisters.

Annabelle's cheeks grew pinker, and she looked a little cross. "There's nothing wrong with this *place,* Mr. Rogan," she said haughtily. "It's a respectable business establishment where men come to drink and . . . be entertained. Everyone has treated me with the utmost courtesy, and . . ."

"Yes, yes, I'm sure. I'm sorry if I sounded . . . but what I really came to ask is if everything is all right. With you and your sister, I mean. I thought that there might be some difficulty, some trouble, or that something had happened to Belinda."

Annabelle turned away with a flounce. "Everything is quite all right, Mr. Rogan, you may be sure. Bee and I are both in excellent health."

Josh let his breath go with a relieved sigh. He hadn't realized how concerned he had been. "She's all right then?"

Annabelle looked at him archly. "If you're speaking

174

about my sister, yes. Is that why you came up here, to ask about Bee?"

Josh, tired of trying to play polite games with her, nodded curtly. "Yes. I thought you might have taken work in the Poke because something had happened to her. I'm glad to know that's not the case."

"Humph!" Annabelle tossed her curls. Everything she did, Josh concluded, seemed to be exaggerated, with an eye for effect. "Well, you certainly disappeared fast enough after you left us at Crater Lake, I must say! We've been in Dawson for weeks and weeks, you know, and Bee never heard from you. You know," she looked thoughtful, "that *could* be the reason she's been so cross and disagreeable. And now, suddenly, you're all concerned. Men always claim they don't understand women, but *I* think it's the men who behave strangely. You simply can't count on them!"

"You may be right," he said, anxious now to be gone. "However, I am glad to hear that you are both all right, and that you're here not out of need, but . . ." He didn't know how to continue without offending her.

"When I see Bee, Mr. Rogan, I'll tell her you asked after her."

"No, no!" He backed toward the door. "I'd rather you didn't, if you don't mind."

Surprise made her face blank. "But whyever not?"

"I have a reason, a very good one, but I don't wish to go into it at this time. Will you do it as a favor to me? Because I saved your sister's life, if for nothing else?"

Annabelle frowned. "Well, since you put it like that." She smiled then, coyly. "Do come back when you have time to visit awhile." Now she looked directly into his eyes, and batted her long eyelashes.

"Of course," Josh said politely. "I should be delighted. Now, if you will excuse me, I have some business to attend to."

"Certainly, Mr. Rogan. But first you must tell me if you liked it."

Hand on the doorknob, he paused. "Liked it? I'm sorry . . ."

"Why, my singing, of course! You said you saw my performance."

He had to choke back a laugh. She was incredible. "Oh, yes! I liked it very much. You have a beautiful voice," he said truthfully, glad of something positive he could say to her.

She dimpled. "The men seemed to like it, didn't they? They applauded so."

"They liked it very much indeed," he assured her.

Determined to end this absurdity, he turned the doorknob, swung the door open, and found himself face to face with Chet Harter. Harter had an expectant smile on his face. At the sight of Josh, the smile was replaced by a look of murderous fury.

Josh's dislike of the man was instinctive and, at any other time, he would have welcomed a confrontation with him, but right now it was important that he not make himself too noticeable. It was too early. This was the worst kind of bad luck.

Stiff-legged, Harter pushed his way into the room, causing Josh to back away from him, something that galled him. At that moment he would have dearly liked to punch Harter right in his arrogant, pockmarked face!

Harter gave Annabelle an angry glance. "What the hell is this? I'm not gone ten minutes, and you've got another man up here!"

Annabelle, face pale, was fluttering her hands. She looked as if she couldn't make up her mind whether to be frightened or outraged. "How dare you, Chet!" she finally managed. "How dare you accuse me like that? Mr. Rogan is an old friend. He was only here to ask after Belinda."

Harter's fists were still clenched, but the expression in his eyes altered slightly. "Asking after your sister, huh? Now, why did he have to come up here to do that?"

Annabelle stamped her foot. "I told you! He's an old friend we haven't seen in months, and he saw me sing downstairs. It was perfectly natural for him to come up to say hello." Harter grunted. "Well, now that he's said it, he can get the hell out." He jerked his thumb toward the door.

Josh held his temper in check. He turned to Annabelle, and bowed. "Goodbye, Miss Lee. I'm sorry if I upset your friend. Thank you for telling me about your sister. Where could I find her?"

"In the tent town. She has a portrait studio there."

Josh forced a smile. "Thank you again, and sir, whoever you are, I'm sorry if I caused you any worry."

Harter did not answer, as Josh turned and went out the door. When Josh was in the hall, the door slammed loudly behind him, and he felt his fists clench involuntarily. If he could only have said what he wanted to say, do what he wanted to do! That was one of the unpleasant aspects about his job. Yes, it was bad luck that Harter had seen him. Now it would be impossible to be just another face in the crowd, and it would make his task more difficult. If only he hadn't gone up to see her!

It only went to prove that women and police work were incompatible.

≈12≈

Turning away from slamming the door after Rogan, Harter scowled at Annabelle. "You say this Rogan is an old friend. Just where did you meet him?"

Annabelle, alerted by his scowl, for once decided to tell the truth, or something like it. "Why, weeks ago. In Dyea. He saved Bee's life twice. Once, when they had that avalanche on the pass, and again on Crater Lake, when she got lost in a snowstorm. We owe a lot to Mr. Rogan, and I think you were perfectly horrid to treat him so rudely!"

Harter appeared to be only half-listening, and Annabelle felt piqued. Why did he ask a question if he didn't bother to listen to the answer?

"So that's what happened!" he said softly, which made no sense at all to Annabelle.

Then, suddenly, Harter smiled and gave her a pat on the rear. "Sorry, dollie. But I might as well let you in on a little secret . . . I'm the jealous type, and I don't want anybody fooling around with my woman. If he's just your friend, that's a whole different thing."

His smile widened, but it didn't look all that sincere, and Annabelle turned away with a petulant flounce. Men! Sometimes there was simply no understanding them.

When he heard the knock on his door, Pugh automatically said, "Come in," but he wasn't even conscious of doing so. His thoughts were elsewhere.

A newspaper lay open on his desk. Soapy Smith had been killed—shot down in a Skagway street by his old friend, Frank Reed—and Soapy's empire was in ruins, as his band of followers ran for cover. It had happened over a week ago, and nobody had bothered to inform him!

Pugh couldn't remember when he had been so depressed by anything. He could feel the moisture in his eyes. It had happened again. Everyone he had ever cared for was eventually taken from him—his parents, his brother, and now his friend, Soapy. Why was he singled out for this loneliness, this pain? Were the gods jealous of him?

"Uh, L.P.? Didn't you hear me? I said I want to talk to you. It's important!"

Harter's presence finally registered, and Pugh pulled himself back from despondency. He said dully, "Oh, Chet. To be sure. I was deep in thought. Have you heard the news from Skagway?"

He thrust the newspaper at Harter, who read it cursorily. "I'll be damned! How'd a thing like that come to happen?"

"Bad luck and bad planning," said Pugh, sighing deeply. "You knew we were close friends, Soapy and I?"

"Yeah, I knew." Harter returned the newspaper. "Tough luck, L.P."

"Yes, and a lesson which we must take to heart. It could happen to us, Chet. The same forces are at work against us. We must proceed with great caution, and we must not get careless."

Harter shifted his weight on his feet, anxious to tell Pugh

his own news. He had never understood the friendship, or what Pugh claimed was friendship, between Pugh and Soapy Smith. Personally, he thought Smith was a small-time operator, who cared more for the game of power than he did for money—in Harter's estimation a grave mistake. Also, he did not quite know what to make of Pugh in his present mood. Unpredictable at best, Pugh, when actively unhappy, could be a dangerous man.

"Uh, you're right about that, L.P. And that brings me to what I wanted to tell you. I just saw Rogan, the federal marshal."

Pugh tensed. "Where?"

"Right here. In the Poke. He was upstairs visiting Annabelle."

Pugh's little eyes hardened. "Oh? And why, may I ask?"

"She says Rogan was looking for her sister. She says they are old friends, on account of he saved her sister's life out on Crater Lake."

Pugh slammed his hand down on the desk. "Didn't I warn you, Chet, what would happen if having that woman here caused trouble?" His voice cut like a knife.

"Who could guess he'd come here?" Harter said hastily. "But no harm done, L.P. His coming here had nothing to do with us."

"How sure are you of that?"

"As sure as I can be," Harter said, with far more confidence than he felt.

Pugh studied him for a moment out of narrowed eyes. Finally, he sighed. "Well, that decides it. The time has come for taking care of that federal snoop for good, before he gets a chance to finish his snooping. He keeps on, I may end up like poor Soapy. You understand me, Chet?"

"I understand, L.P. And it'll be a pleasure to carry out that order." Harter grinned wolfishly.

Pugh eyed him thoughtfully. "Just don't let your enjoyment get in the way of doing an efficient job this time. You've come a cropper once, don't forget. It would be best to make it look like an accident. If that's not possible, then make it look like robbery, or a crime of passion. The most important thing, of course, is that his, mmm, disappearance, not be associated with us in any manner whatsoever. Is that clear?"

"Clear, L.P. I know how to do my job. You don't have to keep telling me, like I'm some greenhorn kid!"

"I'm sure I don't," Pugh said soothingly, "but after what happened to Soapy, we can't be too careful. Let me know when it's taken care of."

Pugh turned away, back to his newspaper on the desk, and Harter left the room, closing the door behind him.

Pugh sadly picked up Soapy Smith's picture, and turned it face down on the desk. "Poor old Soapy." He sighed gustily. "You were just like a brother to me."

That, of course, made him think of his brother, Wendell, and he brooded on the fact that the powers-that-be seemed to go out of their way to destroy anyone close to him.

It was a beautiful day, clear and cloudless, and Belinda was in better spirits than she had been in some time.

She had taken what she hoped were some excellent shots of miners working their claims, and she was anxious to get them developed so that she could see them. Now, she and Charlie were heading back to the tent studio. Belinda, feeling the good tiredness that comes from satisfying work, and Charlie, apparently not in the least weary. Walking several miles carrying a camera case and tripod was hardly even exercise for him, she thought.

She breathed deeply the clear, warm air. Yes, she was feeling great. Her natural good health, combined with the fact that she was doing work she loved, made it difficult to feel otherwise; and yet, just under the surface, lurked the thought of Annabelle, which occasionally pained, as if it were a secret bruise on her mind.

Not that Annabelle was not well. On the contrary, Belinda had had lunch with her just a few days before, and she was blooming like the proverbial rose. No, Annabelle seemed perfectly content, even though her new name, Alabaster White, was being bandied about Dawson. Thank God, Belinda thought, Annabelle had agreed to change her name. Her sister seemed to find nothing wrong with singing in that awful place, but instead seemed to have convinced herself that it was a respectable showcase for her talents.

However, the thing that Belinda found it hardest to understand was her sister's quick change of mood. Only a few weeks ago, she had been apathetic and depressed and, Belinda had thought, scarred for life by her experience with Chet Harter. Now she appeared to have adjusted completely to her new way of life, and Belinda found her attitude incomprehensible. She could not hate her sister, but she could hate Chet Harter for what he had done to her.

She shook her head, making a clucking sound, and Charlie glanced at her questioningly. "It's all right, Charlie," she said. "I was just thinking to myself."

Charlie grinned knowingly. He was growing accustomed to Belinda's frequent moods of introspection, and her strange ways.

Belinda's thoughts went back again to Annabelle. One evening she had stood outside the Poke while Annabelle was performing, and took a quick peek through the batwing doors. What she had seen had appalled her. Oh, Annabelle had been accepted by the audience well enough, but what a motley crowd they were: drunken, raucous, profane, belligerent—Belinda had seen two men thrown out while she was watching—and there was her sister up on that tacky stage, singing as sweetly as if she was in Carnegie Hall, and taking bows afterward, as if she was Adelina Patti.

Belinda supposed she should be pleased that Annabelle was content; and yet it seemed wrong somehow.

Since she tried always to be absolutely honest with herself, Belinda tried to figure out the basis for her unease, and finally came to the conclusion that deep down she thought that Annabelle had demeaned herself in going to Chet Harter, and also that somehow, strangely, it would be more appropriate if Annabelle were to suffer for her mistake, not profit by it.

Belinda shook her head again and laughed. That was ridiculous, of course. She had, in a way, done the same thing as Annabelle—she had let a man take her. Was Annabelle more to blame, just because she, Belinda, did not approve of Chet Harter?

Still, deep down inside, Belinda knew that she felt contempt for the life that Annabelle was leading. Since this feeling was not fair to Annabelle, she would have to try to root it out.

They were in sight of the tents now, and Belinda could see someone standing in front. She shielded her eyes with her hand, and saw the scarlet jacket. Douglas Mackenzie! Suddenly, she wondered if her hair was a mess, or if she had dirt on her face.

Charlie turned toward her, beaming. "Sergeant waiting. Good. Have nice visit. Have tea."

Charlie had taken an inordinate fancy to the custom of having tea, and seized on every opportunity to do so. From somewhere, he had obtained a huge China pot, painted with poppies, and a mismatched collection of cups and saucers. The tea was always served hot and strong, with plenty of sugar and tinned milk, and was accompanied by a huge plate of cookies, biscuits, and jam, most of which found its way into Charlie's stomach.

Charlie was also very fond of Douglas Mackenzie, and to have the sergeant come to visit and serve him tea would really cap off Charlie's afternoon, Belinda knew.

Douglas doffed his hat as they approached, and the strong sunlight did him no disservice. He was a handsome man.

At the thought, Belinda could feel herself tighten. She tried not to think of Josh Rogan, but the thought of him, like that of Annabelle, was always just below the surface of her mind. Whenever she saw an attractive man, like now seeing Douglas, she always thought of Josh, then quickly pushed him out of her mind, for she could not think of him without bitterness.

"Hello, Douglas," she said brightly. "We've been out working."

"So I see." He smiled, holding out his hand to take the small valise she was carrying. "Did you get some good pictures?"

She nodded. "I think so. The light was wonderful. I'm anxious to see them myself."

He followed her and Charlie into the tent, and put down the valise. "There was a letter for you at the post office. I took the liberty of bringing it with me."

He reached inside his coat and took out a long, yellowish envelope. Belinda took it with excitement—and some trepidation. Mail delivery up here was slow and undependable, and she had received very few letters. Who could this be from? She turned it over and the name, *Leslie's Weekly,* leaped out at her. She made a small sound and ripped open the envelope. The two men watched as she read it, then looked up at them with eyes shining with delight.

"Douglas, Charlie, it's from *Leslie's!* They say that because of the great interest in the Yukon and the gold rush, they have changed their minds. They want to order pictures *and* text, if I can provide it on the route, the stampeders, and the diggings. Pictures of *anything* here that might be of interest to their readers. And they'll pay well!" She whirled on Charlie. "Charlie, we must have a wonderful tea to celebrate!"

Charlie beamed. "You betcha. I go to bakery, get fine cake. You say?"

I say yes!" Belinda said happily. "Oh! You'll stay, won't you, Douglas?"

He stood looking at her, bemusedly. "Yes," he said, "but only if you'll promise to look that happy all the time."

Belinda was taken aback for a moment. Then she

laughed, a rich sound of pure delight. I promise, Douglas."
She couldn't remember when she had been so happy. "You
will stay, won't you?"

"I should be delighted," he said.

The tea was a great success. Charlie had outdone himself,
and Belinda wondered what they were going to do with all
the leftover cake.

The bakery shop had just *happened* to have an enormous
chocolate confection, made especially for someone's
birthday, and the cake proclaimed in bright yellow on
chocolate frosting: "Happy Birthday, Moose, You Old
Sumphole!"

For some reason or other, the cake had not been picked
up, and the baker, anxious to get rid of it before it became
stale, had let Charlie have it at a bargain price.

Oh well, Belinda thought, at least it will keep Charlie's
sweet tooth satisfied for a few days.

She lay back in her chair, feeling replete and contented. Douglas was looking at her with a look that she
recognized. Well, why shouldn't he? She was a woman,
attractive enough, she liked to think, and he was a man.
It was a natural enough phenomenon. For a moment she
warmed to his glance, feeling desirable and, yes, a little
aroused. Charlie was out for a moment, fetching hot
water for more tea.

Douglas leaned toward her, about to speak, when a voice
called from outside, "Hello! Anybody here?"

Belinda's heart gave a leap of gladness. It was Josh
Rogan!

Overwhelmed by the stunning onrush of feeling, Belinda

literally could not answer. She didn't want to see him. She wanted to see him desperately. She could feel her body grow fever-hot, and then turn cold, and she became aware that Douglas was staring at her curiously.

She opened her mouth, but no words came out.

It was Charlie who released her from this shattering paralysis. Coming from around the curtain in the back, he trotted to the tent flap and pushed it aside. Belinda heard his voice, as if from a great distance. "Ah, Mr. Rogan! Good to see." And then she heard Josh's voice, again arousing emotions that she desperately wished to suppress. "Is Miss Belinda in? May I talk with her?"

Tell him no! No! For a moment she feared she had shouted the words aloud.

"Sure, Miss Belinda in. Has company. But we have plenty tea and cake. Come in. She glad to see you, I betcha."

Then Josh's wide-shouldered form was pushing into the tent and he was standing by the table, looking down on her and Douglas, with a guarded expression in his strange eyes. He nodded formally. "Miss Lee. It's nice to see you. I didn't realize you had company . . ."

She looked quickly across at Douglas, who wore the same guarded expression as did Josh. The two men studied one another warily, like ancient enemies. Yet, they had just met.

She said quickly, "Sergeant Mackenzie, this is Joshua Rogan, an . . . an old friend."

The two men nodded to each other, but neither offered to shake hands. Now a silence fell, an interminable silence, which Belinda finally felt compelled to break. "Won't you sit down, Mr. Rogan?" she said stiffly, "and have a cup of tea?"

Josh hesitated, then shook his head. "No, I don't want to impose when you have company. I only dropped by to see if you were all right. I talked to your sister and . . ." His words drifted away in apparent embarrassment.

Belinda felt heat rise to her face. She was growing angry—whether at Josh, for coming here, or at herself for letting him upset her so, she didn't know. "It was kind of you to come," she said distantly, in what she hoped was a dismissing tone of voice, but still he hesitated.

"You stay. Have tea." Charlie poured a cup as he spoke the words and handed it to Josh, who took it automatically; the moment in which he could have gracefully left had passed.

He sat down awkwardly and took a sip of the steaming tea.

Douglas cleared his throat. "Are you in the Yukon to look for gold, Mr. Rogan?"

"Yes," Josh replied, but his gaze never left Belinda's face, and she began to feel angrier than ever. Why had he come here? What was his purpose?

"Have you found a place to stake a claim?" Douglas asked. "I understand that most of the promising areas have long since been taken."

"So I've found." Josh turned toward Douglas, staring into his eyes.

The Mountie felt the full impact of Josh's gaze and personality for the first time. A tiny warning sounded in the Canadian's mind. This man was not one to be dismissed out of hand. Was he interested in Belinda? Romantically, that is? It would seem so. Douglas felt antagonism stir.

Actually, Belinda didn't seem too pleased to see him; but then women were often incomprehensible, and it was difficult to know what they were thinking and feeling. Rogan didn't take to *him,* that was plain enough, and that probably meant that he *did* have a romantic interest in Belinda.

Douglas was about to ask Rogan how long he had been in Dawson, when the man turned again to Belinda and said, "Belinda, could I talk to you alone for a couple of minutes?"

Belinda choked on her tea, and put down her cup with a clatter. She wiped her lips with the napkin before replying, "I don't believe that would be very polite, Mr. Rogan. As you very well can see, I have a guest, and I consider it quite rude of you to ask to have a private conversation with me under the circumstances."

Josh set his cup down with force sufficient to crack the heavy China. The hot tea spread its way over the cloth, and dripped off the edge of the table. "Damnit, Belinda, it's important, or I wouldn't ask! Don't play games with me!"

Belinda, her temper spiraling, shoved back her chair and shot to her feet. "Mr. Rogan, I would appreciate it if you would leave. Right now! You may send your apologies later!"

Douglas also got to his feet. He said easily, "That seems clear enough, Mr. Rogan."

But Josh dismissed the other man with a wave of his hand. "Oh, sit down, Mackenzie. This is personal. Between Miss Lee and myself. Nothing to do with you." The look he gave Douglas was insolent. "Or any of your boys in red jackets. Tell me something, Sergeant . . . I've always wondered how you Mounties manage to *ever* get your man.

Hell, with that color jacket, a criminal can see you coming a mile off!"

Belinda gasped, hand going to her mouth.

Douglas's face flushed almost as red as his jacket, and his boyish face hardened. "I'll thank you to remember who you're talking to, Rogan. Or I may forget that you are a so-called friend of Miss Lee, and treat you like you deserve. Now, the lady has made herself perfectly clear. Get out, Rogan, before you get hurt."

Josh tightened up, his blue eyes blazing. Belinda could feel the charge of anger that leapt between the two men. Oh, my God! They were going to fight! How could she stop them?

Josh poked Douglas in the chest with a stiff forefinger. "Look, Mackenzie. You may be the law in these parts, but even the law has no say in something between a man and a woman. I have something to say to Belinda, and I'm damned well going to say it. Now, since it's of somewhat a personal nature, I shouldn't imagine you'd care to hear it, so I suggest *you* leave!"

Belinda saw Douglas's arms tense, and Josh was already cocking his hand into a fist. With a loud slap, Belinda struck the table with her open hand. Charlie, who was standing off to one side, jumped at the sound, and the two men turned toward her in surprise.

"Stop it!" she cried. "Both of you, stop it!" She knew she was shouting, but she didn't care. She glared at Josh. "How can I make it clear to you? I don't want to hear anything you have to say. Do you understand that? Now, this is my home, poor as it is, and I'll thank you to leave it. At once. I don't want to see you, Mr. Rogan, and I don't want to hear from you. We said our goodbyes at Crater Lake, and as far as I am concerned, they were final. You certainly made that plain enough. Now, please leave, before Sergeant Mackenzie has to arrest you for disturbing the peace!"

Josh gazed at her with a pleading look in his eyes and Belinda felt her resolve weaken, then harden again, until she felt as cold inside as the Yukon winter. Josh's face was white with anger now, and without another word he whirled and stormed from the tent.

Belinda turned her head away and caught Charlie watching her with a look of wonder in his eyes. He did not understand, she knew. For that matter, she didn't understand herself. Without looking at Douglas, she sat shakily back down in her chair. With a great effort she pulled her ragged emotions together and faced him. "I'm sorry, Douglas," she said. "I do seem to bring you a lot of trouble, don't I?"

The anger left his face, and was replaced by tenderness. "You didn't bring that about, Belinda. It could hardly be said to be your fault that he barged in here that way. I must credit the man with a lot of gall!"

Belinda glanced around and saw that Charlie was still staring at her. Anger surfaced again, this time directed at the Chilkat. Dear God, couldn't she have *any* privacy? "Charlie," she said in a controlled voice. "Why don't you leave us for a while? Take a walk. Go visiting. All right?"

Charlie nodded cheerfully. "You betcha, Miss Belinda. Be back to make dinner."

Within seconds he was gone, and she felt guilty for losing her temper with him. He had done nothing to warrant it, and to make her feel even worse, he didn't seem to resent her sharp tongue. For a moment she let herself slump wearily, then she felt Douglas's strong hand under her arm. "You're worn out. A scene like that would exhaust anyone. Here, lie down for a little on the cot."

She felt herself being lifted and yielded to the pressure. For the moment it felt good to lean on someone else. She let herself be assisted to the cot; and, indeed, it did help to stretch out and give up the struggle for the moment.

Douglas pulled his chair up to the edge of the cot, sat down, and took her hand. "Just relax, Belinda, and breathe deeply. It will help." His voice was low and solicitous, and his hand stroking hers felt warm and soothing. She closed her eyes, and tried to breathe deeply. She felt a butterfly touch on her forehead, and opened her eyes to see Douglas looking down at her with a naked emotion he did not bother to conceal. Again, he touched her, brushing the tendrils of moist hair back from her forehead.

"You're very beautiful," he said huskily, his voice rough and yet tender.

Belinda felt her breath catch, and her heartbeat accelerated. She made no protest as his fingers moved caressingly from her forehead to her cheek, where they lingered, their touch no heavier than the brush of a feather.

Douglas moistened his lips with his tongue, and she noticed that his breathing had quickened. Her gaze strayed to a pulse on the side of his neck; it was beating strongly, like a tiny bird trapped in a cage. She could feel the heat of his body reaching out to her from where he sat, and her own body grew warm in response.

No, she thought, dimly sensing what was happening, I shouldn't be feeling this way.

But the warmth, lulling, strangely seductive, stole over her as her gaze met his, and their eyes seemed to lock. She was touched by the fact that his expression was so open, so vulnerable; that his feeling for her was there, on his face, for her to see, and savor. Oh, yes, to savor! It was a nice feeling to know that she was wanted; it made her vividly aware of her womanhood.

Slowly, his hand moved down her cheek to the soft, pulsing skin of her throat. His touch evoked a feeling both exquisite and painful—a tender yet tense expectancy that both excited and frightened her.

Now his hand fingered the buttons of her blouse, and then stopped. He groaned. "Oh, Belinda! You're so lovely! I've thought, I've dreamed, of this moment! I can't . . ."

She waited—for what she was not sure. She seemed caught in a dream-like state, incapable of speech or movement.

Douglas dropped to his knees beside the cot and buried his face against her shoulder. His hands clutched her arms in a grip almost painful, and again he cried her name. Tentatively, she reached up a hand and touched the crisp spring of his hair.

After a little he raised his head and looked down into her face. Belinda could see a dim reflection of herself mirrored in his eyes. She did not look away. As his face lowered and his mouth touched hers, she did think of drawing back, but found that she could not. His lips were hot, with the sweetness of honey, and as the pressure grew, she felt her body respond, catching fire. She felt herself being consumed by the hungry, wanting feeling she had experienced in the tent on the ice—with Josh.

For a brief passage of time, the image of Josh's face and the feel of his body moved across her mind like an accusation, and then it was gone, washed away by these other hands, these other lips.

"The tent flap," she managed to whisper.

For a moment the pressure was gone, and she felt desolated. But then Douglas was back, and in the hot darkness she let her thinking self go, yielding to the mindless demands of her body. She let sensation seize her. Somehow, their clothes were removed, and somehow the frail cot accommodated their two bodies, locked together and straining.

Seeking surcease from her body's torment after being once aroused and then deprived these many months, Belinda was shameless in her demands. Douglas was equal to it, and finally the tent echoed to the sound of her muted cry of completion, and Belinda was still, a sighing sound of contentment escaping her lips.

≈13≫

The morning was clear and hot, and already the mosquitoes were out in force, but Two-Step Sam's leathery skin resisted them.

No-Ears Riley, curled comfortably on a low stump, was giving himself a thorough wash. He paused only long enough to give Two-Step a greeting consisting of a rough "werf," before returning to his bath. Josh had left again for Dawson and they had the claim to themselves.

Two-Step coughed and stretched. "Good mornin', Riley.

It's a fine day, ain't it?"

Riley twitched his ragged tail and went to work on his paws. Two-Step rinsed out his mouth with a dipper of water from the pail, then set about making coffee and biscuits and frying some bacon. When the bacon was sizzling, Riley finished his ablutions and sauntered over to Two-Step's side, where he began to rub and purr against his leg.

Two-Step snorted. "You're just like a woman, ya old rogue. A-twistin' and actin' sweet as sugar when ya want somethin'!"

Riley "werfed" and purred all the louder. His yellow eyes were round and innocent-looking.

Two-Step laughed heartily. "Ya earless devil! Well, it'll be ready soon."

When the simple meal was ready, Two-Step set out a small share for the cat, then dug into the rest with gusto. It had been weeks since he had regularly had full meals; and since he knew that he could never be sure what tomorrow might bring, he meant to take full advantage of the present.

He swiped up the bacon grease with his last biscuit, and belched happily. Yep, this was the life. It had been a lucky day when he had run into Josh Rogan. Now he and Riley had food in their bellies and a roof over their heads. Now he had better get to work, so he could earn their keep. Two-Step was no beggar, and he intended to give full value for what he was receiving.

After putting the breakfast things away, he doused the fire and headed for the tent to get his working tools.

It was true that, as Josh had stated, this location had long since been dismissed as worthless, so far as finding color was concerned; but Josh had also said he had a feeling about the place, and Two-Step was not one to discount hunches. He had seen too many such inspirations bear fruit to shrug away a man's dream. And besides, he had nothing else to do. He might as well scout the area, and see if he could find something that everyone else had missed.

With Riley weaving in and out between his feet, Two-Step loped in his inimitable fashion—swearing mightily at the cat—in the direction of the small rise at the end of the claim away from the river.

As the sun rose higher, Two-Step carefully examined every inch of the ground. The cat finally abandoned him and sought a cool place in the shade of a tree, but Two-Step kept on, his old back bent and his nose close to the ground.

At the base of the hill, he found traces of an old stream bed, probably the original course of the existing stream down below. He grunted and hefted his pick. Might as well start here as anyplace.

The sun felt good on his back, warming his ancient bones, and he hardly noticed the sweat that dripped steadily from his nose and chin. It felt fine to be swinging the old pick again, and his body settled into the familiar rhythm, as the dirt flew.

Two-Step Sam was back doing the work he loved.

Josh, his head pounding with the roar of his own blood, stamped down the dusty main street of Dawson, heading toward the Poke. He had never been so angry with himself. How could he have let himself get involved in that kind of situation? Why had he gone to see Belinda, anyway? Annabelle had told him, when he saw her at the Poke a week ago, that her sister was all right. But he had been determined to see for himself. Well, he had seen. Belinda was obviously fine, and she certainly hadn't wasted any time in finding another "friend." He knew this last was unfair, but the presence of the Mountie rankled. It was clear to Josh that the Canadian's interest in Belinda was more than just social.

He took several deep breaths, trying to calm himself. After all, he was supposed to be working. He had a job to do, and it was necessary to remain cool and objective. Cool and objective. Hah! He was in great shape to go snooping around the Poke. He slowed to give himself more time to pull his thoughts together, and by the sheer force of will ordered himself to think of the business at hand.

Over the past week he had begun to put together what looked to be a possible case against Lester Pugh and his henchman, Chet Harter. Gossip, in a mining town, was active, and he had soon amassed a collection of tales, conjectures and complaints against the two men that was damning. However, the number of witnesses who were willing to swear to these incidents remained dishearteningly low. It was the eternal problem of the lawman, and in Dawson it was compounded by the fact that the miners did not want to take the time from their claims to appear in what was certain to be a lengthy trial.

But Josh continued doggedly to collect the rumors, gossip, and a few facts, hoping that he could catch Pugh and Harter in something really serious. He had to admit that Pugh was clever. He worked behind the front of legitimate business operations, and he was careful, very careful.

The wooden facade of the Poke loomed up before him, and he went through the swinging doors.

As he entered the barroom, he nodded to the few men he knew. He was, he thought, beginning to be accepted as a regular. The tall barkeep recognized him, and he had made friends with a couple of the girls, one a rather sad little creature by the name of Child Meg. Child earned her name because of her small size and childishly wistful face. She had huge, dark-brown eyes, a tiny pointed chin, and the whole effect of her appearance was that of a poor waif, abandoned and on her own.

Despite the fact that most men up here liked a buxom woman they could fill their hands with, Child Meg was popular. Her wistful manner and look of innocence made the men feel protective of her, and she knew very well how to utilize these assets.

Still, she wasn't completely hardened—not like some of the women who gravitated to these boomtowns, women so tough they could best a man in a bare knuckle fight—and she was possessed of a certain native intelligence that livened her conversation and made her good company.

As soon as Josh had taken his usual place at the bar, he saw Child weaving her way toward him. She was wearing a big, welcoming smile, and he felt hopeful. Maybe she had some good bits of information for him.

Early on in their acquaintance, he had tipped her well for what he referred to as her "witty conversation." The conversation, in reality, consisted mostly of bits of gossip, which Child passed on to him, but he had been able to sift through it for some valuable stuff. It hadn't taken Child long to make the connection between the large tip and the content of her dialogue; and now she came to him with more and more useful tidbits, all this without Josh once asking her to gather information for him.

"Hello, big guy." Her voice was high and soft, and she blinked her big, dark eyes at him playfully. "How's about buying a girl a drink? I'm near dying of thirst."

"Sure." He turned to the bartender. "Pete, I'd like to buy the little lady a drink. That is, if you serve a lady who's underage."

Pete and Child both laughed. This banter was part of the aura that surrounded Child, and was indulged in by all who knew her. And Josh knew that Child usually drank the real stuff, instead of the colored water most saloon girls drank.

"Why, you promised you wouldn't tell," Child said coyly, lowering her eyelids with their dark fringe of lashes. The drink, when Pete set it on the bar, disappeared quickly, and had to be followed by another before the girl would settle down and talk.

"I've got some great conversation for you, handsome," she said, pressing provocatively against Josh's arm so that her small breasts were warm against his elbow. Josh stirred uneasily. He had never thought of Child in a physical way, but he had been some time now without a woman, and the angry confrontation this afternoon with Belinda had roused thoughts and feelings he had been trying to keep in check.

He moved away slightly and looked down into Child's big eyes. "That's great, Child. Let's see if we can find a table with more privacy."

The table, near the edge of the room, was duly found, and when they were seated, Child leaned conspiratorially toward him. At first she chatted on about trivial things, then she paused and her expression grew solemn. "Josh, I did hear one thing that I thought you might be interested in.

The word is going around that there is a U.S. government man in Dawson, a lawman, but nobody seems to know why he's here. The word is also going around that when they find out who he is, he's going to meet with a sudden 'accident.' if you get my meaning."

As she talked, Child's gaze never once left Josh's face, and he had to wonder if she had guessed who this lawman was. She was bright, there was no denying that, and women's intuition was not entirely to be discounted. He had kept his expression as bland as possible. Now he said, "That is interesting. A lawman, huh? One thing though . . . who are this 'they' who are arranging the accident?"

"You know, Josh. Just they." She gestured vaguely, a gesture that could have meant Pugh and Harter, or could mean anybody in the saloon. Josh desperately wanted to dig deeper, but he knew it would be risky to push too hard.

The color of her eyes had deepened, the lines of her face softening. She said abruptly, "Josh? Why haven't you ever gone upstairs with me?"

The change of subject was so sudden, and so unexpected, that Josh, caught unawares, could only gape at her.

"I mean, don't you like me? We been talking like this for close to a week now, and you've been buying me drinks, but you never once tried to kiss me or make a grab at me. Why?" Her voice was plaintive. "Don't you like me?"

Josh swallowed and managed to say, "Why, sure, Child. I like you fine. You're a pretty girl."

"Then why haven't you taken me upstairs? You don't have to pay me. You've given me enough money already."

Staring into those dark, fathomless eyes, Josh found that he literally did not have an answer for her. Why not indeed?

He was not a man given to patronizing prostitutes, and yet he was not that prudish—he had bedded them in the past, and certainly Child was several cuts above the average.

The memory of that night in the tent on the lake ice could not last a man forever, and it certainly looked as if Belinda Lee had found herself another friend. The repressed anger and frustration began to stir in him again, and he could feel his male member coming to life against his trousers. He moved uncomfortably and felt the feathery touch of Child's hand on his thigh, and then against the front of his trousers. Full desire stabbed through him like a sword of fire, and he saw Child's face blaze with delighted understanding.

"Come on, honey," she said, her voice husky. "Let's go upstairs."

Thanking whatever gods there were for the loose work trousers that helped conceal his condition, Josh followed Child's switching skirts up the stairs. He felt certain that he was the cynosure of all eyes, but when he stole a glance back over his shoulder, no one seemed to be paying any attention. There was a constant parade, both day and night, of men and saloon girls up and down these stairs, Josh knew, but it was different when the man was *him!*

The room upstairs was spare and simple. The curtains were pulled, and the main piece of furniture was a large, four-poster bed.

Child, smiling, came close to him, and standing on tiptoe, lifted her face to his. Her lips were cool beneath his own, and for a moment, he felt a faltering of desire. She was so like a child, but what happened next disabused him of that notion. As their lips pressed together, she insinuated her tongue, hot and eager, between his, lips. As she did so, she expertly undid his belt and the buttons of his trousers, and in an instant, her small hands were grasping his swollen member. Josh shuddered with desire.

Then she stepped back from him, and with quick, practiced movements, divested herself of her gaudy dress. Without the structured clothing, her body was more womanly than might be supposed, with firm but small breasts, a tiny waist that could be spanned by a man's hands, and narrow hips framing the dark V of her womanhood.

As they tumbled onto the bed, Josh was at first afraid he would hurt her, she was so tiny, so delicate; but after a few seconds contact with her supple body, the fear left. She was a tiger kitten, a wild woman, and she made love like a mink, wildly and fiercely. A few moments of frantic frenzy, and it was over. He lay gasping on his back, with Child curled up against him.

For a moment he pondered the wisdom of what he had just done. But then, what harm could it do? However, he wasn't given much time to think about it, for her busy hands were already at work again, caressing and stroking his quiescent organ, bringing it slowly and surely back to pulsing life.

"You know, honey," she murmured in his ear, "sometimes, I just like to love for fun, with someone I like, someone who attracts me. I really liked loving you, Josh. Did you?"

"Yes," Josh replied honestly, "I liked it very much." But as he voiced the words, he didn't feel happy with them. He had liked it, liked the act, and he liked Child well enough, but putting it into words seemed to him a kind of commitment, and he wished to keep himself free from anything of that sort.

He gasped, body arching off the bed. Her practiced hands and lips had roused him to the point where logical thought was impossible, and all he could do was surrender himself to the raging passion she had aroused in his still-hungry body.

It was late when Josh left Child's room above the saloon, but the pervasive summer light gave no inkling of this fact.

There was certainly sufficient light in the hallway for Annabelle Lee to recognize him as he turned away from Child's door. He froze for a moment, then removed his hat.

"Good afternoon, Miss Annabelle."

Her gaze darted to the closed door and back to his face. She sniffed. "Try to remember that I am now Alabaster White, Mr. Rogan." She swept on down the hall and banged her door shut after her.

Josh stared after her in dismay. What if she told Belinda that she had seen him coming out of Child Meg's room?

He snorted at himself. Why should he worry about what Belinda knew, or didn't know? She had the Mountie now.

He clapped the hat on his head, clattered down the stairs, and on outside.

Striding along the street, Josh was both relaxed and somewhat melancholy. He did not feel entirely happy about what had just happened with Child, and he had to ask himself why. After all, he was a man, and a man had certain physical needs. The nature of his business ruled out a really permanent relationship, and so he had resigned himself to making do with what was available. Then why this discontent? He found Child attractive and sympathetic, and she clearly liked him. True, it could be that she liked him too much; but that had happened before, also. And, although he always felt bad when he had to leave a girl who obviously cared for him, Josh had been truthful in the relationship, telling the girl in the beginning that he would not be able to stay, that it must, of necessity, be a short-term arrangement.

Josh wasn't certain that he believed in hunches, but what he felt now gave every sign of being out of the ordinary in origin. He felt that Child would be bad luck for him. Or maybe it was because of Belinda. He could not help but compare this, and all past relationships, in light of that night on the lake with Belinda, which had transcended anything he had ever before known.

Again, he scolded himself for thinking of Belinda. He had a job to do, and he had wasted almost the entire day, first because of Belinda, and then because of Child. Women, too many women! He shook his head.

He was now approaching the outskirts of the main part of town. A hot wind had come up, producing whirls of dust from the road, and stinging his eyes and nostrils. Head down, he trudged toward camp, going over the evidence that he had so far collected against Pugh and Harter. He sighed. It wasn't enough, not nearly enough.

When at last his claim came in sight, he experienced a feeling of relief. A man needs a base, he thought, a place to come back to, even if it is only a tent.

The camp was quiet, no sign of Two-Step Sam or his weird cat. Josh thought briefly of starting the evening meal, but on the off-chance that Two-Step was hunting for something for the pot, he decided to wait.

The hot wind was still blowing, and Josh sought the shelter of the tent. It was too warm inside, from the collected heat of the day; but even so, he stretched out on his sleeping bag and closed his eyes, the better to sift through the information he had already collected, and to plan how to get more. The wind soughed around the tent with an ominous yet monotonous whine, and his thoughts fragmented, as he dozed. . . .

Something was tight against his mouth and nose, something moist and sickeningly sweet, something that fumed into his nostrils, filled his lungs, and numbed his mind. Something deadly . . .

Spiraling down, Josh felt himself falling away into a great hole filled with blackness, turning as he fell. His mind buzzed and hummed, but was capable of no coherent thought.

The darkness took him down, and then he felt himself coming back, in the way a swimmer beneath the water struggles for the surface, but the surface was too far away, much too far away.

He smelled something burning and he felt heat, but that too seemed far away. Then he felt rough hands under his arms, and was aware of being dragged across the ground to the accompaniment of a low rumble of words that made no sense. . . .

"Here now! Here now, younker. Wake up now, you hear me? Come on 'round, boy!"

The words should mean something, Josh knew, but at the moment they were nothing but an annoying rumble in his ears.

"Snap out of it! Come on, boy. Breathe deep!"

Something was slapping his cheeks, jarring his head from side to side, but Josh felt no pain. In fact, he seemed to feel little or nothing. His head felt like it was stuffed with cotton, and there was still that sickening smell coming from somewhere.

His eyes fluttered open, and for a moment he saw the wrinkled face of Two-Step Sam, then the vortex tugged at him again.

His return to consciousness seemed slow and irregular, marked by great ebbs and flows, but finally he grew more aware of his surroundings and of Two-Step bending over him, supporting his shoulders and head, and briskly slapping him first on one side of the face, then the other.

"What the hell?" Josh finally gasped out. "Two-Step? What the hell are you doing?"

Two-Step stopped hitting him and grinned widely. "Well, I do declare, Riley, I believe our meal ticket is a-comin' back. Praise the Lord!"

Josh took a deep breath, then coughed wrackingly. The sickening smell was still present, and it made him feel nauseated. His head hurt abominably.

He tried to struggle to his feet, but finally had to collapse back into Two-Step's arms. What the devil was going on? The last thing he had remembered was falling asleep in the tent.

The tent? He glanced around. Behind him, on the ground was a fairly large pile of blackened wood, and ashes. "The tent?" he asked, looking up at Two-Step.

Two-Step shrugged. "Couldn't save her, younker. She

was a-burnin' like the flames a' hell when I dragged ya out."

"Burning?"

The old man nodded. "Yep, burnin' like a bonfire. I hate to say this, younker, but if I hadn't got here when I had, well, you'd been cooked meat, and not fit for supper!" He cackled. "What happened? Did ya fall asleep smokin' one of them new-fangled cigareets?"

Josh shook his clearing head. "No, Two-Step. I don't smoke."

Two-Step looked thoughtful. "Well then, I guess I should tell you that I smelled coal oil a-comin' from the tent, when I pulled ya out." He looked at Josh sharply. "Is there somethin' ya haven't told me, Josh? Somethin' I should know?"

Slowly, Josh shook his bead. His thought processes were still not functioning properly, but he didn't need all his faculties to know that the tent didn't catch fire by itself. Someone had set fire to it, and that someone had taken care to chloroform him first, so that he would die in the fire. If Two-Step Sam had not gotten to him when he did, it might have looked like an accident. Tents and buildings in this area were always catching fire for one reason or another. People would have shaken their heads sadly about the poor young gold seeker who was burned to death in his tent, but no one would have asked any questions. Thank God for Two-Step Sam!

Josh sat up, and this time managed to get shakily to his feet. "Probably a spark from the morning's cooking fire," he said. He would prefer that the old man not suspect anything out of the ordinary. "Maybe the fire wasn't quite out, and with this wind . . ."

"Might be that you're right," Two-Step said skeptically. " 'Course I clearly recollect puttin' that fire out with a dumpin' of water after breakfast. But then that's just rhe-tor-ical, ain't it? The fact of the matter is, that that fire has rousted us out of a livin' place, and what's more, done away with a good share of our supplies."

Josh swallowed. He still felt nauseated and a little dizzy from the chloroform. Some of the supplies he had stashed in an off-the-ground rock platform, and more were stored in a rough lean-to near the tent. Neither had been touched by the fire, and most of the tools and winter supplies were intact. He said absently, "Don't worry about it, Two-Step. I've got things cached round and about. We'll need another tent, some new clothes for me, and fresh food. I'll go in to Dawson tomorrow and replace what we lost."

Two-Step's old eyes were bright with curiosity. "Must be you're better heeled than most tenderfeet. Most of 'em, by the time they've staked their claim, are flat-busted."

"Don't worry about it," Josh said crossly. "I'll handle it."

"Whatever ya say, younker." Two-Step held up his hands. "Reckon I'd better get at cooking that rabbit I caught. Seems my belly thinks it's suppertime, no matter what Mr. Sun says. Looks like we'll be havin' to sleep out under the stars tonight, though."

As the old man started a cooking fire, Josh studied the pile of ash and charred wood that had been his tent and belongings. There were a lot of questions in his mind, but he felt too woozy to consider them. It had been a busy day; perhaps it would be best to sit quietly for awhile, not thinking of anything much, until his mind cleared and his lungs were free of the chloroform.

He chose a flat rock before the fire and rested his back against the stump that Two-Step had placed there as a seat.

"That's right, younker. Ya rest a bit and get yourself pulled together whilst I stew us this rabbit. I guarantee ya that it'll bring your appetite back for sure, the way *I* cook it. I learned the recipe from an old Aleut woman what lived in Skagway. 'Course it would've been even better if'n I had us some fine bear steaks for our supper, and enough good meat to last us a week or more."

Josh, glad of the old man's chatter since it helped to keep his own thoughts shoved back in his mind, smiled. "I've never eaten bear, old-timer. What does it taste like?"

Two-Step shrugged as he gutted the rabbit and flung its entrails near the spot where Riley crouched. "Kinda sweet-like. More grainy than moose or elk, but it's tasty, *mighty* tasty if ya get a young one that's not toughed up yet. 'Course my old teeth, bein' worn down to stumps the way they be, are getting kinda useless for eatin' *real* meat. Guess pretty soon I'll be gettin' me some of them dentures they talk about."

With an expert twist of his wrist, Two-Step sliced the rabbit in two, down the backbone, and then cut the two halves again into two pieces, which he dropped into the iron pot that hung on a tripod over the fire ring. Suddenly, he uttered that mad cackle of laughter. "Say, you ever hear the story of Old Moses and the bear?"

Josh, feeling a little better now, shook his head, and began to smile in anticipation.

Two-Step poured water from the nearby bucket over the rabbit in the pot, then began to feed fuel to the fire. "Well, sir, it was this way. Old Moses was a real sourdough, one of the first ones, and a mean, sorry old bastard he was, tough as moose sinew and strong as wolf piss. A real loner. He had this claim, way up in the hills, at the head of a stream. Real isolated it was, and he had made a good strike.

"Now Old Moses, besides being mean and onery was greedy as a hongry bear. He took more gold outen that claim of his than he could rightly carry, but he wasn't about to leave his claim to take the gold into town. As long as the vein held out, he was gonna mine it.

"Howsomever, long about October, he started to run out of supplies, 'cause he wouldn't go into town. He jest kept workin', all through September, and of course the snows began to come, and there he was with hardly no supplies and no way a gettin' more.

"Well, no man could say Old Moses wasn't a determined coot. Ever day he went out huntin', and since he was a good shot and tracker, he got plenty of game. Moose, deer, rabbits, and bear. The meat was easy to keep in the freezin' weather, and he was doin' fine, until he started to lose the rest of his teeth. Ya see, Old Moses had been losin' teeth, one by one, over the past few years. Now he was down to about the least amount he could chew with, and he didn't want to take the time it would need to go into town and have false ones made up for him.

"Well, it was during this winter that the last of his teeth went bad, and he had to pull 'em out hisself. So, here he was, snowbound and hongry, with plenty of meat and no teeth to chew it with.

"But, as I said afore, Old Moses was determined. He found some soft tin, from an old pan, and he made him a base to fit over his gums. And then he made himself some gold teeth. Yep, he made them teeth out of solid gold, and set them on the tin base, and for awhile he managed to eat pretty good. But then the teeth wore down, gold bein' as soft as it is, and he didn't want to waste anymore of the precious stuff makin' teeth, so he got another idea."

Two-Step opened a small pouch and threw some salt into the now boiling water. "Ya see, he had this bearskin, head and all, from the bear he had just kilt. Old Moses, he took that bear head, and he took out the teeth, the grindin' ones that is, and he put *them* on that tin base.

"Now they was twice as good as the gold ones, for chewin' that is, and Old Moses made out fine until the spring thaw came. When he finally came down outta the hills with all that gold, he told everybody the tale of how he had et up that old bear, chop and roast, with its own teeth!"

Two-Step threw back his head and let out his cackling laugh, and Josh, despite the recent happenings, or perhaps because of them, laughed too. The old man certainly knew how to tell an entertaining story. But then, as Two-Step turned his attention to the cooking of his rabbit stew, Josh found himself face to face with the thought that he had been trying to avoid.

He had been convinced that no one knew his real identity, and yet, someone had tried to kill him. Since no one had a reason to kill Josh Rogan, prospector, it stood to reason that they must have been trying to kill Josh Rogan, federal marshal. That meant that someone knew who he was, and that in turn meant that he would have to make his move against Pugh and Harter very soon, before someone killed him or before his real identity became so well-known that he would be rendered ineffective.

L ester Pugh seated his huge bulk in the big desk chair, and motioned to Harter and Carl Doober to make themselves comfortable. He went through the ritual of lighting his Turkish cigarette before condescending to speak to Doober, who was still on his feet on the other side of the desk.

Pugh was wound tight with anger, as he slowly lifted the cigarette holder to his lips and inhaled. It was obvious, from Carl Doober's nervous manner, that his appearance here boded no good. Harter had been an idiot to use that pair of half-witted brothers on the pass business, and now it had come back to haunt them. The first thing to do was to find out what this fool wanted, for it was clear that he wanted *something*.

Pugh leaned back and fixed Doober with a bland look. "What is it, Carl? What brings you to Dawson, my boy?"

Doober twisted his battered hat in huge, scarred hands. "Well, Dick and me got into a little trouble in Skagway. Fact is, poor Dick is in jail right now, and if I hadn't been real lucky, I'd be in there with him."

"That still doesn't tell me why you came to Dawson," Pugh prompted, his voice unctuous with concern.

"Well, sir, Mr. Pugh . . ." The man's hands continued to mangle the piece of headgear. "I'm in bad need of some funds, Mr. Pugh."

"Hmmm." Pugh examined the glowing end of his cigarette, then glanced over at Harter as if to say, "You see where this is leading, don't you?"

Harter's glance slid away. He knew that Pugh was furious, and he was beginning to feel uneasy about what the fat man might have in mind.

"And just what has this to do with me, Carl?" Pugh asked. "This lack of money?"

"Well, I thought that since I had done a piece of work for you . . . that is, me and Dick." Doober looked down at the twisted hat, then back up at Pugh. "Well, I thought that you might be willing to stake me until I'm sort of on my feet again, so to speak."

When Pugh did not answer, Doober rushed on, "You know, more'n sixty men were buried in that avalanche at Chilkoot, and everybody in Dyea is pretty concerned about it. I bet that the police would be mighty interested in knowing that that avalanche wasn't no act of nature." He peered at Pugh, his expression sly, and wet his lips. "Not that I'd tell them. No siree! I'd never do a thing like that, but I thought that out of gratefulness, so to speak, for me not talking, that is, you might be willing to let me have a few hundred to tide me over."

Pugh's expression did not change in the slightest, but Harter felt his gut grow cold. He knew that Carl Doober was as good as dead, and the poor fool didn't even know it!

Pugh ground out his cigarette and leaned forward. "I just realized that I've been sorely lacking in hospitality. Would you care for a drink, Carl?"

Doober licked his lips, and his glance shuttled from Pugh to Harter, and back again. "Why, don't mind if I do, Mr. Pugh. That's mighty hospitable of you."

Pugh reached down and pulled open the bottom drawer of his desk, then closed it, shaking his head. "I'm afraid I

213

forgot to replenish my private stock. You must remind me tomorrow, Chet. Shall we repair downstairs, where we can drink in comfort at one of the tables and discuss our business?" He got up, picking up his cane, which was leaning against the desk.

Doober bobbed his head eagerly, and Harter felt a twinge of pity. The poor bastard thought he was going to get the money. Harter knew as well as Pugh that the man was a danger to them and would have to be gotten rid of, but he disliked the way that Pugh was playing cat and mouse with the man. Harter was not sentimental and violent death was nothing new to him, but it was always more or less an unemotional matter done for protection or profit; and the way Pugh enjoyed playing with his victims was distasteful to him. He also thought it an indulgence, posing an unnecessary danger. If you were going to get rid of a man it should be done with neatness and dispatch in a professional manner, not with all this elaborate fooling around. Still, Harter knew he didn't dare say anything. Underneath Pugh's mannered exterior, he was seething, Harter realized, and he also knew that Pugh, when like this, was as dangerous as a coiled rattler; so despite his feelings, he didn't want to risk that anger being turned on him.

Reluctantly, he followed as Pugh sailed through the door, with Carl Doober trotting along behind, looking much like a cur dog trailing eagerly after his master.

Montana Leeds couldn't get to sleep. Since closing time, he had been lying on his bed, tossing and turning, his mind a welter of thoughts and fears.

He had some money saved, even with the outrageous

prices in Dawson, since room and board were part of his wages at the Poke. Also, drunken prospectors were just as apt to give you a few nuggets or a pinch of dust, when they were feeling good, and although Montana did have some qualms about accepting money from men who didn't rightly know what they were doing, he rationalized that the men were going to lose, spend, or give it away in one way or another, and it might as well be to him. So he had enough to return to his wife and children, although not nearly enough to return in the style that he had been dreaming of these many years. But at least he had enough for the fare home, where he could settle down to a respectable job.

But would they accept him? He had not seen his children in eighteen years. Would they be prepared to accept a father whom they hadn't seen since they were babies? And his wife? How would she react? True, he had sent her money from time to time, whenever he could, but would she be glad to see him, or would she tell him to go away again? He couldn't blame her if she did, after all the years he had been away.

He sighed, sitting up in bed. Maybe a drink would help him sleep. He wasn't much of a drinker, but now and then, when a body was tense and wound up tight, a few drinks would dull the tension and help bring on sleep.

In his nightshirt, Montana slid out of bed and felt for his slippers. Putting them on, he left his room and went down-stairs. There was no need for a light; although it was two in the morning, the sun was still bright enough to illuminate the barroom, creating a soft dusk.

Yawning, Montana padded down the stairs and into the

empty barroom.

Going behind the bar, he bent over to get a bottle of the good whiskey from the row under the bar. He had just pulled out a bottle and placed it on the bar top, when he heard the sound of voices, as Pugh and Harter came down the stairs with a third man, whose voice Montana did not recognize.

Instinctively, Montana crouched down behind the bar.

"Well, here we are. Let me see what I can find."

Montana felt his stomach muscles tighten as the sound of Pugh's heavy footsteps approached the bar. He shouldn't have ducked down; he should have let them see him. Now Pugh was sure to think that he was spying on them—or worse. What would he say when Pugh came round behind the bar and saw him crouched there?

But Pugh didn't come around the bar. Instead, he stopped in front of it, and Montana could hear his voice just above his head. "What have we here? A bottle of the good stuff, right here on the bar. Harter, remind me to speak to the night man. He's getting careless, leaving the prime stuff out."

Montana sighed in relief. Thank God he had left the bottle in plain sight!

"And now we need some glasses."

Montana held his breath and closed his eyes, while Pugh went to the other end of the bar and evidently gathered some glasses from the backbar. But there was no outcry. Apparently Pugh didn't see him, since the bar was long and the light dim.

Montana began to breathe again as he heard the sound of chairs being pulled out, and the clink of glasses. It looked like he was safe. It was more than he deserved.

At the table Pugh swallowed his whiskey with one quick toss of his wrist, and smiled pleasantly into the face of Carl Doober. "And now, old friend, where were we? Oh, yes, you thought that, in gratitude for your *excellent* work for me in the past, that I might be willing to stake you to, what was it? A few hundred dollars?"

Doober swallowed whiskey, coughed and nodded. "Well, yes, sir, that's what I thought. Considering everything, all them people caught in the avalanche, you might say."

Pugh nodded benignly. "Just so. And what would happen, when *that* money ran out, might I ask? Is it just possible that you might be back to ask for more?"

Alarm flickered in Doober's eyes, and he began to fidget. He said hastily, "Oh, no, Mr. Pugh, I think you got it wrong. I would never . . ."

Pugh, who had been rocking his chair back on the two rear legs, something of a test for the sturdy piece of furniture, suddenly let the front legs crash down, and he slapped the palms of his hands down upon the table.

"You *think!* I'm afraid that is somewhat of a contradiction in terms. Never in your miserable life have you had a mental process remotely related to a thought! You are a fool and a bungler, Carl Doober, and you have made a sad mistake in trying to blackmail Lester Pugh!"

Carl Doober's eyes suddenly flooded with terror, and in one, awkward, jerky move, he rose from his chair, sending it crashing to the floor.

In the same instant, Pugh also stood up, pressing the button on his sword cane. Before Doober could turn to run, the needle-sharp blade was resting against his chest. He gazed down at it in frozen horror.

Pugh smiled. "Goodbye, Mr. Doober."

Doober had only time to cry out once, like a trapped shoat, before the bright blade plunged into his heart.

Harter found himself turning away before the look of pure pleasure that blazed on Pugh's face.

Montana, in his crouched position behind the bar, had to choke back the bile that he felt rising in his throat. Watching in the bar mirror, he had witnessed the whole thing. Now the figure of the man named Doober collapsed to the floor, as Pugh coolly wiped clean the blade of his sword-cane.

"Less blood than slitting his throat," Pugh said in a normal tone of voice. "Far less mess to clean up. Take him away, Chet, and dispose of the body. Damn this eternal light up here. If it was dark, you could simply slip out and dump him in some alley.

"Yeah." Swallowing, Harter gazed down at the body on the floor. He rubbed at his pockmarked face. "So what do you suggest, L.P.? You killed him, but I don't want to be arrested for it."

Pugh sighed. "You simply have no imagination, Harter. None at all. There are any number of ways to get rid of him." He gazed around the room. "For instance, take that chest over there." He indicated a large, wooden chest against one wall. "Put him in that, put the chest on the wagon, hitch up the mules, and take him out of town. From there on, even you should be able to handle it. Dump him in an abandoned mine pit, in the river." He yawned. "Now, I am going to retire. When I arise later today I expect to find our friend there safely gone, and any signs of his, uh, elimination, washed away. Is that understood, Chet?"

"Yeah, understood."

As Pugh moved ponderously up the stairs, Harter glared after him. The fat, pompous bastard, always leaving the dirty work to me, he thought viciously. Well, it wouldn't always be this way! And when the tables were turned, Pugh would see how *he* liked being the bottom man. He dragged Doober's limp body over to the wooden chest, raised the lid, and with some effort, rolled the body inside.

Montana sat crouched, his gaze riveted on the mirror. His leg muscles cried for relief, and his mind was numb with despair and horror at what he had seen. He forced himself to wait for Harter to finish his grisly task.

Finally, he heard the chest being dragged away, out the door, and he hoisted himself gingerly on protesting legs, so that he could peer over the edge of the bar. The barroom was empty.

Grabbing the nearest bottle of whiskey, Montana hurried to the stairs. Once there, he took them two at a time, and almost ran to his room, where he locked the door behind him.

Dropping onto the bed, he opened the bottle and took a long swallow, as if hoping that the strong liquor would help to ease the pain and horror in his mind.

But it didn't. He had known that Pugh and Harter were corrupt and evil, but what he had witnessed was cold-blooded murder!

The question was—what should *he* do? Quit his job? Tell the Mounties about what he had seen? Or just take the money he had saved and light out?

Agonizing over it, he took another drink, and shuddered.

Belinda stood looking down at the stack of food and gear, checking the list in her mind to be certain that she had not forgotten anything. Now that she had made up her mind to make this trip, she experienced a certain peace of mind.

It hadn't been an easy decision; she was growing fonder and fonder of Douglas Mackenzie. But that, of course, was one of the reasons she had to get away. It was impossible for her to think clearly, make a decision about their relationship, when she was seeing him constantly, and when they were constantly . . .

Belinda still found it somewhat embarrassing to think about the physical side of their relationship. It seemed to her that they came together too often, and that such conduct was somehow—apart from the fact that it was considered wrong by society—unseemly, like being greedy at the supper table. Even thinking about it brought a flush to her cheeks, and a warm stirring in her body, that did not entirely please her.

It was like being an opium addict, she concluded. The more you have it, the more you want it, and it was a trap— she could see that. How easy it would be to drift on, loving and being loved, lost in physical sensation, only to wake up one day and discover yourself married, mother of several children, and the physical part of it gone, eroded away by family problems and hard work. She had seen married couples like that, and it was definitely not what she wanted for herself.

Also, she was not all that sure of her feelings for Douglas. She was fond of him, and she found him physically attractive enough, certainly, but was she ready for a permanent relationship? And if she was, was Douglas the man she wanted to share the rest of her life with? She just didn't know.

That was why she had decided on the trip to the interior. It would enable her to get away from her problems so that she could gain some perspective on them, and also allow her to photograph some of the local Indians, a project which had intrigued her from the start.

Belinda had dispatched her first batch of pictures and text to *Leslie's Weekly,* and she was pleased with what she had submitted. She hoped that the magazine would be, too. Although she had been earning a great deal of money photographing the prospectors, and selling pictures of the Yukon to the miners to send home to their families, this was not what she really wanted to do. She felt certain that after the weekly periodical had printed her pictures, other magazines and newspapers would also want to use her work, and the idea filled her with excitement.

There was another reason for her to be away from Dawson for a time. Before making plans for the trip, she had talked to a builder and arranged for a permanent studio to be built here in town. Her original idea had been to return to New York with the advent of winter, but when she had made these plans, she had had no idea of how long it would take to travel from place to place in the territory. Now, remembering how long it had taken them to reach the gold fields, and with the time limitations imposed by the severe winters, Belinda knew that she needed more time here. She would have to stay the winter, and she would need a warm place to reside, and a studio other than a tent.

The builder had promised the studio would be completed, or very nearly so, by the time she returned.

She smiled to herself, remembering her promise to Douglas Mackenzie, made that day at the top of Chilkoot Pass, the promise that she would only be staying a few months. How naive she had been! Well, she had the money now to buy the supplies needed to last the long winter, and because of the high rate of attrition—many newly arriving prospectors turned around and headed for home when they found that the gold fields were overcrowded—there were ample supplies for sale, and at bargain prices.

Mentally, she crossed the last item off the list—the trinkets that Charlie had insisted she buy. Everything was here. They would be ready to leave in the morning.

The most difficult thing about going had been telling Douglas. He had been hurt, she could tell, and he did not understand why she wanted to trudge miles cross-country, just to photograph Indians. Of course, she couldn't explain that she needed to get away from *him* for a time; that would have hurt him even more. So now he was resigned, but clearly resentful of her decision.

Men! They always said that women were more emotional, less logical and less rational; but in Belinda's experience, it seemed the other way around.

It was odd, she thought, that her first real experience with a man should have been with one who rejected her, and her second was with a man who was reluctant to let her go. In the back of her mind a thought gnawed, a thought that she did not wish to examine too closely. Would Douglas grow tired of her and leave her, too? Logic told her that different men *were* different, and behaved differently; yet it was hard to discount bitter experience.

As Belinda turned away from the pile of supplies, a shadow fell across her, and she glanced up to see a bulky figure towering over her. At first, with the sun behind the figure, she took the man to be Lester Pugh and drew back in distaste, but as he lifted his hat, she saw a thick shock of sandy-gray hair, and a sigh of relief escaped her. It was a stranger, not Lester Pugh.

The stranger bowed politely. "Could you tell me the way to the nearest hotel, ma'am?"

Relief made her smile. "Yes, of course. Just continue down the street, until you reach the Poke Saloon. There is a hotel just next to it."

"Thank you very much, ma'am."

The man bowed again, replaced his hat, and turned to follow her directions. He was carrying a huge Gladstone bag in one hand, and a small-handled trunk in the other. He carried them easily. He was dressed in city clothes, and Belinda shook her head, smiling. He certainly didn't look the type to be at home in the Klondike, but then, she supposed, neither did she.

Her thoughts returned to the trip. Charlie had managed, with his usual amazing efficiency, to obtain a horse and a mule for the trip. The horse was definitely past his prime, but he was large and solidly built, and Charlie had assured Belinda that he could plot steadily for miles without tiring.

The mule, a mean-eyed animal on the smallish side, was full of energy, but had his own ideas of where he wanted to go. Charlie assured her that he could manage the beast, and Belinda, who was grateful to have any means of transportation other than her own two feet, took him at his word.

They could, since the river flowed in the direction they wanted to go, use a raft or a boat for the trip downriver, yet that would have left them afoot for the return trip; and Belinda agreed with Charlie that the horse and mule were a better choice.

When Belinda had asked Charlie about the Indians in the interior, and inquired if he had relatives there, he had smiled broadly.

"Have cousin who married out of tribe. She married Athabascan man and live in village downriver." He shook his head. "Too bad you not have time to take picture my village near Dyea, Miss Belinda. Tlingit much better than Athabascan. More interesting. Tlingit have big village. Build lodge, make totem, have potlatch. Athabascan poor. Follow the game. Not sea people like Aleut, Eskimo, and Tlingit . . ."

Listening to Charlie expound, Belinda had realized how little she knew of the native races of the area. She had assumed that all Indians were of one kind, one tribe. It was only during this discussion that she learned that the Chilkats, Charlie's own people, were also a part of the Tlingit tribe.

Now, she looked around at the empty space where the tents had stood. Except for what they were taking along on the trip, everything had been packed and stored in town, for when she returned, she hoped to be able to move into her new building. There was nothing left to do now but to check into a hotel for the night.

Charlie came hurrying up, beaming. "You get good night's sleep, Miss Belinda. Charlie here first thing. Six o'clock morning, with horse, mule, and gear. You betcha?"

Belinda smiled, and nodded. "You betcha, Charlie. I'll be ready."

"Good!" Charlie bobbed his head, and hurried away, his bandy legs showing daylight between them as he walked.

Early as it was, Belinda decided that she had best get to bed. Tomorrow would be a long day, and she needed a good night's sleep. She walked up the street to the hotel, almost sorry that she had asked Douglas not to come by. She had told him she was retiring early, and he had reluctantly agreed. Once in the hotel room, lying on a strange bed, she wished he was there, to hold and comfort her. She flounced onto her side, and tried to punch up the limp pillow, angry at herself. A perfect example of what she had been thinking about. Douglas was a habit already!

She clamped her eyes shut, and willed herself to sleep.

Annabelle carefully placed the photograph in the third frame of the silver triptych, then stood back the better to admire it.

The picture was of herself, and Annabelle thought it was excellent. She was wearing one of the dresses she wore when she performed, and was holding a large, feather fan. The pictures in the other two frames were of her mother, taken a few years before her death, and of Belinda.

Looking at her own likeness, Annabelle had to admit that Belinda was good. She had captured just the right expression of innocence and coquetry—what Annabelle thought of as her best expression.

Belinda had taken and developed the picture two days before, so she could have it finished before her trip. She had made several copies, and Annabelle was going to ask

Chet to mount one on the sign that stood outside the Golden Poke, proclaiming the merits of "Miss Alabaster White."

Annabelle smiled at her image. Things were going better than she had expected when she came to Chet Harter, her luggage in her hand. Most of what she had told Belinda, that day in her room here, was true—Chet wasn't really a bad sort, as long as she agreed with him and let him think he was having his own way.

Annabelle was accustomed to agreeing with men. It was a woman's lot. And Chet was generous to her, buying her anything she expressed a desire for. Of course she hadn't told Belinda some things; for instance, that when Chet was drinking, he was occasionally a bit rough, or that she suspected he wasn't completely faithful to her. But again, these were the kinds of things men did, and women had to close their eyes to them. From what Annabelle had seen and read, all women did just that.

She faced about as the bedroom door opened and Chet Harter came into the room.

"Look, Chet!" She picked up the picture and held it out. "It's my picture. Bee took it. Isn't it grand?"

Harter took the picture and studied it without much interest. "Looks good, sugar. Just like you."

Annabelle picked up the copies of the photo from her dresser. "And see, she gave me several copies. I thought maybe you could mount one of them on the poster outside the Poke. It would look nice, don't you think?"

She stopped, puzzled. He was staring at the pictures in her hand, with a very strange expression on his face.

Tentatively, she put her hand on his arm. "Chet? Honey,

what is it?"

"Copies?" he said slowly. "You have copies of the same picture?"

"Of course." She held them out. "See? This way, I can give one to the newspaper, if they ever do a story about me, or give them to my friends or . . ."

Harter's eyes were hooded when he looked up. "Can your sister make copies of just any picture, like this?"

Annabelle nodded. "If she has a negative, she can make as many as she wants."

"Negative?"

Annabelle, at the risk of angering him, could not help but giggle. Clearly he knew little or nothing about photography, but then she knew she couldn't make an issue of this, even if it was rather funny.

She smothered the giggle and said with a straight face, "You see, Chet, when a photographer takes a picture, it is taken with a plate, or with that new-cut film, like Bee uses. Then she does something to the film, or plate, and it has this backward picture on it, all kind of funny and dark. Then she makes prints of the picture from this plate, or negative, as they call it. It's all kind of complicated. Bee could explain it much better than I can. Heavens, I don't know exactly how it works, and wouldn't know even as much as I do, except that's all Bee talks about, day and night." She laughed merrily. "Anyway, that's why a photographer can make a lot of pictures, from just one negative."

Harter's expression was forbidding. "I see," he said, and returned the picture. "I have to go out. I'll be back later."

And without another word, he strode from the room.

Pouting, Annabelle placed the framed picture back on her dresser. He was certainly acting strange!

She shrugged. Oh, well, there was no use worrying about it. She did wonder if they were still going out to supper at that new restaurant which had just opened. Chet *had* promised.

Apprehension rode Harter like the shadow of a circling vulture as he hurried out of the Poke, and started for Belinda Lee's studio. There was one way to make sure there would be no more pictures, and that was to destroy all of her "plates," or "negatives," or whatever the hell she called them. The sure way to do it was to burn down her tents!

As he strode down the board sidewalk, he almost collided with a tall, wide-bodied man strolling leisurely along. Harter was about to give the man a piece of his mind, when he noticed how big he was and how easily he carried himself. Harter contented himself with a surly growl and a twist of his shoulders to show his displeasure, and continued on his way. Damned if the big bastard didn't sort of look like Lester Pugh.

Harter's thoughts returned to Belinda Lee and the pictures. Maybe he was worrying over nothing, yet he had the uneasy feeling that there was still a photographic record of Chet Harter standing off the Chilkoot trail only seconds before the avalanche erupted. It could raise questions if the photograph ended up in the wrong hands. Harter's neck got a constricted feeling, as if a noose was being tightened around it.

He wanted to take a really good look at the woman's setup, and decide where a fire could best be started. He would do it tonight, in the brief span of darkness, and the problem would be solved for once and all. If Belinda Lee—the trouble-making bitch—happened to be inside at the time, well, that would be all to the good. She would be out of his hair for good; she wouldn't be coming around all the time, filling Annabelle's head with foolishness.

He had a good thing going with Annabelle; she was, as far as was possible, the perfect woman for him—beautiful, docile, eager to please. In his own way, Harter was rather fond of her. But after her sister's visits, she was different for a few days, a little restless. Harter found no contradiction in the fact that he was quite willing to kill the sister of the woman he professed to care for.

Now, the tents should be just about here . . .

He skidded to a stop and looked around in bewilderment. They should be right here, next to the tent with the sign that said LAUNDRY DONE, but instead another, large, white tent was in that spot.

Angrily, he rang the cowbell, which hung outside the laundry tent, and waited impatiently until a small, stooped woman came to the tent door. "Yes, what can I do for you?"

"Didn't a photographer, a Belinda Lee, have her tent next to yours?"

The woman nodded. "She sure did, and a lovely girl she is, too . . ."

Harter cut the old woman short; he hadn't come here to listen to a tribute to Belinda Lee. "Then where's her tent? Where's she gone?"

"Why, bless me, she's gone off on a photographing trip.

Left day afore yesterday. Downriver to the Indian villages, she said. Says she wants to get some pictures for that magazine in New York. Why anybody would want to look at pictures of Indians, I don't know."

Harter kept his frustration barely under control. "What'd she do with her things? Why'd she take down her tent?"

"She stored all that somewheres in town, but I don't know where. She's building a real studio here in Dawson, or having it built. I understand that when she comes back, she's going to move into that. Do you want to leave a message? I promised I'd take any messages for her."

Harter said, "No, thanks, lady. No message. I appreciate your help."

He smiled at the woman—a baring of teeth that caused her to draw back in alarm—and strode off.

"Damn! Goddamn the rotten luck!" he said viciously.

There was only one thing to do now. He had to go after her, and make damned sure that she never came back. If she was dead, there would be no one who would be likely to draw any conclusions from any prints of the picture that might remain.

Harter knew that he did not dare tell Pugh. The fat man was already a little peeved at him because of Annabelle, and he had given Pugh his assurances that he, Harter, had destroyed the only copy of that picture. If Pugh learned that it was possible another one existed . . .

He shuddered. No, the only way he could stay in Pugh's good graces was to eliminate Belinda Lee, and confront him with the accomplished fact. Once that was done, all of their immediate problems would be taken care of. Now that the federal marshal was out of the way—the thought

of that fire brought a gloating smile to Harter's face—
Belinda Lee was their only problem.

When she Was taken care of, Harter thought smugly,
Pugh should be in a very good mood, and with Pugh that
was something to be greatly desired!

≈15≈

Although the morning was bright and sunny, there
was a bit of a nip in the air, a foretaste of the winter
to come.

Belinda and Charlie had been traveling for several hours,
and Belinda, astride the bony old horse, was feeling
relaxed, as she gently swayed in the saddle.

This was their third day on the trail, and Charlie had
assured her that they should reach the Indian village very
soon now. They had met very few other travelers, as they
followed the Yukon River.

Belinda knew now that she had been right to make the
trip. Just getting away from Dawson had given her a new
perspective, and she felt less tense than she had in some
time. Oh, the problem was still there, and she knew that she
would still have to resolve it, but somehow human problems seemed very small in this primitive wilderness, where
man or woman was only a tiny, vulnerable speck on the
landscape.

They rode on for another hour before the Indian village
came in sight.

Belinda saw first the crude houses—frameworks of
poles covered with light brush and bark—set back from the

water, in a bend of the river. The rough shelters looked incredibly flimsy, and Charlie, as if he guessed what Belinda was thinking, gestured at the camp. "This not permanent camp. Only summer camp. Have stronger wickiups in winter, covered with caribou hides. Sometimes have log houses. Not like Tlingit village. Tlingit village much better."

Belinda, smiling to herself at Charlie's favoritism of his own, urged her horse forward.

At first there seemed to be no one in the village, although here and there a fire burned low in a fire ring.

Besides the fragile wickiups, she saw platforms erected, on posts and in the trees, obviously used as caches for food and other supplies. On the ground near the river she could see nets spread to dry. A strong, rank odor of fish hung over the village, and Belinda coughed and wiped her eyes.

"There's nobody here, Charlie," she said.

Charlie grinned. "Oh, they here. You betcha. They just looking. Make up minds whether we friends. Just wait. They come soon."

With these words, Charlie hunkered down in a squat that he seemed to be able to hold for hours. Belinda, less trained in stoicism, sat restlessly on her horse, occasionally brushing away the flies and mosquitoes when they grew too bold.

For some little time there was no sound except for those made by birds, animals in the brush, and the wind in the trees; and then, a shadow moved in the door of the largest wickiup and a man stepped out.

He was taller than any of the Chilkats whom Belinda had seen, less stocky in build, and swarthier in complexion. He was also less Oriental in appearance, looking more like the pictures that Belinda had seen of the Plains Indians back in the States.

He was dressed in a white man's shirt and leather breeches, and his feet were bare. His coarse dark hair was cut off just below his ears, and looked as if it could use a good combing.

Charlie arose from his squat and held up his hand, palm outward toward the other man, who repeated the gesture.

They began an exchange that Belinda could not, of course, follow. And after what seemed an interminable time, Charlie motioned to Belinda to get down from her horse. She did so, and was escorted without further cere-mony to the large wickiup in the center of the village.

Belinda had to stoop to enter, and once she had, the odor coming from inside almost made her turn back. A com-posite of spoiled meat, fish oil, and human excretions caused her nostrils to constrict and her eyes to start watering.

Swallowing, she willed her unsteady stomach to behave, and went on into the dwelling.

On the floor in front of her was a raised pallet piled with hides and blankets. On this dais sat an ancient Indian male, dark face seamed with deep lines. He was dressed in an embroidered leather tunic and trousers, which had defi-nitely seen better days, but his white hair was neatly plaited and bound with colored bands, and he seemed to be cleaner than the first man Belinda had seen.

The old man motioned for Belinda and Charlie to be seated, and Charlie immediately hunkered on the ground, which was more or less covered with caribou skins.

Belinda, with some difficulty, sat down, crossing her legs like the old chief before them.

Then, for what seemed like hours, the two men talked. Some of the time Charlie would translate, as when there was a direct question asked of Belinda—why she was here, what she wanted to do here—but most of the conversation was between the two men, and Belinda, numbed by the heat and the smell inside the wickiup, began to feel woozy.

Finally, when she had begun to think that she must leave the wickiup or be sick, Charlie got to his feet and gave her a hand up. Charlie made the same hand sign to the chief that he had made to the first Indian, and on impulse, Belinda did the same.

The old chief looked startled, but Belinda thought that she detected a tiny gleam in his eyes that might have been amusement.

When they were outside once again, she drew a deep breath. "Thank God! I couldn't have sat still in there for another minute! Why on earth did it take so long?"

Charlie grinned. "Must have palaver. Polite talk. Must tell news, tell what is going on up river. Must give presents. Take time."

Belinda nodded. "It certainly did that. Well, what did he say? Will he let us stay awhile?"

Charlie bobbed his head. "Sure, you betcha. We stay. 'Cause we bring own food. Poor tribe here. Hard to get enough food. They give welcome feast for us tonight, but not afford to feed extra people many days. Chief say we can set up our wickiup there, near trees."

Belinda looked to where he was pointing, a clear space somewhat isolated from the other structures.

"And what about the pictures? Did you explain that I wanted to take pictures?"

Charlie nodded again. "Chief say he tell others to let you do this. Now Miss Belinda see why Charlie ask you bring trinkets? You take picture, give present. Some Indians afraid of picture box. Think it bad magic. But you give present, they happy. Everybody happy. You betcha?"

Belinda laughed. "Everybody happy, you betcha."

Josh strode along the main street of Dawson with some apprehension. This was his first trip into town since the tent had been fired, and he walked warily. Someone knew who he was, and now there was no safety, even in the midst of the crowded streets.

He had puzzled long over the identity of his would-be killer, and had finally decided that his attacker had to have been sent by either Pugh or Harter. Unlikely as it seemed, somehow they must have learned of his identity. They were the only ones who had anything to gain by his death. Or perhaps it was Harter alone. Perhaps he was one of those suspicious, jealous men who mistrusted any man around their sweethearts or wives—although that seemed a bit far-fetched, as Harter, insofar as Josh knew, had only seen him the one time in Annabelle's room.

At any rate, he intended to go to the Poke and make himself fairly conspicuous, and watch for any telltale expressions of surprise on the faces of the men he knew.

Although it would have been much quicker to have approached the Poke from the other end of town, Josh found himself walking past the tent city. He did not care to examine the reason for this approach too closely; and as he passed the place where Belinda Lee's studio and tent should be, he allowed himself only a quick, sideways glance.

This one glance stopped him in his tracks. The tent and studio were not there! There was another, large tent in their place.

Worried now, he picked up his pace. What could have happened? Where had Belinda gone?

He pushed his way through the crowd thronging the street, and made his way to the Poke, trying not to think any further ahead than the next few minutes. He would find Annabelle, and she would tell him. It was probably nothing serious. Maybe Belinda had moved into a hotel, nothing more than that.

Inside the saloon, he headed at once for the stairs. He was halfway across the barroom, when he felt a hand on his arm.

He turned impatiently and looked down into the upturned, elfin face of Child Meg.

"Hello, big fellow," she said softly. "You seem in an awful hurry. Don't you have time to have a drink with a friend?"

Josh tried to keep the impatience out of his voice. "I'm sorry, Child. I didn't see you. Look, I have something to do, some important business to take care of. I'll be back in a few minutes, say a half-hour. All right?"

Child stuck out her lower lip in a pout. "Well, all right. If you promise it won't be more than that."

Josh's smile was forced. "I promise, Child. Now, don't go away."

Without waiting for her answer, he turned and headed

for the stairs. There was no answer to his first knock on Annabelle's door and his heart sank. She wasn't in! But he knocked again, louder, and after a few moments the door opened and Annabelle peeked out.

"Why, Mr. Rogan!" She smiled charmingly. "I didn't think you'd be calling on me again. Come in!"

Hoping that Chet Harter wasn't with her, Josh entered, taking off his hat.

Thankfully, Annabelle was alone. There was a China tea service set out on a small, round table, and Annabelle gestured toward it. "Will you join me in a cup of tea, Mr. Rogan?"

Trying to maintain his poise, Josh shook his head. "I just came to ask you something, Miss Lee. It's about your sister . . ."

Annabelle pouted attractively. "You horrid, horrid man. The only time you come to see me is to talk about Bee! Well, what is it this time?"

Josh took a deep breath. "I just came through tent town, and I noticed that her tents were gone. Could you tell me why, and where she's gone?"

Annabelle gave a deep sigh, and swished over to the table and the tea things. Carefully, she poured herself a cup of tea before answering. "She's gone on a trip, that's where. She and that Indian went along the river, so that she could take pictures of some of the Indians, or something. She had the tents taken down and stored, along with her other things, because she's having a permanent studio built here in town. She'll move into that when she comes back."

"Oh." Josh felt foolish in his rush of relief. There was nothing wrong with Belinda, and as was becoming his habit, he had made a bit of a fool of himself worrying over her.

Annabelle turned to pick up a picture from the dresser. "See this picture Bee took of me before she left? Isn't it good?"

Josh scarcely glanced at the picture. "Yes," he said, "it's very good."

Annabelle gave a rueful laugh. "But maybe I shouldn't show it to you. I showed it to Chet yesterday, and I haven't seen him since." She set the picture back on the dresser, with slightly more force than was necessary. "And we were supposed to go out to dinner at that new place, too. Men!"

Josh, trying to make some sense out of this flood of words, blinked at her. "What?"

"He just disappeared," Annabelle said crossly. "I got all dressed up and everything, and he never came back. He hasn't been back yet, and he didn't leave any word for me, either. I just don't know where he is!"

For some strange reason, Josh thought of Belinda being stranded in the snowstorm on Crater Lake, and a creeping cold gripped him. Something was wrong here, very wrong. "And this was yesterday, you say? Just after you showed him the picture that Belinda took of you?"

Annabelle nodded, her curls bobbing. "I showed him the picture, and we talked about putting a print of one of the pictures of me on the billboard outside the Poke." She giggled. "Do you know that he didn't even realize that you could make more than one picture from a plate?" Her expression turned thoughtful. "He acted kind of funny when I told, him, even though I didn't tease him or anything like that. And then he went rushing out, without telling me where." She shrugged. "It's aggravating!"

Josh was cold all over now. He asked, "When did Belinda and the Chilkat leave?"

Annabelle thought. "Three days ago."

"And Harter left yesterday? About what time?"

"Oh, around noon, I guess. Anyway, that's the last time *I* saw him."

"Thank you, Annabelle," he said, putting on his hat. "I hope your friend Harter comes back soon."

Annabelle smiled. "So do I. I'm getting pretty bored here all alone." Her face brightened. "But then, I always have my singing."

Josh nodded, his mind already on other things. He said absently, "That's good."

As he walked out the door, Josh was trying to think how he could verify the fear that was growing in him. He had no facts to back it, yet he was gut-certain that Harter had taken off in pursuit of Belinda and Charlie—for what reason he couldn't begin to guess.

However, one thing was sure. Harter meant them no good, no good at all!

At the dinner-feast in the Indian village, served in her and Charlie's honor, Belinda was very glad they had brought along their own provisions. The meat she had seen tossed into the stewpot looked rank and wormy, and some of the other ingredients looked even less appetizing than the meat.

During the meal, she pretended to eat, while Charlie ate hugely to the apparent delight of their hosts.

Afterwards, there was dancing, in which Charlie joined,

and Belinda, after asking the chief's permission, took pictures of the dancers, and of the chief and his many wives. She did not forget Charlie's advice, and was liberal with gifts to one and all.

By the time the festivities came to an end, Belinda was weary yet happy. She had been on the trail since early morning and her body cried out for rest, but she felt at peace.

Carefully stowing the exposed film into the storage case, she crawled into her sleeping bag in the tent which Charlie had erected earlier. This trip was going to be very good for her, she knew, both professionally and emotionally.

They remained at the Indian village for two days, during which time Belinda was everywhere with her camera, photographing the Indians at work and play, and discovering some marvelous character faces among the older men and women.

Again, as she had been so often on this trip, Belinda was grateful for the fact that she had decided to use the new cut film instead of wet or dry plates. On a side trip, like this one, it was so much more convenient, so much lighter to carry. Her only concern was that she would run out of film before she had photographed everything that caught her fancy. She was also glad that she had sent a request to her supplier in New York for more film, at the same time she had mailed her pictures and text in to *Leslie's Weekly*. She would certainly need more film by winter.

On the morning of the third day, Charlie packed up their things, and after a long and ceremonious farewell, they moved on to the next village, which Charlie had told her was not too many miles distant.

As they headed toward the river, and the river trail, the sky grew overcast and a chill wind came up.

Belinda, feeling the wind through her thin jacket, called over to the Chilkat, "Charlie, is it going to get worse?"

Charlie shrugged. "Cannot tell. This funny time of year. Weather start big change soon, you betcha. Winter. Brrr!"

Belinda laughed, and shivered. "But it's only August!"

Charlie shrugged as he plodded alongside the mule. "Summer short here. Only work few months. Then all freeze. Like iron. Miners back in Dawson heading out already. Back to Dyea for winter supplies. Just make it back time snow flies. Maybe.

"Then we had better get our supplies too, hadn't we? As soon as we get back, that is?"

Charlie nodded. "Yes. But then we stay in town. Easier for us. But still need to lay in food and things. Supplies get low in winter. Stores run out. Best be ready. Charlie already give Mr. Hooper, at general store, winter order. All taken care of, you betcha."

He looked over at Belinda with a shining smile and, not for the first time, Belinda felt a wave of affection and gratitude toward the stocky brown man. Someday, she was going to have to do something really nice for him, something that would show him how she felt, but until then . . .

With an answering smile, she said, "You are a wonder, Charlie. I'm lucky to have you working for me."

Charlie ducked his head modestly, but she could see that he was pleased.

As the day wore on, the sky grew darker, and the wind increased to the point where Belinda had Charlie stop and get her heavy coat from the pack.

After a brief stop for a cold lunch, they went on, heading into what appeared to be a coming storm.

To Belinda's surprise, Charlie now picked up the pace of the animals until he was trotting briskly alongside the reluctant mule, and Belinda, seeing his grim face, assumed that he was worried about finding a sheltered spot for tonight's camp.

But as the hour grew late, and several likely looking spots had been passed up, she began to wonder. Finally, tired and saddle-sore, she called out, "Charlie? Can't we stop for the night? I'm getting awfully tired!"

Charlie pulled the mule in alongside her horse. "We go little longer, Miss Belinda," he said seriously, and his face, usually sunny and open, wore an expression of concern that Belinda had never seen there before. "You try get horse go faster Please?"

A little disturbed by his intensity, Belinda did not question him as he let the mule drop back to a position behind her horse. For the first time she saw Charlie as something other than the jovial child of nature she had always thought him. Also, she wondered why he had taken the position behind her. Always before he and the mule set the pace.

She urged her horse into a faster gait, to which the animal reluctantly acceded, breaking into a trot that jarred Belinda's body and made her bones ache.

They had gone perhaps another mile at this speed, and were approaching a part of the trail very near the river, when the shots rang out. Two of them, one right after the other. Belinda had only time to glance hastily back over her shoulder, before the sound of the second shot made her horse rear and break into a lurching gallop.

What she saw in that single glance was like a blow to her heart. She saw Charlie clutch his chest, an expression of pain and surprise on his face, as he stumbled backward toward the river's edge. He was falling, as the force of her mount's rearing snapped her head around to the front, and then she saw nothing except a blur of green and brown as the animal thundered away from the trail and into a stand of trees. As the branches whipped past her, one of them, like a brutal arm, swept her roughly from the saddle, and the ground struck her. A swirl of pain clouded her senses.

Dimly, she was aware of hearing more shots, the high-pitched scream of the mule, and then the shout of a man. Charlie?

Then consciousness faded, and there was only a pain-filled darkness.

It had only taken Josh a few hours to learn that Harter had hired a horse from Dawson's one stable, and had told the hostler that he might be gone for several days. He had, Josh also learned, taken along two full saddlebags of food, a blanket roll, and a rifle. He had left the stable around two o'clock the afternoon before.

Still not absolutely sure, Josh then headed toward the tent town, where he talked to Belinda's ex-neighbors on both sides. One had no real information, but the woman who operated the laundry told him that a man answering to Harter's description had been there, yesterday, asking after Miss Lee.

That clinched it for Josh. True, his judgment didn't seem to be the best where Belinda Lee was concerned, and true, he did tend to fret needlessly in her behalf; but it was just too much of a coincidence that Chet Harter should have departed town in a hurry just after discussing Belinda's picture-taking process with her sister, and just after learning Belinda's destination from her neighbor.

He was now certain in his mind, and in his gut, that Harter, for whatever reason, was in pursuit of Belinda. He thought again of the incident on Crater Lake. Was it possible that the attempted murder of the Chilkat bearer had been done so that Belinda would be left to die in a blizzard?

Well, the reason wasn't important at the moment. It was still early afternoon. If he hurried, he could cover several miles before dark.

The livery stable had only one horse left, a swayback bay, but Josh took it gratefully and rode it back to his camp, which was on his way. He found Two-Step Sam busily at work on the far side of the claim.

Josh told the old man that he would be gone for a few days on business, then packed his saddlebags with provisions and ammunition. He tied his blanket roll and slicker behind the saddle, and he was ready to go.

The woman at the laundry had told him that Belinda and Charlie intended to take the river trail, stopping at Indian villages along the way. They were three days ahead of him, and Harter was almost two days ahead. Josh just hoped to God that Harter hadn't caught up with them yet and carried out his intent.

He rode hard for five days, scarcely stopping to rest. On the afternoon of the fifth day, he rode into the teeth of a gathering storm, but he knew he was close behind Belinda and Harter now, and impatience prodded him.

The Indians at the village he had passed through early

that morning had talked freely about the beautiful white squaw and her picture box. They had also talked of another man, who had remained outside the village, skulking about, probably not even aware that the Indians had seen him.

This news had filled Josh with a cold dread. He must catch up to them soon, but the storm was not going to help. He would have thought that they had made camp by now. It would be the natural thing to do; but evidently they were still moving on, and Josh was puzzled as to the reason. The Chilkat was wise in the ways of this country, and the smart thing to do, with a storm brewing, was to make a snug camp and wait it out.

Josh urged the bay to move faster, but the animal was growing tired. They both needed a rest.

And then he heard a sound, carried back to him on the wind—the unmistakable sound of a gunshot. He drummed his heels against the flanks of the bay, and the animal reluctantly complied, breaking into a half-hearted gallop.

Now he heard the sound of a second shot, coming from somewhere on the river side of the trail ahead.

He rounded a bend in the trail just in time to see the Chilkat stagger back, hands to his chest, before falling headlong into the river. Up ahead was Belinda, astride a rearing horse. Even as Josh saw her, her horse bolted in fear. Josh had just the one glimpse of Belinda's white face and frightened eyes, before the animal plunged recklessly into the copse of trees to the right.

All this happened in an instant, and just as quickly Josh's brain sorted through what he had seen, and decided on a course of action.

He couldn't try to save Charlie without exposing himself to the gunfire of the hidden shooter; and if *he* was killed, Belinda would be left to the mercy of the marksman, who had to be Chet Harter. It could be no one else.

Josh was already sliding off his horse. He dropped the reins, and leaving the animal standing on the trail, he ran a crouching, zigzag course for the cover of several large boulders, which lined the river at this point.

Harter, Josh was reasonably sure, was concealed somewhere on his right. Crouching down behind a boulder, pistol drawn, he scanned the landscape for a sign of movement. For several moments all was quiet, but as he leaned forward to move in closer to the river, a bullet chipped the rock by his head. Josh dropped back out of sight, grinning tightly. He had seen where the shot had come from, and he knew his surmise had been correct—Harter was to the right of the trail.

Carefully, he edged around the boulder in the opposite direction, and ran flat out for the cover of another, closer to Harter. A bullet splintered rock behind him, but he made it safely. Once behind the boulder, Josh peeked around to see the brim of a man's hat, and part of a leg, clad in dark trousers. Josh aimed at the exposed leg and carefully squeezed off a shot.

The bullet sped true and Harter yelled, jerking his leg out of sight. Josh heard what he hoped was the man's rifle clattering to the ground. At once he was out from behind the sheltering rock and running toward Harter keeping what scant cover he could between himself and the other man.

Then, just in time, he caught the glint of light on a rifle barrel behind the rocks, and he threw himself headlong behind a low rock, as several bullets kicked up dust within a few inches of his head. He felt as exposed as if he was naked, but at least he was close enough now to hear the other man swearing steadily in a low voice.

Josh poked his head around, aiming his pistol at a crevice between the rocks hiding Harter. He fired, and was rewarded by a muffled cry.

Again all was still, save for the sound of Josh's own ragged breathing. Then he heard Harter's voice, "Rogan? That *is* you, ain't it?"

"It's me, Harter."

"I'm hurt bad, Rogan. Help me."

Josh said suspiciously, "Throw out your guns, and I'll be happy to oblige."

There was a brief silence before Harter answered, and when he did, his voice sounded weak. "Can't. Can't move my arms. You got me in the chest. I'm bleeding bad. Christ, man, you wouldn't leave me here to die?"

Josh thought hard. Harter could be faking. On the other hand, it wasn't necessarily his job to kill Chet Harter, but to bring him to justice for his crimes. Josh's own inclination was to let the murdering bastard lie there and bleed to death. He had killed the Chilkat, had tried once before to kill Belinda, and might very well have succeeded this time . . .

He sighed. Hell, he couldn't do it. If he had killed him cleanly in a fight, that would have been one thing, but this was another. It wasn't his way.

"Rogan?"

Josh didn't answer. Instead, he began to crawl toward the boulders concealing Harter, circling to the right. There was one space about ten yards wide with no cover; he would be completely exposed. Josh drew a deep breath and crawled on. He had covered about half the distance when he heard a movement, and knew that Harter had been lying. A shot grazed his temple, as he started to roll sideways. The bullet had only laid his scalp open, but as he tried to get his feet under him to spring to one side, he felt his ankle twist and buckle under him, and he sprawled to the ground.

From his position on the ground, he saw Harter break from behind the boulders. From his awkward sprawl, Josh snapped off a quick shot that struck Harter's gun arm. Harter yelped and dropped his pistol.

Josh, dizzy from the head wound, snapped off another shot, but this one went wide and Harter, limping, his arm dangling, vanished into the trees.

Josh tried to give chase, but as he came to his feet, pain like a knife thrust tore into his ankle, and he fell again. He watched helplessly; Harter was getting away, and there was nothing he could do about it. He managed to raise himself on one elbow at the sound of hoofbeats, and saw Harter, clinging to the back of a horse, ride out of the trees and onto the trail. Josh's own horse was racing away in front of Harter's, and in a few minutes both animals were out of sight around the bend of the river.

Josh collapsed back onto the rocky earth until his head cleared, and he felt strong enough to get to his feet. His ankle was already swollen and hurt like the devil, but he had to find Belinda.

He struggled to his feet with the aid of a tree. Braced against it, he glanced around. The mule lay unmoving across the trail, evidently killed early on, and there was nothing else in sight. No Belinda. And the Chilkat was gone, if not killed by Harter's bullet, surely swept to his death in the icy waters of the Yukon.

Josh shouted, "Belinda! Where are you?"

He listened with bated breath, but there was no answer.

He would have to look for her. Painfully, he hobbled toward the trees where she had disappeared. Every step was an agony, but doggedly he dragged himself along.

Once into the woods, he cut a stout branch with a fork at one end. Using this as a crutch, his progress was a little easier. Just when he was convinced that he could go no further, he found her, stretched out on the ground beneath a small tree. There was no sign of her horse.

She looked terribly small and frail lying there, her body crumpled and still, and her face white and covered with blood. His heart began to hammer. There was so *much* blood! It seemed to be flowing from her head, and a groan was wrenched from him as he dropped down beside her. He could detect no signs of breathing.

Had he failed her at the last minute? Was she dead?

B elinda opened her eyes to pain and biting cold. Her body ached as if she had been beaten, and her head, when she tried to move it, throbbed like a toothache.

The sky had darkened even more while she had been unconscious, and the branches of the tree above her head whipped and rattled in the rising wind.

As full awareness flooded back, she groaned, and finally raised her head. And then she saw the figure, slumped back against the trunk of the tree. "Charlie?" she said hopefully.

The figure stirred, the head coming up. Ice-blue eyes looked into hers, and she gave a muted cry.

Astonishment rendered her speechless for a moment, and she had to swallow before she could speak. "Josh? What are *you* doing here? Where's Charlie?"

"I'm sorry, Belinda. He's dead, I'm afraid."

The memory of her last sight of Charlie, staggering backward toward the river, filled her mind. "Oh, no! No, it can't be!"

Josh said gently, "I'm sorry, it's true."

She began to weep, the tears leaking out of her eyes, and a thickness clogged her throat.

Josh smiled at her wearily, his lean face pale under the trail dust. Dried blood had caked on his forehead. He inched closer to her, and she saw him grimace and reach for his ankle. He was hurt, and in pain! What had happened, how had he come to be here?

With an awkward hitch, Josh finally pulled himself close, and he put an arm around her shoulders, drawing her against him. She clung to him, clung to his warmth and reassuring maleness, letting herself be pressed against his chest until the breath almost left her body.

"I thought you were dead," he said in a hushed voice. "You looked so white and still. I thought he had killed you, too."

"Killed?" She raised her head. "I remember now. There were gunshots, and I saw Charlie . . ."

"Yes." He nodded. "I arrived just in time to see Charlie go off the bank into the river. The water's swift along here, and he *was* shot. I know how fond you were of him."

Belinda wiped the tears from her cheeks and tried to quiet her sobs. "What happened, Josh? Who was it, firing at us, and how did *you* get here? I don't understand any of this! Who would want to kill Charlie? And you said that you thought he had killed me, too. *Who?*"

Josh pulled her head back down onto his chest and smoothed her hair. "We haven't time now. I'll tell you everything as soon as we're settled in for the night. Right now, if you can manage, you're going to have to do the walking for both of us. There's a hell of a storm coming up, and we will both die from exposure if we spend the night sitting here."

Belinda sat back and looked around. "My horse?"

He shook his head. "Gone. However, the mule is out there on the trail. It's dead, but your supplies are still on its back. Do you think you can get them off, and bring everything here?"

She nodded, grateful to have something to do that would keep her mind off the questions that crowded her mind.

As she started to her feet, Josh held her back. "Wait," he said, his expression tender.

She stared at him without comprehension. Gently, he cupped her face between his big hands and drew it to his own. As his lips pressed hers, the memories of that night in his arms warmed her body and senses. Oh, she had missed him! Say what she might, and fight it as she had, the truth of it was she had missed him terribly. She did not fight the feeling, but let herself relax into the kiss.

When he released her, Josh was smiling. "That's for just being alive, and because I need something to warm me while you're gone."

Despite all that had happened, Belinda found that she could smile, too. A tense, weary smile, but a sign of life, she thought.

Carefully, she rose to her knees, and then to her feet. Her body was sore, but everything seemed to be in working order. Her head hurt abominably, and she was dizzy for a moment as the effort of standing upright caused the painful lump on her head to throb. She could feel the dried blood on her face, but at least motion didn't start the wound to bleeding again.

Thrusting her hands deep into her jacket pockets, Belinda walked toward the trail.

It took her several trips to lug the contents of the mule's pack over to the tree, yet she felt better for the exertion. The sky was very dark now and threatened rain any minute.

Following Josh's instructions, and with him giving what assistance he could, they got the tent up, hammering the pegs in deep and further securing the tent to the trunk of the tree. Fortunately, the tree was on a slight rise, which would help if the rain was heavy enough to saturate the ground.

Josh showed her how to cover the tent floor with the tarpaulin, and she made a fairly comfortable-looking bed in the center of the tent, surrounded by the supplies, which Josh instructed her to stack around the perimeter of the floor.

While the wind tugged and pulled at the tent's canvas sides; they crawled inside and fastened the flap behind them. Away from the wind, it seemed much warmer. Josh collapsed with a groan onto the pile of blankets and sleeping bags, drawing up his leg in pain.

Belinda, barely able to see in the dark, fumbled with the kerosene lantern, and finally got it going. In the warm, flickering light, she examined Josh's foot and ankle. The foot was grotesquely swollen, and Belinda cringed away at its frightening appearance.

Luckily, Josh had managed to slit the boot and get it off before the swelling made that impossible, but the woolen stocking was horribly extended. Gently, as carefully as she could, Belinda tried to peel the stocking away, but found that she couldn't manage it. Josh grunted slightly and handed her a long-bladed knife.

Belinda cut the stocking away, exposing a foot and ankle that looked more like some gross sausage than a human appendage. She couldn't suppress a cry of pity when she saw it. Josh raised up and gazed down at the swollen foot.

She looked at him, appalled. "What can we do? I didn't bring any medical supplies!"

He gave a resigned shrug. "Not much, I'm afraid. I don't think it's broken, just badly sprained, and there's not very damn much you can do in such cases, except stay off your feet for a time. I didn't do it any good, I'm sure, by walking on it after I twisted it."

Belinda sat back on her heels. The walking, she knew, had been to find her. How much she owed this man!

"If you'd heat some water, Belinda, we might soak it. That'll help a little with the pain. Then I'll prop it up, and that's about all we can do. I'm afraid that I'll have to depend on you to do a lot of things until it's better."

Belinda dropped her gaze. "It's the least I can do. After all, you hurt it helping me."

Not wanting to empty their canteens, she took the one

cooking pan and hurried down to the river to fill it. It was much colder, and the low clouds were blue-bellied and moving fast. A few flakes of snow feathered her cheeks on the way back. Josh had the small stove going on her return. Belinda set the pan on to heat.

Then she said determinedly, "Now, tell me everything. What you're doing here, all of it. I'm going mad with curiosity."

Josh didn't hesitate, but told her the story, or at least most of it, starting with his discovery that her tents were gone, and his conversation with Annabelle. The only thing that he omitted was the fact that he was a U.S. marshal, and that he had had Harter and Pugh under surveillance for some time.

Before he had finished, the water was hot and she soaked his ankle and foot. By the end of his story, she had the foot dried and propped up on a roll made from one of the blankets, and Josh was resting more comfortably.

Her cheeks pink from bending over the stove, Belinda fixed them a simple meal from the supplies. Her mind felt loose, her thoughts in danger of running wild. One second she would be thinking sadly of Charlie, and how near she too had come to death, and in the next she would be thinking of the night to come, she and Josh alone in the tent, and a rush of both apprehension and desire would set her hands to trembling.

I must keep talking, she thought crazily. As long as they talked, nothing could happen. Could it?

The food was prepared and she handed a filled plate to Josh who began to eat greedily. "God, this tastes good," he said through a mouthful. "I've hardly had time to stop to eat, or sleep, for days. I didn't realize I was so hungry."

Belinda, picking at her own food, didn't reply. She had been hungry when she started to prepare their supper, but now her appetite was gone. Also, she was puzzling over something Josh had said earlier.

"Josh, you said Annabelle told you Harter acted strangely when he found out more than one print could be made from a negative, and it was just after that that he rode out after Charlie and me. It sounds pretty strange, don't you think? I mean, I believe what you said, that Harter wanted to kill me, not Charlie. But what would my pictures, or the printing of pictures, have to do with it? It doesn't make sense!"

Josh, full now, lay back on the blankets. "I don't know, Belinda. I only know that Harter had to have *some* reason for acting as he did, and the only clue seems to have something to do with your pictures. Do you remember that day when you were lost in the late blizzard, on Crater Lake?"

Belinda shivered and pulled one of the blankets up around her shoulders. "I certainly do! How could I ever forget?"

"Well, we never did learn why your bearer was attacked. Your sled had been searched, and your things strewn all over the ice, but nothing was taken. Remember? It made no sense at the time, and it still doesn't."

She pulled the blanket closer. "You mean, it wasn't some kind of an accident? That, well, that someone clubbed the bearer, just so I would get lost in the storm, and die?" She shook her head. "No, I can't believe that. It's just too incredible!"

Josh shrugged. "Maybe there was something in your sled that someone wanted, and maybe they just didn't care if you lived or died."

"But what could I have that anybody would want? I only had what every other person going to the Klondike had . . . supplies, food, the necessities."

Josh raised his closed hand, forefinger in the air. "Ah, but you had one thing *more,* your picture-taking equipment, and the pictures you had already taken."

"But a lot of that was on the other sled, at least my negatives were."

"And maybe that's why nothing was taken. Maybe what they were after *was* the negatives."

Belinda was bewildered. "But Josh, a picture? Somebody tried to kill me because of a *picture?* And you're saying that's why Chet Harter tried to kill me today? That doesn't make any kind of sense!"

"You won't get an argument from me on that, but it's the only reason I can come up with, crazy as it sounds." He yawned suddenly. "Well, I'm too tired to think about it now. I don't know how long it's been since I slept, and tonight I'm going to make up for it, wind, snow, blizzard, come what may."

"You don't think Harter will come back, to try and finish it?"

Josh began to pull the blankets up around him. "No, he's badly wounded himself. His arm looked useless, and I think I got him in the leg, too. He's lost all stomach for it. He's on his way back to Dawson, if he can make it that far, or at least to that Indian village. It will be some time before Chet Harter is in shape to try anything again . . ."

The last words trailed off and Belinda saw that he was asleep, his face relaxed and his expression peaceful. One hand was outflung, half-open, and gently she touched it. He didn't stir.

She sat for a long time, studying his face in the lantern light, her thoughts switching directions as capriciously as the wind whining around the tent. He looked so young, so vulnerable, now that sleep had hidden those penetrating eyes and relaxed his mouth.

Although Belinda understood his need for sleep, a part of her vacillating mind kept hoping that he would wake up. She didn't want to admit it to herself, but another part of her knew that she wanted him to make love to her. Her thoughts went back again and again to the night they had spent together on Crater Lake, and the memory brought a flush of heat to her body despite the icy wind seeping into the tent.

Shivering, she raised the blankets and slipped in beside him.

It was warm, like being in a nest, and she curled up next to his body, hoping that her nearness might rouse him, but he slept on. She moved closer still; he only stirred and muttered in his sleep.

Oh, she was wicked, wicked! He was dead-tired, and hurting. He had been riding for days without rest, and all because of her, and here she wanted to wake him. She was shameless, a wanton-hussy. But oh, the thought of his arms around her, of his body next to hers . . .

She lay for what seemed hours in a torment of desire, and then without being conscious of it, slipped into sleep, one arm thrown across his body.

When Belinda awakened, it was to the awareness that

someone was removing her clothing, piece by piece.

Startled fully awake, she sat bolt upright, as the memory of yesterday's events crashed in on her. Her jacket had been removed and her blouse was off one shoulder, exposing her breasts to the chill morning air. In the dim light filtering through the canvas, she saw Josh smiling at her. He looked fit and rested, and his eyes sparkled.

She let out the breath she had been holding and sank back upon the blanket. "For a moment I didn't know where I was."

He only smiled and pushed the blouse farther off her shoulder, so that his fingers could caress the soft skin of her breasts. She shivered as he gently stroked the nipple.

She tried to frown, saying, "Oh, *now* he wants to make love! In the daylight, when it's time to get up." But she did not push his hand away, and he kept on with his slow exploration of her flesh.

"It's the best time, my sweet," he whispered. "Didn't you know that?"

It was strange, she mused, how the ice-blue of his eyes could turn warm and tender in moments like this.

She gasped aloud, as he bent to her, his lips seeking her mouth. She had no will to object. The feeling of the night before came back, and all of the secret places of her body seemed to throb.

"Oh, Josh!" she said against his throat. She wanted to tell him that she had missed him, but she held it back. It would be an admission of weakness, and she didn't want to show him that.

"Sweet, sweet Belinda! God, how I've missed you! How I've dreamed of you!"

His lips pressed again on hers, and it was as if a kind of electric current flowed between them, so sweet that it made tears come to her eyes. It made her feel vibrantly alive, as if a vital part of her, awakened that night on Crater Lake, had remained dormant, awaiting the touch of his mouth.

His hands were moving down now. His fingers brushed across her stomach, and she sucked in her breath and waited without breathing, for him to continue. He did not and it took her an agonizing moment to realize that he had encountered the barrier of her belt and trousers. With a mutter of impatience, she helped him undress her, then assisted him with his own clothes.

There was a trying moment when she pulled his trousers down over his swollen foot, and Josh moaned with pain; but then that was past, and they were together, body to body, under the blanket.

His hands were rough and warm as he stroked her back and buttocks, and then he bent his head to take her nipple into his mouth. The touch of his lips was again electric, and she shuddered.

"Oh, Belinda! Sweet, it's been too long!"

Then, with a kind of rough tenderness, he was atop her, and Belinda felt the prod of his sex along her inner thigh.

Eagerly, she opened for him, pulling him into her with hungry insistence. Josh moaned softly as he penetrated her. The joy that Belinda felt at his entrance was more than sexual. It was as if the physical act was part of a greater joining, the meeting of spirit and mind as well as body.

Whatever happened after this, she thought joyously, even if he had to leave her again, was worth it. At least she had this.

And then all rational thought fled, as their bodies flowed together, straining toward that moment of sweet, shattering rapture when they would be totally one.

Afterward, as they lay quietly on the blankets, Belinda experienced an enervating melancholy. They would have a few days here—Josh wouldn't be able to walk for a week, maybe more—and then what would happen? Would it be the way it had been after Crater Lake? Would Josh go on his way, his mysterious way, and she be left alone?

She remembered what she had thought a short time ago, that it was worth it. Well, perhaps it was. What did they say about love? That it was better to have loved and lost than never to . . .

She sighed, and Josh raised his head to look over at her.

"Belinda? I want to tell you this now, so that there won't be any more misunderstandings. I love you, and you're the only woman I've ever spoken those words to."

"Oh, and I love you, too!" Belinda felt as if her heart would explode. Giving him a radiant smile, she stretched her hands toward his face, but he caught them and held them fast, his expression sober.

"No, Belinda, wait until you hear all that I have to say."

Her smile began to fade. What was he going to tell her? What he had once before, that he could make no commitment, and that he could not explain the reason why?

Josh saw her expression and shook his head quickly. "No, no, my sweet, it's not what you're probably thinking. It's just that there are some things that I have to explain, and some things that I *cannot* explain, just yet. You're going to have to trust me, and wait for me, if you will, until

I . . . well, I do what I have to do."

Gaze clinging to his face, Belinda listened skeptically.

"First of all, there is something that I must do here, in Dawson, and I am still not at liberty to explain. To do so might place you in danger, but would also violate the rules of . . . uh, my employer. At any rate, until my job is finished, I won't be able to see you often, or spend much time with you. What I am here to do must come first."

"Then it's just like the time you left me at Crater Lake," she said dully, all the joy gone out of her.

He grasped her by the shoulders and shook her gently. "No, you goose, that's what I'm trying to tell you, damnit! It's not like that at all. Things are different now. Between us, I mean. When this is done, well, let's just say that I'll be free to do what I want, and what I want is to marry you!"

Belinda was momentarily taken aback. She had been so prepared for the worst, that she hadn't dared even hope for the best. She flung her arms around his neck, and kissed him with such passion that he was soon aroused again, and the next few minutes were spent in intense celebration of their declared love for each other.

It took a week for Josh's ankle to heal sufficiently for him to travel. During that time, Josh and Belinda did not stray far from the tent under the tree. The storm that had come up that first night blew itself out the next day, and the snow that had fallen melted when the sun came out. The weather warmed, making the days pleasant again.

The days passed all too quickly for Belinda. Never had she been so happy, and Josh, too, seemed content to just be with her.

They stretched out their supplies with fish caught in the river, and with small game for which Josh made traps. The rest of their time was spent in love-making and talking, telling all the secrets that lovers share.

They didn't see another living soul during the entire time they were there.

When Josh's ankle was strong enough to walk on, they packed up what gear they could carry and headed down the river for the Indian village.

Progress was slow. Josh's ankle was still tender, and they were both carrying heavy loads, as there was Belinda's photographic equipment to tote, as well as food and blankets. She absolutely refused to leave her equipment behind.

They rested at the village for two days, and managed to persuade the Indian chief to loan them the only horse in the village and an escort to see them back to Dawson.

They traveled a little faster after that. Their gear was loaded onto a travois-like sled, and Josh and Belinda took turns riding the horse, while the Indian trotted alongside.

Belinda was looking forward to reaching Dawson. She would have liked to stay forever with Josh in the little tent under the tree, but since she could not, she was now impatient for him to finish whatever it was he had to do, so they could be together.

Josh, on the other hand, approached Dawson with something akin to reluctance. His ankle still pained him, and he would have to move about gingerly for a time yet; and it was important, once back in Dawson, that he be able to quickly bring about a successful conclusion to what he had been sent here to do.

He didn't know how badly Chet Harter was hurt, but he

knew that the man was still alive, and he was bound to be angry and vengeful—no matter that he had tried to kill Josh and Belinda.

Also, it seemed clear now that Harter knew who Josh Rogan was, and if that was so, Pugh knew as well. They were out to eliminate him and he had to get them first, preferably not with a gun, but with a warrant for their arrest, based on hard evidence—which he did not yet have, damnit! If only some of the people involved, people who had suffered at their hands, would come forward to testify as to what they knew!

Josh had experienced something very special this past week, something which he did not want to lose. He did not want to die *now*, when the future held such promise.

If he was a different type of man, he might say to hell with it—quit now, and leave Dawson with Belinda. Go somewhere else and start over in safety. But he was committed to do a job, *this* job, and if he was to live in peace with himself, he had to finish it. Then he could resign in good conscience, tell the gray man in Washington what he could do with his job, and settle down to enjoy the good life with Belinda.

≈17≈

Chet Harter lay in the big bed in Annabelle's room above the barroom, scowling at her. She was arranging her hair at the carved dressing table.

His arm and leg hurt like hell, and anger boiled just beneath the surface of his mind. Damn that federal snoop,

Rogan! Harter had thought the bastard was dead, killed in the tent fire. And damn the Lee woman, too. The pair of them were going to be sorry they had ever heard the name of Chet Harter.

He ground his teeth and shifted in the bed, his leg throbbing. The shot had gone through cleanly, breaking no bones, but the bullet in his arm had shattered both muscle *and* bone, and would require much longer to heal. Well, at least he was alive, and no one except Pugh and Annabelle knew that he was here.

After the fracas on the river, he had managed to make it to the Indian village, and the old medicine man there had patched him up sufficiently so that he had been able to get back to Dawson and a real doctor.

It had been a nightmarish trip, getting back here, but the real hell had been facing Pugh, and telling the fat man the bad news. Pugh was now convinced that Chet Harter was a prize bungler. Harter seethed at the memory of the things Pugh had said to him, all in that cold, precise voice, like a schoolmaster with a classroom of dolts.

Well, when this was all over, Pugh would pay, too. His debt was long outstanding, growing every day.

Harter lay back among the pillows. His day would come. He had plenty of free time now, and nothing to do but think. He would dream up a plan, a plan that would take care of them all.

He watched irritably as Annabelle pinched her cheeks to heighten their color. Even she angered him now, in his present mood.

"Come here!" he said harshly.

Annabelle looked at him in the mirror. "What?"

"Come here, I said. I feel in the mood for a little personal attention."

She fluttered her hands. "But your leg, your arm? You can't . . ."

His smile was cold. "There are ways of doing things that a nice girl like you doesn't even know about. But I'll teach you, dollie. I'll teach you!"

She came toward him hesitantly, and when he saw her frightened expression, his smile widened, and he began to enjoy himself.

From the stairs, Montana Leeds surveyed the interior of the Poke. It was an ordinary evening in the place—crowded, noisy and a little rough. Even while Montana noted this, his thoughts were busy elsewhere.

He had been in a quandary ever since he had witnessed the stabbing of the man named Doober more than three weeks earlier. Each day, he recalled it in vivid detail, and each night, it haunted his dreams.

He should go to the Northwest Mounted, he knew that; but if he did, would it accomplish anything? No body had been reported, and the man had evidently been a stranger in town, with no one to miss him. What was he supposed to tell the Mounties? That Lester Pugh and Chet Harter had killed a man in cold blood, while he, Montana Leeds, crouching like a shivering coward behind the bar and made no move to interfere?

He liked to think of himself as being as brave as the next man, yet Montana shivered at the thought of the look that would come into Pugh's eyes, if he ever learned that any employee of his had carried tales to the Mounties!

Anyway, how could he prove the crime with no body? It would be foolish to try; worse, it would be suicide. And besides, he had almost enough money now to leave here. So why rock the boat, even if it was loaded with garbage? In a month or two, he could clear out and forget this place, and Lester Pugh, as if they had never existed. If only his conscience would be as practical!

He sighed, feeling scorn for himself. He glanced at his pocket watch. It was time to announce the show, a chore that had fallen to him this week, since the bartender who usually did it was home sick.

Putting the watch back in his pocket, and smoothing down his hair, Montana walked on down the stairs and across the barroom to the small stage.

He went through the usual extravagant praise of Alabaster's talents, and the crowd gave its usual ovation. The little lady had certainly become popular.

As the curtains drew back, Montana stepped down into the audience, and found himself a place from which he could watch. He really enjoyed Alabaster's singing; her voice was as pure and sweet as spring water, reminding him of another time and place, and Alabaster's fair skin and dark hair reminded him of his wife, Mary, when she was young.

The piano player began his introduction, and Montana waited in pleasant anticipation for Alabaster to appear. He hadn't seen much of her lately, since Harter had returned from an unexplained absence, with his arm and leg wounded.

Privately, Montana wished that whoever had shot Harter had been a little more accurate and eliminated the man entirely. Harter was the kind of person the world was better off without; and it was a shame that a sweet child like Alabaster had gotten involved with him.

A wave of grumblings passed over the room, rousing Montana from his thoughts, and he realized that the piano player had been playing for some time, and that Alabaster was not yet on the stage. The crowd was growing restive.

Where was she?

And then she was there, stepping lightly out of the wings, a vision in pink and white, carrying a large, white feather fan in her right hand.

As she lowered the fan to sing, Montana felt his stomach tighten. What in the name of heaven had happened to her face? Even the heavy theatrical make-up could not hide the purple bruise that marked her left cheek and eye.

The audience, drunk and boisterous, didn't seem to notice or care, but Montana felt himself growing tight with anger. It had to be Harter. The son-of-a-bitch had struck her!

Bravely, Alabaster went on with her song, but her usual flair was missing; she sang mechanically, and although the voice was as pure as ever, the feeling was just not there.

She ran off the stage immediately after her last number, as if she wanted to be seen as little as possible. As she left the stage to the usual accompaniment of cheers and shouts, Montana hurried after her. He wanted to catch up with her before she returned to her room, and Harter. He caught her just as she reached the top of the stairs. "Alabaster! Miss White!" he said, reaching for her arm.

She cringed away from him, and he swore at Harter under his breath. More gently, he said, "Don't be alarmed,

Miss White. I want to help you."

She looked at him uncertainly, her eyes suspiciously bright, and then she threw back her head. "Why, that's very nice, Mr. Leeds, it really is. But why would you think that I need help? Everything's fine, just fine!"

He shook his head impatiently. "You know that's not so, Alabaster . . . Miss White. Somebody has hurt you, that's plain, and I mean to see that it doesn't happen again."

She blushed, and covered the left side of her face with her hand. "Oh, you mean my face! Why, nobody hit me, Mr. Leeds. I fell! Yes, I tripped and fell against my bedroom door. Silly me! I know it must look awful!"

She smiled and blinked her eyes in instinctive coquetry, and Montana's heart went out to her. He took a step closer. "Look, Miss. If you're afraid he'll hurt you for talking, or if you're afraid he'll hurt me for interfering, don't be."

She shook her head. "No, Mr. Leeds, it's nothing like that at all. Now if you'll excuse me I have to change costumes."

There wasn't anything Montana could do but step aside and let her go. He watched as she walked down the hall to her room, opened the door, and went in. Before she closed the door, he heard Harter's voice raised in anger.

He half-turned away, then halted, torn, by indecision.

As Annabelle closed the door behind her, she felt as if she was closing out all hope. Still, she couldn't unburden herself to Montana Leeds. He couldn't help her—Chet would have him fired if he interfered. Besides, it would only make Chet angrier, and he would then take it out on her.

"What the hell do you think you're doing?"

The bark of Chet's voice reminded her that she was leaning against the door with her eyes closed. She moved away from the door, wearing a bright smile. "I was just resting a bit, Chet. Singing can be a lot of work, you know. Well, they really loved me tonight, just as usual." She began stripping off the long gloves. "And I sang the song about . . ."

"Who the hell cares what song you sang? Come here and straighten up this bed. I feel like there's a whole pile of tailings in here with me!"

"Of course, honey."

Anxious to keep him placated, Annabelle threw down her fan and gloves and approached the bed. The sheets were full of food crumbs, and she swept these to the floor, tightened the sheets, and fluffed the pillows.

Harter, grunting, got back onto the bed, settling back against the pillows. He stared at her. "That's the new dress, huh?"

She nodded, pleased at his interest. "Do you like it? I think it's very flattering."

She turned, showing off the back and sides, and when she again faced him she saw the now-familiar light in his eyes. Oh no, not again! Before, she had found pleasure in their being together, even if Chet, now and then, was inclined to be a little rough. But now that he was bedridden, it had changed. He grew more and more demanding, and brutal, every day; and the things he forced her to do!

Annabelle shuddered. She hadn't known people did things like that, and she didn't like it. Still, she had not objected until yesterday, when the thing he had asked of her was particularly revolting.

She fingered the bruise on her cheek, and thought about the way he had looked at her when he hit her, eyes narrow and filled with a sort of glittering pleasure that she could not understand. Chet had told her once that he distrusted Pugh because the man enjoyed hurting people. It was strange that he didn't recognize the same trait in himself.

His harsh voice broke into her thoughts, "Come here, dollie. Let's have a little comfort, hmmm?"

Annabelle tried to draw back but not quickly enough. He caught her wrist with his good hand, squeezing so hard that she gasped.

"I've got to change," she stammered. "Let me hang up this dress and . . ."

Harter smiled, a rictus of the lips. "Nah. I want you to do it with the dress on. It'll add something. I've never had it done by a woman in a fancy dress like that before."

Inexorably, she was being pulled toward the bed. Despite her fear of what he would do to her if she fought him, Annabelle held back, twisting wildly in his grasp.

"No!" she cried out. "Please, Chet! No!"

"Come here, you silly bitch," he said between gritted teeth. "You'll do as you're told, and damn well like it!"

With a mighty yank, he pulled her onto the bed, and then released her. As she tried to scramble away, he struck her, backhanding her across the right cheek. Her head snapped back, and she screamed with pain.

As she slumped across the bed, she dimly heard the sound of crashing wood. She raised her head to see the bedroom door standing wide open, and the figure of Montana Leeds looming in the doorway, his face dark with rage.

Harter sat up in bed and winced. "What the hell!"

Montana made it to the bed in two steps, and reached down to take Annabelle's arm. "Come on, Alabaster, I'm taking you out of here."

Annabelle came to her feet, tears running down her bruised face. Sobbing, she allowed herself to be pushed behind Montana's broad back.

Harter said furiously, "You must be crazy, Leeds! If Pugh learns of this!" He struggled to rise, but the wound in his leg prevented him. "You get your stupid face out of this room, and I might, just might, forget this ever happened!"

Montana's body began to shake. All the things that he knew about Harter came boiling up in his mind. "Listen, you bastard! I'm taking Miss White out of here, and you'd better forget about trying to stop me, or *I'll* forget that you're crippled and bust the hell out of that slimy face of yours!"

The violence in his voice was frightening, and Annabelle saw Harter blanche and draw back on the bed.

Montana turned to her. "Come on, Alabaster. Let's get out of here. I'll have one of the girls come up and get your things."

He took her arm and began to propel her toward the door, but catching a glimpse of the triptych on the dresser, Annabelle pulled back. "Wait! Just a minute, please!"

Darting to the dresser, she folded the silver frame and hugged it to her breast, then let Montana shepherd her from the room. Feeling empty and disconsolate, she allowed him to lead her where he would, which proved to be his room: neat, small, and sparsely furnished.

Montana eased her down onto the bed, where she sat,

unmoving, holding the picture in her lap.

Why couldn't things go right for her? Everything she attempted seemed to fall apart. Thank God for this nice man. If he hadn't intervened, Chet might have marked her face forever. Tears squeezed from her eyes and down her cheeks. Things had seemed to be going well, at least, relatively so. And then, this business about the picture, and Chet's going away, and coming back wounded, which he refused to talk about. Annabelle thought that his being wounded had changed him, but now she faced the fact that bed confinement had only brought to the surface what had been there all the time. Chet Harter was a cruel, stupid man, and she had been too blind to see it.

What would her mother say if she was alive? At the thought of her mother, the tears came faster, and Annabelle opened the frame in her lap and looked at the pictures through swollen eyes.

Montana, standing over her, patted her awkwardly on the shoulder. "Now, now, Alabaster, don't you cry. I'll see that Chet Harter doesn't come near you ever again."

Annabelle wept all the harder. "I'm not Al . . . Alabaster!"

His deep voice sounded embarrassed. "Well, that's all right, my dear. I never figured it was your real name. Not many people up here do use their real names. Matter of fact, Montana isn't my real name, either."

"Oh!" she wailed. "I'm so ashamed! My sister tried to warn me, but I wouldn't listen. What would my mama say if she could see me now?"

She closed the frame in her lap, and Montana asked, "Is that a picture of your mother?"

She held it out to him. "Yes, on the left side."

Montana held the delicate frame gently in his big hands, and thumbed it open. There was a long silence as he stared at pictures within. "You say this is your mother, and your sister?" he said in a strange, choked voice.

Annabelle nodded without looking at him.

"And your real name? What might that be, if you don't mind my asking?"

"Annabelle. Annabelle Lee."

"Oh, my God!" he said in a whisper.

There was such a long silence that Annabelle, despite her unhappiness, grew curious. She glanced up. Montana's face was very pale, and she could see his Adam's apple move as he swallowed.

"Belinda?" he whispered. "And Mary?"

Annabelle said in astonishment, "Mary? That's my mama's name! How . . . ? How did you know my mama's name?"

Montana tore his gaze away from the triptych and looked down at her. There were tears in his eyes.

"Why, girl," he said in a wondering voice. "I'm your daddy, yours and Belinda's. I am Morgan Lee!"

Josh, his ankle bandaged inside his boot, sat with his leg propped up on a stump, as he went over the notes in the battered notebook.

He had left Belinda in Dawson, at her new quarters above the new photo studio, which was not quite ready to open for business as yet.

When they had first reached town, she had wanted to report Harter's attack to the Mounties, and it was only with a great deal of difficulty that Josh had managed to dissuade her.

Since he had not been able to tell her his real reason—that if Harter was arrested now, it might be very difficult to prove Pugh's criminality—he put it to her on the basis that going to the Mounties might place Annabelle in danger, since in all likelihood, Harter was back in Dawson and hiding out at the Poke.

Viewing it in this light, Belinda had reluctantly agreed, promising to wait at least a few days, until Annabelle could be gotten out of the Poke and away from Harter. She had also agreed not to try to see Annabelle on her own, as this might trigger Harter into violence; she had promised to hold off until they had a talk, and worked out a solution to the problem.

And so now, here he was, desperately trying to figure out a way in which the situation could be brought to a successful conclusion.

In the distance he could hear the sound of a pick axe, as Two-Step banged away at the half-thawed permafrost that his fire had partially melted. Sinking a mine shaft in the ground here was no easy task. The permafrost kept the ground frozen from fifteen to forty feet beneath the surface all year round, and it was necessary to build a fire about six feet long and four feet wide, keep it burning for about ten hours or so, and then dig up the thawed earth—a slow and laborious process. Even in the summer only the top few feet of earth thawed.

Josh didn't know why the old codger was pushing himself so hard. The claim was worthless, and he had told the old man that he didn't need to work so hard, but Two-Step was a hard man to argue with. The old devil was stubbornly independent, and hard to talk out of something.

Josh sighed, and again studied his notes. There was enough here, he was sure, to put Pugh and Harter away, if he only had a witness or two to back him up. Without at least one good witness, the case could easily be thrown out of court, and all this time and work would have gone for nothing, while Pugh and Harter remained free to ply their criminal trade.

Josh thought of Henly, the prospector whose claim he had visited after Two-Step came on the scene. Henly had seemed to have plenty of information as to what went on in Dawson, and Josh suspected that he knew even more than he had told. Could Henly be convinced that he should become a witness for the State?

And the business of Harter and Annabelle's pictures? What had *that* been all about? Josh sighed, folded the notebook, and put it away, as No-Ears Riley slunk up to him and planted his forefeet firmly on Josh's thigh.

"Yawrp?" said Riley questioningly.

Josh, who had begun to understand the animal a little, grinned and ruffled the fur on Riley's head. "Hungry, are you? Well, let's see what we can do about that."

In the slat cooler, hung from between two slender saplings and draped with damp rags, Josh found a stub end of cooked bacon. Cutting it into pieces, he put it on a stump for the cat.

Riley gave him a grateful, "Yawrp," and settled down to eat, while Josh cleaned his knife and put it away. He had about decided that there was only one thing to do.

He would make one more sweep along the river, and try

to collect as many witnesses as he could. Then, with his own and Belinda's testimony against Chet Harter, he would move against the pair, arresting both.

In Montana Leeds's room, Annabelle stared at him in blank astonishment. She could not believe what she was hearing. "What?"

"I'm your daddy, Morgan Lee."

"My daddy! *You're* my daddy?"

"I find that hard to believe, too." He shook his head in wonder. "But if this is a picture of your mother, and her name is Mary, and if your name is Annabelle, and your sister's is Belinda, why then I sure enough am your real and natural father!" Tears welled up in his eyes, and he held his arms out tentatively.

Annabelle, at first numbed by the shock of it, began to feel a growing sense of awe. Her father! This big, kind man was her father—the father she had always longed for. With a glad cry, she threw herself into his arms, and he hugged her gently, rocking from side to side.

At last, with tears still in their eyes, they broke the embrace and stood back. They both felt a slight embarrassment.

"Well now," he said awkwardly, "since you can't stay here, maybe I'd best try and find a room for you over at the hotel."

Annabelle shook her head. "No, Montana . . . I mean Daddy . . ." The word sounded strange on her tongue. "No, I'll go to Belinda's. She had a building constructed down the street, while she was away, a studio with living quarters above. I don't know if she's back from her trip yet, but even if she isn't, I can stay there. Will you have one of the girls bring my things?"

He smiled. "I sure will. That is, I'll have one of the girls get your things together, and then I'll bring them over myself." He stroked her hair. "Just think, *my* daughter! I can hardly wait to see your sister, and your mother. How, how is Mary? Does she ever talk about me?"

Annabelle turned her face away, tears flooding her eyes. "Oh, Daddy! Didn't you know? She's . . . she's gone. It's been three years now."

Morgan Lee's face paled and his eyes filled with pain. "I waited too long. I always meant to go back, every year I meant to make the last away from my home and family. But I waited too long. That's the story of my life. My timing has always been terrible."

Annabelle put her hand on his arm. "She loved you, Daddy. Even through all those years, she talked about you and never spoke badly of you," she lied. "She always said that you would come back some day."

He said brokenly, "I've been a hell of a husband and father, haven't I? I wouldn't blame you, or Belinda, if you didn't want to speak to me again."

"Daddy . . . Look at me." When he looked into her eyes, Annabelle said sincerely, "I'm more happy than I can say to have found a father after all these years. Belinda will be, too, you'll see." Yet, she wasn't all that sure—sometimes, Belinda could be so uncompromising and unforgiving in her pride.

Belinda was putting up curtains in the small sitting room in her new quarters above the studio, when she heard the footsteps on the outside wooden stairway coming up the side of the building.

It sounded like more than one person, and for a moment her heart beat irregularly, fear coming up into her throat. What if it was Chet Harter? Or someone else bent upon doing her harm?

Since returning to Dawson, she had felt constantly on edge, startled by sudden sounds and almost paranoid in her wariness. She could not forget poor Charlie, and the shot that had come out of nowhere to catapult him into the river. She had never realized how truly valuable Charlie was until now, now that he was gone. He had stood as a buffer between her and the hardships of the life here—bandy-legged and short, but stalwart.

Belinda had promised Josh that she would not go to Douglas Mackenzie about Harter until Annabelle was safely out of harm's way, but all of her instincts cried out for revenge. Harter had killed Charlie, and had tried to kill her! He belonged in jail! She did not feel right about the waiting, although she recognized the necessity for getting Annabelle out of danger before they tried to flush Harter.

But *when* was Josh going to do something about getting Annabelle away? They had been back in Dawson two whole days now, and she hadn't heard one word from him.

The footsteps had now reached the landing outside her door, and then there was a knock on the door, which caused her heartbeat to accelerate again. Should she keep silent? But maybe it was Josh!

"Who's there?" she called out, ashamed to hear her voice quiver.

"Bee? It's me, Annabelle. I'm so glad you're here! Let

me in. You're not going to believe what's happened!"

The doorknob rattled, and Belinda, her fears replaced by delight, ran to open the door. Thank God, it was Annabelle, and she was all right!

She flung the door wide, then gasped aloud. It was Annabelle, all right, but Annabelle as Belinda had never seen her. Her cheeks were purple with bruises, and her eyes were red from weeping. Strangely enough, her eyes also had a look of happiness. She threw herself into Belinda's arms. Belinda stared in bewilderment at the man with her—a tall, broad-shouldered, middle-aged man, who was looking at her in the strangest way. Whatever was going on?

"Oh, Bee! Oh, just wait until I tell you what's happened! It's so wonderful, you'll never, never believe it!"

Belinda looked in confusion from her sister to the tall man, and back again, finally remembering to step back so that they could enter the room.

"I'll never believe what? You've said that twice, and what happened to your face?"

The stranger closed the door behind them, smiling at her in a way that struck Belinda as paternal.

Annabelle, in a flurry of impatience, clutched Belinda's arm. "Bee, do you know who this is? Can you guess?" She reached out her other hand to take hold of the stranger's arm.

Belinda, feeling like Alice in Wonderland, could only shake her head. "Of course, I don't know who he is!" she said crossly. "How can I, since I've never seen him before in my life?"

"That's where you're wrong." Annabelle smiled secretively, and drew a deep breath. "This man is our father, Morgan Lee!"

Belinda blinked, thinking, She's out of her mind. She's been in an accident or something, and she's not thinking straight.

Annabelle smiled tremulously. "I found it hard to believe, too, but it's true, Bee. We found out when he saw Mama's picture. Tell her, Daddy. Tell her it's true!"

The tall man stepped forward, holding his hat in his hand. "I . . . I know that it's hard to believe, and harder to accept, Belinda, but it is true. I married Mary Clanahan in 1875, and we had a baby girl we named Annabelle. Two years later, we had another daughter we named Belinda. That's you."

Belinda, feeling faint, reached blindly for a chair. "This . . . this is unexpected," she said slowly. Then she smiled. "But you do look pretty much as I remember you . . . *if* I really remember you!"

He returned her smile. "And you both turned out prettier even than I would have expected. You, Belinda, look an awful lot like your mother, my dear Mary, may she rest in peace."

A great sadness came over his face and he looked away.

"Why didn't you ever come home?" She couldn't quite bring herself to call this man father. Not yet. "All those years . . ."

He sighed. "I always meant to, you know. Every year, I would say to myself that I had to stop chasing after rainbows and return to my family, but somehow I never did. Good intentions never lived up to. That's the sad story of my life. Can you ever forgive me for all those lost years? I swear to you that I've always loved you!"

He looked at them, pleadingly, first one, then the other, and Annabelle burst into tears and flung herself into his arms. "Oh, yes, Daddy, yes!"

Belinda, hesitating, searched her mind and heart. He had been thoughtless, and selfish, but should *she,* because of the years lost, deprive them of all the years that were to come, when they could be a family?

"You do have a lot of gall, you know," she said stiffly. "Asking us to take you back after all those years."

"I know," he said humbly. "But if I didn't have a lot of gall, I probably wouldn't be alive today, the kind of life I've lived."

Belinda laughed, then spread her arms wide. "Welcome home, Daddy!" She stepped into his arms. Morgan Lee squeezed both his daughters to him.

Their reunion was interrupted by the sound of footsteps on the stairs again, and a knock on the door. Belinda, secure now in happiness, went unafraid to answer it.

Douglas Mackenzie stood on the landing, his wide-brimmed hat in his hand, his red coat brilliant in the sunlight. "Belinda! Someone told me they saw you, that you were back in Dawson. Why didn't you let me know?"

His expression was reserved, but Belinda knew that he was far from happy with her. She took his hand, and drew him inside. "Douglas, the most wonderful thing has happened!"

He followed her into the room, but his expression was still guarded. "What wonderful thing is that?"

She smiled. "Douglas Mackenzie, I would like to present you to my father, Morgan Lee."

Douglas slanted a look of surprise at Morgan, who nodded affably and said, "Sergeant Mackenzie and I have met before."

"Yes." Douglas was frowning. "Montana Leeds, the manager of the Poke. Am I right?"

Morgan spread his hands. "Both the name and the position are now in the past tense."

Douglas turned his frown on Belinda. "You never told me that your father was here in Dawson."

"That's quite true. Because I didn't know he was in Dawson, until today. I just found out two minutes ago. It's a long story, and it will take a bit of telling, but I assure you that this is our father. We've been apart for a very long time."

Douglas said somewhat stiffly, "Well then, perhaps I'd better go. You'll want to celebrate your reunion . . ."

Belinda squeezed his arm affectionately. "Don't be silly, Douglas! Stay and celebrate with us. You're my friend, and I hope that you'll become friends with Annabelle and my father. Besides," she became serious, "I have something to tell you. Something important. Now that Annabelle is safe, I can tell you. I couldn't before."

He looked at her curiously and seemed to relax slightly.

Men were strange, Belinda thought. Their pride was so easily wounded. Douglas had not wanted her to go on the river trip, and he had been hurt and angry that she had gone anyway, against his wishes. Now the fact that she had been home for two days and had not told him obviously upset him further. She could only hope that he would not say, "I told you so," when she told him of Charlie's death and her own escape. Would Douglas understand that she had been forced to wait until Annabelle was safely away from Harter? She hoped so.

She nodded to Annabelle. "I'll put on some tea, and I have some cookies from the bakery. We'll have a real party!"

Douglas was looking around. "Where's Charlie? He's the one for tea. I didn't see him around downstairs, either."

Belinda was evasive. "Charlie's not here, and the downstairs studio isn't quite ready yet . . . I'd better put the water on for tea."

She hurried into the small kitchen, so that Douglas couldn't hammer at her about it. As she put the kettle on, Belinda's eyes filled with tears. If Charlie could have been with them now, it truly would be a festive occasion.

While the water boiled, she got out the cookies and serving dishes. As she arranged things on the tray, the kitchen door opened, and Annabelle swept in. She hugged Belinda with an openness that Belinda hadn't seen in her sister in a long time.

"Oh, Bee! I'm *soo* happy!" Annabelle said. "After all these years, we have a father!"

Belinda patted her shoulder. "Me, too, Annabelle. And it's nice to have you here. I wish you'd stay."

Annabelle looked down at her hands. "I guess you'll get your wish, since I'm leaving Chet. He's beat on me for the last time." Gingerly, she touched her bruised face.

Belinda sucked in her breath. Angrily, she said, "Chet Harter did *that* to you?"

Annabelle nodded. "I'm afraid so. I've tried to tell myself that he's not really that way, not mean and cruel, that it's only because he's hurt and bedridden, but . . . well,

I know better now, Bee, and much as I hate to say this, you were right about him."

Belinda held her sister close and patted her shoulder as if she were a child, then pushed her back and looked deep into her eyes. "Annabelle, there's something that you should know. I know how Chet Harter got those bullet wounds. He was trying to kill me. He *did* kill Charlie."

Annabelle drew in her breath with a shuddering sound, and her eyes got huge and round.

Belinda continued, "He followed us all the way from Dawson. I would be dead now if Josh Rogan hadn't come after me. The only reason I haven't gone to the Mounties, is because Josh said we should wait until we were sure that you were out of Harter's reach. Thank God, you came here on your own! Now I can tell Douglas."

Annabelle bit her lip. Her face was pale under the purple bruises. You're sure it was Chet? I can hardly believe . . ."

Belinda looked at her closely, "Of course, I'm sure! Josh saw him, and he's wounded in the leg and the arm, isn't he? That's because Josh shot him. Why do you ask? What's the matter? I should think you'd be glad that Harter's going to be punished for all that he's done!"

Annabelle nodded quickly. "Oh, I am, I am! It's just that it all seems so . . . so strange. Why should Chet want to kill you? What possible reason could he have?"

Belinda shook her head. "I honestly don't know, Annabelle, although I think it has something to do with a picture, or pictures. Other than that, it's all a big mystery. Oh! There goes the kettle."

"I'll take care of it." Annabelle waved a hand. "You go on back and entertain the men. I'd . . . I'd like to be alone for a bit, anyway."

Belinda stared at her sister, but Annabelle averted her gaze. She motioned again and said in a choked voice, "Please, Bee?"

Belinda shrugged and left the room. The two men were deep in conversation when Belinda reentered the other room. They seem to like one another, she thought, relieved.

Douglas glanced up and smiled. He seemed more at ease now. "Your father has some incredible stories to tell, Belinda. He's seen a lot of things in his travels."

She laughed. "The better to entertain us during the long winter nights coming up. I'll be looking forward to hearing them. But Douglas, I have something much more serious to talk to you about. I want to file a complaint against Chet Harter for murder and attempted murder."

Douglas reared back, frowning. "Are you serious, Belinda?"

She nodded. "Dead serious. Harter killed Charlie," her voice began to tremble, "and he tried to kill me."

As briefly as she could, she told them of what had happened, leaving out only the details of the time spent alone with Josh. Even so, Douglas's lips tightened when she related how they had had to camp together until Josh's ankle was well enough to walk on.

"This Rogan . . . he's the chap I met in your tent one day, the one who tried to cause a scene?"

Belinda nodded silently, the memory of what had happened immediately after that scene bringing a flush to her cheeks.

"Not a very reliable chap, it seems to me," Douglas said musingly. He cleared his throat. "Be that as it may, he saw

Chet Harter kill your Chilkat, and is prepared to testify to that fact?"

"Certainly," Belinda said firmly. With Annabelle safe, there was no reason for not telling Douglas, and certainly no reason not to arrest Harter before he became alarmed and fled Dawson. "So I want him arrested," she said slowly. "He's an evil man, and God only knows what else he has done in this town. You saw Annabelle's poor face. Well, he did that, too!"

She was interrupted by another knock on the door. This time she opened it to see Josh Rogan, and her face stretched in a welcoming smile. "Oh, Josh! Come in, darling, come in!"

Josh seemed taken aback by her enthusiastic greeting, and she laughed. "This is a happy day for me, Josh, but it's going to take a little while to tell you about it. First of all, Annabelle's here. She came on her own, by herself . . . well, not really by herself. But come in, and I'll explain the whole thing!"

Belinda thought that Josh seemed wary during the introduction to her father, and the presence of Douglas Mackenzie seemed to disturb him. And when she had told her story, she expected a smile and a word of congratulation, but instead she got a scowl of disapproval.

"You mean you talked to this Mountie about Harter?" His voice was harsh.

"Of course." Belinda knew that her tone was defensive, but then Josh was questioning her like some criminal! "Why shouldn't I have? Annabelle is safe now!"

All of a sudden, the atmosphere in the room was tense and uncomfortable, and Belinda could not understand why.

Without thinking, she looked at Douglas with a helpless gesture.

He stepped forward. "Yes, Rogan, why shouldn't she have told me? Didn't it happen the way she said?"

Josh glowered at him, then slumped back in his chair. "Yes, it happened the way she told it. That isn't the problem."

"Well, what *is* the problem?" Douglas said in a hard voice.

Josh sighed. "The problem is that if you arrest Harter now, there will be no way to get to his boss, Lester Pugh, no way to tie him into this crime and Christ knows how many others that pair of vultures have committed over the past few years. You see, I want to bring Pugh to justice as well as Harter. Pugh is the brains of the pair. If you arrest Harter now, Pugh will just find another second-in-command, and conduct business as usual, and there will be more deaths, more robberies, God only knows what else!"

"Just what has that to do with you?" Douglas demanded. "If you have evidence that Lester Pugh has committed a crime, it is your duty to turn it over to me. Why haven't you done this, Mr. Rogan?"

"Oh, hell!" Josh said in disgust. "I guess it doesn't matter now! Mackenzie, I'm a U.S. marshal. I've been on the trail of Lester Pugh and Chet Harter for months now. I came up here, to Dawson, to collect evidence to build a case against them."

Douglas Mackenzie's face turned a blazing red. "If that is true, and I'm not saying that I believe you for a minute, why didn't you contact my office? This *is* our territory, you know, although you Americans all too often act as if it belongs to you!"

Josh shook his head. "Because I was working under-cover, and it was thought best, by my superiors, that I work alone. When all the evidence was collected, I would have contacted you. And as far as my bonafides go, get in touch with Washington. They'll vouch for me."

"Vouch for you or not, that still doesn't give you any authority in Canada."

"Goddamnit, man, I know that! But are we going to quibble over that? Pugh and Harter are a plague on the face of the earth! Are we going to quarrel over jurisdiction, or try to rid both our countries of this pair?"

Douglas stared at him for a long moment. Then he gave his head a little shake and said tightly, "But you don't have enough evidence to move against Pugh. Is that correct?"

Josh sighed. "Almost, but not quite. What I need is a wit-ness. Just one good witness to some of Pugh's crimes." He pounded a fist on his knee. "I'm so close . . . if you arrest Harter, the whole thing will blow up in our faces. I'm asking you, Mackenzie, to give it a few days. Just a few more days."

He looked pleadingly at Douglas and the Mountie glanced away, his jaw set stubbornly. Both men were keyed up and tense, and Belinda, who had been following the exchange closely, was afraid they might come to actual blows. She hadn't been particularly surprised at Josh's rev-elation that he was a United States marshal, but she was a little piqued that he hadn't seen fit to tell her. What was the big secret?

Where was Annabelle with the tea? Maybe that would break the tension.

She was just swinging around to go into the kitchen, when her father stepped forward, his expression somber and his shoulders squared. He said, "You won't have to wait, Sergeant Mackenzie."

Josh swiveled his head to glare at the older man and Morgan Lee raised a hand placatingly. "And you don't have to look any longer for a witness, Josh, because I'm your man."

Josh's eyebrows rose. "You, Montana?"

"No longer Montana, Josh. I'm Morgan now." His brief smile was wry, and then he sobered facing the Mountie. "I should have come to you a long time ago, Sergeant, but I had a number of reasons for not doing so. At least, I told myself that I did. Now, none of those reasons matter. I'm prepared to stand up in court and swear that I saw Lester Pugh and Chet Harter murder a man by the name of Carl Doober, and stuff his body into a trunk. Now all you have to do is find the body, and that *could* be a problem!"

∽18∾

Annabelle came out of her reverie with a guilty start when Belinda pushed open the kitchen door. The tea had long been brewed, and was growing cool as Annabelle sat, chin in hand, eyes focused on the flowered China pot.

"Annabelle! What on earth's the matter with you? We've been waiting for the tea!"

Annabelle straightened up, her eyes looking as if they had just been awakened from sleep. "I'm sorry, Bee. I'll bring it right in."

When she put the tea tray down on the table in the other room, Annabelle was struck by the look of excitement on the faces of the others. "What is it?" she asked, feeling as if they were all in on some marvelous secret that she alone was not privy to.

Belinda smiled and put her hands on her sister's shoulders. "Our father is going to be a witness for Josh, that is, for Josh and Douglas. Now they will be able to arrest both Lester Pugh and Chet Harter, and charge them with murder! We, and the town, will be free of them forever! Isn't that wonderful?"

Annabelle forced a smile. "Of course. I couldn't be happier."

But somewhere, deep down, she knew that this was a lie. She wanted to ask again if Belinda was certain that her attacker, and the murderer of Charlie, was Chet Harter, but she didn't dare.

Although Annabelle knew well enough that Chet could lose his temper—she touched the bruise under her eye—she found it difficult to believe that he had done what Belinda and Josh Rogan said he had done. There was just no sense to it. True, it shouldn't matter to her. She wasn't going back to Harter, and he *had* abused her; and yet, what woman wanted to think that she had spent time in the company of, and had taken pleasure in the arms of the kind of a man who would commit such acts. It was very confusing, and thinking about it was making Annabelle's head hurt.

Still, she didn't want to spoil the mood—they all seemed so jubilant. So, she poured herself a cup of tea and sipped it as the others discussed how they would handle the arrest of Pugh and Harter, as soon as they had found someone named Carl Doober.

She didn't really want to listen, and so she tuned out most of the conversation, only coming back to the immediate present when the men got up to leave.

Josh and her father appeared to be leaving together, and as Josh took her sister's hand, he said, "Now remember, we'll use you as a clearing house. If any one of us learns anything at all, he'll report it here, and leave a message for the others. We're going to start early, so be sure you, Belinda, or your sister, are home all day long. And pray that we find Doober's body soon, before something else happens, or before Pugh gets wise to the fact that we're about to nail him."

Belinda smiled up at him with an expression that Annabelle had never seen before on her sister's face. The realization struck her like a slap in the face—they were in love! Also, it was plain to see that they had been lovers. Instead of cheering Annabelle, this knowledge made her feel depressed and a little resentful.

As she carried the tea things into the kitchen, she heard Douglas Mackenzie telling Belinda goodbye, and her resentment grew. Belinda always made things turn out *her* way. She had two good-looking, nice men practically fighting over her.

When the outside door shut, Belinda came into the kitchen. "Do you want me to help with those?"

Annabelle shook her head. "No, it's fine. I'll do them."

Belinda took her by the shoulders and turned her around. "Annabelle, what's wrong? You're acting strangely."

Annabelle shrugged her hands away. "Oh, it's nothing.

I'm just tired, I guess. It's been a long day, and a lot has happened."

"Well then, leave the dishes. We'll do them in the morning. Right now, I want to go through my prints and see just what I've sent off to *Leslie's Weekly,* and what I haven't. I want to get another batch into the mail tomorrow."

"No, I'll go ahead and do them. It's nice and peaceful here in the kitchen, and I need to think."

Belinda leaned over and kissed her. "Of course, dear. Whatever you like. I'll be in the other room if you need me for anything."

Carefully, Annabelle washed the dishes, her raw emotions soothed by the mechanical, monotonous task.

She was almost finished when Belinda again pushed open the kitchen door. "Annabelle, do you remember that picture I took at Chilkoot Pass, the one of the avalanche?"

Annabelle thought for a moment. "Oh, yes. It was one of the first ones you developed."

"That's right. I know I had it when we were in the tents, but now I can't find it, and I've looked everywhere. The last time I saw it was when I was looking through my original prints that day in the tent, the same day that . . ." Her face flushed, and she turned back toward the other room. "Oh, well, it doesn't matter that much. I can always print another."

The door closed behind her, and Annabelle put away the dish cloth. She felt drained, weary, and quite sad. She had better get to bed; a good night's sleep would probably improve her spirits. In the parlor she found Belinda on the floor with a large, wooden box open beside her, and pictures spread all around her in a circle.

Just then, someone knocked on the outside door.

Belinda looked up, face flushed from her labors, and Annabelle waved a hand. "I'll get it, I'm up."

"Open it on the chain. Don't let anyone in until you see who it is."

Annabelle nodded and opened the door a crack, leaving the chain bolt fastened.

A small boy with a stiff brush of tow-colored hair stood outside the door, with his hat in one hand and an envelope in the other. "You Miss Lee?" he asked, in a surprisingly deep voice.

"Yes, I'm Miss Lee."

"Miss Annabelle Lee?"

She nodded. "Yes."

He held out the envelope. "I have this message for you, ma'am."

Annabelle unchained the door and held out her hand. The boy gave her the envelope. It felt stiff and cold in her hand.

"I . . . I don't have anything for you," she said hesitantly.

He grinned. "Oh, that's all right, lady. The gent give me that also give me this!" He held up a coin. "Goodbye, lady."

"Goodbye, and thanks."

Annabelle closed and bolted the door, then stood staring down at the plain envelope that bore her name printed in bold letters.

From behind her Belinda said, "What is it?"

"I don't know."

"Well, open it, silly!"

Annabelle slowly began to pry open the sealed flap, using her fingernails. Inside was a single sheet of paper, upon which was written in a sprawling hand: "Alabaster, doll: I am sorry about what happened this afternoon. I did not mean to hurt you. I guess it was just kind of like cabin fever got to me. Please come back. I need you, dollie. Love, Chet."

Carefully, she folded the note, replaced it in the envelope, and turned to find Belinda watching her curiously.

"Well? What is it?"

"It's just a note, for me." Annabelle put the envelope into the front of her dress. She didn't want Belinda to know who it was from.

But Belinda, with her usual perception, seemed to know what was in the note. She stood up from her nest of pictures, and crossed the room. "Annabelle . . . it's from Chet Harter, isn't it?"

Annabelle felt herself flush. She said crossly, "Well, what if it is?"

"He wants you to come back to him?"

Annabelle nodded. "He says he's sorry."

An annoyed look crossed Belinda's face. "Annabelle, Annabelle! Sorry doesn't cost anything. Will sorry bring back poor Charlie? Will it heal your face? Will sorry erase the fact that he tried to kill me? You know that Josh and Douglas are going after him and Pugh as soon as they find the body of the man Daddy saw them kill. Surely you can't be thinking of going back to that man!"

Annabelle's gaze slid away. She felt a deep resentment at Belinda's sharp tone. "Of course not," she said softly. "It's just that I'm a little sorry for him."

Belinda threw up her hands. "Oh! You are impossible!" The man's a thief, a murderer, and a bully, and you still feel sorry for him!"

"I lived with him," said Annabelle, with as much dignity as she could muster. "It's hard not to feel something for a man you've lived with."

"And whose idea was it to go live with him?"

Belinda's face softened. "I'm sorry, Annabelle. I didn't mean to sound so harsh. Why don't you go to bed? You must be tired. Tomorrow, we'll have to be up early in case one of the men drops by with a message. Oh, I hope they find the body soon, and then this will all be over." She leaned close to Annabelle and kissed her cheek.

Annabelle smiled weakly. She knew that Belinda meant well, yet her attitude rankled. It was infuriating when Belinda talked to her in the condescending tone she would use to a naughty child. It was all she could do to keep from snapping back.

She left Belinda with her pictures and retired to the bedroom, but it was a long time before she was able to sleep.

Belinda was awakened by the sound of morning activity in the street below. She stretched hugely, and glanced over at her sister, lying next to her in the big double bed.

Annabelle's face was serene, despite the awful bruises, and her hair spread like a dark river over the white pillow slip. When Belinda had finally come to bed, her sister had still been awake, she knew. Poor Annabelle! What was to become of her? Would she be able to put all this behind her and make a new life for herself?

Belinda looked at the clock on the nightstand. It was

after eight. She had better get dressed. The men would already be out searching for the remains of the murdered man. One of them might drop by at any time with a message.

She slid out of bed, and pulled on a wrapper and slippers. One reason she had gotten to bed so late was because of the print of that picture taken at Chilkoot Pass. The last time she had seen the picture was on the day that Annabelle first went out with Chet Harter, and Belinda had the suspicion that there might be some connection between the picture's disappearance and Chet Harter's sudden interest in photo processing.

So, she had looked up the negative in her files, and had used the not quite finished darkroom below for the first time. The result of her efforts was several copies of the avalanche picture, which she had studied minutely with a magnifying glass.

She remembered noticing, when she had looked at the picture the first time, a small figure at the top of the picture near the top of the pass, and last night she had studied it carefully. Even under magnification, the man's features weren't clear enough, but it *could* have been Harter, and his presence at that particular point was highly suspicious. Belinda could hardly wait to tell Josh what she suspected.

By the time Annabelle awakened, Belinda had breakfast on the table, but Annabelle, sitting at the table in her wrapper, only toyed with her food.

"You have to eat," Belinda said gently. "You're getting terribly thin and pale looking."

Annabelle smiled, but it never reached her eyes. Belinda poured herself another cup of coffee. "Are you still thinking of him?"

Annabelle's face closed up, but she nodded. "Yes, I suppose so."

Belinda said urgently, "Annabelle, don't torture yourself so! You have to put him out of your mind."

Annabelle's eyes were wide and dark with emotion. "Chet says he needs me, Bee!"

Belinda sighed in exasperation. "Oh, Annabelle! That's the eternal ploy of men. They know women can't resist being needed, and they play upon it. It's far more likely that he's worried about your being here with me, and wondering if you've told the Mounties that he's back in town."

"Bee, that's unfair! Don't you think that he really might miss me?" Annabelle's eyes swam with tears. "Or don't you think that I'm the kind of woman a man might miss?" She knuckled the tears from her eyes. "Besides, I don't think he's as bad as you say he is. I don't think it was him who tried to kill you, and who killed Charlie. You never actually *saw* him, you said so yourself!"

"But Josh saw him, Annabelle. Not only did he see him, but he shot him, in the arm and the leg. And he has been shot, you can't deny that."

"And I suppose that everything that Mr. Josh Rogan says is God's gospel truth?"

Belinda was really annoyed now. It was impossible to have a sensible conversation with Annabelle when she was like this. "I've found no reason to doubt him so far," she said with some asperity. "He's certainly been truthful with me."

Annabelle folded her arms across her breasts. "Then I suppose he told you about that girl at the Poke, Child Meg,

297

and what he was doing coming out of her room! I suppose he told you that?"

Belinda felt as if a glass of ice water had been flung in her face. "What he does with his private life is no concern of mine," she said with forced calm. "Josh is a normal male, and I would assume he was doing the normal thing, with this Child Meg, whoever she is."

"She's a cheap dance hall girl!"

"And what have you been, Annabelle, for some weeks past?"

With a gasp Annabelle's hand flew to her mouth, and she came to her feet.

Immediately contrite, Belinda said, "I'm sorry, Annabelle. I had no right to say that."

But Annabelle was already hurrying from the room. Belinda started after her, then paused, resuming her seat. It had been a nasty thing to say, but let Annabelle stew awhile. Maybe it would make her see Chet Harter for what he was.

Most of the morning passed in strained silence, as the sisters cleaned the new apartment, unpacked belongings, and stayed out of each other's way. None of the men came by, and Belinda fretted. Did this mean that they had found nothing?

Also, her thoughts kept returning to what Annabelle had said about seeing Josh come out of this saloon girl's room. The thought of what he might have been doing there made her feverish with jealousy, and yet she was furious with herself for feeling so. After all, she had known another man, Douglas Mackenzie. How could she, in all fairness, be angry at Josh for having another woman? This had happened before the interlude on the river. Still, the thought rankled, illogical though it might be.

A little past noon, Belinda knew that she had to get out for a bit. She made a list of things she needed and dressed to go out. When she was ready, she found Annabelle in the parlor, staring out the window at the street below.

"Annabelle," she said, "I have to pick up a few things. You'll have to stay here while I'm gone, in case the men come by with a message. All right?"

Annabelle nodded, but did not turn away from the window.

Belinda sighed and touched her sister's shoulder tentatively. "I'm sorry, Annabelle. I didn't mean the things I said. It's just that I love you, and don't want to see you hurt."

Annabelle turned then. "It's all right, Bee. I'm no longer mad at you. You go along now, I'll be fine."

Belinda hesitated. "Keep the door bolted unless you're sure it's Josh, Douglas, or Daddy. Just those three."

Annabelle smiled wanly. "Yes, Bee. I'll keep it bolted."

"I'll be back in about an hour."

Annabelle watched from the window as her sister went down the stairs and out into the dusty main street of Dawson. Belinda meant well, but she simply did not understand. Maybe it was because no man had ever really needed her. And there was something else pulling Annabelle back to the Poke—the memory of her singing and the roaring, foot-stomping reception the miners gave her. It was unlike anything that had ever happened to her, and if she didn't return to the Poke, she would never experience that adulation again.

She knew what she was going to do.

Waiting until Belinda was well away, she hurried into the bedroom and picked up the silver triptych. After looking at it for a moment, she replaced it on the dresser and went to the closet where she borrowed something of Belinda's—an old gingham sunbonnet that would hide her bruised face from casual glances.

When it was tied firmly under her chin, Annabelle slipped out the door and down the steps. When she reached the wooden sidewalk, she began to walk briskly in the direction of the Poke.

The shopping took a little longer than Belinda had anticipated. The stores were unusually crowded, and she had to visit several establishments before she could buy all the things she wanted. As she finally approached her new building, she saw the tall figure of Morgan Lee coming toward her, moving fast.

She stopped at the bottom of the steps and waited for him. When he reached her, his face was flushed with excitement and he was smiling broadly.

"They've found the body," he said without preamble, and Belinda knew that he was speaking of the dead man.

"Where?" she asked, beginning to experience some of the excitement herself.

"In the bottom of a ravine about a half-mile south of town. He was shot in the chest, like I said. Harter, or someone, had tried to cover the body with dirt and brush, but the wolves had been at it, and it was mostly uncovered when we found it. The Mounties are bringing it back to town now, and sometime today they'll be arresting Pugh and Harter." He rubbed the back of his neck and stretched. "Damn! It's been quite a day. Do you suppose you could spare an old man a cup of coffee and maybe a sandwich? I don't *dare* go near the Poke until those two have been jailed."

Belinda smiled at him. He was her father, yet he was so like an overgrown boy in his enthusiasm. "Of course, Daddy, I'd be delighted. Come on up. Annabelle's inside."

He took most of the packages from her and followed her up the stairs. On the landing in front of her door, Belinda took out her key and, turned it in the lock, then tried the door. It did not open. Puzzled, she turned the key again and this time the door opened. She went in, with Morgan Lee behind her.

She motioned for him to put the packages on the wooden sink in the kitchen and called out, "Annabelle, we're home!"

The rooms were silent. She called again, "Annabelle, where are you?"

There was still no answer, then Belinda realized why she had not been able to unlock the door. It had already been unlocked, and in turning the key she had locked it.

"Oh, no!" she cried, dropping her purse and running into the bedroom.

The bed was neatly made, and the silver triptych stood upon the dresser. Where was Annabelle? She feared she knew the answer to that, but did not want to face it. Slowly, she walked back into the parlor.

"Belinda, what is it?" Morgan asked after one look at her face.

Belinda fought down a suffocating feeling of dread. "She's gone, Daddy. I'm afraid she's with Chet Harter."

"No!" Morgan's cry was a bellow of surprise. "She couldn't be! Not after what he did to her. Why would she go back?"

"She received a note from him last night," she said dully. "He begged her to come back. Annabelle said that she wouldn't but she seemed to feel some kind of loyalty to him, because he *needed* her. Maybe she felt that she should warn him. I don't know, Daddy, I just don't know!"

"My God, do you know what this could mean? If she's warned him, then he and Pugh will be prepared, and it will mean a gunfight. Not only could she be killed, but God knows how many others!"

Belinda sighed. "I know. And Annabelle will be right there in the middle of the whole thing."

Morgan came to her. "Maybe he'll let her leave first. If he's got any decency at all . . ."

Belinda laughed, and the sound was bitter in her ears. "I wouldn't count on that, Daddy. You know him, what kind of a man he is. He'll probably hold her for a hostage. I somehow don't see him as a man who would put decency above survival."

Morgan's shoulders slumped. "I'm afraid you're right, but we can only pray that you're wrong. I'd better get down to Mackenzie's office and warn them. They should know this before they move on the Poke."

He turned to go, then came back and kissed her cheek. "You stay here now. Having one of my girls in jeopardy is enough. I'll get word back to you as soon as possible, about how things are going. And try not to worry. Things will work out, I know they will. Annabelle will be all right."

He spoke the words with such sincerity and assurance that Belinda could *almost* believe them.

In the room shared by Annabelle and Harter, above the saloon, a great deal of activity was going on.

Chet Harter, swearing and groaning, was attempting to get into his clothes. The bandage on his leg made it difficult, and finally Annabelle had to cut the trouser leg to the knee. When he was finally dressed, he was pale and sweating.

Child Meg, who had also been pressed into service, was packing Harter's bag, and he snatched it from her with an obscenity when she was finished.

Child and Annabelle exchanged glances, and Annabelle could see a question in the smaller girl's eyes, a question to which Annabelle did not know the answer. Why had she come? She had thought Chet would be grateful that she had come to warn him, and that he would bid her a warm good-bye before he and Pugh rode away; but she had quickly been disabused of that notion.

As soon as she had seen Chet lying there in the bed, sullen and mean-faced, she knew that she should not have come; still, she had plowed ahead, warning of his possible arrest, thinking of it as a gesture for the time they had had together. But Chet, showing not the least bit of gratitude, turned on her with a viciousness that was frightening, accusing her of running to her sister and Josh Rogan with the news of his whereabouts, completely ignoring the fact that his own behavior had driven her away.

He had struggled to his feet and yelled at her to get his

clothes, which she had done. In between spells of cursing he told her that they were leaving now, this very minute, and she had better get herself into some trail duds.

"No, I'm not going with you! I came to warn you, you can't expect anything more of me. I'm staying here, at the Poke, where I can sing."

She broke for the door, and he caught her arm in a cruel grip. "And where you can sing to the Mounties, eh?" he said unpleasantly. "Yes, you're coming along, you stupid bitch! You'll be my passport out of Canada. They won't dare harm me, if I'm holding you hostage!"

"No, please, Chet!" she cried. But as he raised his heavy fist, she began to tremble and gave in. Quickly, she opened her closet and began to throw on clothes for the trail. Filled with dread and despair, she fought back tears.

And now, now they were ready to go. Harter took her arm for support and limped toward the door.

Before they reached it, the door flew open, and Lester Pugh, red-faced with rage, burst into the room. "Harter, I have something to say to you . . . " He stopped at the sight of Annabelle. "What is *she* doing here? You told me she had left!"

Annabelle managed to say, "I came to warn Chet . . ."

Pugh fixed Harter with a glare. "And you were leaving without warning me, is that it?" His lips set in a cold sneer. "Such devoted loyalty should be rewarded, Chesley."

Harter had backed up to the bed and dropped down onto it, his face pale. "Now just a damned minute, L.P. We were just coming to get you, weren't we, Child?"

Child gave a start, then nodded quickly. "That's right, Mr. Pugh. Chet asked me to go fetch you," she said softly.

"I was just fixing to leave when you came in."

Pugh didn't even spare her a glance, but continued to glare at Harter. "It so happens that your warning is a little late. My sources have already informed me that the federal snoop and Sergeant Mackenzie are bringing in the remains of our erstwhile friend, Carl Doober."

"Hell," Harter interjected, "what's the big deal about that? They can't prove who killed him."

Pugh snorted. "One of your bad flaws, Harter, is that you underestimate your opponents. My sources also reported that the Mounties have a witness, Mr. Montana Leeds by name. Another example of great loyalty."

Annabelle couldn't keep herself from crying out at the mention of her father, but neither man seemed to notice.

"They are coming here, probably on their way now." Pugh's voice was deadly. "I am leaving at once. I came to tell you that you have failed me again, Chesley Harter, and you shall regret it, that I promise you, but I will have to attend to it another time, when I have more time to devote to it. If I killed you now, I wouldn't be able to fully enjoy it."

As Pugh turned ponderously toward the open door, Harter said quickly, "What do you mean, *you're* leaving now? Ain't we going together?"

Pugh's lips tightened. "Since you were evidently going to leave me behind to face the wrath of the Northwest Mounted, I don't really think that I can trust you. No, I think that this is the parting of the ways for us, Chesley, at least for the present. May you always be looking back over your shoulder, for be assured that I will be seeing you!"

"Wait!" Harter leaned forward, grabbing Annabelle

around the waist. True, he had intended to leave Pugh to face the music alone, but now that the fat man was aware of what was up, it appeared to him that it might be better if they stayed together. He knew that he was in no condition to make the trip alone, and Pugh was smart and tricky. "I've got the girl. I'm taking her along, as a hostage. Even if they catch up with us, she could be our passport out."

Pugh hesitated, pursing his lips in thought. "Perhaps you're right, for once. All right, but be ready to leave in ten minutes. I have arranged so that any pursuit will be some-what delayed."

He chuckled, sounding more like his old self, and Harter relaxed a trifle.

"So, Chesley, a truce for now. We need each other, and we will put our differences aside for the moment. Survival is more urgent."

He rolled out the door, and Harter gave vent to a huge sigh of relief. He looked at Annabelle and gave her a wink. "You heard the man, dollie. Let's go."

Annabelle, so frightened now that she was almost calm, did as she was told. She finally knew the stark truth—if she didn't do his bidding, Harter would kill her without a qualm.

She lent her support to him, but it was too much for her on the stairs. Child Meg, seeing the problem, got on the other side of Harter, and together they got him down the stairs. Annabelle was surprised to see the Poke empty. Then she realized that it must have been Pugh's doing. He had chased everybody out and locked the doors.

At the bottom Harter leaned against the stair post to catch his breath. He didn't bother to thank Child.

Annabelle could not remember ever paying much attention to the dancehall girl in the past, but now she felt a gratitude for the girl's assistance, and even a strange kinship. It was as if the mere fact of their being women drew them together in some unexplainable way.

She said, "Thank you, Child."

Child nodded gravely, pressed her hand briefly, and then ran back upstairs.

Harter bellowed, "L.P., where are you?"

"In the kitchen," Pugh's voice said from the back.

They found Pugh supervising the packing of food into saddlebags. The last bag was being filled as they came in.

Suddenly, Pugh motioned for silence. "Listen. Do you hear it?"

Harter and Annabelle listened. Annabelle was puzzled; she could hear nothing.

"Hell," Harter said, "I don't hear a thing!"

Pugh bent a hard look on him. "That's just it, my stupid friend. At this time of the day the street out there is usually deafening with noise."

Harter shifted uncomfortably on his wounded leg. "So? What does it mean?"

Pugh shook his head, his expression grim. "It undoubtedly means that Rogan and the Mounties are outside, waiting for us to emerge."

Harter hobbled over to the window, and moved the curtain an inch to peer out. He wheeled back, his pockmarked face white. "Not a soul in sight, and that's sure as hell not normal. You're right, L.P. So, what do we do?"

Pugh's smile gleamed with self-satisfaction. "We are going to take advantage of my foresight. I have made preparations, just in case something of this nature should occur." He turned about to motion to the two men who had been packing the food. When they were gone, he said, "Now, you'll see!"

Moving over to where the huge kitchen table squatted in the center of the room, he gave it a mighty shove and the heavy piece of furniture slid protestingly out of its accustomed place.

In the floor, beneath the spot where the table had stood, Annabelle could see the outlines of a trapdoor.

With a heave, Pugh flipped it up, and for the first time Annabelle realized the strength of the big man. He might be fat and look soft, she thought, but under that bulky exterior, there were muscles to be reckoned with. The thought frightened her, and she wasn't sure why; but then Pugh himself frightened her. He was a cold man, the kind of man, she felt, who was capable of the most evil acts. In that moment she knew that she was far more afraid of him than she was of Harter, for although Harter might treat her roughly, she knew that she had some power over him, even if it was only the power of her body. She sensed that she could influence Chet to some extent, but somehow she was sure that no one could influence Lester Pugh.

Pugh's face was flushed when he straightened up from lifting the trapdoor. "Now! Down there with the pair of you!"

Annabelle hesitated, but seeing Pugh's expression start to turn cold and threatening, she reluctantly began to lower herself into a black hole that seemed bottomless.

Step by careful step, she backed down the ladder nailed to the side of the hole. Although she was shudderingly afraid of the darkness below, Annabelle was more terrified of Pugh. She could hear the two men moving about above, and she felt a chill of fear. Was it possible that they would close the trapdoor, and leave her to perish down there in the dark?

This didn't seem too likely, yet her instinctive dread made it appear possible. But then, at last, her feet touched bottom, and as they did so, a lighted lantern poked into view above her, illuminating Pugh's huge face, hovering over her like a moon.

Annabelle said nothing, but accepted the lantern, and held it high as Pugh dropped the saddlebags and gear down into the underground room, then Harter made his way down the ladder, step by cursing step.

Despite all that had happened, her heart went out to him. He must be in considerable pain from his leg, but at last he was beside her, limping and groaning, and they both waited in silence as the fat man, almost filling the width of the trapdoor, made his way down the ladder, moving with an almost delicate sureness of step.

He had pulled the trapdoor closed after him, and as soon as he reached the bottom of the ladder, he motioned them forward.

Annabelle, holding the lantern high, had already looked around the small room, hoping to discover a way out, so she could make her escape before the men joined her.

In the wash of yellow light she had seen nothing but cases of liquor and racks of dusty wine bottles. A wine cellar. There was no sign of an exit.

What was Pugh's next move? Was it just to hide down here and hope that the Mounties wouldn't find the trapdoor in the kitchen floor? If that was it, then perhaps she could cry out, or make some kind of a noise when she heard footsteps on the floor above.

But she soon found that she had underestimated Pugh, for he was already at work on the far wall, which was lined with wine racks. After some maneuvering, one entire wine rack swung inward, disclosing another, lower, narrower opening that led into further darkness.

Pugh waved Harter and Annabelle forward, and Annabelle, holding the lantern in one hand and a bundle of blankets in the other, was again forced to go first. As she bent over to enter the opening, she again experienced that strange calm that had overcome her before, as if she was now beyond mere fright, and her automatic responses had taken over.

Walking in the half-stoop necessitated by the low ceiling of the tunnel was uncomfortable, and Annabelle could hear Harter and Pugh grunting and puffing behind her. She walked as quickly as she could, trying not to think of anything but coming to the end of the tunnel, and at last it appeared—a wall of dirt not five feet in front of her.

The sight of the wall filled her again with panic, and she almost gagged on the scream that caught in her throat. They were walled in, trapped!

But before she could give vent to her mounting panic, she saw the ladder, just like the one in the other room. Pugh pushed past her, without a word, and went up the ladder first. At the top, he bent his arms and heaved upward.

Slowly, a section of the roof above the ladder gave with a grating sound, and moved up and away. Light, gray as dishwater, spilled down onto them. Pugh climbed out with grunting effort and disappeared. A moment later, his great, pale face appeared at the edge of the hole.

"Hand up the supplies," he ordered.

At once, Annabelle and Harter complied. When everything was above ground, Pugh gestured and said, "Send the girl up!"

Gladly, Annabelle climbed the ladder, emerging into what appeared to be a combination stable and storage shed. There was hay on the ground, and various kinds of gear-sleds, traps, harness, et cetera.

Pugh closed the second trapdoor after Harter had climbed laboriously through. The fat man dusted off his hands, and grinned at them smugly. "As you can see," he said to no one in particular, "it pays to be prepared. Now we'll get the horses and be gone, out the back here." He gestured in the direction of the rear of the building. "We'll be gone, while they're still looking for us in the Poke."

He turned and strode toward the rear, where Annabelle now saw three stalls. Two of them contained sleek, well-fed horses that snorted and shied away from the lantern light and the sound of their voices.

"Where'd you get those?" Harter's voice sounded grudgingly impressed. "I didn't know you had any horses! When I went after the Lee woman, I had to hire a horse, and a sorry nag it was, too!"

"A smart man always has secrets, Chesley," Pugh chuckled. "However, as you can see, I was only counting on two of us. The girl will have to ride double with you, Chet, for obvious reasons. You, girl, help me with the saddles. Chesley, it seems, will be of little use to us for awhile."

Obediently, Annabelle put down the lantern and went toward the fat man. Although she had little or no idea of what to do, fear of Pugh made her attentive and she tried to follow his instructions. It seemed to take a long time, but at last the two horses were saddled and ready to go.

There was still no sound from the direction of the Poke, and she wondered what Josh Rogan and Douglas Mackenzie were doing. She had no hope now that she would be rescued before Pugh and Chet Harter took her away. But what did it matter, she thought drearily. She had brought this whole thing on herself.

What was the matter with her, anyway? Why did her feelings veer so wildly? Why couldn't she do the right thing, the sensible thing, just once, instead of getting herself into situations that only hurt her and those she loved? If I ever get out of this, she thought, I'll do better. I really will! Right now, the important thing was that there be no shooting, that nobody get hurt because of her, and that, she knew, depended on them getting away unnoticed.

She was recalled from her thoughts by Harter's snarl of pain, as Pugh helped him onto one of the horses. Pugh then motioned to her, and with the aid of a wooden box, he helped her mount up behind Chet. Annabelle's flesh crawled where Pugh had touched her, although his touch had been as impersonal as a machine's.

She watched as Pugh, with the aid of the same box, mounted the other horse. The horse was the largest of the two, but even so the animal sagged and whinnied as Pugh's huge weight settled into the saddle. Annabelle knew little of horses, but she could not help but wonder how long the animal would bear up under Pugh's enormous bulk.

It was too late to wonder or worry now. Now she could only pray that they would not be seen. She thought she could not bear it if someone was killed due to her stupidity.

Pugh, astride the horse, was pushing open a tall door in the rear of the building, and the light, blinding after the dimness of the building, poured in.

Glancing back as they rode away, Annabelle could see nothing but the building they had just quitted; the Poke was hidden from view.

There was no hue and cry, no one took any notice of them, and within a few minutes, the horses were plodding through the crosshatch of streets, heading toward the outskirts of town.

Annabelle, clinging uncomfortably to Harter's back, felt tears flood her eyes. Dawson wasn't much; she had hated it from the beginning. However, it held life and people, and she wondered if she would ever see the town *or* her sister again.

≈19≈

Although her father had cautioned Belinda to stay in her rooms, she was too keyed up and restless to remain there.

Morgan Lee had not been gone more than thirty minutes, when she could restrain herself no longer and set out for the Poke.

Belinda knew that it would be dangerous to approach too near, and she didn't want either Josh or Douglas to know that she was in the vicinity, for she realized that that knowledge could well jeopardize what they had to do. But she could not, simply *could* not, stay there in her rooms, while all those she cared about were involved in something as violent and dangerous as this.

The street was its usual busy self, and Belinda, from her post in the shelter of a two-story building a block away, noticed nothing unusual about the appearance of the Poke. Evidently, Josh, Douglas, and her father had not arrived yet; and then she saw them, or rather she saw Douglas coming up the street, stopping people and talking to them.

After each brief conversation, the people quickly left the street. Some of them—she could see their faces as they hurried past—looked frightened and upset.

Then she noticed other Mounties doing the same thing. In a surprisingly short time the street was cleared, and no one remained except Douglas and his men, who were now moving up the street toward the Poke. Guns drawn, they moved quietly, and stayed close to the buildings on either side of the street.

Now Belinda saw Josh and her father come around the side of one of the buildings and intercept Douglas. She strained to see more clearly, and then on sudden impulse, she turned and went quickly up the outside stairway of the building.

A shingle on the building advertised a dentist, an attorney, an assayer, and a doctor. There was a short hallway off the door on the upstairs landing. Only one door stood open—the dentist's office. It was on the side of the building that would overlook the Poke.

Belinda peeked into the waiting room. The room was empty except for a tall, heavy-set man, evidently a patient, standing at the room's one window. He did not even turn as Belinda rushed over to stand beside him. From the window there was a perfect view of the Poke, and the Mounties advancing on it.

A quick glance told Belinda that Josh and her father, along with one of the Mounties, were situated so that they could watch the rear door of the saloon building, while Douglas and the others were deployed in the front. It would be impossible for Pugh and Harter to emerge without being seen. Would they give up? Belinda wondered. If they did not, would they fight, perhaps using Annabelle as a hostage?

Her hands clenched painfully at her sides. Dear God, please let Annabelle come out of this unscathed. If she did, Belinda vowed never to interfere in her sister's life ever again.

It was very quiet now on the street below. Far up the street, Belinda could see the crowd of people, held back like a dammed river, stirring restlessly. Through the open window a fresh breeze blew, stirring the curtains on either side, lending an incongruous contrast to the tense scene below.

Belinda and the stranger stood for what seemed a long time without speaking, yet the scene below did not change. An occasional movement of one of the Mounties, the stirring of the crowd in the distance, were the only signs of motion; and then Belinda noticed that a red-jacketed figure was inching along the front of the Poke, moving toward the swinging doors.

Belinda waited tensely for a gunshot, cringing with anticipation, concerned for the man who crept along the building. But no shot came, not even when the Mountie reached the wooden steps. She heard the man beside her draw in his breath, and knew that she did likewise, as the Mountie squatted alongside the batwing doors. She held her breath as he reached out and pushed at the doors. They did not give; evidently they were locked.

Then, with fast, coordinated movements, he leaped to his feet, pistol cocked in one hand, and kicked out solidly with one booted foot. The doors splintered and burst inward. Belinda could hear the sound from where she stood.

And still no shots, no sign of Pugh or Harter.

She watched breathlessly as the Mountie disappeared inside the building. In a moment she heard him call out. At his hail, Douglas Mackenzie stepped out into the street and motioned his men forward. They rushed the building and burst through the doors.

A period of time passed, an interminable time, and Belinda noticed that her back felt stiff and that her feet were tired from standing. The man next to her moved, sighing, and turned to her with a smile.

"Well, it looks as if there's not going to be a fracas, after all."

His voice was deep and resonant, and Belinda, startled, gazed up into his face with a flash of recognition. It was the same big man who had asked her for directions to a hotel the day she left for the Indian village with Charlie. He struck her as a nice sort.

She said, "Yes, it looks that way, and am I ever glad!"

He nodded pleasantly and left the room, but Belinda remained by the window, determined to see it through until the end.

In a few minutes the Mounties, led by Douglas, emerged from the Poke, and Douglas shouted to Josh and her father, who came around the building and joined them.

Belinda was naturally relieved that there had been no gunplay, and yet she was puzzled. Obviously, Pugh and Harter were not in the building, but where were they? And where was Annabelle? Was she in the Poke or not?

Whirling away from the window, she rushed down the stairs and into the street. The Mounties who had been restraining the citizens moved off, and people began streaming back into the streets.

Belinda hurried toward where Douglas, Josh and Morgan Lee were standing together. Josh glanced up and saw her, and his eyes brightened. She started to smile at him, and then the memory of what Annabelle had told her about the saloon girl came into her mind and her glance jumped away.

Douglas also saw her, and he scowled. "Belinda! Your father assured me that you were safe in your rooms!"

She ran up to take his arm. "Don't be angry, Douglas. I stayed out of the way. It was just that I couldn't stand not knowing what was happening!"

Morgan put his arm around her. "They weren't in there," he said despairingly. "And nobody will admit to having seen them leave."

Belinda looked up into his face. "Annabelle? What about Annabelle?"

He shook his head. "She isn't there, either. No one's there, except a couple of the girls. Child Meg told us that she was with them when they got ready to leave, but she remained in her room upstairs, and she has no idea when they could have gone. Or where."

At that moment a voice called to Douglas from inside, and he ran into the saloon.

"But they were there, and this *Child Meg*," Belinda placed cutting emphasis on the name, "helped them get ready to go?" Morgan nodded.

Acutely aware of Josh listening, Belinda said, "They went downstairs and simply disappeared?"

Her father nodded again. "That's what Child told us."

Belinda shot a quick glance at Josh, and caught him frowning at her. "Well," she said tartly, "I don't see how you can put much credence in the word of a girl like that. A saloon girl. She's probably lying to protect them. Everybody knows that they're no better than they should be!"

Morgan scowled at her in disapproval. "Now, Belinda, that's neither here nor there. The girl would have no reason to lie. I know Child, she's not a bad person."

Belinda, already ashamed of her outburst, looked away. "I'm sorry, Daddy, you're right. It's just that I'm so worried about Annabelle."

Her father patted her shoulder. "We all are, my dear, we all are."

She looked up, caught Josh's quizzical glance, and looked away quickly. "What are you going to do now?" she asked.

Before Morgan could answer, Douglas strode out of the Poke, looking angry and disgusted. "Well, at least we've found out how they escaped so easily. There's a trapdoor in the kitchen that opens to a wine cellar below, and from that a tunnel leads underneath an outbuilding in back. They evidently had horses there, and they rode off as neat as you please, while we waited out here in the street for them to come out!" He shook his head. "Well, they only have about an hour's start on us if we get moving." He glanced at Josh. "I suppose you'll insist on coming along?"

Josh grinned. "You'd better believe it."

Douglas nodded glumly. "And you, Mr. Lee?"

Morgan said, "I have to know what happens to my little girl. I didn't find my children just to lose one of them again."

Douglas shrugged. "Very well. I guess I can find horses for both of you. It shouldn't take us more than a half-hour to get the horses saddled, and our gear packed." He faced Belinda. "Belinda, I want you to know that I will do everything in my power to get your sister back safe and sound, and I'll see to it that those two men are brought to justice. I give you my solemn promise."

She took his hand. "Thank you, Douglas. I know you'll do all that's humanly possible."

He looked very much as if he'd like to kiss her, but then his glance went quickly around the circle of watching eyes, and he colored. "Well be back as soon as we can," he said, tipping his hat in farewell.

"Wait!" she cried as he began to turn away. "I'm going with you. You're not leaving me behind!"

He set himself, his face grim. "Don't be ridiculous, Belinda. You can't go with us. You're a woman."

Sudden anger flared like a flame, and before she could stop herself, Belinda snapped back, "Ridiculous, is it? I happen to know that I'm a woman, Sergeant Mackenzie. I have been one for some time. I fail to see what that has to do with my going with you."

Douglas seemed taken aback by her outburst, and looked first at Morgan, then at Josh, as if appealing for support. Morgan shrugged and spread his hands. Josh turned his face away, but not before Belinda saw that he was grinning; and that made her even angrier.

Douglas was saying, "But surely you see that it's impossible?"

She shook her head in determination. "I don't see anything of the sort. I traveled five hundred miles across all kinds of rough country to get here, so why should this trip be any more difficult?"

His face was almost as red as his jacket now. "Because we will be in pursuit of two dangerous criminals!" he snapped. "There may be, in fact there certainly *will* be, violence, people getting shot. We have a job to do, and knowing that we have you to look after and worry about will make that job all the more difficult!"

Belinda's voice shook with her anger. "Just furnish me with a horse, Sergeant Mackenzie, and I'll worry about myself. You won't have to look after me."

She looked quickly at her father, then at Josh, to see how they were reacting. Josh was smiling broadly now, his blue eyes dancing. Damn him! He was enjoying this!

"You are not going, Belinda, and that is final!" Douglas said coldly. He gestured. "Let's go, men."

She said firmly, "If you won't let me go with you, then I'll follow along behind. How will you stop me from doing that? Shoot me? Put me in jail?"

He gritted his teeth. "I would like to put you in jail, believe me. You are a stubborn, contrary female, Belinda Lee!"

"Since you've got her figured out so well, Mackenzie," Josh said amusedly, "you might as well let her tag along. If you don't and she follows us, we'll all *really* be worrying about her. I'll look after her, so she won't be a problem to you or your men.

Douglas turned his glare on Josh, but there was really nothing he could say. He was defeated and could only nod, reluctantly.

At any other time, Belinda would have appreciated Josh's taking her side, but in her present state of mind, she was aware only of his condescending attitude, shown by the words, "I'll look after her." God! Men were impossible, forever treating women as if they were children, lovable and fun to play with, but never accepting them as adults. When Josh looked over at her, clearly expecting approval, she could only glare at him, at a loss for words.

"Oh, hell and damnation!" Douglas said disgustedly. "Let's get on with it. We've wasted enough time already."

"What in the bloody hell!" Douglas threw his hat down into the dust in front of the empty corral, and for a moment, Belinda thought that he was going to jump up and down on it. The gate hung open, and dust still hung thick as fog in the air. There was not a horse in sight, only a red-faced and apologetic Mountie, who had been left behind to man the office during the raid on the Poke.

"I'm sorry, sir," the young Mountie stammered. "I'm sorry, but I was in the office, behind the desk, and by the time I heard the noise they were off and running! I didn't even see who opened the gate, just heard a shout, and then the sound of the horses thundering away."

Belinda drew back slightly into the shelter of Morgan's arm. Douglas had the expression of a man who had reached the end of his patience. He thundered, "Take four of the men and round those horses up, get them back here, and I mean *now!* Is that understood?"

"Yes, sir! At once, sir!" The Mountie saluted and headed for the main building at a dead run.

Douglas turned to the others with a weary gesture. "You might as well go and collect your own gear. It will be at least an hour or two, maybe more, before we get the horses back. Meet me back here in an hour."

He strode away with a heavy step, and Belinda found herself wanting to call after him. But what could she say? She wasn't sorry that she had insisted on going with them. She wouldn't have been able to stand the suspense of waiting here in town, not knowing what was happening, and she had a right to go. Her sister was involved, and surely if Annabelle could make the trip, she could do no less.

Morgan touched her shoulder. "I have to trot over to the Poke to collect my belongings. I'll meet you at your place in a half-hour, all right?"

She nodded and started off, just as Josh said, "Belinda?"

She ignored him, pretending that she hadn't heard him, and strode briskly toward her rooms, but in a moment he was beside her, stopping her with a hand on her arm.

"Belinda, come on now! What is all this? You have all the warmth of an ice floe today. What's the matter?"

Belinda opened her mouth to speak, then closed it again. She had been about to confront him with the fact that he had been seen coming out of Child Meg's room; but if she did that, she would have to tell him that it was Annabelle who had seen him, and she didn't want him to think that her sister had been spying on him. So, although she ached to lash out with hurtful words, she said, "I don't choose to talk about it," and walked on.

She heard Josh mutter a curse under his breath. Walking away, she strained to hear his footsteps following her. None came, and her spirits dropped.

Why didn't he come after her?

She knew that if he forced the issue, she would tell him what had angered her, and he could explain it away.

He must not care very much for her, if he gave up this easily!

Josh stood staring after Belinda, his mind seething. Women! How could a mere man ever hope to understand them?

He and this girl had just spent what he considered the happiest time of his life together, and she had been as sweet and warm as fresh milk. Now she had turned a cold shoulder to him, for no reason that he could fathom. This was just what he needed as they set off after Pugh and Harter. Well, he would just have to put all personal problems, including Belinda Lee, out of his mind for the present. He had a job to do, and while he was doing it, she would be just another member of the party to him. Afterward, he would try to straighten it all out. Damn her, anyway! And after he had urged Mackenzie to let her go with them!

He stalked away in the direction of his claim. It was a fair walk, and he had to get his gear together for the trip.

And yet, as much as he tried, Belinda still lingered in his

thoughts. Women!

"Women!" Lester Pugh muttered the word like an imprecation.

The damned girl had been sniveling and carrying on ever since they left Dawson, and Pugh's nerves, already stretched to the breaking point, could not take much more of it. Harter, the idiot, seemed to be taking no notice of it, even though she was riding on the same horse with him.

"Silence, woman!" Pugh thundered in a terrible voice.

He caught a flash of the girl's white, startled face as she turned it toward him, and then hid it against Harter's back. Pugh snarled under his breath.

They had been making steady but agonizingly slow progress ever since leaving Dawson, and Pugh knew that they would have at least a few hours lead, for it would take the Mounties nearly that long to round up their horses.

He smiled to himself as he thought of the consternation of that snotty sergeant when he learned that his corral was empty. Of course the Mounties would probably make better time once they were on horseback, since they would not be slowed down by riding double, as were Harter and the woman. Pugh had to admit that his own animal carried an equal burden. Somewhere along their route they would have to scrounge up an additional horse for the girl, and a larger, stronger animal for himself.

He groaned. It had been years since he had been astride a horse, and although he had not forgotten the skills required, his weight and bulk made him extremely uncom- fortable. But there was no alternative, and Pugh, who actively disliked physical effort and shunned it whenever possible, was prepared to do anything necessary to survive—even if it meant riding a jolting horse several hundred miles to Dyea.

He eased his weight in the saddle and groaned again. Reaching into an inside pocket, he took out a handful of hard candies and crammed them into his mouth, carefully shielding his action from the pair on the other horse. Sucking on the sweets, Pugh began to scheme. Since they obviously could not stay ahead of their pursuers for any great length of time, he must think of a way to outsmart them.

The pursuit party finally departed Dawson. It had taken some time to round up the horses, and by the time they could leave, Pugh and Harter had a good three hours start.

Douglas and Josh rode in the forefront, then Morgan and Belinda Lee, followed by a pair of Mounties, who seemed to Belinda young enough to still be in school.

Douglas Mackenzie had decided to take only two additional men, as he thought it would be unwise to leave Dawson unprotected in their absence.

Since their exchange in the street back in Dawson, Josh and Belinda had not spoken, and it was a quiet and subdued group that rode out on the trail to Dyea, following the river.

There had been some discussion as to which direction the fugitives might have taken. Although the approach of winter made it doubtful that Pugh would have headed inland, Douglas knew that the man was devious and bold—perhaps devious enough to risk the long, rougher inland journey in the hope of fooling them into taking a false trail.

However, Josh thought otherwise. He was convinced that Pugh would take the closest route to Dyea, the fat man's home base before he had come to Dawson this spring. He convinced Douglas of the soundness of his reasoning, and only a short way out of town, he was proven right. They met a traveler who reported seeing two men who answered Pugh's and Harter's description, heading out of town on the road to Dyea. One of them was riding double with a young girl.

This news cheered Douglas considerably. "We should be able to make up those lost hours," he said confidently. "Harter and the girl are evidently riding double, and Pugh weighs at least as much as two normal people. They can't be moving very fast."

Josh shrugged. He said dubiously, "Maybe."

The Mountie gave him a furious glance. Josh realized that Douglas Mackenzie thought him opinionated and hard-headed; but he knew Pugh, far better than the Mountie, and knew that the fat man was not to be underestimated. He had proved that with his hidden tunnel and the stampeding of the horses. That showed shrewdness and foresight. They might be traveling slowly, but Josh was sure that Pugh would think of something to give them an edge, and he really dreaded whatever it might be.

Behind Belinda and her group, far enough back to be out of sight of the last member of her party, came a lone rider, a tall, heavy-set man dressed in city clothes and wearing a derby hat. Despite his city clothing, he rode well and his horse, a big bay, moved along easily. In the dry air, it was easy to keep track of the party ahead, as their passage was marked by a cloud of boiling dust. The man's expression was relaxed, and he hummed to himself as he rode along.

∽20∾

By the time darkness came that night, Pugh was tired, sore, and cross in equal proportions. When they finally halted for the night, which was coming earlier now with the advent of autumn, it was only with difficulty that Pugh was able to get down from his horse.

The final straw was Annabelle Lee, silly creature, who sat there atop her tired horse, after Harter had managed to slide to the ground, as if waiting for someone to help her.

Well, Pugh decided, he had better get things straight with her right from the start.

They had stopped in a small clearing, a short distance off the trail. The spot was sheltered and secluded, a natural campground.

Harter, evidently in some pain, had collapsed on the ground in the shelter of a large rock. Pugh spared no sympathy on the fool; he had brought it all on himself through sheer stupidity.

Meanwhile, the silly girl just sat there on the horse, drooping over the saddle and looking helpless.

Just like a damn woman! Pugh massaged his aching buttocks, and glared at her. A pretty piece, he thought, but like all women, useful for only one purpose. If he didn't need the protection she might provide them, he would gladly have disposed of her right now. Part of the anger he felt toward Belinda Lee spilled over to Annabelle, and he determined that when they were safely away, he would eliminate at least the sister in his possession, although perhaps he would enjoy her first.

It had been a long time since he had mounted a woman. The urge didn't come upon him as often as it used to, when he was younger and thinner; still, now and then he felt the need of carnal relief. And speaking of appetites, by God, he was hungry!

"You!" he roared suddenly, causing both Harter and the girl to jump. He aimed a finger at Annabelle, and then pointed to the ground. "Get down off that horse and let him rest. There's work to be done, and since Chesley is in no condition at the present, *you* will have to take his place!"

Annabelle's eyes widened. "Me?"

"Yes, you! Who else is there? Now, down off that horse and get busy!"

Annabelle gazed down at the ground with tears in her eyes. She had never been much of an outdoor type, and she was unfamiliar with horses and riding. The ground looked a very long way off, yet she could see that she was going to receive no help from Chet, who was slumped there on the ground, and Pugh evidently meant what he said.

Timidly, she slid to the right, trying to reach the ground with one leg. As her body weight shifted, the horse whinnied and reared, causing her to fall heavily to the ground, landing with a bone-jarring thump on her right side.

"Not that way, you nitwit!" Pugh bellowed. "Never get off a horse on the right side. Incompetents, I'm forever cursed with incompetents! Now, get yourself up and fetch some water from the river."

Annabelle picked herself up, tears of hurt and humiliation filling her eyes. She dusted herself off, carefully avoiding eye contact with Pugh.

"Enough waterworks, woman!" she heard him say.

"Get the water."

Annabelle looked around bewilderedly. What was she supposed to fetch it with?

"The pot, you idiot girl! The pot! In the saddlebags."

It took her several minutes of effort to remove the saddlebags from the nervous horse, then to find the pot. Stumbling with pain and weariness, eyes still blurred with tears, she headed toward the river.

As she filled the small pot from the fast-moving river, Annabelle wondered dully whether or not she should try to escape. Just drop the pot and run. But if she did, what could she do? Where would she go? They were miles out of Dawson, she couldn't walk back. True, someone would eventually come along, since this trail was well-traveled, but that might take some time, and she was, Annabelle realized, ill-prepared to cope with the hazards of nature. This time of the year a blizzard could hit any time. Besides, there were wild animals ranging the countryside. She had seen the huge, brown bearskins, and the hides of cougars, heads snarling in ferocity. No. She wouldn't try to escape. It would be foolish.

By the time she brought the water back to camp, Pugh had unsaddled the horses and thrown down the blanket rolls. He looked flushed and angry, and the thought came to Annabelle that he greatly resented having to perform these homely chores.

They made a cold supper from the supplies. Pugh ate as much as both she and Chet, and following it up with a large bar of chocolate, which he took from his own pack. He didn't offer to share the candy. Annabelle wished he had, since she could have done with a bite of something sweet;

but she was too intimidated to ask. What a mean and selfish person he was!

She and Harter managed to make a bed for themselves with the blankets spread over pine boughs, and Annabelle did not question the fact that it was apparent the bed would have to be shared between them. Now that darkness had come, the air had grown chilly, and she knew that they would be warmer together.

Also, despite her anger at Chet's behavior back in Dawson, compared to Lester Pugh he seemed almost kind. He appeared to be subdued by weariness and pain, and certainly not of a mind toward any carnal intentions, so she climbed under the blankets with him, grateful for his body heat. She watched as Pugh, using twice as many blankets as he had allowed them, wrapped his huge frame in them, and rested his head on his saddle.

It was still dark when Annabelle heard Pugh's bellow, ordering her to get up, and she felt almost as weary as when she had lain down.

Pugh was already up, his blankets rolled, and he was saddling his horse. "Get Chesley up," he said shortly, jerking his thumb at Harter.

Annabelle sighed and shook Harter's shoulder. Finally, he came awake with considerable grumbling and cursing.

When they were both on their feet, Pugh gestured to their horse. "Get him saddled up. We've got to get moving."

"Don't we have time for some breakfast?" Annabelle asked, despising the quaver in her voice. She was hungry, dirty, and utterly miserable. When she took a few steps, the muscles of her inner thighs protested painfully, and she found that she could not walk without limping.

"Chew on some hardtack. That will have to hold you," Pugh said curtly.

In the growing light, Annabelle could see traces of some dark substance around his mouth. Chocolate, she thought; he's been eating chocolate on the sly. The great pig. And we have to eat hardtack! In that moment she began to actively hate Lester Pugh, yet she was still in great fear of the man.

Dispiritedly, she rummaged in the supplies until she found the hard biscuits and took two for herself and two for Harter. She also found a slice of ham, and noticing that Pugh was not looking, defiantly took that also, giving half to Harter, who was still partially asleep.

In a short while they were on the trail again, and Harter called out to Pugh, "How far behind us do you think they are, L.P.?"

Pugh shrugged. "They too would have had to stop at dark last night. I would imagine they spent a good two or three hours rounding up the horses. However, they will be moving at a faster clip. They may not be more than an hour or two behind us right now."

The big man spoke calmly, but Harter swore and struck the saddle horn with his fist. "Damn! What're we going to do? If they're that close on our ass, they'll catch up to us in no time."

"We're going to delay them," Pugh said.

"And how're we going to do that?" Harter's voice had a whine in it.

"By blocking the trail behind us."

"Hell!" Harter exploded. "What good will that do? They'll just go around."

Pugh chuckled, but there was little humor in the sound. "Where I intend to block the trail, Chesley, that will be difficult."

There was no more conversation until they reached a long, narrow canyon, where the trail paralleled the river as it plunged through a rocky defile.

The sun was well up now. Annabelle felt the effects of the sun, as well as the cumulative pain of sore muscles, and she was hungry. She asked plaintively, "Can't we stop soon and eat?"

"Yeah," Harter said. "I'm hungry, too. That bite of hardtack this morning only made me hungrier."

Annabelle saw Pugh cram something into his mouth before he answered. "All in good time. A little hunger never hurt a man, and since you got us into this predicament, Chesley, it ill becomes you to complain."

The fat pig! Annabelle clamped her lips shut to keep from shouting at him. He had been eating on something out of his pockets since they broke camp. No wonder he was so unconcerned about food!

Harter twisted and stretched in the saddle. Annabelle thought that he seemed stronger today; he must be healing. The thought cheered her, chiefly because she sensed that a weak Harter made her position even more dangerous.

As she had so often this morning, she looked behind them, hoping to see some sign of pursuit, but there was nothing except the dust raised by their own passage. What if there *was* no one after them?

She noticed that the trail was narrowing even more, the

Yukon River close on the left and a cliff rising high on the right. Far below tumbled the rapids, swift, white, and cruel-looking, with rocks like bared teeth projecting from the swirling water.

It was beautiful, but very wild, and she clung with frightened strength to Harter's waist, praying that the plodding horse would not make a misstep.

Up ahead, Pugh seemed to be pulled in upon himself, back rigid, and she had a sudden insight that he too was afraid. Instead of cheering her, this only made her even more afraid. Somehow, she doubted that very many things frightened Lester Pugh.

Annabelle closed her eyes tightly, hoping that they would soon be through the canyon, but she opened them again when the horse suddenly stopped and nickered.

She saw that Pugh had turned ponderously in the saddle, and raised a hand in the signal to halt.

What was he doing?"

"Get down off the horse," he shouted over the thunder of the water below.

Annabelle did not understand. Did he mean Harter, or both of them?

"You, girl, get down from the horse!"

My God! He meant her! Her heart began to hammer in her breast, and she felt her hands grow moist.

Why did he want *her* to dismount? "Why?" she called out as loudly as she could.

His face darkened with quick anger. "Down!" he bellowed. "Get down. Goddamnit, do as I say, you silly bitch!"

"Chet?" she said tentatively. "Why does he want me to

get down?"

Harter shook his head slightly. "How the hell should I know? But you'd better do as he says."

"Chet?" she said again. "Can't you help me? Can't you at least ask him the reason?"

Harter gave a low, harsh laugh. "Right now, I can't even help myself. Now do what he says before he *really* gets mad. A Lester Pugh really mad you don't ever want to see, believe me!"

Harter's words held a desperate urgency, and Annabelle realized that he too was fearful of the fat man, and it was useless to hope for him to speak up in her behalf. There was nothing to do but get down off the horse. She remembered what Pugh had yelled at her last night. The left side, she must dismount from the left side, and that was the side next to the precipitous drop to the river far below.

She looked down. There was room enough beside the horse to stand, but not if she fell, as she had done last night. She felt dizzy.

"If I fall, I'll go into the river," she whispered to Harter. "Can't you help me down?"

He grunted and extended his left arm. "Hang onto that."

Carefully, she wrapped both hands around his rigid arm, and with that support, she managed to get safely to the ground. Quickly then, she edged around the restless horse and walked ahead to the space between the two horses, where there was at least *some* room.

Pugh, still facing about in the saddle, stretched toward her with something in his hand. "Here!" he said.

Cautiously, Annabelle moved forward and took it. It was a package made of four cylinders, with four wicks on the ends; the wicks were fastened together, forming one very long wick.

Her mind a blank, she stared at the package in bewilderment. "What is it?"

"That, you nitwit, is a neat little package of dynamite that I brought along. Another example of Lester Pugh's foresight!"

At the word, "dynamite," Annabelle gave a startled leap and almost dropped the bundle, managing to hold on at the last instant.

Pugh's face lost a little color. "For God's sake, woman, careful with that!"

In a faltering voice, she said, "Dynamite? What on earth am I supposed to do with this?"

Pugh smiled down at her coldly. "That is our means of delaying pursuit." He raised one beefy arm and pointed to a spot above them on the sloping canyon wall. "See that outcropping there, on that ledge? Now, you're going to scale that slope and plant the dynamite just there, under that ledge, the overhang, you see?"

Annabelle swallowed, her stomach turning to ice. What could he be talking about? She couldn't believe what she was hearing. She couldn't climb that cliff!

"I asked if you see, if you understand." Pugh's voice cut into her bewilderment like a whip.

"I see," Annabelle said weakly, "but I don't understand. I can't possibly climb that cliff."

"What?" Pugh said. "I can't hear you over the river."

"I said I can't climb that cliff!" she shouted in sudden rage and fear. "And why should I do your dirty work for you?" For an instant she had a mad impulse to fling the dynamite into the river; but the look on Pugh's face, and the very real possibility that he might kill her if she did, stayed her hand.

Pugh, with a sudden lunge that caught her unawares, leaned down from his saddle and seized her arm. She gazed into his huge, pale face, his teeth clenched and small eyes as hard as stones. "You will climb that cliff, you idiot girl, and you will do it quickly. When the dynamite is placed, you will strike a lucifer to the fuse, and then you will get your tail back down even more quickly and back on that horse. If we ride hard, we will get safely away, out of the canyon before the dynamite goes off!"

Annabelle, made desperate by her fear, shouted, "I won't do it!"

Pugh tightened his grip on her wrist until she thought she would faint from the pain.

"Your friend Harter, because of his own stupidity, is unable to do it, and I, for obvious reasons, am unable to do it, but you, my girl, have no problems of either disability or size, and if I say you'll do it, you shall do it. Now, in case it should enter that silly head of yours to place the dynamite, but not set the fuse burning, I warn you now that if the dynamite does not go off when we are out of this canyon . . . then, I shall kill you both, you and your precious Chesley there, and push your bodies into the river. Do you understand me, girl?"

Annabelle nodded dumbly, and Pugh released her wrist and handed her a small tin of matches.

"Now, up the cliff with you."

As she reluctantly turned to face the rock wall, holding the dynamite in one hand and the matches in the other,

Pugh shouted again, "Idiot, stick the dynamite into your waistband, and the matches into your pocket! You can't climb with your hands full. God save me from incompetents!"

Breathing in great gulps, Annabelle did as he ordered. The dynamite wouldn't fit into her waistband, but she managed to button it inside of her blouse, and she put the match tin into her pocket.

The rock wall at first looked unclimbable, but as she studied it more carefully, Annabelle saw that there were small chinks, ledges and slopes where she could, hopefully, gain purchase. Reaching up to where a piece of rock projected above her, she wished that she had been one of those active children, more like Belinda, who had loved to climb and who had done so often, until Mama had forbidden her to indulge in such unladylike pursuits.

Oh, Belinda! How she missed her!

"Get a move on, goddamnit!" Pugh boomed behind her.

With an explosion of breath, Annabelle hoisted herself up to the first foothold on the cliff face and began to climb. Inch by agonizing inch, she moved upward. Time seemed to have stopped, and there existed only the present, where she was constantly reaching, clutching, stretching, and straining for hand and footholds.

Dirt fell into her upturned face, and she felt tears come to her eyes. Angrily, she blinked them away.

Her hands burned and bled, and her knee hurt where she had bruised it on a rock. She dared not look down, but beneath her she could hear the rushing roar of the river.

Several times she almost gave up, but fear of Pugh's wrath kept her climbing.

At last she reached the ledge Pugh had indicated, and was able to pause for a moment in relative safety. She risked a glance down, and saw the figures of Harter and Pugh impossibly far below her, their faces turned upward like pale moons. Dizziness gripped her, and she swayed, and tore her gaze away.

"The dynamite! Place the dynamite!"

Pugh's bawl sounded thin and far away, but obediently Annabelle pushed the package of dynamite into a corner formed by the ledge. She took the tin of lucifers from her pocket.

For a time she crouched there, staring at the long fuse and the match in her hand, wondering if she dared disobey Pugh's instructions. No, she had to do it. She was certain that Pugh meant what he had threatened, that he would kill her and Chet, if she did not do his bidding. And it was not as if the landslide would really harm anyone. It would delay them, but not hurt them. There was no choice—she had to do as she had been told.

Carefully, she struck one of the large matches and held the flame to the end of the fuse. The fuse spluttered and flared, and the flame began eating its way toward the dyna-mite.

Staring at the sputtering flame, she did not move until she heard Pugh's faint shout, "Get back down here, girl! Now!"

All at once panic struck her, and she began scrambling back down the way she had come, reaching blindly for footholds and handholds with trembling feet and hands.

In her haste, she missed a foothold near the bottom and hung for a moment by only her hands. Then, miracle of miracles, her foot found a niche to support her, and in a few seconds more she was on the ground.

Pugh's horse was already moving at a gallop down the trail. Annabelle managed, with Harter's frantic help, to climb up onto the horse behind him.

Harter urged the animal into a trot with a yell threaded with terror, and Annabelle clung to his waist, her face turned against his back, her body trembling from exhaustion, and her pulse pounding with fear.

As they pounded down the trail, despite the fear, despite her torn hands and trembling muscles, she felt exhilarated. Although she had never been one to examine her emotions very closely, she could not help but wonder why her spirits were so high. And then it came to her that it was because she had at last done something, something difficult and hazardous, and she had brought it off! Never mind that she had done it for a bad cause, and at the command of a man she had come to hate; she had still done it, using only her own strength and skill. In that instant of understanding, Annabelle felt that, strangely, she had come to know Belinda much better. This was what it felt like to accomplish something difficult on your very own!

The explosion came just as they rode out of the mouth of the canyon, and even though she had been expecting it, Annabelle jumped and cried out at the tremendous boom of the exploding dynamite, and the accompanying crash and roar of falling rock. The earth under them shook and trembled, and a great cloud of dust rose behind them.

Pugh was looking back over his shoulder, and he actually smiled at her. "That should delay them for a bit," he said complacently. "Now, I have to think up something to delay them even further."

From the top of a small rise, Josh looked through a pair of binoculars at the trail, sloping away in the distance. Just at the far edge of visibility, he could see, through rolling dust, two tiny specks moving away. "That's them," he said. "It has to be."

Douglas Mackenzie held out his hand for the glasses and put them to his eyes. "They're not more than an hour ahead of us. If we pick up our pace, we should be able to catch up to them by this afternoon."

Josh nodded. That was his estimation as well. He and the Mountie had worked out a kind of wary truce. Each would rather have been handling this on his own, but each also knew that this was impossible under the circumstances, and so he was making the best of it. A sort of mutual respect had even sprung up between them, and although they occasionally had different ideas on procedure, so far they had been able to work things out.

They had both kept a wary eye on Belinda. Josh knew that the redcoat was hurt and angry because Belinda and Josh had been together all that time on the river, and it would have amused Josh, except that he knew how *he* would feel if the situation had been reversed.

At any rate, Josh had his own problems. Since the trip began, Belinda had been treating him like a stranger. What on earth was wrong with the woman? Less than a week ago, she had told him that she loved him, and now he couldn't manage a civil conversation with her! It was beyond him. What the devil was he supposed to have done? If this was an example of what he could expect from her after marriage, perhaps they should forget the idea.

With a mental shrug Josh forced his thoughts to another tack. He shouldn't be worrying about personal concerns; that could lead to carelessness, and just one careless moment could get a man killed! His mind should be on the business at hand, and the business at hand was catching Lester Pugh and Chet Harter, to put them where they could no longer prey upon innocent people.

Riding alongside Josh Rogan, Douglas Mackenzie's thoughts were also straying into areas where they had no business to be. He sent a quick glance over his shoulder at Belinda. She was relaxed in the saddle, her thoughts obviously turned inward. He felt an actual physical pang as he stared back at her. She was so lovely, so spirited and strong, and he wanted her so *damn* much!

He knew that his stiff-necked attitude was not the way to win her, but he did not seem to know how else to act. The thought of Belinda being with *him,* with Josh Rogan, all those days while they were away from Dawson, filled Douglas with rage and frustration. He ached to ask her what had happened. Had she been *with* Rogan? Had she let him make love to her? Thinking about it almost drove him crazy.

There was one cheering fact, however. Since they had started on this journey, she had shown no sign of any special feeling for Rogan; on the contrary, she had seemed quite cool toward him. That should mean *something.*

Douglas knew that he shouldn't even be thinking of all this now. This was neither the time nor the place. Yet he couldn't seem to help himself. It was what came of having a woman along on this kind of a trip!

Belinda, busy with her own thoughts, roused only enough to give her horse a toe in the ribs, when Douglas called out for them to pick up the pace.

Her thoughts were not really all that welcome, yet she could not seem to escape them. Belinda was angry with herself for the way she had been acting toward Josh, letting her jealousy prod her into saying things she afterward regretted, but she didn't know how to go about healing the breach. Now he was unhappy with her, and she supposed she couldn't really blame him. This was certainly no time to go about trying to make up. They were getting close to Pugh and Harter, and it was clear that both Josh and Douglas had their thoughts on that moment when they would catch up to the pair.

No, the best thing she could do for the time being was just keep out of their way as much as possible, and let them go about doing their jobs.

"Are you all right, Belinda?"

She started at the sound of her father's voice, and managed to dredge up a smile for him.

It still seemed strange to her, calling this man Daddy, but it pleased him, she knew. She also knew that Morgan was deeply concerned about Annabelle, and she was, too. Annabelle wasn't accustomed to rough treatment or outdoor conditions. How was she surviving this trek?

"I'm sure that Annabelle is all right," she said reassuringly, reaching out to him with one hand. "Surely they won't harm her, since they need her for a hostage . . ."

All of a sudden, as if a wrathful god had smote the earth

with a giant fist, an explosion ripped the air, causing the horses to rear and whinny and setting Belinda's heart to pounding.

The sound wave was shockingly loud, and in the distance a cloud of dust boiled up.

"My God! What was that?"

Belinda realized that it was her own voice calling out. No one answered; they were all busy trying to control their horses and staring ahead in the direction of the explosion. Finally, the echoes of the explosion died away, but the horses still pranced nervously.

"Daddy?" Belinda looked over at Morgan Lee.

He shook his head, his face worried. "I don't know. But I have a feeling that whatever it was, it means no good for us."

Belinda looked ahead again, and saw with dismay that he was right. The dust was settling now, and about a half-mile ahead the trail simply disappeared, hidden by a great landslide.

Behind them, out of sight around a bend in the trail, the large man on the big bay stopped, too. He held the bay reined in as the sound of the explosion died away, and the faint babble of excited voices drifted back to him. He waited until he heard hoofbeats going away, then he loosened the reins and clucked to the bay, sending it on ahead.

The great pile of rubble blocked the canyon trail, making it impassable.

Belinda, gazing over to where Josh and Douglas sat their nervous horses, could feel the anger and frustration of the two men. Josh's jaw was clenched, and Douglas's face was white with suppressed fury.

"Well," said Morgan Lee, "what do we do now?"

Josh's voice was harsh as he answered, "We go around it, over the top. If necessary, we climb up out of the canyon. It would sure as hell take a month to dig our way through *that,* even if we could manage it. Mackenzie?"

"Much as I hate to say it, Rogan," Douglas said heavily, "but you're right. We don't have any choice. Damn that fat man!" He struck the saddle horn with his fist. "We underestimated him!"

"We? *You* underestimated him . . . all right, all right!" Josh held up his hands. "We haven't time to quibble over something like that. Let's get moving."

Morgan was staring up at the vaulting canyon wall. He sighed. "We'll lose a lot of time," he said to Belinda. "We may never catch them now."

She nodded, feeling depressed and shaken. He was right, but obviously there was nothing else to do.

Up ahead, Josh was already turning his horse about, with Douglas close behind him. Spurring their horses, they led the way back out of the mouth of the canyon, and shortly they turned their mounts up the rocky slope. These were not real mountains here, more like high hills, but the slope was steep and there was no trail as such.

Belinda knew that the going would be slow and treacherous, and that they would fall farther and farther behind Pugh and Harter. And Annabelle.

Behind them, the man on the bay watched from among the trees as the group, with the Mountie in the lead, came back out of the canyon. For a moment it seemed they were heading back to Dawson. Then they started their horses uphill. After a moment the man on the bay sighed and sent his horse after them, always careful to stay out of sight.

Annabelle's rear had lost all feeling. Pugh, evidently in better humor since they had blocked the trail through the canyon, was humming under his breath, stopping now and then to pop a piece of candy into his mouth.

Harter, despite his wounds, didn't seem too uncomfortable. He rode stolidly, head nodding, but his body was firm in the saddle and Annabelle concluded that his wounds must be healing well.

Trying to shift her weight to relieve some of the numbness, she leaned forward to speak quietly into his ear. "Could we stop now, Chet, just for awhile? The canyon is blocked. They won't be able to catch up with us any time soon."

Harter merely grunted and twitched his shoulders like a fly-pestered horse. He might be feeling better, but he wasn't talking much, seeming content to remain in his role as a semi-invalid.

She tried again, "Chet! Do you suppose you could get Pugh to stop so we can rest?"

This time he answered, "Not yet. I think L.P. wants to reach the way station first."

"The way station?"

But again he would not answer, and she had to wait until a building came in sight before she found out what he was talking about. The way station proved to be a cluster of rough buildings and a corral, built on a section of the trail a distance back from the river, and it was protected from the weather by a low hill on the north.

However rough it was, it looked good to Annabelle. She slid down from the horse with less awkwardness than she had heretofore displayed—experience was an excellent teacher—and unembarrassedly rubbed her numb bottom. There was no one in sight anyway except Pugh and Harter, and both seemed too deep in their own thoughts to notice her.

Before dismounting, Pugh walked his horse over to the makeshift corral, and studied the two horses inside. Only after giving them a good inspection did he ride on over to the lopsided veranda and dismount. Annabelle thought he seemed well pleased about something.

He beckoned to her. As she stopped warily before him, he said in a low, menacing voice, "A word of warning, girl, before we go in there. If you so much as let out a peep in there about the circumstances of your being with us, you're dead. Is that quite clear?"

She nodded wordlessly.

He bared his teeth in a mirthless grin. "Nobody in there will give a damn about you anyway, except maybe to climb all over you." He chuckled. "Consider yourself fortunate that you have two such gallants as Chesley and myself along to preserve your honor!"

Her gaze was filled with loathing, but Pugh ignored it and motioned them inside.

The interior of the building was much like the outside, rough-hewn and crude. Despite the smell of dirt and old grease, Annabelle's stomach spasmed with hunger. They were growing low on rations, and Pugh was extremely miserly in doling the food out to Harter and Annabelle, although he practiced no such restraint when feeding himself.

They were able to order a simple meal—a stew, made of some meat Annabelle couldn't identify. She acquitted herself well, cleaning up her plate and asking for seconds.

When they had finished eating, Pugh engaged the owner in conversation. The owner of the establishment was a lank, cadaverous individual, with a drooping, gray moustache and a fringe of greasy, gray hair. He was the only other person there, and he ignored Annabelle as if she weren't present.

Annabelle, finished with her food, grew restless sitting on the hard bench. "What is he doing?" she asked Harter, with a nod at Pugh.

Harter smiled slightly. "Oh, he's making some arrangements. Come on. We'd better go outside."

Puzzled, Annabelle followed him outdoors.

"Wait right here," he told her and, turning, walked around the side of the building, out of sight.

In a few minutes he returned. "The old man is the only one around. Be back in a minute."

This time he disappeared into the building, and Annabelle, sensing that something was going on but not knowing what, began to grow uneasy.

When Harter came back, Lester Pugh was with him. Harter's face was set in grim lines, but Pugh's round face wore a look of smiling satisfaction, and he was jauntily swinging his cane. Annabelle stared at them questioningly, but both men ignored her as they went down the rickety veranda steps and made for the corral. She hesitated for a moment, then hurried after them.

As Annabelle watched, Harter turned loose the horse Pugh had been riding, sending it galloping into the trees, then led out the two fresh mounts, which they saddled. The three horses were led back to the main building, and Pugh brusquely ordered Annabelle to fill the saddlebags with fresh supplies from the kitchen.

Annabelle wondered if the owner had agreed to this, but she knew better than to ask questions. She had already learned that the best way to get along with Lester Pugh was to cause as little trouble as possible.

Going around back, she went into the filthy kitchen and searched the cupboards for what she could find. There wasn't a lot, yet it should be enough to get the three of them to Dyea; at least she *hoped* that was where they were headed. She packed the food hurriedly, expecting that any second the owner would storm in and demand to know what she was doing. No one came, and at last the saddle-bags were full.

Carrying one set of bags, she went through the building this time. The main room was rather dark, as little light was admitted through the small, grimy windows set high in the wall. There was a strange, almost frightening silence in the building, and she quickened her steps as she crossed the room where they had just had their meal. As she passed by the end of the bar, Annabelle thought she saw something out of the corner of her eye. She paused, peering through the gloom, her curiosity stronger than her fear. It looked like a man's feet on the floor. Moving closer, she timidly peeked around the corner.

There, lying on the floor with his head and shoulders in a pool of his own blood, was the owner of the way station, his eyes bulging in death. His throat had been cut.

Annabelle stifled a scream. Feeling the food she had recently eaten rising in her throat, she grasped the saddle-bags in both hands and ran stumbling toward the door.

As she burst outside, she saw Pugh and Harter resting on the steps. They looked up as she ran onto the porch.

Pugh smiled at her, his eyes glittering coldly. "Well, such haste to please is to be commended, Miss Lee. Now, if you will bring the other saddlebag out, we can proceed on our way."

Annabelle shook her head mutely, the memory of the dead man's eyes filling her mind. She gasped out, "The owner . . . he's dead in there!"

Pugh made his eyes round. "Is that right now? Some brigand must have slipped in and slit the poor man's throat."

Harter laughed nervously. "Hell, L.P., I'll get it."

Annabelle watched numbly as he limped into the building. She dropped down onto the steps and buried her face in her hands. She could hear Pugh laughing softly, and a fear such as she had never known seized her. If he could kill a man as casually as this, what would he do with her once she had served her purpose? Would Chet help her? He must have been with Pugh when the murder had taken place; they had come out together. No, she could expect little help from Chet Harter.

A shudder wracked her body, and her stomach felt cold and hollow, despite the food she had just put in it. She had her own horse to ride now; maybe she could escape, but that notion died almost as soon as it was born. She didn't know how to ride that well, and they would be watching her more closely now.

Annabelle hadn't been to church in a long time, but silently now, her eyes closed, she began to pray.

Belinda was weary to the very bone. She rode slumped in the saddle, knowing that her horse would follow the animal in front. She wished that Josh or Douglas would call a halt so she could rest, but she was sure they wouldn't stop until darkness came and travel was impossible.

She didn't dare say anything; after all, it was she who had insisted on coming along, claiming that she could take care of herself. She didn't regret that she had come. It was just that she was so tired and disappointed. But then they all must be equally so.

She looked over to where Morgan Lee rode, a little to the side and behind her. His face was drawn, and gray with dust, and for the first time she was aware that he was not a young man. She could not see the faces of Josh and Douglas, as they rode ahead of her, but the weary slump of their shoulders told a story of their own.

It had taken them a great deal of extra time to backtrack out of the canyon to a point where they could toil up along the hillside, making a wide and arduous detour around the blocked trail.

Belinda had heard Josh and Douglas talking about a way station somewhere ahead. Douglas seemed worried that Pugh would obtain fresh horses there, which would give him an additional advantage. It was plain that both Josh and Douglas were discouraged and frustrated, with tempers short. Feeling alienated from both men, Belinda stayed out of their way as much as possible, remaining close to her father.

Even if things had been different, there wouldn't have been much time for socializing. They rode hard all day and then stopped when darkness forced them to. On the treacherous terrain they were traveling, it was not possible to ride at night. Since they did not have to worry about anyone spotting their fire, they had a hot meal at night, which was eaten rapidly, so that they could get to sleep. In the morning a quick, cold meal was eaten, and by the time there was enough light, they were on the trail again. Belinda had trouble remembering how many days had passed—they all ran together in a haze of fatigue and discomfort.

At night she dreamed of herself and Annabelle, dreams of their childhood long ago. Sometimes, she dreamed of Josh, dreams that made her awaken full of embarrassment and annoyance.

And then they reached the way station—a cluster of small, crude buildings, that looked awfully good to Belinda.

They all seemed to perk up at this sight of human habitation, and even the horses picked up their pace, probably sensing feed and a rest. The place looked strangely deserted. There were no horses in the corral, and no one was in sight in the yard, nor did anyone come out to greet them.

Of course the owner could be inside, but Belinda experienced a queer uneasiness, almost a premonition. Evidently, Josh felt the same way, for he reined in beside Douglas and said something to him in a low voice. Nodding, Douglas motioned for the rest of them to fall back and wait. Dismounting, Josh and Douglas approached the main building with guns drawn, and disappeared inside.

It seemed to Belinda that they were in there for a very long time, and she felt herself dozing in the saddle under the stillness and the warmth of the sun.

Then they emerged, and Douglas called to the pair of young Mounties.

Belinda glanced over at her father. "What do you suppose is the matter now?"

Morgan Lee shook his head. "I don't know, but I have the feeling that it's nothing good."

As they watched, the two Mounties conferred with their superior on the veranda. Then they went inside, and Josh and Douglas walked toward Belinda and her father.

"What is it?" she asked of Douglas, who was looking up at her, his face grim. "What's wrong?"

"There's no use in stopping here," he said. "Pugh and Harter got here first, and have taken the horses and whatever food there was."

Belinda could sense that there was something he wasn't telling her. Staring past him, she saw the Mounties come out of the building carrying a long, blanket-wrapped bundle. She felt her stomach turn a flip-flop. "They killed someone," she said flatly. "It's not . . . not Annabelle?"

"No, no," Douglas said quickly. "It's the man who owned the place. I've stopped in here in the past. Jed was a good chap, in his way." His jaw set. "Another death Lester Pugh will have to account for."

"If you ever catch him," Belinda said, her glance going to Josh, who had been standing by silently. Now his gaze locked with hers, and Belinda felt a deep stirring of her emotions. She wanted desperately to speak to him, to reestablish communication, but he was turning away toward his horse.

Douglas was saying, "We'll catch him, don't worry, Belinda."

Belinda, gaze on the blanket-wrapped body being carried by the Mounties, thought: But will it be in time to save Annabelle?

Riding along the shore of Crater Lake, a ground squirrel dashed across the trail, causing Pugh's horse to rear.

The frightened animal tried to retain its balance, but Pugh's great weight, shifting in the saddle, brought the horse to its knees. The sound of its breaking leg was clearly audible in the still air.

The horse screamed and Pugh, swearing mightily, clambered off the animal and glared at the offending leg. Still swearing, he stripped off the saddlebags. He turned a cold face to Harter. "Shoot him."

Harter pulled his gun and fired a bullet into the animal's head. The horse sprawled to the ground without a sound. Annabelle uttered a muted cry and looked away.

They were in a semi-sheltered area, and Pugh looked around. "We might as well camp here. It will be dark soon, anyway. In the morning I'll take your horse, Chesley, and you can take the girl's."

Harter, accustomed to listening for the nuances in Pugh's speech, took note of the last phrase. Just what did the fat man have in mind? He looked quickly at Annabelle to see if she had noticed Pugh's choice of words, but she was staring off across the lake. Apparently, she hadn't heard.

Harter swung down off his horse, showing more hesitation and discomfort than he actually felt. His wounds were pretty well healed, and he was feeling reasonably fit, but he had been careful not to let Pugh know this. He knew that at some point before too long, Pugh would try to exact vengeance for what he considered Harter's betrayal, and Harter wanted all the odds he could manage on his side.

They were not too far from Chilkoot Pass now, and as far as Harter could judge, their pursuers weren't close enough to have a prayer of catching them before they reached Dyea, and the first ship out.

From the way Pugh was talking, he apparently thought it was no longer necessary to have Annabelle for a hostage. He planned to leave her here. Alive or dead, Harter thought, that was the question.

Well, Lester Pugh, the fat bastard, might be a mite surprised to find out that Chet Harter had plans of his own.

First of all, maybe *Pugh* would be left behind, not Annabelle. Harter's lips twisted in a cruel grin. That would be a shock to the bastard, a shock that he had had coming for a long time.

Annabelle, after all, suited Harter well enough. She was docile, easily dominated, and she was good in bed. Also, she was the most beautiful woman he had ever had, and he liked the image that being seen with her gave to him. She had class and that was something Harter didn't often get in a woman.

Yeah, she looked great on his arm, and other men envied him when they saw him with her. She was an asset, that's what she was, and so was more valuable to him than Pugh, who had now turned into a threat.

Yep, there was no contest. Pugh had gotten them through this far, and now they didn't need *him*.

And then there was the money that Harter knew Pugh had, both on his person now and in the safe in the saloon in Dyea. Pugh didn't suspect that Harter knew about that. He not only knew, but he had the combination to the safe! It was a lot of money, enough to set up a nice little operation somewhere else, some place where they had never heard of Chet Harter.

Harter flexed his arm. The muscle had softened a little, but there was enough strength there to pull the trigger of the heavy pistol he wore. Yep, tonight old L.P. was going to get the surprise of his life!

Pugh sprawled on his broad back, his head resting on his saddle, so he could keep an eye on Harter and his woman. His belly was full, and his mind was busy. He was well content. Things had worked out, largely because of his own leadership, his own cleverness.

He would soon be back in Dyea, where he could buy safety in the form of a ship to take him away from this frozen wasteland, back to civilization. He had had enough of the primitive way. The gold rush was drawing to a close, anyway.

He thought fondly of the piles of greenbacks and gold locked in the safe in his place in Dyea—enough money to do him nicely for a long time, until he could set up another organization.

Now he had some loose ends to tie up. He peered out from under his hat brim at Harter and the girl. She was a pretty thing. So young, so tender! Even now, after weeks on the trail, she was still damned attractive.

Pugh felt a faint stirring inside himself, and smiled. He was not often plagued by lustful urges, but tonight, with freedom within his grasp, with the satisfaction of revenge upon Chet Harter an extra fillip, he felt the prod of desire.

Perhaps he *would* enjoy the girl before disposing of her. Why not? After all, he deserved a small indulgence after all these days of hell. Yes, he might just take the girl. A bit of relaxation would do him good.

He switched his gaze to Harter, who was sprawled on his blanket. Chesley was obviously still handicapped from his wounds. Well, soon he would suffer no longer. If he didn't need the girl, he didn't need Harter either. Now was the time to rid himself of both, and it would be a real pleasure to see the surprise and terror on Harter's face when he realized that Lester Pugh was stamping paid to their account.

He sat up, stretched mightily, and called out, "Chet? Come here, will you? We have to make some plans."

Harter stared at him warily, and Pugh smiled inwardly. Finally the man got to his feet and came toward him. Pugh got to his feet as well. He was pleased to note that Harter had left his gunbelt behind on the blanket. Good! He was careful to leave his sword-cane in plain sight, propped against his saddle.

Pugh took Harter gently by his good arm, and started to lead him away from the campground.

Harter did not resist, only asking, "What is it, L.P.?"

Pugh whispered, "It's about the girl."

They were out of Annabelle's hearing now. Harter stopped and faced him. "Yeah, I guess it is time we talked about her. What do you have in mind for her?"

Pugh tugged at his lower lip. "What do *you* suggest?"

Harter shrugged. "Oh, I don't know. I thought I might keep her around, at least for awhile. She suits me well enough."

"It struck me that was what you might be thinking. What would you say if I told you that I think we should kill her?" Pugh kept his voice mild.

Harter's tone was also low-key, which surprised Pugh, who had expected him to blow up. "Why, I'd say we ought to discuss it, L.P. I'd say that was the democratic thing to do."

Pugh snorted, stung to a quick answer. "Democratic! What has democracy to do with us, Chesley? I am in charge here, as I have always been. You work for me! I make the decisions, and I give the orders. And I say she dies!"

Harter's features, which had remained bland, now contracted into a snarl, and Pugh saw his wounded arm move, far quicker than he had thought possible. In an instant, Pugh was looking at the long, glittering blade of a knife, held near his throat.

Pugh's mind went cold, and he cursed himself. He was a fool! He had done what he had so often cautioned Harter against—he had underestimated his opponent. His mind, spurred on by the knowledge of how close he was to death, started clicking furiously, examining and discarding possible options.

Harter was sneering, his face so close now that Pugh could smell his breath. "So you're the big cheese, eh, L.P.? You give the orders, and I march, huh? Well, this time you've overreached, *old friend!* Did you think I was dumb enough to come over here with you without a means to defend myself? Now it's my turn, fat man, and I'm going to let some of the air out of that blubber-gut of yours. I've been waiting for this for a long time. First, let's get a little farther away from the camp. I don't want to upset Annabelle. I want her to be nice and relaxed when I come back, so we can celebrate the end of Lester Pugh!"

He shoved Pugh roughly forward and Pugh, feeling the cold blade of the knife against his neck, made no protest.

Then, as they moved in tandem, Harter with his arm around Pugh's shoulders and the other holding the knife at his throat, Pugh stumbled slightly, throwing them off-balance for just an instant. Pugh's hand darted into his coat pocket to grasp the small derringer he had hidden there.

At that short distance he could not miss and the shot caught Harter in the stomach, blowing away tissue and blood, which Pugh, with distaste, felt gush over his hands and chest.

He watched with almost clinical curiosity as Harter, an expression of comic disbelief on his face, dropped his knife and clasped both hands around the hole in his belly.

As Harter fell, Pugh whipped around to look back at their camp. The girl had jumped up at the sound of the shot and was standing there, trying to peer into the dark. She took a single step and halted, her apprehension evident in the way she stood, like a wild animal alerted by a stalker's footsteps.

Well, Pugh thought gleefully, she has a lot to be apprehensive about!

He chuckled and prodded Harter with the toe of his boot to make sure that he was dead.

A nnabelle had been aware that Chet had risen and walked away from his blanket, but she took little notice. She was upset over the death of the horse and that, coupled with her fatigue, lured her toward sleep, where all her troubles could be forgotten for a few hours.

She was almost asleep when the sound of a shot startled her awake. She jumped up, looking around with frightened eyes, but she saw nothing at first. After a little while she saw the dark blur of a figure coming toward her across the camp area. Was it Chet? She had already noted that Pugh was also gone. What did the shot mean, and who had fired it?

As the figure came nearer, the light from the gibbous moon revealed that it was Pugh, not Chet.

Annabelle felt her skin crawl, as the figure came steadily on without speaking a word. "Mr. Pugh? Where's Chet?"

And then he was beside her, towering over her, gross and menacing. He laughed, a high-pitched sound that sent chills dancing down Annabelle's spine.

"Chesley is no longer with us, my dear. He has gone on,

so to speak, to meet his ancestors, if he has any. It is just you and I now, girl. Just you and I."

Chet dead? Realization struck her like a slap. He had murdered Chet, and she was left alone with this monster!

Too late, she tried to flee. His big hands had her by the shoulders, and he forced her to her knees on the blanket.

"Yes, just you and I, my girl, and I feel the need of feminine attention."

There was something in his voice that made her skin crawl, and she tried desperately to break his hold. His hands squeezed her shoulders with crushing force, and with no apparent effort, he pulled her toward him against his chest.

"Now," he said, laughing, "I really don't care to have to exert great effort in my love-making, so I would prefer that you not fight it. To convince you of my sincerity, I warn you that if you try to resist, I shall kill you, as I have just killed your paramour. I like my women cooperative and compliant, and if I must dispatch you to assure myself of such circumstances, I shall do so. It does not make all that much difference to me!"

In the faint light, Annabelle could see the gleam of his smile. His face was close to hers, and she could smell the sweetness of chocolate on his breath. He couldn't mean what he seemed to be saying! She felt herself shudder.

Pugh laughed again and took one hand from her shoulder to fumble with her blouse, and then, with more strength than she thought he possessed, he ripped her blouse open, sending the buttons bouncing away.

Annabelle felt the crawl of his fingers, like slugs, on her breast. As his moist, hot breath fanned her ear, a feeling of loathing so strong as to be overwhelming seized her.

No, she thought. By God, no!

Whether he killed her or not didn't matter anymore. Death would be preferable to being raped by this revolting pig of a man. The thought of him penetrating her body was more than she could stand.

Somewhere in the back of her mind was the thought, not clearly formed, that she had been a victim for the last time. Remembering something she had overheard one of the saloon girls say, Annabelle reached for Pugh's face, long nails raking the puffy flesh of his face, and at the same time she brought her doubled-up knee into the soft area between his legs.

Pugh screamed, a high, womanish sound, and bent over, grabbing for his wounded parts.

Annabelle, as soon as his hands fell away, jumped to her feet. As she did so, she caught the moon-gleam on Chet's gun in its holster on the blanket a few feet away.

As Pugh rolled about on the ground in agony, she ran quickly to the blanket and scooped up the pistol. She jerked it out of the holster and whirled, pointing it in Pugh's direction, holding it as steady as possible in both hands.

She knew that it was necessary to put one finger on the trigger, and this she did, drawing a deep breath in an effort to calm her racing heart and galloping pulse. Pugh, still moaning, climbed painfully to his feet. The moon came out from behind a cloud, and she could see that his face was bleeding where her nails had gouged him.

And then suddenly he stopped his moaning and stared at her, still and cold as some predatory creature poised to attack, and she tightened her grip on the gun.

"Don't come any nearer," she said in a shaking voice. "Or I'll shoot!"

Pugh said nothing, but continued to stare. "No, you won't," he said finally. "You don't know how to use a gun, and even if you did, you couldn't kill a man in cold blood."

He took a step toward her, and Annabelle felt panic rise up in her throat. Was he right?

He smiled, an evil baring of teeth, and took another step. Frantically, Annabelle willed herself to pull the trigger. She felt the little curved piece of metal move beneath her finger, but there was no explosion. Pugh was laughing outright now. He reached toward his pocket, moving ponderously toward her.

Why hadn't the gun fired?

Then Annabelle remembered watching Chet at target practice. The hammer. The hammer had to be cocked!

As Pugh's hand went into the pocket of his jacket, Annabelle thumbed back the hammer and again pulled the trigger. A terrible explosion made her ears ring, and she felt herself propelled backward by the force of the shot.

Pugh was staring at her in astonishment, but he didn't seem to be hurt. She had missed him! She aimed the gun again, pulling back the hammer.

Pugh hastily raised his arms above his head, showing empty hands. His face was a white moon above the dark of his clothing. The tableau held for an endless time, neither speaking. Then Pugh gave a fatalistic shrug and dropped his hands, turned his back on her, and began to walk over to the tethered horses.

Annabelle found it difficult to think straight. Should she just let him go like this? Should she shoot him in the back?

No, she couldn't. When he was attempting to rape her, she would gladly have killed him. But not like this, not with his back turned. Not in cold blood.

"Stop," she said in a faint voice, when he was standing beside his horse. "I'll shoot if you try to get away!"

"I don't think you will," he said calmly. He stepped over to pick up his saddle, his back still to her.

The heavy gun shook in Annabelle's hands. What was she to do? She couldn't kill him, and she couldn't let him get away like this. And then she knew what she *could* do. Cocking the pistol and aiming carefully, she fired a shot into the ground before the tethered horses.

Pugh jumped and the animals whinnied, pulling loose their tethers as they reared, pawing the air. Another shot over their heads sent them stampeding into the trees. Pugh spun around, his face white with rage and frustration.

For an instant then, Annabelle faltered, but she steadied the gun and kept it pointed at Pugh. She made her voice as firm as it was possible for her to make it. "I'll kill you if I have to, Mr. Pugh. I want you to believe that. Now, take off your coat, very slowly, and drop it to the ground."

Pugh hesitated, seething, and she raised the pistol until it was centered on his heart. Slowly, he removed the coat and dropped it.

"Now, kick the coat away from your foot."

Sighing, he obeyed.

Annabelle paused. Now what should she do? She couldn't keep the gun on him until help arrived, and she didn't dare approach him close enough to tie him, even if she had something to tie him with.

Pugh sensed her hesitation. "I have a solution, girl," he

said, his voice condescendingly polite.

"A solution to what?"

"Your dilemma," he said scornfully. "It's plain that you have no stomach for killing me in cold blood, and it is also obvious that you don't know how to render me helpless until your *friends* arrive. So I offer you a solution. Let me go."

She shook her head vehemently, and he shrugged, smiling slightly. "Think, girl. It's the only practical solution. You have no idea how long it will be before the others get here. Let me go. I'll be afoot. What harm can I do?"

A chill breeze blew with some force off the lake, and Annabelle shivered.

"May I have my coat?" Pugh asked politely.

"No!" Annabelle shook her head. "You have something in the pocket, I'm sure. The gun you shot Chet with, probably."

"You do have some brains," he said with grudging admiration. "So I will back away, and you search the coat, removing the gun and whatever else you think I might use as a weapon. When that is done, you let me take the coat when I leave."

Annabelle thought hard, searching for a catch in his proposition. She finally nodded, feeling foolish that she should be taking directions from the man she was holding at gunpoint.

Pugh backed away, and Annabelle advanced cautiously to where the coat lay. She stooped and searched the coat blindly, never once removing her gaze from him. She found a derringer and three chocolate bars in the right-hand pocket of the coat, and Pugh's long cigarette holder in the left. She removed the derringer, and in a burst of defiance, the chocolate bars. Then she backed away and let Pugh retrieve his coat and put it on.

"Now, if you will allow me to take some supplies?" He started toward the saddlebags.

"Wait!" she cried. "I'll get them out."

Again never taking her eyes from the fat man, she walked over to the saddlebags. Fumbling in them, she took out a bag of hardtack, a packet of jerky, and some dried salmon. She tossed the packages to him, along with a canteen.

Pugh stooped to pick them up. "May I take a blanket?" He grinned. "Surely you're not so heartless as to wish me to freeze to death?"

Annabelle nodded wearily, wishing him gone so that she could rest and try to pull herself together. She felt that her mind and strength were slipping away, stretching to the breaking point, until soon something would snap.

She watched closely as Pugh selected one of the blankets and wrapped the supplies in it, making a sort of sack. Finished, he said calmly, "Now may I take along my cane? Often I need it for walking."

Again, she nodded. Awkwardly, she peeled away the wrapper from a candy bar and put it into her mouth, chewing.

Standing up with the cane, Pugh stared at the remains of the chocolate bar in her hand and licked his lips. "I am confident that we shall meet again, girl. I'm looking forward to it!"

With the cane in one hand and the blanket bundle in the other, Lester Pugh turned and walked away. Annabelle stared after him, the gun still pointed at him, until the darkness had swallowed him up.

When he was out of sight, she gave a shuddering sigh and dropped down upon her blanket. She was trembling uncontrollably. She wanted to cry, but her eyes felt dry and raspy. She kept the gun cradled in her lap. Would he wait for her to fall asleep and sneak back? She couldn't stand up to him if he did. Her strength was gone.

But surely, he would not. The horses were gone, so he had nothing to gain. Certainly his pride was stung at being bested by a woman, but to risk everything for revenge was stupid, and whatever else Pugh was, he was not stupid.

Still, Annabelle could not shake her apprehension. He could be out there right now, circling around behind, waiting until she dozed so he could kill her. This fear kept her sitting there with the gun, eyes straining against the dark, until exhaustion overcame her and she lay down, one hand still gripping the gun.

She was still asleep the next morning when Josh Rogan, Douglas Mackenzie, Morgan Lee, the two Mounties, and Belinda rode into the clearing.

"Annabelle!" Belinda's cry startled the horses.

Annabelle lay on her right side on a blanket, her right hand loosely holding a large revolver. She was very still, only her hair moving in the light morning breeze off the lake.

Belinda started down from her horse, but Josh was quicker, catching her in his arms. His expression was worried. "Wait, Belinda."

She knew that he was thinking the same thing she was,

and she looked at him with dread.

And then Annabelle moved, turning over onto her back. She opened her eyes and sat up. When she saw Belinda and the others, a cry escaped her. In the next instant, she was running toward Belinda and her father, her arms outstretched.

The two girls clung together in tearful reunion. "Oh, Bee!" Annabelle cried as she hugged her sister fiercely. "I thought I would never see you again!"

Belinda held her tightly, the love she felt for her sister filling her heart; and then Morgan Lee was holding them both, and Josh and Douglas were barking questions. Belinda could not understand what anyone was saying.

A fire was built, a hot meal prepared, and Josh, out of some secret pocket in his saddlebags, produced a bottle of whiskey. He splashed liberal portions into their tin coffee cups.

Annabelle told her story and Belinda could only listen with mounting amazement. "*You* set the dynamite?"

Annabelle dimpled. "Yes! Hard to believe, isn't it? I wanted to leave it there without lighting the fuse, but I didn't dare. Pugh would have killed me!"

Josh shook his head. "Annabelle, you're a wonder! I don't think anyone could have handled themselves better. Now that Pugh is afoot, catching up to him should be only a matter of time, a short time."

Douglas, Belinda noticed with some amusement, seemed to be looking at Annabelle with an interest he had heretofore not showed. "Miss Lee, it was very clever of you to think of driving off the horses. You've helped shorten the chase considerably, I'm sure. I don't see how Pugh can possibly reach Dyea before we catch up to him."

Annabelle dimpled again, smiling demurely. Her cheeks were pink, and despite the accumulated grime of the weeks on the trail, Belinda thought that she had never looked lovelier. She was glad for her sister. Annabelle had, for the first time in Belinda's memory, shown initiative and fortitude, and the experience clearly had been good for her.

Douglas and the other Mounties were observing Annabelle with frank admiration. Belinda felt a twinge of jealousy at Douglas's admiration, and then was ashamed of herself. Why shouldn't he turn to Annabelle, if he felt attracted to her?

Her gaze sought out Josh, and found that he was staring at her in question. She smiled, tentatively, and those blue eyes brightened as if someone had turned on a flame behind them.

He moved over beside her. "Do you feel better now?"

She nodded, her hand coming out to grip his.

Now that she knew Annabelle was safe, Belinda felt spent, as if she had been existing on nerve alone for the last weeks, and yet she knew that the ordeal was not yet over. They still had to capture Lester Pugh. Only then would it really be over. Only then could they all get on with their lives.

Belinda and Annabelle sat and talked into the afternoon, while the men buried Chet Harter. Belinda had never felt so close to her sister.

By the time the burial was completed, it was growing dark, and it was decided they would spend the night here. There was no longer a sense of great urgency. With Pugh afoot, time was on their side.

That night, despite her weariness, Belinda could not sleep. She was very conscious of Josh, lying wrapped in his blanket only a few feet away, and she ached to be able to go to him and crawl into the comforting circle of his arms. She had been foolish, she knew. This whole recent thing between them was her doing. Why, oh why, did humans cause themselves so much pain?

She sighed, smiling softly to herself. The sky above was brilliant with stars, and the air was cold and tangy as she drew it into her lungs. It was good to be alive. It was good to know that those she loved were safe, and were here with her. Death, with all its attendant tragedy, was a spur to the living; a reminder that life was sweet, with all its problems.

Certain that she would not sleep at all, Belinda sank slowly into the most restful slumber she had known in weeks.

The big man on the bay had camped not far away, out of sight but close enough to see their campfire, now dying down.

He had not made a fire for himself, but he had plenty of food and drink, and he was reasonably comfortable now, warm and snug wrapped in his blankets.

Under cover of darkness, he had crept close enough to the other camp to overhear some of their conversation as they sat around the fire, and he knew that his search was almost over. It had been a long journey, and it had taken much time. There were other things he would much rather be doing, but this was a debt. Something he owed himself, and the past. Something that must be taken care of before he could, in all good conscience, go about living his own life.

He sighed deeply, and gave himself up to sleep.

Lester Pugh walked alone through the night. The darkness was not complete, and there was enough light to enable a man on foot to make his way.

The blanket, which held his meager supply of food, was slung uncomfortably across one shoulder, but Pugh's step did not falter, although his breathing was coming heavier, the farther he progressed. He was climbing, toward the summit, and Chilkoot Pass.

He was reasonably certain that those behind him would not travel by night, and this could give him a small advantage, but it was not enough. There was still a distance to travel before reaching the pass. All he needed was a chance to reach Dyea and his cache of money. Just a few hours headway, but now, afoot as he was, his chances of that seemed slim.

Still, he refused to give up. No matter what happened, he would not give up—*that* was the sign of greatness. And something might turn up to help him yet; a clever man always managed to turn adversity to his advantage.

Busily, his mind foraged for possibilities; and then he saw the campfire, flickering in the darkness like a warm, beckoning finger of light, and Pugh smiled. Another traveler. The gods were being kind, perhaps in atonement for the brutal fact that he was again alone, betrayed by his cohorts—the price he seemed always doomed to pay for greatness.

Quickly, Pugh placed the blanket roll on the ground.

Slowly and quietly for such a large man, he approached the fire, sword-cane balanced in his right hand. There was only one man at the fire—a hard-bitten sourdough in a battered hat and leather vest, stirring some sort of food in an iron skillet over the fire.

Pugh's nostrils dilated. The hot food smelled appetizing, and his stomach rumbled. He could smell the coffee, too, boiling in a can. The old man seemed absorbed in his task.

Eagerly, Pugh scanned the campsite. Disappointment chilled him, when he could see no horse. Damn! The old fool was afoot!

And then he heard a familiar stamping, and heard an animal blow. A wide grin split his face. Fate was again with him. He was going to make it!

He hefted the sword-cane and flicked the button to see if it was in working order. With a snicking sound the blade sprang out, shining dully in the faint light. Moving quickly but still quietly, Pugh approached the sourdough from the rear. The old man didn't hear him until Pugh was upon him. At the last instant the sourdough turned. Surprise widened his eyes as the sharp blade bit into his throat, and he died never really knowing what had happened.

When the man's body was pulled away from the fire and hidden under a pile of brush, Pugh made a decent enough meal for himself from the food the sourdough had been cooking. He washed it down with bitter coffee, wishing he had some of his chocolate to finish off the meal.

Damn that girl to hell! She had had no cause to steal his chocolate! He hated her for that more than anything else.

Finished, he went looking for the horse. It wasn't a horse, but a mule. Pugh cursed vilely for a few moments before he accepted the fact that a mule was better than walking.

The animal stared at him with ears pricked, as Pugh placed the worn saddle upon its back and heaved himself up. The mule was at first reluctant to move out under Pugh's great weight, but a couple of pokes from the sword-cane made it lively enough, and soon it was jogging briskly along the trail.

Not a fitting mount for a great man, Pugh thought, but even the wisest of men often had to adjust to circumstances—that was the key to survival.

The mule would not be as fast as the horses of those behind him, but by morning he would have increased his lead and, with any luck at all, he should reach the summit ahead of them.

Softly, he began to hum under his breath, an old nursery tune that he and his brother used to sing as children. Ah, it was sad that he was alone again. If only he and Wendell had not been separated as children . . . but there was no use in thinking of lost relations and friends. He must go on alone, bravely, to eventually assume the mantle of greatness that fate had decreed should be his.

Belinda and her party came upon the murdered sourdough in the middle of the morning.

Belinda and Annabelle stood off to one side, while the men buried another of Pugh's victims in a shallow grave and said the proper words over the departed.

Pugh had to be stopped! If he was not, there was no justice in the world, Belinda thought, as tears flooded her eyes. That poor old man! He hadn't done anything except have something that Pugh wanted—in this case, a horse. How many people would Pugh murder before he was captured?

After the burial, they did not linger, but once again struck out on the fat man's trail.

Neither Josh nor Douglas said anything, but Belinda knew that they were worried. Pugh was mounted again, and it was quite possible that if he had traveled all night— which he apparently had—he might get to the pass before them, and then down to Dyea.

Douglas kept them moving at a fast pace all the rest of the day. They did not even stop for a meal, but ate in the saddle, washing the smoked salmon and biscuits down with water from their canteens.

It was close to dark when they finally rode up to the Mountie check station on the top of Chilkoot Pass.

A cold wind had begun to blow and the trampled earth, barren of vegetation where thousands of feet had trod, looked desolate and forbidding. There were patches of snow and ice on the ground; the long arctic winter was not far off. Even as Belinda reined her horse in, flakes of snow began to fall. Shivering, she slid from the saddle, and let the reins drop to the ground. Her horse hung its head wearily.

She could hear the creak of the freight cable as it moved slowly around the winch. She looked down the long slope, but there were no climbers in sight now. Campfires burned on the flats at the bottom of the steps, and the smell of fried fish hung in the air. She glanced around as Morgan and Annabelle came to stand beside her.

"Has Pugh gotten away again?" she asked tiredly.

Morgan shook his head. "I don't know. At any rate, he's sure not here."

Douglas and Josh had gone into the Mountie tent station on their arrival. Now they came bursting out of the tent, and ran to where the huge apparatus housing the winch for the freight cable squatted, looking like some kind of iron insect. Belinda could hear their voices raised in excitement.

She exchanged glances with her father and Annabelle, and by mutual assent they hurried over to the winch housing. The man who operated the winch was pulling back on a large lever, while Josh and Douglas peered down the slope, which was partially obscured by snow flurries.

Belinda strained to see what they were looking at. About halfway down the length of the cable, dangling from it, was a dark bulk swinging in the wind.

"What is it?" she demanded. "What's the excitement?"

Josh turned to her, his face alight. "It's Pugh!" he shouted above the whine of the winch. "The Mountie in charge of the check station said Pugh got here about a half-hour ahead of us, and took the cable down. The operator is reversing the cable, to bring him back. We've got him at last!"

"Oh, Josh!" All reserve gone, Belinda threw herself into his arms. He kissed her soundly, and she returned the kiss passionately, before she remembered that others were present.

Embarrassed, she tried to draw back, and saw Morgan smile wistfully. Annabelle nodded encouragingly, but Douglas's expression was tight and cold. Belinda felt a moment's sorrow over the fact that she had hurt him, but her happiness was too great for her to remain sad for long.

Douglas would find someone else. Perhaps even Annabelle. The thought made her smile.

Josh laughed softly. "We'll celebrate later," he whispered in her ear, and she felt herself blush.

"It's all over!" she cried to Annabelle, taking her sister's hand. "I can hardly believe it!"

A high, whining screech cut off her words, and the man operating the winch was thrown backward.

Bewildered, she asked, "What is it? What's happened?"

Josh said in dismay, "The winch has stuck! He can't wind the cable back!"

23

Lester Pugh, huddled in the blanket that had contained his supplies, swung slowly back and forth in the growing darkness. He shivered in the occasional snow flurry.

The leather sling hung askew from the creaking cable. Still, the discomfort should not last long. Just a short time more, and he would be down below, and on his way to Dyea. He rubbed his hands together under the cover of the blanket, and permitted himself a smile. He had arrived at the check station just as darkness began to gather, and the last of the day's stampeders were making their way up the steps.

The freight cable was not in use, and the operator, who remembered Pugh from previous trips, was more than happy to rig up the special harness and send him on his way. Now, it was too late for any pursuit to catch up with him. Trying to go down the steep steps in the dark would be too dangerous. As for the cable, he had in mind to disable it once he reached the bottom, and that would give him ample time.

Pugh shifted his bulk in the uncomfortable harness, carefully not looking down at the ground as he glided over it, like a great bird soaring in flight.

Yes, he was safe now, and someday he would return to gain his vengeance on those who had persecuted him. At some time, at some place, Pugh was convinced that he would see them again; and they would suffer at his hands! He smiled to himself in anticipation, then reached into his coat pocket for one of the small cakes that the Mountie in command of the check station had so kindly given him.

As he pushed the sweet morsel into his mouth, the harness jerked forward and then back, the straps biting into his stomach and buttocks.

Choking on the cake crumbs, Pugh grabbed at the ropes that held the harness to the cable. He was swinging wildly, and it was apparent that the cable had stopped. Some malfunction of the winch, no doubt.

And then he felt the movement. He was traveling backward, back up the mountain. It couldn't be! But he was.

Twisting around as far as he could in the harness, he stared back over his shoulder. At the top of the pass, outlined against the somewhat lighter darkness of the sky, he could discern several figures milling around the winch housing.

A great rage filled him. They were reeling him in, like some hooked fish! The indignity of it!

Abruptly, the cable stopped again, with a clang that

reverberated along its length, causing it to sing like a harp string; and once again Pugh and his harness were set into violent motion. When the swinging had abated somewhat, Pugh again glanced up. The figures were scurrying about busily. He gave a terrible smile. Fate was on his side again! Obviously the winch apparatus had jammed, and they could not reel him in. His smile faded. Just as obviously, he could not get down. Sunk deep in thought, he reached absently into his pocket for another cake. He would find a way. He had so far, hadn't he?

His mind busy with the possibilities, he bit into the cake.

"Damn!" Josh struck his fist against his thigh. He stood with the others staring at the cable, and its swinging burden, down below. "Can you fix it?"

The operator shrugged. "I don't know. It would be far easier in the daylight. It jams like this every now and then."

"It would happen *now!*" Josh shook his head angrily. "Pugh must have the luck of the devil! Every time we seem to have him, he does something unexpected, or something happens in his favor!"

Belinda took his arm, squeezing it against her side. "But this time he can't go anywhere, she pointed out. "Maybe we can't get at him, but he can't get away, either. Even if we have to wait until morning, he'll still be there."

Josh sighed. "You'd think so, wouldn't you? But will he? I tell you I'm getting superstitious as far as that man is concerned. I wouldn't put it past him to find some way of getting down, even if he has to grow wings and fly!"

Douglas gave a wry laugh. "I understand how you feel, Rogan. He *is* a slippery devil. But even the devil himself, if he weighed close to three hundred pounds, couldn't get down out of that harness to the ground, not at that height. If the winch can't be fixed tonight, well, we'll just wait until morning and bring him in then."

"Yes, and in the morning the trail will be swarming with gold seekers, unless we station someone down there to block off the steps, and *that* will cause a ruckus. I tell you, I have a bad feeling about this."

Somberly, they all moved over to the edge of the incline and gazed down. The dark bundle that was Lester Pugh swung slowly back and forth, back and forth, like some sort of dreadful pendulum.

Swinging above the earth in his harness, Pugh was busy. He had managed, not without considerable effort, to pull the blanket from around himself, and using the blade of his sword-cane, he was cutting the tough fabric into narrow strips, strips that when tied together would reach the ground, or near enough to it. Pugh stopped for a moment to rest his hands, and to put the last cake into his mouth. It would have to last him until he reached Dyea, which he was now confident he would do.

On the mountain, lurking back out of sight of the cluster of people around the winch housing, stood the man who had been trailing them since Dawson. He was staring down the slope, frowning in thought. He stood there until the others grew tired of waiting, and crossed in a group to the Mountie tent station. The only person left was the winch operator, laboring over the winch by lantern light.

The stranger strolled over to the housing, making a noise

378

so that he would not startle the operator. He asked, "Do you think you'll get it working soon?"

Without looking up from his work, the operator shook his head. "Doubt it. She's jammed real good this time. I'm afraid it'll be morning before she's fixed, when I can see what I'm doing."

The big man returned to the spot where he could look down the mountain. He could just make out the large form of Lester Pugh, swinging from side to side. Then he sucked in his breath, squinting down, as a cooking fire on the flats below flared up, revealing what Pugh was doing.

The stranger reached a sudden decision. He swung about and began scouring the area. He started to despair of finding what he sought. Then he found it, leaning against a small lean-to used to shelter the station's wood supply.

When he returned to the cable housing, he carried a heavy, double-bladed axe over his shoulder.

Quietly, he stepped up behind the sweating winch operator. With a surprising gentleness, he raised his hand and brought it down in a swift chopping motion upon the smaller man's neck. The man dropped to the ground without a sound.

The stranger moved him gently out of the way, then took up a stance beside the cable. Raising the axe, he brought the blade flashing down with all his strength, across the cable.

Sparks flew, and strands of metal parted with a whining sound as the cable vibrated violently. Once more the axe rose and fell, and again the cable sang. The remaining strands parted and the cable sprang away, whipping down the mountainside like a great snake.

From down the mountain came a wailing human cry, and then all was silent.

The man with the axe shuddered, and let the axe fall to the ground. He removed his hat and stood gazing down the mountain, hat over his heart, his lips moving as though in silent prayer.

"What was that?" Belinda, startled by a high, whining sound and then a distant, eerie cry, almost dropped her mug of tea.

The others, frozen in various positions while refreshing themselves with hot tea and small cakes provided by the Mountie in charge, looked at one another with questioning eyes.

Then, while Belinda's words still hung in the air, both Josh and Douglas bolted for the door, colliding with each other as they reached the narrow tent door at the same time. The rest followed quickly, and in a few moments they were all standing by the winch housing, staring at a tall man who stood there, hat over his heart. The winch operator stirred on the ground nearby, groaning. He sat up, looking around dazedly.

"My God!" Morgan Lee said in a hushed voice. "Look!"

Belinda and Annabelle followed his pointing finger. The cable that should have stretched down the mountain was gone. Only the ragged edges of several strands protruded from the cable end still on the winch.

Below, the mountain was ominously quiet.

Josh looked at the tall man, who had not moved. Josh picked up the axe from the ground, staring at the ruined blades, and then looked again at the stranger. "Who the hell are you?"

The man replaced his hat and turned slowly. "Why, I am Wendell Pugh," he said softly. "I am Lester Pugh's brother."

Several Mounties made the trip down the steps in the dark, to fetch Lester Pugh's body. The trail of lanterns, moving slowly down the steps in the darkness, was an eerie sight to Belinda, who watched from the top of the steps.

Later, she overheard one of the Mounties describing Pugh's body when they found it. "He was laying there, just off the trail, his neck broken, and his head crushed like an egg where it had hit a large rock. His eyes were open, and there were cake crumbs on his mouth. One arm was out-stretched, like he was reaching out for something. I think the thing that got me was the surprised look on his face, like he couldn't believe what was happening to him. It was almost enough to make me feel sorry for the chap. There were strips of blanket scattered around him, some tied together."

Belinda was glad that Pugh was dead, glad that it was finally over, and yet the idea of death itself was sobering. She and Annabelle sat close to one another, in the Mountie tent, while Josh and Douglas questioned the man who said he was Pugh's brother.

Belinda, recalling having seen the man in Dawson, stared at him curiously. There was a family resemblance. If Lester Pugh had been of normal weight, he would have looked very much like this man, except for the difference in expression. This man had a gentle mouth and kind, though tired eyes. He did not look at all like a man capable of killing.

Josh leaned forward. "You claim to be Wendell Pugh, the brother of Lester Pugh?"

The man nodded. "I am, sir."

Josh shook his head in puzzlement. "But why? Why did you do what you did? We'd have brought him in in the morning, when the winch was fixed. Why did you cut the cable?"

The man sighed, and for a moment lowered his eyes. Then he made a weary gesture and said, "I don't know if you'll understand, but I do owe you an explanation.

"As for your bringing him in, that would not have happened. He was about to make good his escape. I had a glimpse of what he was doing with his blanket. Lester always had a way of escaping the consequences of his acts. It was almost spooky. I simply couldn't let him do it again.

"I haven't seen Lester in many years, not since we were small boys together, living with an aunt. Even then, he was an . . . an unusual boy. Brilliant, but self-absorbed, and totally unable of putting up with being thwarted at anything."

Wendell Pugh shook his head. "He was younger than I, but I have always wondered if he wasn't responsible for the death of our parents . . ."

Douglas made a sound of disbelief, and Wendell Pugh nodded, smiling faintly. "I know, it is hard to accept, that a boy that young could imagine or do such a thing. But, as I told you, Lester was unique. You see, on the day they died, our parents had, for reasons which aren't important, confined Lester to his room, as a punishment.

"They were going out on the lake, to try out a new sailboat, and had been making preparations all morning. That same morning, I saw Lester sneak out of his room, go to the kitchen where a picnic lunch was being prepared, and then into the shed where the boat was kept. Since I wasn't a lad for tattling, and since I felt some sympathy for Lester's punishment, I didn't say anything.

"Later that morning, our parents were drowned when their boat sank. When the boat was brought to the surface, it was found to have a large hole in the bottom, under the seat. It was thought they might have run aground upon a rock, or some such. No one could explain why they hadn't still made it to shore safely, since both were expert swimmers, but at any rate, it was officially declared a regrettable accident, and Lester and I were left alone.

"At the time, I thought nothing of Lester's lack of grief, for as I told you, he was an unusual lad, and was not given to outward displays of emotion. Then, one day, I ran afoul of his displeasure.

"Since we had been living with our aunt, Lester had become unbearably selfish, and given to ordering me about, even though I was the elder. One day, he had tried my patience with his churlish behavior, and I struck him. It was only a light blow, but Lester was outraged. Later that day, however, he seemed to be over his pique, and even asked me to go out in the punt with him."

Wendell Pugh spread his hands almost apologetically. "To shorten a long story, when we were out in the middle of the lake, Lester caught me with my back turned and pushed me into the water. Since I was a good swimmer, he tried to assure my demise by striking me on the head with the oar.

"This time, his scheme didn't work. Being somewhat larger and stronger, I wrestled the oar from him, and managed to pull myself back into the boat. When we reached shore, Lester immediately started screaming for our aunt, and when she arrived to find me half-conscious, he claimed that I had fallen overboard, and that he had saved me!

"My aunt, however, was not a stupid woman. She already had her own suspicions about Lester, and when I told her my version, in private, she sent me away, with some friends who were visiting at the time. A middle-aged, childless couple, who very much wanted children.

"I never saw Lester again, until several weeks ago, when I came to Dawson in search of him."

There was a long silence after the man had finished. Finally, Josh shook his head. "It's hard to believe," he said in a low voice, but Wendell Pugh heard him.

"Yes," he said wryly. "If you read this story in a book, you would say that it is melodramatic. But life often is, you know."

Douglas, his eyes narrowed in thought, hitched his chair closer. "Tell me, Mr. Pugh, why, after all these years, and after what you claim happened, did you come in search of your brother?"

The big man sighed, and gestured to the tea pot. "May I have a cup? I'm very thirsty."

"Of course." Douglas poured a mug of tea.

Wendell Pugh drank heartily, then wiped his mouth with a handkerchief. "Now, where was I? Yes. Well, several years ago, my adoptive parents died, leaving me comfortably off. Then, two years back, our aunt, mine and Lester's, died, leaving a considerable fortune, more than I ever imagined she possessed. She left the entire estate to me in her will, never mentioning Lester.

"But after the funeral, I began thinking about my brother, wondering what had happened to him and what kind of a man he had become. Perhaps he had changed. People do. Perhaps he was no longer the selfish boy who could not brook frustration. I became obsessed with finding him, to learn what he had become. If he had grown up to be a decent citizen, I would share the fortune with him. I finally found him, in Dawson."

He sighed heavily. "Needless to say, when I found him, he had not changed. On the contrary, he was even more evil, more despicable than he had been as a child. Watching him, I learned of your interest in him, gentlemen. When he fled Dawson, and you gave chase, I felt compelled to follow, to be in on the conclusion.

"On the trail I saw what happened. I saw the men he killed, saw you burying them, and I knew that he must be eliminated. Dear God, I dread to think of how many deaths my own brother has been responsible for!

"Then, when the cable jammed, and I heard you speak of waiting until morning, I had a feeling that this would never come to pass; that once again Lester would somehow slip away, and be free to continue on his murderous way. That was when I cut the cable.

"I'm glad it's all out." He slumped back. "The rest is up to you, gentlemen."

When he had finished speaking, there was a long silence. Finally, Josh and Douglas exchanged glances.

"Well, Mackenzie," Josh said, "do you want to take him

into custody? It's your bailiwick."

Douglas looked surprised, then shook his head. "Why, no, you're wrong, Rogan. The dead man was an American citizen, as is this man, and the body was found on the American side. So, I really don't think it's my bailiwick. How about you?"

Josh shrugged. "Nope, not me. I just resigned my job. So, what do we do now?"

"I guess we'll just have to let him go," Douglas said with a grave countenance.

Wendell Pugh looked at each man in turn. "You're making sport of me," he said slowly.

Josh shook his head. "No, sir, not at all. You're free to go your own way. And off the record, we owe you a vote of thanks. But don't tell anyone I said that. I would have to deny it."

Relief crept slowly into Wendell Pugh's eyes, and then he reached out and grasped Josh's hand. "Thank you, sir. And you as well, Sergeant Mackenzie."

He rose from the table, and almost stumbling in his weariness, left the tent.

Josh watched him go. "There's one thing we can't do," he said thoughtfully. "We can't free him from the guilt that he will carry about for the rest of his life. He's a good man, and he'll never be able to forgive himself for what he did, necessary or not."

He smiled at Belinda, and a glow of warmth filled her as she smiled back.

He said, "We're going to have to leave first thing in the morning for Dawson." He pressed her hand. "If we don't, we'll never make it back before winter freezes everything solid."

Belinda turned in Josh's arms, and pressed her lips against the soft, reddish-gold hair that matted his chest.

Without opening his eyes, he pulled her close and kissed the top of her head; she could not remember ever being this happy.

Tomorrow, they were to be married—or today, since it would soon be morning. Josh, who was no longer a U.S. marshal, had promised that they could stay in Dawson at least until spring, so that Belinda could take pictures, of the town, and the miners, in winter. After that? Well, that was in the future, and they would worry about that when they came to it.

She stretched, reveling in the feeling of her naked body moving against clean sheets, and the lean length of Josh's body.

She was still a little stiff from the rigors of the return trip to Dawson, but since they had used the river, thank God, there had been little horseback riding! Even so, it had not been without its hardships, since they had had to battle a couple of blizzards, making it back yesterday, just as the first big storm of the winter buried Dawson under a foot of snow.

But now, now she was warm and snug in Josh's arms. Her father and Annabelle were staying at the hotel, leaving them alone in the rooms above the studio.

The owner of one of Dawson's better saloons was leaving for Nome; word had spread of a fabulous new gold strike there. He had his saloon up for sale, and Morgan Lee was going to buy it, with the intention of turning it into a respectable place providing good dining and fine entertainment.

Belinda smiled to herself. Annabelle was to provide the entertainment; she was to be the star. She was already bursting with ideas for costumes, material, and new songs. There seemed little doubt that Annabelle Lee—*not* Alabaster White—would soon be the toast of Dawson.

Belinda found it all a little confusing. She had been brought up to believe there were certain things a woman did not do, and performing in a frontier dancehall was certainly one of them. If a woman did something of that nature, she was considered a soiled dove, an outcast from society, doomed to a life of unhappiness. And yet, here was her sister doing just that, and not only glorying in it, but being thought none the less for it.

Of course, Belinda thought contentedly, what I'm doing without the benefit of matrimony does not have society's approval. And yet, she was happy, blissfully happy!

So thinking, she ran the palm of her hand down across Josh's chest, across his flat stomach, and found the source of much of that happiness. It stirred under her touch, and Belinda laughed throatily.

"You're insatiable, woman," Josh growled in her ear. "Do you know that?"

"You mean I'm shameless?"

"Something like that, yes."

"Well then, in that case, I must live up to my bad reputation, mustn't I?"

Mouth fastened to his, hands busy, she moved onto her back and drew him to her.

Passion restored again after their night of love, Josh

responded to her urging. "Yes, you shameless hussy! That's what you are, Belinda Lee . . ."

"Belinda Rogan" she muttered, "as of this afternoon."

"Absolutely without shame," he said, and moved into her with a long stroke.

Belinda clenched her fingers around his upper arms and rose to meet him, and the world went away. Everything ceased to exist for her except this room, this bed, this man, as she was swept up in ecstasy's sweet oblivion.

When awareness seeped back, Belinda noticed that night had passed while they had loved, and a new day was dawning—her wedding day!

Lying beside Josh, she twined a finger in his chest hair. "Darling, do you know you have a beautiful body?"

He grunted without opening his eyes. "You don't say that a man's body is beautiful. A woman's, yes, but not a man's."

"And why not?" She raised up on one elbow. "Why can't a man's body be beautiful?"

"All right, all right!" He flapped a hand at her. "So I have a beautiful body. What of it?"

"Well . . . speaking as a photographer, I'd like to take a picture of you in the nude. It's never been done, as far as I know, by a woman photographer. Nude women have been photographed, but never men . . ."

"What! Are you out of your mind?" He reared up. "You will *never* get me to pose naked for that camera of yours!"

She said serenely, "Don't say never, Josh darling, that's a long time. Just think about it. You'll come to see that . . ."

She was interrupted by a thunderous pounding on the

outside door.

"What the hell!" Josh raised his voice to a bellow, "Who is it?"

The pounding stopped, and a voice rumbled, "It's me. It's Two-Step. Open this darn door, younker. I've got something important to tell ya. I been waiting for ya to come back, so open this darned door, before I kick the fool thing in!"

Josh groaned. Hopping out of bed, he wrapped one of the blankets around him and hurried into the other room. Belinda listened to the sound of voices. Then Josh returned to the bedroom, with a sourdough in tow and a . . . a cat! Of all things, a cat, and one with no ears! The cat stalked about the room, sniffing at everything.

Josh gestured resignedly to the old man. "This character, Belinda, is my partner, Two-Step Sam, and that object on the floor is No-Ears Riley, his cat. This, Two-Step, is Belinda Lee. Before the day is over, she'll be my wife."

Two-Step bobbed his head. "How do, ma'am."

He seemed to think nothing untoward about Josh and Belinda sharing the same bed, and she relaxed, really looking at the sourdough. His face was aglow, his eyes sparkled, and his grin was wide. He was carrying a large, leather bag, which seemed to be quite heavy.

Josh said impatiently, "All right, Two-Step. Now what's so damned urgent that you have to barge in here and . . ."

Two-Step pushed past him, toward the bed. Belinda, suddenly uneasy, shrank back, pulling the blankets up to her chin.

Josh said, "Two-Step, what are you up to?"

The old man ignored him; he lifted the bag by the end

and dumped its contents onto the bed.

Belinda stared in hushed awe at the glittering objects scattered on the bed. Gold! Pure, sun-bright gold! No-Ears jumped up onto the bed, and picked his way daintily among the nuggets.

Belinda picked up one of the nuggets and stared up at the sourdough. "Where did you get all this?" Her voice came out a whisper.

Two-Step gave a cackling laugh. "Why, on our claim. Where else?"

Josh stared at him, his mouth open. "On *our* claim? But that's impossible! That claim's no good. Everybody knows that."

Two-Step cackled again. "Then everybody is wrong, 'cause it has the best color these old eyes has ever seen! Found this in the old stream bed, and there's plenty more where that came from. We're rich, younker, me and ya and old Riley there. And the little lady, too, I reckon."

Josh dropped down onto the bed beside Belinda and picked up a nugget. "I will be damned! I don't believe it, I simply don't believe it!"

Two-Step was still talking, " 'Course we got one problem, younker. Last night's blizzard froze the ground solid as iron. We just ain't going to be able to dig on that claim until spring thaw. Them nuggets there on the bed, that's about all there'll be until spring.

"Then we'll just have to make do, Two-Step," Josh said.

"But all that gold down there, more color'n I've ever seen," Two-Step said mournfully, "and I can't get to it. It's going to be a long winter!"

Josh and Belinda locked glances, and both began to

laugh, rich, full laughter. Startled, No-Ears jumped down from the bed, and stalked about the room, tail elevated in disdain.

Face suddenly solemn, Josh placed a finger across Belinda's lips, stilling her laughter. In a voice meant only for her, he said, "I'm looking forward to a long winter, aren't you?"

Belinda nodded, wordlessly.

Josh leaned toward her. He took away his finger, and replaced it with his lips.

Center Point Publishing
600 Brooks Road • PO Box 1
Thorndike ME 04986-0001 USA

(207) 568-3717

US & Canada:
1 800 929-9108